PSYCHO

PSYCHO

Stuart Pearce

The Autobiography

with Bob Harris

HEADLINE

First published in 2000
by HEADLINE BOOK PUBLISHING

10

A catalogue record of this book is available from
the British Library

ISBN 0 7472 7204 2

Typeset by
Letterpart Limited, Reigate, Surrey

Printed and bound in Great Britain by
Mackays of Chatham plc, Chatham, Kent

HEADLINE BOOK PUBLISHING
A division of Hodder Headline
338 Euston Road
London NW1 3BH

www.headline.co.uk
www.hodderheadline.com

DEDICATION

To my wife Liz and daughter Chelsea

ACKNOWLEDGEMENTS

Stuart Pearce and Bob Harris would like to acknowledge the help of Liz, for her patience, Stuart's family, Kevin Mason, Jonathan Harris, Ian Marshall, Lorraine Jerram, and all at Headline.

contents

prologue

There was no mention of a penalty shoot-out. The prospect had simply never crossed the minds of the players and I'm not even sure whether it crossed the mind of the manager. It wasn't just another game. This was a big one, a very big one, and all of our thoughts were on the 90 minutes ahead. Every player was focused on what he had to do, his role in the team.

In that situation, you just think about the game and nothing else. When the 90 minutes comes to an end, and there's still another 30 minutes of extra time to go with tired minds and tired bodies, that's when mistakes are made. The concentration has to be even stronger. When the referee blows the final whistle, the winding down process begins immediately, the jangling nerves begin to relax. The game is over. You have given it your best and it has finished as an honourable draw. Then the realisation dawns – penalty kicks. Everything you and your team-mates have worked for over the past months rests on five individuals taking penalties and a goalkeeper who you hope is going to stop at least one of the opponents' spot-kicks.

In those two or three minutes before the penalty-takers are announced, you suddenly have to concentrate, regain your focus as quickly as possible, especially if you are chosen or put yourself forward as one of those under the microscope, as I did.

The players gather in the centre circle, encouraging, showing solidarity for each other. There is anxiety among the chosen five and a perceived relief among those who do not have to shoulder the responsibility. The goalkeeper is away at the end of the ground where the shoot-out is to take place, bouncing around knowing that he, above anyone, has nothing to lose and absolutely everything to gain.

I keep my socks up and my pads in to try to stay in game mode. Others prefer to lie down and draw a deep breath, relax those cramping muscles but I stay on my feet, take a drink and keep my mind as sharp as I can. The job isn't over yet; it's only finished when we have won on penalties and that is now all that matters.

All you need to do is walk 50 yards, take a penalty and score. That's the worst part of it, that bloody walk from the halfway line. Why do they make you stand there, so far away? God only knows which masochist decided that. It is clearly someone who has never been in this nerve-jangling position because it heightens the tension to an unbeliev-able degree. The stadium is a complete blur as you take that seemingly endless walk. I was not aware of the crowd or of anyone talking to me. I had already decided in which direction to shoot. But you talk to yourself. You tell yourself not to sidefoot the ball to give the goalkeeper a chance. It is now down to the simplest of equations – you against him.

When you are in a tight corner like this, a crisis situation, the usual decision is to go for your best penalty, to play your strongest card. Drill it because even if he goes the right way, if there is pace on he might not be able to keep it out. After this basic concept there are two other choices to make – whether to aim straight down the middle allowing for the certainty that the goalkeeper will move, or whip the ball across him.

Suddenly you're there. While you have been making the long walk there has been a feeling of detachment that only disperses when you grab hold of the ball, which is either bouncing around or, more often than not, thrown with unnecessary pace by the goalkeeper who is trying to gain a psychological edge. The nerves which have been racking your body disappear when you finally reach the penalty area and pick up the ball. You are on familiar territory, like the seasick sailor who at last sees the land ahead.

But it is still a dream world. There are no individual noises from the crowd, just a muffled blur. You try to flood your mind with positive thoughts. You tell yourself that you are the favourite, that you are 12 yards out with everything stacked in your favour. Make a good strike and if the goalkeeper picks the wrong way it will look like one hell of a penalty.

The pressure is truly on. No one has missed so far and the burden of not only your team-mates and your family, but also an entire nation is weighing heavily on your shoulders. Football is supposed to be a team game but now you're on your own. There is no hiding place in a football stadium for a penalty-taker in a shoot-out.

You put the ball on the penalty spot. It's only about six inches in diameter and you put it on the extreme edge nearest the goalkeeper. Silly as it sounds, it gains an inch and every player does it. Much more important is to find a high point. The last thing you want is a sunken penalty spot and you quickly seek an upgrade. You look for every possible advantage, no matter how tiny.

Having finally placed the ball, you walk back, totally ignoring the goalkeeper, taking nothing in, keeping the mind focused. I know where I'm going to put the ball and I won't change my mind. I never have before and never will, no matter what the circumstances. Any hesitation now is lethal.

I know that the goalkeeper will be hoping for that unnerving eye contact. He has nothing to lose and you have everything. I have to take a quick glance when I reach the end of my run, just to make certain that he isn't standing by one of his posts or hasn't gone for drink. You will look a fool in front of the world if you run up and shoot without looking and are called back to do it again. But there is no searching for his soul through his eyes. In most cases during 90 minutes and extra time, I am more than happy to stare into someone's eyes and throw down the challenge but all I want to see now is his profile. Come penalty shoot-outs, I'm more than a bit shifty. If I look in his eyes, that would move the advantage to him. When you are in combat, you have to play your strongest hand.

I walk back to the edge of the penalty area, just far enough to be able to get the right pace on the ball. Then, at last, you are on your run up, and there is no going back. Half a dozen steps between you and glory or abysmal failure. I know what my job is. I know exactly where

I want to hit it. Keep your eye on the ball . . . keep your eye on the ball. One . . . two . . . three . . . four . . . five . . . six . . . and strike. It's like a golf shot, the moment you make contact you know whether it's good or bad, hit or miss.

CHAPTER 1

the penalties

Turin, Wednesday, 4 July 1990

The ball flew straight and true and German goalkeeper Illgner dived to his right but he was aware enough to get his legs in the way and the ball rebounded back into play. My world collapsed. I had been taking penalties for as long as I could remember but now I'd missed the most important penalty of my life, in the semi-final of the World Cup.

If the walk from the centre circle had been long and nerve-racking, the walk back was a nightmare as the first onrush of tears pricked at my eyes. I had given away our advantage. We had won the toss and elected to take the first penalty, which Gary Lineker tucked away. Peter Beardsley and David Platt scored, but the Germans were unshakeable. Brehme, Matthaus and Riedle beat Peter Shilton. Now at 3–3, the advantage swung heavily towards the Germans. All I could do was pray that Thon evened the balance and missed his. He didn't, of course, and it was up to Chris Waddle to keep us in it and at least force the Germans to take their fifth penalty. He put the ball into orbit and we were out of the World Cup, facing a third-place play-off against Italy instead of the final in Rome against an Argentinian team we felt sure we could beat.

I don't blame Chris. I don't blame anyone but myself. It was my fault that England were not in the World Cup final. Friends surrounded me; special friends including Des Walker along with my other Nottingham Forest colleagues Steve Hodge and Neil Webb. But it scarcely eased the pain. Mark Wright was the first to come up, quickly followed by Terry Butcher. They put their arms around me and told me not to worry. My Forest team-mates knew me better than the others and knew that I would be in no mood to talk.

I noticed as I walked off that Gazza and a few others had gone over to the fans to applaud them for their support. I would normally have been there with them because I appreciate the effort the fans make, the time and money spent, to come and watch England play. I am from a working-class background and I know it means a lot when the players go over to say thank you. But on this occasion I couldn't do it. I felt guilty because I'd let them down. Neil Webb threw me a towel because I was sobbing my heart out. I had it over my head like a convicted criminal leaving a courthouse. I had never cried on a football pitch before. The towel hid the tears. I didn't want them to be seen in public; crying is something you do behind closed doors. Once Chris had missed and I knew that we weren't going any further, it was a case of getting away from the arena as quickly as possible. I wasn't running away to hide because I'm not that way inclined. It was just that I could do no more, we had lost, we were out and I didn't want to shed my tears in front of the cameras and the thousands in the stadium.

As I reached the touchline, our manager Bobby Robson was there. I had let him down too. He was gutted like the rest of us. We all knew that this was our final; get through this one and we would win the World Cup. We knew we had enough about us to go all the way. The confidence was building game after game following a bad start. Bobby came over, gave me a tap and said, 'Unlucky son.' But it's not always words. Des Walker, who knew me better than most, came over and he didn't have to say anything to me. He knew how I felt and I knew what he was thinking. It wasn't a case of 'how are you doing' and 'don't worry'. Of course I was going to worry. It made no difference that Chris Waddle went on to miss as well. I was the one who missed first and piled all the pressure on him. As far as I was concerned, it was my fault, my responsibility that we lost. Chris Waddle's penalty was irrelevant. As soon as I missed, if the Germans scored twice we were out.

To this day I admire everyone who goes up to take a penalty in those circumstances, especially the Germans. Every time we have come up against them they have held their nerve, even in our own backyard.

Credit to them, it shows a lot of mental strength. I don't know whether mental strength helps you score a penalty or even whether practising does, but you have to admire teams who manage to hold their nerve more often than not in something they call a lottery. It is not such a lottery for them.

I took penalties for my club so I had not bothered practising. Anyway, in those days penalty shoot-outs were the exception rather than the rule. It changed, of course, as time went on with penalty kicks deciding cup matches at every level from European Cup finals to World Cup finals. As they became more frequent, managers became cuter, putting on good penalty-takers in the final minutes as substitutes.

I could practise 100 penalties in the morning but it wouldn't help me score from the spot at ten o'clock that night when it mattered. There was a lot of criticism levelled at Glenn Hoddle for not insisting his team practised spot-kicks before the World Cup against Argentina in France eight years on, but I'm not sure that was justified. If I were to level a criticism it would be that the penalty-takers and the back-up were not named before the game. Then it would be up to the individual to go off with a goalkeeper and practise if that was what he wanted. To my mind, a match situation cannot be recreated no matter how hard you try.

In Italy I volunteered to take the third penalty but Bobby Robson felt that the fourth was the most important and wanted me, as a regular penalty-taker, to shoulder the responsibility for that one. The team's penalty-taker, in our case Gary Lineker, takes either the first or the last. What you need most of all is five people who want to take the penalties, without having to break their arms to persuade them. Then you have to look around for others if it goes beyond there.

The five penalty-takers that summer's day in Turin really picked themselves. Bobby knew and we knew who would be taking them – Gary Lineker, Peter Beardsley, David Platt, myself and Chris Waddle, all confident in our own ability to score from 12 yards. I don't think Paul Gascoigne wanted to be one of the five, although he would have taken his place afterwards, offering to take the sixth – a brave option. Des Walker wouldn't have wanted to take one, not because he was scared but simply because he was not a good penalty-taker. He readily admitted that he had scored just one goal in his entire career. No one in the team had a bigger heart than Tony Adams but he, like Des, wouldn't be one you would expect to take a penalty. No one has his guts but you would say to yourself surely there is someone better than him. There were those who did and those who didn't and we all knew who they were without going into great debates. That was not what happened with Glenn in France. His five penalty-takers weren't the logical choice. But ask anyone close to the team in 1990 and they would say that we had the correct five.

I have often wondered what would have happened had we put Dave Beasant in goal in time for the penalties. He's a big bloke, fills the goal. He had come out as a replacement for the injured David Seaman and brought with him a great reputation for saving penalties, including in a Cup Final at Wembley against odds-on favourite Liverpool. On the other hand, I couldn't remember the last penalty Peter Shilton had saved.

Who knows? Maybe the day will come when there's a specialist goalkeeper on the bench and you bring him on in the same way that you bring on a penalty-taker in the last few minutes. Imagine the psychology of the situation. It would certainly give the opposition food for thought because the move would be a very obvious one and they would be thinking, 'Oh, oh, what have we got here?' They would see this big monster coming on and the first-choice goalkeeper, captain as it happened, going off. I know I would be thinking the worst.

Martin O'Neill did it for Leicester City in the League Cup when he brought off injured Tim Flowers and sent on Pegguy Arphexad who had saved penalties in the competition before. He is shrewd is Martin O'Neill. I noticed on the way to winning the competition he made late substitutions to send on penalty-takers.

But it would have been a brave manager who took off Peter Shilton for that reason. He had been magnificent for England for 20 years and had more than played his part in taking us as far as the semi-finals. I still wonder if big Beasant might have saved one of those spot-kicks. Peter claimed he went the right way for every penalty but you can do that once the ball has hit the back of the net! He could offer an even better argument by saying England would have had a better chance if they had taken me off.

As I was leaving the field in Turin, Thomas Berthold, the German right wing-back whom I had been up against for the last two hours, came up and wanted to swap shirts. I wasn't in the mood to do it there and then and I told him to come into the dressing-room afterwards and I would look after it then. The last thing I wanted to do was to wear a German shirt as I walked off the pitch.

I was massively disappointed for myself and seeing the look on Bobby's face did not help. It was his last chance with England and he must have thought that he was about to emulate Sir Alf Ramsey and win the World Cup. I had let the nation down, but most of all I had let him down. He was and is a good man. Everyone who knows him and especially those who played for him like him and I have never heard a bad word about him.

As I reached the sanctuary of the dressing-room there was a tap on my shoulder and Doc Crane was telling me that I had been picked for the drug test. My immediate reaction was to hell with it. I won't do it. I'm not getting involved in that. But it was just the Doc doing his job.

The dressing-room was like a morgue. There were a lot of tears. Myself, Chris Waddle and some of the others were sobbing. I sat there thinking that I had let them all down even though it was evident that they were not thinking that way. The grieving was interrupted when a couple of the Germans came in, including Berthold. They were most civil and polite but a couple of our lads took offence. Steve Hodge shouted at them, 'Fuck off out of here.' He was distraught and thought they had come to rub our noses in it but I told him to leave it and exchanged shirts as promised.

Peter Shilton was the other England name to come out of the hat for a drug test and, having taken on board extra fluids, we went to the medical room where we joined the two Germans who had been nominated. Had an outsider walked in they wouldn't have known who were the winners and who were the losers. That's how respectful the Germans were. There was no question of them gloating over their victory. Shilts was lucky. He walked in, had a pee and walked out again leaving the three of us sitting there waiting for something to happen. The two Germans said nothing about the missed penalty; they just kept their own counsel and respected my silence. I appreciated that for I was in no mood for chitchat. I wasn't just low, I was double low. I'm not sure that the English would have behaved as well. I guess if the roles had been reversed, we would probably have been jumping around, laughing and celebrating. I appreciated their professionalism when I thought about it later. They had achieved a massive honour but, at the same time, they clearly knew how I felt. I had my head down all of the time and didn't take in their faces. I couldn't say who they were, but right now I would like to thank them.

I learned a good lesson. When we beat Spain on penalties in Euro 96, I celebrated the goal but when we won I went up quietly and shook hands with the Spanish players who had missed. I didn't want to be rubbing it in. I also congratulated the Germans when they beat us one match later. I cried then, not just because we had lost but because I had made up my mind that I was going to retire whichever way the result went. I thought it was my last international game.

It took the two Germans almost half an hour to give their samples but I was so dehydrated that still nothing happened. I was in there for a good hour and a half and still not able to take a leak. We were probably losing six pounds a game during the World Cup in the heat of an Italian summer, and despite drinking litre after litre of water I was just soaking it up like a sponge. In the end, I walked around the deserted stadium with Doc Crane for company, just the pair of us walking around having a quiet chat. Seventy-five minutes earlier I had been on that pitch in the midst of the action, and here I was now with my belly swollen and sloshing round with water. What I really wanted at that moment was to be with the rest of the team, commiserating and supporting, a group of blokes together in a time of mutual despair that only we could fully appreciate.

When I did finally have that long-awaited leak and returned to join them, they were all sitting on the coach waiting for me. I can't even remember whether I apologised to them. I was gone. The first to come up to me again was the manager who told me to keep my head up and not worry. I sat down on my own and Terry Butcher came and sat by me. I cried all the way back to the hotel. I was glad that it was Butch. I knew what he said was coming from the heart because he had the same attitude and passion for the game as me. It must have been hurting him as well; he knew that this was his last tournament. Even so, I would have preferred to sit on my own in my abject misery but he sat there for a good half an hour talking to me and doing what he thought was right.

There was a meal laid on at the hotel when we returned but I just went straight up to bed. I was rooming with Des Walker, as usual, and for once it wasn't him keeping me awake with his incessant chatter. We were old room-mates. He liked to stay up late and talk and I liked to go to sleep. I would usually doze off, wake up every half an hour or so and say 'yes Des' 'no Des' until he went off to sleep. But it pays to have a friend alongside you to share the load. He knew when to talk and when not to talk – and boy could he talk. This time he kept silent and that tells me volumes about the man.

I couldn't get to sleep anyway thinking about the game, and having started to pee I couldn't stop. I was going every half an hour and I didn't want to keep Des awake. After going half a dozen times I got hold of one of the old tin wastepaper bins and put it by the side of the bed. Every time I wanted to go I just rolled over and urinated out of the bed straight into the tin. Poor Des, it must have sounded like a machine-gun at first and then a waterfall. All you could hear was the noise made by the tin and come the morning I had virtually filled it. All I can say is that it was a good job that the bin had a good seal on it! Des claims he slept through it all.

The next day the management had arranged for the team to meet up with our wives and families at another hotel. I had not seen Liz or my father and mother, Dennis and Lil, since before the game. I apologised to them when we met and immediately filled up again. But that was to be the end of my tears. Football beckoned with a third-place play-off game against the hosts Italy in Bari.

It is always a massive let-down for a player to face what is a consolation match when you feel you should be in the final and this one turned out to be an even bigger disappointment for me because Bobby Robson decided to leave me out. Had I been a bit more experienced and a bit older I would have stood up to the manager and told him forcibly, 'There is no way you are going to leave me out of this game after what happened to me.' Certainly Peter Shilton did. Bobby was going to play Dave Beasant instead but this was going to be Shilton's last game. He said he wanted to play and was reinstated. He had 125 caps and had the right to say it. But I was young and had too much respect for Bobby Robson to start throwing my weight around and he decided for his own good reasons to leave out both myself and Chris Waddle, saying that he wanted to give the patient Tony Dorigo a game and that Chris was looking tired.

It concerned me that people would think I had wanted to be left out and was hiding after missing the penalty. Quite the opposite was true. I wanted to go out and show how well I could play. I wanted to prove to everyone that I wasn't afraid. I believe that had I said so, Bobby Robson would have played me for at least part of the game.

It would have been selfish of me not to let Tony Dorigo play. He had been with us all the way through, his parents were there and he was especially keen to play against the hosts because of his Italian ancestry. Nevertheless, it remains a regret, and I missed a cap.

We all stripped and sat on the bench anyway. The pressure had gone and it was a carnival atmosphere, although we lost 2–1. At half-time we stayed out and had a kickabout and it was so relaxed that I walked over to the touchline and talked to Liz in the crowd.

There was another twist to the tale when the physio came on to the pitch and gave me a shout that I might be going on. Bobby and all the staff were in the medical room with Mark Wright who had one of his socks and boots off. I heard Bobby say, 'I don't give a fuck. Get your boot back on and get out there for the second half.' It was not the first time Mark had complained on the trip and Bobby was adamant that he should go out and run it off. I should have said then, 'Get him off and get me on. I'm desperate. He doesn't want to play. I do.'

It was back home the next day and I thought that Chrissie and I were going to be lynched when we arrived back at Luton airport. We had heard a whisper that there were a lot of people waiting for us and I was dreading it. All I wanted to do was to go home to Nottingham because I knew that with my relationship with the people and the football fans I would have no hassle. Nottingham is not a hotbed of football and they would let me get on with my life, leave me alone and let me have my own time.

An open-topped bus was waiting to take us from the airport to the Hilton Hotel at Junction 11 on the M1. Both Chris and I sat downstairs out of the way. We were taking no chances. But we need not have worried. There was not one bad word from anyone. The support was tremendous. What should have been a 15 minute drive took us almost five hours so dense were the crowds. Talking to Chris about it now, it is still unbelievable the way people rallied round. I am sure it is the British spirit. It was just incredible; everyone got behind us and I couldn't understand it because I expected to be hammered. In Italy, we were insulated from how people were feeling about the World Cup. I am not much of a newspaper reader and, anyway, things are hyped up.

When we realised there wasn't a lynch mob waiting, Chris and I quickly made our way to the top of the bus. People had turned up to say well done and that we had been unlucky the way we went out. It would have been rude to stay downstairs. At least I wasn't wearing a pair of plastic tits and a false bum like Gazza at the front of the bus; I preferred to be a little more sedate at the back.

I don't think you should glorify losers but I have to admit that reception gave me a huge lift. Maybe it was because we lost gloriously and went out trying. I must have received over 500 letters of support and I replied to every one. It was the least I could do but it was still a total surprise. There was not one nutcase or a single anonymous slagging. I expected at least one from Chris Waddle telling me that it was my entire fault.

Admittedly, some people made up for it the following season with chants of 'Pearce is a German' and I was the one with the target on my back. But I had taken something positive from that dreadful time and had by far my best season for Forest, in fact my best season in football.

I scored 16 goals with not a penalty among them; Nigel Clough was taking them successfully at the time. He took over before we went to Italy.

Brian Clough didn't say a word about the World Cup when we returned. His main concern was that the four of us would come back from Italy thinking that we were big hitters. I can't remember having any dialogue with him other than asking for some extra days off as there were only eight days between the day we returned and going back to pre-season training. He told me that I couldn't because he had signed a contract committing us to a trip abroad.

I thought I had cleansed myself of that penalty miss in Turin long before my goal from the spot in the shoot-out against Spain in Euro 96 but watching the video now, I'm not so sure. My emotional reaction was the culmination of several things – scoring a goal for England; the competition being on our own soil; and thinking the tournament was going to be my last for England. Perhaps there was also something lingering deep down from Turin.

When Terry Venables first rang me up, I'm sure he hoped I would retire when he told me that I would not be his first choice left-back. I responded that if he thought I was good enough to be in the squad, I was prepared to sit in the stand if necessary and wait for my chance. I think that shook him. That was in 1995 and I spent a lot of time watching Graeme Le Saux play at left-back. He played reasonably well for his country and it was only his injury that got me back in. I was lucky. I wouldn't wish that on anyone but so often in football one person's downfall is another's bonus. I would much prefer to stand up, fight my ground and put him out of the team by my own form.

Terry left the door open for me to walk away from England but I'm glad I never did. Come that penalty against Spain I was well pleased that I had hung around on the off chance.

This was a completely different situation from that warm, pulsating night in Turin. When I was walking up this time I knew that the entire stadium was behind me. It was tangible. The whole of Wembley was buzzing. But I was also aware that half the people in the stadium were thinking, 'Oh no, not him again,' while the other half were probably saying to themselves, 'Don't let him miss this time.'

Afterwards Liz asked me why it always seemed to be me on the spot. My response was that I would rather take one than send a mate of mine up for him to miss. Liz was sitting with her brother and they apparently just looked at each other when I made my way to the penalty area. Neither said a word. No one knew I was going to take a penalty that day, not even me.

Terry had told us to practise spot-kicks prior to the game but it hadn't been sorted out who would take them and in what order. Practice was crazy anyway and far too light-hearted to be of any real use. One of us would put the ball down to take a penalty and Paul Ince would steal up and hit it. It ended up with Incy taking more penalties than anyone else. The only thing we knew for sure was that Alan Shearer would be taking one because he was the nominated penalty-taker. When Terry came off the bench to sort it out, I made a beeline for him and said that I wanted to take the third one.

'Are you sure?' he asked.

I had never been surer of anything. If he had said no I would have fought it. I don't know whether I surprised him but I felt that I had, just as I did when I said I was prepared to sit in the stand and wait my chance.

When I scored, my reaction wasn't stage-managed. It was a release of pressure and if you looked around the stadium you could see the relief and joy on every English supporter's face. Like me, they probably celebrated that particular penalty more than any of our others. It was a great feeling of elation but after my initial celebrations it was a case of being a bit humble, remembering how proper the Germans were.

No one deserved credit more than David Seaman, the Arsenal goalkeeper. Not only did he make the save that took us past Spain but he was also our best player throughout the tournament. I congratulated him quickly but didn't get involved in the mêlée. I went off to find the Spanish lad, Nadal, who had missed and shook his hand, trying to keep a civil head on it because I remembered what had happened to me. I drew the line, however, at going into their dressing-room. I hadn't been invited and sometimes it can be misconstrued, as it was by Hodgey when Berthold came in for my shirt.

When we went back to the training pitch on Monday morning to prepare for the German game, I already knew my strategy if it went to penalties. I told Terry Venables that I wanted to take the third one again. It would have been extreme cowardice to score against Spain and then not take one against the Germans. I knew that the Germans would be thorough. They would have watched every video of every penalty-taker and noted in which directions they shot. It was my belief that the German goalkeeper, Andreas Kopke, would dive the way we took our penalties against Spain. I sought out our penalty expert Alan Shearer and explained my theory to him and asked him, 'Are you going to change direction if it goes to penalties?'

'I'm not going to tell you,' he replied.

'Well, cheers mate,' I said. 'I'll watch you anyway as you take the first penalty.'

Maybe he had heard the chants around the grounds that I was a German and didn't trust me after my miss in the 1990 World Cup.

Of course, it went to penalties. I was sure that my theory was right because a German goalkeeper would be so professional that he would know which way he was going to dive against each penalty-taker. If a player took one which went to the goalkeeper's right against Spain, he would dive to his right.

Alan took the first and he chose the opposite corner to his penalty against Spain; the goalkeeper went the other way. I thought that was going to throw a spanner in the works. If the second penalty-kicker, David Platt, went for the other corner as well, what would the goalkeeper think then? I was in a quandary until Platty took the penalty. He went the same way as before – the goalkeeper guessed right but failed to save it. That put my mind at rest and I went up thinking if I went in the other direction I would score.

Don't get me wrong, the pressure was on – it always will be at that level – but in David Seaman we had a goalkeeper who was playing so well. He had already saved Gary McAllister's penalty against Scotland as well as Nadal's against Spain and he was such a colossus I just couldn't see him being beaten. That's not meant as any sort of slur on Peter Shilton six years earlier; it was just that Seaman was in such prime form I couldn't see us being beaten if we scored our penalties. I simply couldn't see him letting five penalties in and even now when I watch it on the video I cannot believe he did not stop one of them.

To be honest, the pressure had lifted in comparison with the game against Spain when I felt the weight of the world on my shoulders. The pressure was still there but it was different, and I had convinced myself that provided I changed corners I could even side-foot it in. That's how confident I was of scoring.

I went through the usual routine and hit the penalty with far less force than usual. In fact, if Kopke had gone the right way he would have saved it; it would have been a doddle. He could almost have headed it out. The BBC's Barry Davies said on the commentary, 'What a penalty! What a great penalty!' It was not a great penalty; it was a shite penalty but the goalkeeper had gone the wrong way. I had done my homework and it had paid off. It was a great feeling that it had worked. I knew that this time the advantage was mine. It gave us a chance of going to the final but it didn't give me the same feeling as the goal against Spain.

Hassler, Strunz, Reuter, Ziege and Kuntz took tremendous penalties and although Dave Seaman got near to a couple he couldn't save any of them. Our first five were rattled away with equal authority as Shearer, Platt, myself, Gascoigne and Sheringham all scored. Then came Gareth Southgate. How my heart bled for my young friend.

Before we came together with England, we didn't know each other at all but straightaway we hit it off. He is an excellent professional and that's something I admire in a player. The way he talks is very mature and he is not a beer-swilling player who is going to be a bad influence on the game. I was impressed with Gareth. He puts his heart and soul into his profession and we struck up a good friendship.

So when he missed his penalty, I went straight up to him to console him. Andy Moller completed the *coup de grâce* with another fine penalty and we were out. He even showboated a bit, puffing out his chest in a parody of Gascoigne. Who could blame him. They had come in the three lions' den and bitten our heads off again. I have to give them total credit. They came into our backyard and scored six out of six penalties. You have to applaud their bottle.

I swapped shirts with winger Thomas Hassler and joined the others in a lap of honour that gave me my best footballing memory. Euro 96, with my family being there, the atmosphere in the stadium and the closeness of the team, brought a joy greater than I had ever experienced, and walking round Wembley thinking I was never going to do this again or represent my country again brought the tears. I was there as understudy to Graeme Le Saux and only played because of an injury. Every time I pulled on an England shirt it was a bonus to me.

I hadn't gone straight from school to a football career. I had worked for a living and I walked around Wembley thinking to myself, 'I'm an electrician and here I am at one of the great football moments in English history.' This was something I loved doing. It wasn't a game of football; this was my life. I have a wife, Liz, and a daughter, Chelsea, but this was different and the pride I had in playing for England and the thought it would never happen again made me very emotional.

Gary Lineker made a statement when he retired saying that he had more important things in his life – his wife and his family – and that football was just something he had done. I am not like that at all. I find that attitude as alien as probably he finds mine of football being something far more than just a game that you play for fun. People might find that attitude odd but I'm convinced a lot of supporters and players share it. Anyway, I'm not sure I totally believed Gary. He loved the game. I suppose some love it more than others and some of us have a great passion for the sport. Looking back on my career, I still have that great surge of passion and pride.

We saw our families to commiserate and then we boarded our bus. Just before we pulled out from Wembley I asked Terry if I could say something over the microphone. I told the other lads it had been an honour and a privilege to play with them, it was my last game and that I was retiring. As a footnote, I added, that I wasn't retiring from football and would still be around the Premier Division to kick shit out of them.

Back at the hotel, we ordered beers. Our football had finished, there was no third-place play-off, so we were on holiday. We stayed up for most of the night. Sleep was impossible after that with so much adrenalin still flooding through our bodies. Terry told us we could go home if we wanted to but we all stayed, had a meal together and then got drunk together.

Gareth went straight up to his room to telephone his family and then came and joined us in the bar. As he walked in, Tony Adams booed and hissed at him and that broke the ice. Gareth was under a cloud, an awful cloud, and Rodders (Adams) had done the right thing. Everyone laughed and it lightened the atmosphere.

As everyone finished their dinner and drifted out to the bar I was left talking to Gareth. We had a long chat and I hope it helped him having me there. The others could only imagine what he was suffering but I knew for sure.

There were more than a few who took offence when Chris Waddle and I joined Gareth in a television advert that raised a laugh out of the three of us missing crucial penalties. As far as I was concerned, the penalty trauma was in the past. The ghost had been vanquished and banished when Pizza Hut asked me to do the advert, offering me £40,000, a considerable sum of money for what amounted to one day's work. I couldn't really turn it down. To be honest, if it had been straight after the 1990 World Cup I wouldn't have done it. Wild horses wouldn't have dragged me within a mile of television cameras.

But in 1996, for me it was just a spin-off of being a professional footballer. I found it very amusing and so did Chrissie. I think Gareth did as well. He had his doubts about doing it but the two of us persuaded him. 'It's old hat,' we said. 'Everybody misses penalties. Go for it.'

Call me a hypocrite or worse – when he asked me if I would have done it just after the 1990 World Cup, I told him I would. In my defence, in 1990 the entire issue of penalty shoot-outs was new. They hadn't happened that often. By the time Gareth missed his, there had been lots of such dramas all around the world at every level. Also, if he hadn't agreed, there would be no fees for Chris and me! Selfish?

Maybe, but most people took it the right way and I don't think it harmed Gareth at all. Sometimes in our game you have to laugh at yourself and this was some sort of relief for all of us.

It was hardest for Gareth in every sense – he was the butt of the joke and he was the one who had to keep eating the pizzas. The pizza he was seen eating in the advert had to look hot and steamy so someone kept blowing cigarette smoke on it. Imagine how awful that was for a non-smoker and fitness fanatic. Chris and I kept cocking it up on purpose so that he had to take yet another bite. We had him on about 20 takes before we relented.

The advert was shot in a studio in Park Royal starting at eight in the morning. I left at seven in the evening. It was exhausting. Gareth had more to do than the rest of us. Chris finished his part and shot off, and when I left the poor boy was still hard at it, shooting the scene where he stood up and walked into a post. He had to stay for another two hours, bumping into two Germans, and he finally went home at around nine, tired and feeling sick from all the pizzas he had to eat.

Of course, the simple way out would have been not to volunteer to take penalties in the first place. Certainly that was Liz's feelings. Why, she asked, did I continually put myself in this position? It was because I had been taking penalties for so long and I did so because I could strike the ball well. It dated back to my childhood. When you are a kid and you hit the ball firmly, you tend to take all the free kicks and penalties as I did from schooldays onwards. It is also part of my character and I have always wanted to do it. At most of my clubs I have also been captain and it is a natural extension of that responsibility.

It's easy enough to take a penalty when you're 3–0 up but the higher the stakes the harder it becomes. One of the first misses I remember was in the County Cup in a Sunday League for a very strong team called Bourne Hall. Apart from myself, we had John Humphries who went on to play for Wolves and Charlton, and Gary Waddock who played for Queens Park Rangers. Most of the others were attached to Watford. I was one of the lesser lights in the side. That day the pitch was thick mud. We were awarded a penalty, I didn't hit it hard enough and the goalkeeper saved it. To this day the coach will remind me that I missed a penalty that cost us a game when he would have put money on me to score.

At Wealdstone when I was 18 and in my first season, we played AP Leamington with so much on it that the winners would stay up and the losers would be relegated. It was a bigger deal than normal because who went into the newly formed Alliance Conference and who didn't depended on the result. It was even more massive for me as I was being paid £15 a week for doing something I loved. It was a baking hot day, the last game of the season, we were 1–0 up and cruising. We had a lad on loan from Millwall named Jimmy Swetzer. I had not heard of him before and I have not heard of him since. He missed a penalty; we lost and went down.

That was my first experience of what a missed penalty could do. Had he scored we would have been two up and we would never have lost but he was on loan and probably didn't care too much one way or another. The rest of us were stuck with the outcome and I was there for 12 months trying to get out of the Southern League and back into the Alliance.

There was a repeat scenario when I was playing for Coventry. We needed to win our last three matches in the 1983–84 season to stay in the top division. Nowadays every game finishes at the same time on the last Sunday but it was not the case then. We beat Luton 1–0 when Brian Kilcline scored a goal in the 82nd minute, thundering one in from the edge of the box. We went to Stoke in the next game and I scored from the spot in the last ten minutes, whipping one across the goalkeeper like the one I took against Spain. Then Ian Painter had a penalty at the other end. He took a long run up, smashed it against the underside of the crossbar and it bounced up so high that our goalkeeper Steve Ogrizovic caught it on the way down. Had that gone in and the game finished in a draw, we were down regardless of our last result.

On the last day we were due to play the league champions Everton on a Sunday at Highfield Road. Everyone else had finished so we knew that a win would keep us up. We won 4–1. You could smell the booze on the breath of the Everton players. We were sure that they had been out on the Saturday night to celebrate. We were trying our hearts out but if the game had been played a month earlier when they were chasing championship points, they would have wiped the floor with us. They had lost seven games all season. We won three games in the last week and yet previously we had won just 12 games all the rest of the season. In retrospect, the two penalties in the Stoke game proved to be critical.

Another crucial penalty in the Stuart Pearce scrapbook was in the quarter-final of the League Cup against Arsenal in the late eighties. We were 2–0 down at the time and I missed from the penalty spot. We scored after that and were playing well enough to have taken something out of the game. I thought we could have won if I had scored. I can be the most philosophical player in the world when someone else is taking and missing penalties.

Free kicks are all part of the same thing but without the pressure of taking a penalty. You are expected to score from the spot but if you score from a free kick outside the penalty area you are hailed as a hero. There is nothing I relish more than a free kick just to the right-hand side of the penalty area. At Forest, Nigel Clough was brilliant at winning free kicks in that zone. He wanted the ball to feet and when he was touched from behind he would go down. We set the wall up so that we had someone masking the ball from the goalkeeper, so I got in a lot of strikes and goals at that time. I scored from one in the semi-final of the League Cup against Coventry City. I curled the ball in from wide and it hit the underside of the bar, beating Oggi. It put us in the final and gave that particular Forest team the first bit of silverware for Brian Clough.

In those days we were being awarded two, three and sometimes four free kicks in good positions every game. Even if the goalkeeper saved from them, more often than not there would be the pickings for the others to follow up on. Nigel wasn't a diver but he was very clever. He was ahead of his time because that's how it's played now when, at the merest contact, down the forward goes. You have to be cute.

I hear and understand the arguments about cheating and diving but to me it's clever play. I never take a dive and if I did I would probably look such an idiot the referee would laugh and play on, or book me. Much of the time, as the laws stand now, if you are stupid enough to make that lunging tackle, you have to expect the worst. When Paolo di Canio goes down and wins a penalty for West Ham, I would never ever criticise him or any other player for diving. If it were me who conceded the penalty, I would probably blame myself more than the forward. I would probably have a little moan at him at the time but you have to think to yourself that if you can't win the ball then don't make the tackle.

People used to say that I wouldn't be able to cope with the new interpretation of the rules at either club or international level, but you have to learn and adjust. In the end, it makes you a better player.

CHAPTER 2

yak jensen, the three-time loser

I was never a big lad. If anything I was a bit small and skinny and, consequently, there was no queue of top clubs knocking on my parents' door in Kingsbury, a free kick away from Wembley Stadium. In fact, I was a pretty normal sort. I played semi-professional football at Wealdstone on a Saturday afternoon, went down to the local pub on a Saturday night and turned out for my mates' team, Dynamo Kingsbury Kiev, on a Sunday morning.

I wasn't supposed to play for them because of my contract with Wealdstone but these were my best mates, most of them schoolmates, and I didn't want to miss out on the fun. We cooked up the scheme that I would play in goal under the assumed name of Yak Jensen. I had to look the part, of course, and I wore a spectacular tangerine and black goalkeeping kit complete with an embroidered number one along with the name Jensen. A pair of long black shorts that came down to my knees completed the outfit. It was hardly a case of hiding my true identity – if I wasn't spotted in that get-up I certainly was when I went upfield for corners and free kicks. I did lots of stupid things like standing on the penalty spot to take crosses with four defenders on the line. I would also throw the ball out to the wing and then chase it myself, taking on opponents because I was confident that I was better than most of the players in that league.

Not everybody appreciated this colourful 'Russian' interloper and now and again someone would take offence, come across and whack me down as I tried to push the ball past them. 'That will teach you to come out of your goal, Jensen,' I heard more than once. I knew that if

I had played under my proper name, sooner or later I was going to get collared. Even so I was taking a risk but I enjoyed every minute and one season I even finished top goalscorer in the team with seven. It was a great laugh and was simply an extension of Saturday night out with the lads.

All good things have to come to an end and, sure enough, one winter Sunday morning one of the rivals caught up with me. I had come to the edge of my box and was caught on the side of the leg. I didn't think much of it at the time and carried on playing even though it was a bit sore. Wealdstone's training was called off on Tuesday because of the bad weather and it wasn't until I went in on the Thursday that I began to realise that something was wrong. It was still icy so all we did was run up and down. The leg was worse but I said nothing. We were due to play at Runcorn on the Saturday and when I went out for the warm-up it became obvious that it was far more serious than I thought. As I went to turn, it felt as though someone had thrown a lump of mud at the back of my leg with quite a smack. It turned out that I had fractured the small bone, the tibia, and when I turned it snapped completely.

I limped into the dressing-room and told the manager, 'I think I've broken my leg.'

'What?' he said.

'I think I've broken my leg. I thought at first it was one of the boys messing around and throwing something at me but there was no one near. I think it's broken.' He wasn't convinced.

'We've only got one substitute with us. Do you think you can go out and give it a go? See how it goes.'

I agreed. It was only a small bone, not load bearing, so I thought I could get away with it. I lasted five minutes before I had to give it up and as I limped back to the bench along the touchline one of the Scousers leaned over the barrier and yelled, 'You soft Southern twat.' He thought I'd gone off because I'd bumped into someone.

I went off for an X-ray and the hospital confirmed my worst fears. I was out for six weeks and that was when I decided that Yak Jensen should hang up his goalkeeping gloves and return to the anonymity of the Russian plains.

I really missed the Sunday football; not that it stopped me meeting up with the lads. We continued to sink our pints together at the Plough in Kingsbury, usually going on to the Preston in Preston Road. We used to drink a fair bit and lads being lads we got into the odd scrape or two. I have to hold up my hands and confess that I was as bad as the rest of them. I blotted my copybook enough to have three convictions against me.

The first offence was taking and driving away a car. A group of us had been to a nightclub in Acton and left so late that there were no tubes and we couldn't get a cab for love nor money. In our weak defence it was not like the modern car theft, which is a serious offence and a real stigma, but more of a minor misdemeanour. We were desperate to get home and when we spotted an ancient Escort, we piled in. We thought that when we got home we could telephone the police anonymously and tell them where it was, or even drive it back to where we had found it the next morning. As jack-the-lad teenagers you tend to think silly things like that.

The three of us jumped in the car, turned the ignition using someone's house key and shot off. We were so naïve. We were only a couple of miles from home when, sure enough, the Old Bill saw these three kids batting along in an old motor, flashed us to stop and nicked us. I took control of the situation and said to the other two not to say a word and under no circumstances to tell them our real names. They nodded but as soon as the copper asked, 'What's your name?' I immediately replied, 'Stuart Pearce, sir.' So much for the hardened criminal.

I was gutted. I went to Harrow Magistrates Court where I was fined £100 and handed a year's ban from driving. I was thoroughly ashamed and very grateful that my parents hadn't heard about it. But I hadn't thought that one through either and, sure enough, a brown envelope popped through the front door with Harrow Magistrates Court emblazoned across the back. Naturally, my mum and dad opened it and discovered that their son was a convicted criminal.

The boys down the pub, who had been through the experience before, told me that the secret was always to take your chequebook with you to court so that you could pay the fine on the spot. That way no bumf is pushed through the front door. It was a little late for all that good advice and I suffered a serious grilling over the escapade from my parents with my dad even calling round my eldest brother Ray to try to find out if I was truly going off the rails.

It would be nice to say that I learned my lesson and trod the straight and narrow afterwards but I didn't and shamefully admit I was done twice more, once for being drunk and disorderly and then for criminal damage. At least I learned one lesson and neither my mum nor dad knew anything about offences two and three – well they didn't until they read this!

My mates to this day will say that there are two Stuart Pearces – the footballer and the lad they know. Certainly I proved that I could be as stupid as the rest of them. The difference now, however, is that I am a professional in the limelight and I know that I have to watch my step even though I still have a few beers, a laugh and take the piss with the best of them. They don't let me forget how I became a three-time loser.

As usual, the demon booze was at the heart of the matter and my second brush with the law came after a visit to a local nightclub when a friend of ours, behaving a bit over the top, had his collar felt. Showing admirable solidarity, we followed him down to the nearest police station. When we arrived he was already banged up in the back. Undeterred we approached the duty sergeant and asked if Mr Mitchell was there. When he confirmed that he was, we politely asked for the waiting room only to be told that there was one but we couldn't use it. With that the sergeant turned his back and disappeared into his office. Of course, we found the waiting room and went in to sit it out until they released our mate. We were soon discovered by a constable.

'You lot can't wait in here,' he said.

'Why not?' I asked. 'It says waiting room and we're waiting for our friend.'

He didn't like our attitude. 'One more word from any of you lot and you're nicked as well.'

Sure of my rights, I answered indignantly, 'You can't do that.'

He could and he did. He pointed at me and said, 'You'll do,' and promptly nicked me for being drunk and disorderly. I wouldn't have minded but I wasn't even drunk! I couldn't believe that I'd been arrested. It was embarrassing to be done on such a charge when all I wanted to do was sit in a waiting room.

That is not the end of this sorry tale of criminal activity. A week later the Sunday team went out for our usual dinner dance. That was a fancy name for meeting down the local, in this case the Green Man, where we each chipped in a fiver, more than enough to start the kitty with pints at 50 pence. I was delegated to collect the whip, make a note of the drinks and fetch them from the bar. On the way, I had a bright idea. I suggested to the barmaid that since every time I came up it would be the same order, if I paid her the same amount as the first round each time, it would save us both a lot of time and trouble. She was happy with the arrangement unaware that I had a little scam going. I paid the 13 or 14 quid for the 20 or so drinks and the next time I simply read off the list but added myself a drink at the top, another in the middle of the order and a third at the end and still paid the same money. I would take up one of the boys, ask him what he was drinking, and we would stand there and enjoy the first one on the house while she filled the remainder of the order.

Needless to say, I was several drinks ahead of the rest when we finally lurched out of the pub and staggered down Wembley High Road, past the Hilton Hotel and into the Greyhound on the corner. Football supporters will confirm that it is a rough-and-ready pub now but it was even rougher in those days. They had a live band and we played up to it, doing forward rolls on the dancefloor and generally larking around.

The dinner part of the evening followed at closing time, when we were uncorked into Wembley High Street to look for a curry house or fish and chip shop. It was then that, in my wisdom, I decided to climb a traffic light. Don't ask me why because to this day I haven't a clue. As if that wasn't daft enough, once at the top I decided to remove the little plastic cone, all under the surprised eyes of two policemen who watched the entire cameo. So I was nicked again, caught as they say 'bang to rights'.

I should have been set for a night in the cells to sleep it off but there were about 20 of us and the others followed us down to the station. Clearly the police were worried that they might have a minor riot on their hands and they let me straight out in response to the football-like chant of 'let him out, let him out' at the counter of the Wembley Police Station. They charged me to attend Harrow Magistrates Court, would you believe, on the same day that I was due to appear at the same place for my alleged drunk and disorderly charge!

I duly went to court and was asked whether I pleaded guilty or not guilty to the charge of being drunk and disorderly. I answered, 'Well, to be honest, I'm not guilty but I have got to plead guilty because I can't afford the time off work to fight the case.' The magistrate was clearly perplexed at this unusual response.

'I can't work this out. Are you pleading guilty or not guilty?' he said.

'I'm innocent but I'm pleading guilty.'

This was real John Grisham stuff but he wasn't impressed with my innocent look and, trying to hide his smile, he banged his gavel and fined me £25.

There are six or eight courts at Harrow and I thought that the chances of me going back to the same court and appearing before the same judge were remote in the extreme.

Who says that lightning doesn't strike twice? Thirty minutes later I was back in front of the same magistrate. The look on his face was worth the price of the first fine alone. It was a picture. He asked me what had happened this time and I answered that I had enjoyed a few drinks and climbed a traffic light and lifted the top off and that I was very sorry. Criminal damage sounds really bad when you are up in front of the beak but when you have had a couple of drinks, or more, and climbed a traffic light, it's not the worst offence in the world. Is it?

The magistrate asked me what had made me do it. Having just fined me for being drunk and disorderly he had hardly any need to ask and I mumbled the facts again, that I had had a few drinks and that I was sorry, really sorry. I was ready for him to throw the book at me for this, my second charge in half an hour, but he fined me £15 and added

77 pence for the cost of the part I had 'damaged'. I was much relieved and immediately wrote out a cheque totalling £40.77 while blessing a magistrate with a sense of humour and a grasp of reality.

My parents never did discover about that double whammy and I didn't class myself as a bad person even though I had a triple strike against me. Drunk and disorderly, stealing a car and criminal damage makes me sound a real tearaway, an absolute rogue and a hard case but I wasn't at all. What I was really guilty of was being all too ready to act the fool and be distracted – just as my old school reports said.

Strangely my football remained totally professional, believe it or not, and nowadays it's only once in a blue moon that I go past my limit and never when football is in close proximity.

Fortunately, I was never one for getting involved in fighting or anything physical like that. One or two of the lads were known to the local police and, later, when a fight broke out in a pub where we were drinking I slipped out of the door and was stopped by a couple of the local policemen, who knew I played for Wealdstone. They warned me not to get involved with that particular crowd, as they would surely land me in trouble. I took that advice to heart. I had been in enough grief.

The ones I meet up with every year were certainly not the worst of the worst but friends I have remained in touch with since our days together at school. Everyone is grown up now and a lot more sensible . . . most of the time. What amazes me is that none of this has come out over the past 20 years. Obviously my mates aren't into the kiss and tell business with the tabloid newspapers.

It was all part of growing up and while it's not something to be proud of, I can look back and laugh about it. I can relate to some of the young footballers that land themselves in trouble nowadays.

Although I liked a drink I can't say that I was ever a big drinker. We had a drink on a Saturday night like everyone did in my age group and it was the company and the laughs that meant more than the alcohol. It was all part of my background and I only did what most of the other kids did in those days. Some were caught and some were more fortunate.

★ ★ ★

I was born in Hammersmith Hospital on 24 April 1962, the youngest of four children. My eldest brother, Ray, is 17 years older than me, my sister Pamela is 14 years older, and my other brother, Dennis, ten years older. Dennis is the only one I can remember being at home.

Dennis is not sport-orientated at all, and neither is Pamela. Pamela is a child of the sixties. She was into women's lib and stuff like that and quite a headache for the old man by all accounts. When he asked her how she got home from school, more often than not she would tell him that she had hitchhiked. He was a bit old-fashioned and that sort of gay abandon tied him up in knots at times. As far as he was concerned, she was a girl and he couldn't treat her in the same way as her brothers. Now she teaches at Tottenham Tech.

Ray, on the other hand, is heavily into sport. He played football but his real love was boxing. He was a London ABA champion. My father was very disappointed when Ray got his girl pregnant and packed up boxing to marry her. He thought Ray had a real chance of making something in the fight game; it was not so much the pregnancy that upset him but the fact that Ray gave up boxing! That was when Dad started pushing me into football. He pushed me hard because he wanted me to do well but also because he's like that anyway – a bit obstinate and stubborn.

I have never gone into details with Ray over why he quit. He was matter of fact about it at the time. He enjoyed boxing but once he had the responsibilities of a wife and family he packed it up and started taking an interest in football refereeing. He progressed through non-league into the Football League and ran the line in top matches. The big age difference between us meant that when he was asked the usual questions about whether he had any relatives in the game he answered quite truthfully that he had not.

In fact, a trivia question that would flummox even the most knowledgeable football fan is when did two brothers take part in the same game with one playing and the other officiating? It happened to us when he ran the line in a Nottingham Forest League Cup-tie at Brighton. He disallowed a goal for Brighton! I had no fears, however, about his honesty. He would have erred on the side of Brighton rather than favour me.

No one knew, apart from the Forest team. It was funny running up the wing and having my brother alongside me on the touchline. He could have booked me because I kept taking the mickey out of him – 'Oi, you ginger dickhead,' is one thing I remember calling him. Perhaps it was a good thing that he never became a league referee because it would have come out eventually that he was my brother.

As can be guessed by the age gap I was an accident, something my parents have told me many times. It must have been quite a shock. Once you have had the kids and seen them grow up, I'm sure that the last thing you want is for another one to come along with the nappies and all the other things you thought were long gone.

We lived in a terraced house in Latimer Road, Shepherd's Bush, with an outside toilet. We were not on the poverty line and I'm a million miles from being a deprived child but it was bloody cold going outside to the toilet in the middle of winter and when I had a bath it was in a tin tub in front of a coal fire. Other than that, I can't remember a great deal about Shepherd's Bush or the fact that we were so close to Queens Park Rangers' ground. The odd thing sticks in the mind, though, like waking up in the middle of the night and finding Mum and Dad not there. I ran out into the street to the next-door neighbour who took me to the local pub where my parents were having a drink and a game of darts. They took me home and put me back to bed. I must have been very young but the memory is etched vividly on my mind. If that happened now, there would be hell to pay but in those days they weren't the only ones to leave the front door on the latch and ask the neighbours to keep an eye out.

We moved to Wood Lane, Kingsbury, near Wembley, when I was five, which was an ideal time for me as it coincided with me going to Fryent primary school. My father worked hard, clocking up the overtime to ensure that we lived as well as possible. He was a waiter up in London, working on the railways, at Quaglinos and at other restaurants, but he found time to play football for a Waiters XI. If you listen to both my father and my father-in-law, they were both the iron men in their teams but then I have yet to meet someone of 50 or 60 who owned up to being the little farty one on the wing, the one who used to scream when he was tackled. They were either a great goalscorer or the iron man of defence. I find it quite comical. My old man loved his football, was honest and a grafter but never progressed beyond the waiters team.

Dad worked hard to pay off the mortgage in Kingsbury. He would be up in London as early as six in the morning, travelling either by train or, if he was lucky, being dropped off by my mum. Sometimes he didn't finish until midnight. Ridiculous hours. There were times when Mum would have to get me up in the middle of the night, and drive me up to the West End to collect Dad because he couldn't get home any other way. Mum worked as well. She was a dinner lady at my primary school; that suited me because I always got extra chips.

Dad's belief was that you paid your mortgage off whatever the circumstances. John Beresford, whom I knew at Newcastle, told me that there was a young striker he played with at Southampton, James Beattie, who was bought as a reserve from Blackburn Rovers. He had a Porsche and a half share in a boat but rented a flat! We were laughing about it because we were both brought up by parents who force-fed us their own ideas, like all parents do. Sometimes when you reach your 30s you think what a load of rubbish they talked, but there was some good advice in there. I'm with my dad all the way where bricks and mortar are concerned. It has always been my philosophy, too, to get the house paid off.

As soon as the mortgage was settled, Dad packed in the job in London. It was the only reason he had worked so hard and as soon as it was done he became a postman in Wembley. He used to work on the post in the morning and come to watch me play football in the afternoon. In fact, both Mum and Dad would regularly come to watch me play. Dad couldn't drive so Mum used to take him in the Morris Minor and they would both watch whether it was a school match or a district match. Dad was marvellous the way he backed my football. He was so keen to see me get on that if he was doing nothing he would even clean my boots. With my brother no longer boxing, my football became the focal point of his life. He was living the football through me. The important factor was that both my parents were very supportive and helped me whenever they could. As I grew older, I sometimes played and trained with Ray but it was my dad who put his hand in his pocket to buy the boots and other equipment I needed. He even wrote off to our old local club and got me a trial.

'How would you like to play for QPR?' he asked me one day. I told him I would love to and he broke the news. That was very exciting for a 13-year-old kid.

We were very successful at Fryent Primary in Kingsbury – champions of London one season, losing just one match in the year. We also won the League and Cup in Brent but lost the Middlesex Cup 3–2 with the opposition's games master refereeing and being a bit liberal with the timekeeping.

At that time I always played centre-half – never, ever at left-back – but the first medal I won was as a goalkeeper in the third year of primary school, before I got into the school team. It was in a six-a-side tournament with third and fourth years. Each side had to have at least one third-former in the side and I was picked to play in goal.

It was my first medal and the feeling was unbelievable. I took it home and just looked at it. I guess that's when I developed my taste for winning trophies. Winning that medal really meant something. Times have changed. When I do presentations for kids these days, I find myself giving out so many trophies. When I ask did they win the cup or the league, the answer invariably is that they won neither; they are just awarded a trophy each year. There are medals for the Most Improved Player, the Leading Goalscorer and even for Turning Up Each Week and so it goes until these kids walk away with armfuls of cups. I had to play all season to win a trophy if we were lucky, and we were also given a medal.

I still have that first medal along with all my other school medals. They are side by side with my World Cup medal, all together. Obviously some mean more than others do but every one has its own personal memory. Sadly, I don't display them anymore because the police warned that things like that might attract burglars. I could lose a video or a television but I couldn't stomach losing an England cap, my World Cup medal or Littlewoods Cup winner's medals. It's a shame I can't show them but I can't take the risk. Other players have pictures of themselves in this game and that covering the walls but I suppose I have grown beyond that. I would rather have a nice print of a horse on the wall. It is more traditional and better for the room rather than a picture of me kicking a football.

I won about 70 cups and medals while I was at school – and not just for turning up. At my senior school, Claremont High in Kenton, we never lost a single home match. Quite a few of us went together from junior school to senior school so we had a good understanding and a very good spirit. We had a very good side but I was the only one to come through and make it at professional level. Gary Waddock was the only other one from my district to make the paid ranks. It wasn't ability; it was dedication.

When I was at school I was very small, probably the smallest in our team. That was probably what held me back in terms of being spotted. Who wants a tiny centre-half? I couldn't win all the headers so I had to make up for that by trying to win everything on the ground. That was when I started left-back for the county team. I was always one of the better players in all the teams I played for – not the best, but one of the better players. I put that down to pushing from the old man plus a lot of self-belief.

Dad bought me a briefcase when I went to senior school, which was probably the worst thing he could have done as you were immediately seen as a wally kid. That soon had the shit kicked out of it not only by other kids but also with some help from me to make out I wasn't one of those wallies!

Football was everything to me in senior school. We had one or two matches a week. They used to kick off at around 2.30 so the team used to miss the afternoon lessons, especially if it was away from home. All sport meant a great deal more to me than my academic work and as well as football I was picked to play in the school rugby team. Although I was very small, I could kick the ball over the posts for the conversions and penalties. Rugby wasn't really my game but I didn't mind because it meant I missed more classes. This sometimes happened three times a week with two football matches and a rugby match all during school time! In the summer I threw the javelin for the athletics team and I admit now that I did most of it to avoid as much school as I could.

Yet I never bunked off. I never missed one day of school when I was able to go and, in fact, I quite enjoyed it. I loved history, as I do now. We studied the twentieth century and even now I am a keen student of the Second World War. Looking back, I wish I had taken a little more notice of geography because of my love of travelling and visiting different countries. I also wish I had learned cookery for the times when I lived on my own. I gave maths my best shot but it was far from being my best subject, and if I had known I was going to be an electrician it would have been useful to do carpentry.

Dad wanted me to do well at lessons and all that but it was football where he most wanted me to succeed. Out of the four kids, Ray is an electrician like me and intelligent. He sometimes belies that by acting the fool but he is bright. If any tricky jobs had to be done, a big boiler house or anything like that, the council would call him in straightaway. He taught electronics at Willesden Tech. Dennis joined National Cash Registers from school and is still with them now. He is heavily into computers, working at Lloyd's of London as I write. With Pamela also teaching, I am so far from them intellectually it's untrue. I don't know whether the old man knew that.

I am one of those people who have kept my old school reports. (Without seeming too pathetic, I've also got the match reports of games I played in. I don't know whether that says something about me or not.) Every year my school reports were the same – maths C, English C, games AA. The comments were pretty standard, too, with 'too easily distracted' and 'too ready to play the fool' the most common. Lessons didn't mean a great deal to me and when you are not that intelligent you seem to slip even further away from it.

Both my parents were very understanding and I have no doubt that their support helped me come through.

Watching me play became something of a hobby for them. You wouldn't know what the other parents looked like because they would be working when the games were on. Mum and Dad continued to watch as I moved on to Sunday football and then non-league with Wealdstone and into the professional game.

As a teenager I was a firm QPR supporter and went regularly to Loftus Road. My hero was that brave aggressive defender David Webb. This was just after the Rodney Marsh era under Dave Sexton, with Don Givens, Stan Bowles, Dave Clement, Gerry Francis, Frank Gillard, Frank McLintock, John Hollins, Don Masson, Phil Parkes and the rest. I could name the whole team and the substitutes.

They finished second in 1975–6. I watched them a lot that season and was there for the last couple of games they needed to win to take the championship. Although we beat Arsenal and Leeds at home, we missed out when we lost 3–2 at Norwich, which allowed Liverpool to nip in and take the title. We had a small squad and needed one or two more to have won it.

I had friends who supported Leeds United and I would regularly watch them, too. We travelled to Elland Road and to games in the Midlands and all over London, of course. They were a fantastic side under Don Revie and I loved watching them. They were so good, it's hard to pick out favourite players from the likes of Jack Charlton, Paul Madeley, Terry Cooper, Allan Clarke, Paul Reaney, Billy Bremner, Norman Hunter, Johnny Giles, Eddie Gray, Peter Lorimer and all the rest. I remember having tears in my eyes watching them lose to Chelsea in the FA Cup final replay at Old Trafford when Dave Webb scored with a far-post header. He was no hero of mine that day! I even used to wear sock tie-ups with Peter Lorimer's name on them because I fancied I had a big shot like him.

I eventually left school at 16 having earned a CSE grade one in social studies and CSE in geography. I was never going to be academically gifted. I was average. It was hardly preparation for the big wide world.

I started work in a warehouse and attended day-release classes to become a qualified electrician. After the problems of school, I really enjoyed going to college and doing the work. I applied myself a little bit more and sailed through it, probably doing a lot better than some of the others in the class. I began to realise that maybe I was not so daft as I thought I was at school, especially compared with some of the others.

I qualified not just as an electrician but as an advanced electrician. That, however, was as far as I got. I became a little lost in the advanced mathematics that followed and, as it became a bit like hard work, I tailed off my studies.

As I got older, I became a lot closer to Ray. As I've mentioned, we used to play football together, especially in the Rolls-Royce six-a-side competition. He had that same instinct to win at all costs that I have and he could be a bit nasty in the tackle when he wanted; worse than me.

Mum is very relaxed and laid back, the same star sign as me and fairly quiet until something rouses her. I think I took some of that from her and the strong will to succeed from my dad. The old man is a bit more serious; my mother is more of a fun person, always ready for a laugh. They played an equal part in my development in their own way.

They were there for my first game at Coventry and followed me through the years, especially the big games. Once I moved to Newcastle it became more difficult and they stopped coming regularly. It was a long way for them to come from their home near Bury St Edmunds where they moved about a year after I joined Coventry.

The family have remained close without having to talk to each other every single day. It can sometimes be weeks between calls but the relationship remains solid. My parents see a lot of my brothers and sister and we all get together when we can. That's difficult at traditional family times such as Christmas because I tend to be playing, training or preparing for a game.

I probably have less in common with my sister than with Ray or Dennis but that is understandable because she has little interest in sport and is a college lecturer. I go to concerts with Dennis and talk football with Ray. I guess we are a pretty normal family.

I realise now how lucky I am that I have been able to do something for a living that I love and to get paid enough to fulfil some of the ambitions of my life. I know full well that had I been an electrician I would be working on a building site, probably married to a different girl.

I appreciate what the game has given me. I was good at football but I believe that it was my professionalism that dragged me through even at school level, then on to non-league and the professional game. I think I was born with it because I can see it as a family trait. Dad and Ray were my role models. I believe I could have been taken away from the bosom of my family and still have developed in the same way because it is within me. You are what you are and you have what you are born with. I guess I was lucky that the very thing I loved doing could also provide me with a well-paid career.

I have experienced a lot of different things because of football, travelling and meeting people who would otherwise be well out of my sphere, such as the Sex Pistols. I know some would say who the hell would want to meet them but they were my heroes when I was a boy because I loved their music. Now I can go and see bands, go backstage and have a laugh and a joke with them, but if I was not a footballer I wouldn't get that opportunity and they wouldn't want me.

I am privileged to have this life. Once I became a footballer, my horizons opened up and these experiences shape you.

CHAPTER 3

to hull and back

My first taste of football with a professional club came when I was 13. It was also my first experience of rejection!

I was offered a trial by Queens Park Rangers after my father had written to them and after they had watched Gary Waddock and me playing for our district side. We trained at a gymnasium in Eastcote on a Friday night under a coach named Brian Eastick. Mum drove me there and back every week. It lasted for six months.

I was invited back for the following season and given the time, date and venue, but when I arrived at the training ground on the given date there was no one there other than Chris Geeler, one of the staff coaches.

'Oh, it's not today,' he said. 'We'll let you know when it is.'

It was the classic case of don't call us, we'll call you. But I was far from devastated; I didn't really enjoy those Friday nights. A few of the lads were a bit cocky; they thought they had already made it. I felt more comfortable playing for the school and with my mates on a Sunday morning.

I also had an option to go to Arsenal about the same time, again after being spotted with the district side. Some of the boys went to QPR one week, Arsenal the next and Crystal Palace in between, but I felt that one club at a time was enough. I told them that I was already training with QPR.

After the west London club gave me the elbow, I never really had a sniff. I find it quite strange looking back that it all went so quiet because I didn't suddenly become a bad player. I can only assume that I was improving with age and my physique developed. I reached the end of my schooldays having achieved quite a bit, winning lots of medals and going almost to the top in local representative terms, just failing to make the London team after reaching the final 22. But that was it. Suddenly there I was, a 16-year-old in love with the game and no team to play for. I can understand how so many players drift away from the game at that stage when work, women and booze begin to intervene.

I have to confess that it hit me with a jolt when I left school. I found I no longer had any real belief in a career in football and hadn't a clue what to do with myself. It was evident that A levels and university were not an option. Initially I was interested in joining the police or one of the armed services because they offered an active, outdoor life that fitted in with my interest in sport and lack of interest in desks and offices.

As the time approached to make a decision, we had career talks at school and as a result I went for interviews with the Old Bill – this was before my convictions – and with the army. My priority was the police but the army interview came up first and I went off to Brentwood in Essex for a weekend of tests that I cruised through, especially the physical tests over the assault course. The only mistake I made was that I was too honest. I told them that I couldn't make a decision at that moment because I had an interview with the police the following week and if I passed that I would join them and if not I would join the army. The recruitment officer didn't like this at all and told me that clearly I wasn't interested enough and turned me down there and then. At the time they were overwhelmed with recruits and could afford to be selective. Nowadays they drag people in off the streets from what I hear.

I went to the police recruiting as planned, passed all the physical tests and failed the interview! It was a lot harder to get into the police force at the time and to this day I don't know why I failed. Maybe it was my lack of confidence or my shyness that counted against me. No one bothered to tell me. What I did know was that I was up the creek without a paddle as my two chosen careers had been blown away in the space of a week.

I had left school by this time so I had to do something. Then I spotted an advert in the local paper for a spares clerk at a warehouse in Stonebridge NW10, working for the Binatone Radio and TV Company. I got the job but I was far from convinced that it was right for me.

In fact, on the day I was due to start work I went back to the school. It happened to be the day when those who wanted to stay on enrolled and I went back to see what was going on. On the second day, I went in to work and told them I had been ill. Some start to my working life!

I didn't have a clue what the job entailed until I started. I was a spares clerk for about a month and then they moved me to another department. I was basically the odd-job warehouseman. In those days, school leavers tended to stay in their first job but this was a dead-end job, manual labour with no real future.

Fortunately, my sister came up with the idea of going to college to qualify as an electrician like Ray. She advised me that if I applied, the firm couldn't turn me down. It was a real crossroads in my life. When I started, I found I was one of the brightest there, something I had never been at school. I was there because I wanted to be there and not because I was made to go.

There were other boys from the firm on day release, studying radio and television engineering as that was what the firm specialised in. It was only when my half-term report came in that they discovered I had taken a different course in electronics. But my report was really good with 100 per cent attendance and excellent marks, and when I suggested that perhaps there would be jobs with the firm as an electrician, thankfully they allowed me to carry on.

It would have been so easy to walk away from serious football then, as so many youngsters do when they leave school. There were other attractions – the pub, music, girls. I suppose I was a year away from just playing for a Sunday pub side. Luckily, Geoff Carson took a hand.

He was the school caretaker. He had a daughter in our year and took a keen interest in the football team, often ferrying us about. He recommended a few of us to local club Wealdstone. Someone from the club took a look and invited us to go down there. Had it been just me on me own I don't know that I would have even bothered. There's no doubt that it was Geoff Carson who put me on track.

When you finish school and you have no club to go to, you have a job and maybe a bit of private work on a Saturday, then football tends to be pushed into the background and standards drop. Even though I was playing for the youth team and occasionally the reserves, it was a big club and not football to be taken lightly.

My perspective on life now is due in no small part to coming through the non-league set-up. It's probably why I don't make a song and dance of what I have achieved. I certainly don't see myself as a big-time Charlie and the fans do seem to identify with me. I'm a tradesman who has struck it lucky. People are still surprised that I can do things other than play football. We had a man in fitting a washer and when a socket needed changing I told him to leave it and that I would do it. He was amazed when I told him that I was an electrician.

I count myself fortunate that I have travelled the entire journey, missing out virtually no stops in between other than perhaps not having played in the lower divisions. But five and a half years of non-league more than makes up for that. I have seen every level and I thoroughly appreciate what I have – it's all the sweeter for having started at the bottom.

I attended a Wealdstone dinner recently and I was surprised when I was told that I had played 242 games for them in those five years. Add that to the 600-plus as a professional and it makes for a long time in football.

If I hadn't gone to Wealdstone I don't know what I would have done, probably gone and played with the rest of the lads in the pub team on a Sunday morning and watched QPR on a Saturday afternoon.

Come the end of that first season there was the usual massive backlog of fixtures and the old pros didn't fancy taking days off to travel to all points north and south. It meant the team was short of a left-back and I was told I was making my first-team debut away to Dorchester at barely 17 years of age. This was the breeding ground for the player who was to develop some years later. These weren't friendly kick-abouts. They were very, very physical. It wasn't a case of me kicking the winger, more the other way round. The old pro against the young whippersnapper – they used to kick the shit out of me. You had to learn to look after yourself at places like Altrincham where it was very rough. I was a bit quick but also a bit naïve.

I couldn't have been too bad, though, because I ended up being offered a two-year contract by manager Alan Foggarty when that first season ended. It was £15 a week plus bonuses – an absolute fortune at the time and a massive addition to my salary as a warehouseman.

I passed my exams at college and applied for a job with Brent Council. Ray was working for them at the time. I went for the interview confident that with that year at college and my good results – not to mention the fact that my brother worked with them – I would have a good chance. I was right and I was taken on board. It was a blinding job because I could always get away to play for Wealdstone in their midweek games. If we were playing at somewhere like Scarborough, the team coach would leave at lunchtime and they would not only let me off but would put a couple of hours' overtime on my timesheet.

While I was ducking and diving between Brent Council and Wealdstone I was invited for a trial at Hull City who were managed by former Welsh manager Mike Smith. I hadn't been in the Wealdstone first team for much more than a season when the rumour machine began to suggest that I might have a chance of picking up a league club. I let it be known that I might be interested and the next thing I knew John Watson and I were invited to travel north for the trials.

John was the Wealdstone and England non-league captain. He was 27 at the time and pretty settled in his ways while I was around 18 and very unsure of what might lie ahead. John had a good job, also with the council, as a stonemason. He had family in London and was earning a good wage with Wealdstone. I had my doubts about whether he would be interested and when I couldn't find him at the station in London I assumed that he had backed out and I began to wish I had done the same. Being a shy young lad, I wasn't that keen on going on my own. But when the train arrived at Hull, he stepped off it two carriages away.

We travelled up on the Tuesday and trained that day. We trained again on Wednesday before playing away to Grimsby in a local derby. John was brilliant, absolutely superb, head and shoulders above everyone else on the pitch. He always was whenever he played in any big game. I was average.

We had dinner with Mike Smith on Tuesday night and went to his office at Boothferry Park on Thursday morning to talk about signing. I chatted to John first and he wasn't that keen because of what he had back in London. I decided there and then that I was going to say no as well. Mike Smith did his best to persuade me, even offering to find me a job on the local council when I told him that I wanted to keep on with my trade! But I had made my mind up and turned it down. Then when John came out he told me he was thinking about it! I thought I had done it all wrong because had John said yes I would have gone as well. In the end, neither of us went.

In my first full season at Wealdstone we were relegated and Alan Foggarty, the manager who signed me, was sacked. He was a nice guy from Birmingham. He had been around for years, a cigar smoker and a spitter. We used to have our team meetings on the back of the bus where we would all gather round and he would say things like, 'The centre-half has just split up with his wife. I live near him and I know he's upset about it so have a pop at him about his missus.' Another time, he said about a useful opponent, 'He's just lost his job. Have a go at him about being out of work.' He knew bits about everyone and was always ready to make use of it, or rather have us make use of it by winding up the opposition.

I was sorry for him, devastated for myself. What if the new manager didn't fancy me? I remember vividly Alan Foggarty coming round the dressing-room to say his goodbyes and saying to me, 'I will see a lot more of you.' I hadn't a clue what he was talking about; I thought that maybe he was going to invite me around for dinner or something. I felt very sad because I liked him, looked up to him, and he had given me my chance. But he was a survivor and I still see him from time to time, scouting for managers including Dave Bassett.

It was certainly an experience playing at Wealdstone. I recall a trip to Bangor in North Wales. It was too far to go by coach and so we all travelled up together by train instead. We played the game and afterwards four of us collected a whip and slipped off to find a pub so we could get crated up with lager for the train journey back home. We were in our suits and club ties and walked straight into a pub full of bikers. We weren't going to turn round and walk away so we brazened it out, expecting a hiding at any minute. Perhaps we were too brave because we had a few beers, picked up the crates – and missed the train by five minutes! The porter told us that there was no other train back to London for three hours, so what else was there to do but go back to the bikers pub and carry on drinking.

We finally caught the later train to London with enough lager for nigh on 30 young men. It proved to be a monster journey. There had been a derailment outside Crewe and this delayed our train so badly that it was eight o'clock in the morning when we arrived. We didn't care. In fact we had drunk so much beer that we didn't care about anything until we turned up for training on Tuesday when we were slaughtered by the rest of the team for missing the designated train. To make matters worse, the team had travelled back in a train without a buffet so they had nothing to eat or drink, fuming at the thought of the four musketeers with their money and their beer.

That was the joy of non-league football. It was full of characters. Roy Davies was one of them, a bit of a lad who was always pulling stunts. Roy went from Hayes to Torquay and on his debut on the left wing for his first league club he picked up a woollen bobble hat thrown on to the pitch by one of the fans, carried on his run and got on the end of a cross from the other wing with a diving header with the bobble hat still on.

You can imagine what an influence he was on us at Wealdstone with a mind like that. When we had a testimonial match for his big mucker Wally Downes from Wimbledon they had a couple of mackintoshes and streaked across the pitch. I was a bit impression-able and this incident stuck in my memory. When Brian Roberts had a testimonial at Coventry I thought that I would resurrect the stunt. Our manager Bobby Gould was getting ready to come on in the second half as a bit of a gimmick when I collared our 6ft 3in centre-forward Brian Withey, another former non-league man who went from Bath to Bristol Rovers before joining us, and told him to meet me in a few minutes. We both put on flasher's macs, skimpy white briefs and old men's masks. We waited until the ball went near Gould and raced on, flashed him and raced off again. It was quite impressive; we probably looked naked from the stands. Gould knew very well that it was his players involved but, because of the latex masks, he didn't know who. Such was the interest that the local newspaper, the *Coventry Evening Telegraph*, ran a competition to name the two flashers for a prize of a couple of tickets for our next game (which someone did win!).

At least that was all a bit of fun. The same could not be said about some of our non-league encounters. One time at Scarborough for instance we were involved in a very rough match indeed. It has to be said that we were giving more than we were taking. The tackles were becoming naughtier and after one particularly evil one our captain John Watson jumped up, chinned an opponent and was promptly sent off. A Scarborough player slid into our goalkeeper who was carried off just before half-time with concussion and took no further part in the game. With only one substitute there were precious few options open to us and I finished up in goal for the second half, reviving memories of the Russian Yak Jensen! We were two goals down by that stage but still playing and trying to squeeze a result from an impossible situation. I was watching a corner at the other end when I spotted our centre-half whack their centre-forward on the halfway line. Unfortunately for us I was not the only one; a linesman saw it as well and off went our central defender. Then there were nine.

It was quickly getting out of hand. After another bad tackle, another of our players had gone and there we were with me in goal behind seven outfield players. I conceded two more goals, one a screamer into the top corner, and we lost 4–0. As we trailed off towards the dressing-room we were being booed and jeered by the local supporters when our manager Ken Payne, who was under pressure for his job at the time, ran on and headed straight for me.

'Well done son,' he said, 'you've grown up today.'

I didn't know what he was on about. We had been hammered, had three players sent off and here he was telling me I'd grown up. Then, as we walked along the touchline, he turned round and started shouting at the home fans, 'Fuck off you wankers,' and waving two-handed, two-fingered gestures in their direction. I couldn't wait to get off the pitch. Just another day at the office.

On another occasion we were playing Barnet in a traditional Boxing Day game with a morning kick-off. This was another nasty one. Before I arrived our big annual punch-up was with Wimbledon before Wimbledon went into the League. The lads told me that you could guarantee a 2–2 draw and six sent off. Barnet had taken over as our grudge match and on this day the linesman had given decisions which hadn't delighted the home manager, a certain character by the name of Barry Fry. Barry, hardly a shy retiring flower, finally had enough and set off up the line after the linesman carrying a bucket of ice-cold water and tipped it over him. It's the sort of thing you don't see anymore. Nowadays he would be banned *sine die*. Barnet was always a flashpoint game but that day we were united in our mirth at Barry's antics.

We managed to hoist ourselves back up into the Alliance only to be relegated again, leaving the way for the renowned Alan Batsford to take over. He was a strict disciplinarian and his reputation preceded him, having taken Wimbledon into the League. Everyone was dreading him arriving but I have to admit that he did a lot for me. There were a couple of ex-league players who thought they were Jack-the-lads and I ended up being influenced by them, messing around. Batsford quickly pulled me and told me that it was high time I got out of my pram. It was only when I thought about what he had said that I realised the message he was putting across. He was right; it was about time I grew up. So I did and it was Batsford and his joint manager Brian Hall who sold me into the League.

Batsford was deaf in one ear, caused when he was caught on the ear during practice, some say deliberately. The boys reckoned he could tune into Radio Luxembourg on his hearing aid and, in typical football fashion, they used to get on his deaf side to give him some verbals without fear of reprisals.

When I tell people I played against Alex Stepney they are amazed but he was in goal for Altrincham when they won the Alliance twice. He was about 41 then and I was 18 so there was a massive age difference. He has always been my trump card when footballers gather together and swap stories about who they have played against. When I drop Stepney's name in they reckon it makes me around 90.

We were all PFA members at Wealdstone. Every year we would put on our hired dinner suits and head off for the annual Professional Footballers Association awards dinner to brush shoulders with the big stars. The tables were seeded so we were almost out in Park Lane, so far away from the action it was ridiculous. It became a standing joke. It was almost as if we were at a different function. We were, of course, in awe of the big stars who, in those days, attended in numbers. Nowadays there seem to be more hangers-on than footballers. I haven't gone for years because I end up signing more autographs than after a West Ham United game. But it was good in those days and after the speeches and awards we would all mix together and have a drink. One day Alan Batsford said to me, 'I want you to come over and meet Kenny Sansom. He's a friend of mine.'

As much as I admired Kenny, I wasn't that keen, as an electrician and a non-league left-back, on being introduced to the current England left-back and a superstar of his time. But Batsford insisted and introduced me, saying, 'This is Stuart Pearce. He's a good left-back.' Kenny stood there with a bottle of champagne in an ice bucket in one hand and his glass in the other, waiting to join his mates. He was very good but it became even more embarrassing a few seconds later when Batsford added, 'He'll have your place soon.' It was a flippant remark and Kenny must have been thinking, 'Yeah, sure he will.' The great irony was that when I did break through into the England team, it was Kenny whom I replaced. I never did remind him of that embarrassing conversation at the Hilton Hotel in Park Lane.

I didn't make the non-league England team. I came close after we won the double of Southern League and Southern League Cup to get back into the Alliance. We had a good team and the next season we finished third and could have won it but for giving away silly points. The chairman was so confident that he told us he had put £500 on us to win the League at 14–1 and if we won he would take us all to Florida for an end-of-season jolly on the proceeds. We had a saying as we ran out of the dressing-room door on a cold Saturday afternoon: 'Win today – Tampa Bay.' But we ended up blowing it.

I had a fairly good season and I heard that the England selectors were having a look at me in an FA Trophy tie at Wycombe Wanderers. It was a heavily sloping pitch at Wycombe and in the opening minutes one of their players came flying down the hill towards me. I put my head in to clear the ball and he just missed taking my head off with a flying boot. He would have caught me if I hadn't pulled my face away sharply. It was nasty and Roy Davies promptly chinned him while I stamped on him for good measure. There was an instant free-for-all as the referees ran up to sort it out. He sent Davies off having seen him throw the punch, but he hadn't spotted my indiscretion and said nothing. I had got away with it but the crowd had seen and every time I went near the ball they gave me plenty of stick.

This incident clearly sowed seeds of doubt about me with the selectors but they invited me, all the same, for a trial at Nuneaton where we played a Combined Universities side. A mate of mine, a wages clerk at the council, drove me to the Midlands so I could sleep on the way. I had a good game and the only moment of indiscretion was when I bollocked one of my team-mates for not giving me the ball. They were all very proper and the manager told me that there was no need for that. I was pretty pleased with myself all the same and thought I had given myself a chance. When I went into the bar to find my mate who was driving, I discovered he had bumped into the manager of South Liverpool and some of their team who had come to give support to a couple of their players. He was out of it, absolutely steaming and I finished up having to drive him all the way back. What's more, I didn't get picked, probably partly because of the stamping at Wycombe and partly because I had mouthed off at one of my own players but mainly because Altrincham, top of the League at the time, had a left-back named John Davidson who, quite frankly, was better than me. I was up and coming and might have pushed him the next season if I hadn't turned professional but there was no doubt in my mind that he earned his place.

In fact, my disciplinary record in what was a very tough league was pretty good. I learned to look after myself not only then but even before that when I used to play in the park against older boys. I was small and had to learn to protect myself. I am what I am. I haven't manufactured myself. I have always been that way and able to punch my weight. I grew a little more when I left school but I had to be able to handle myself in a physical league.

The dream of every non-league club is a run in the FA Cup. It not only brings in much-needed money but also puts the players under the national spotlight. I was in the Wealdstone side on both occasions when we reached the FA Cup first round proper, drawing Southend one year and Swindon Town a couple of seasons later. We lost both times. We tried to rough them up a bit to even the balance and both of the professional teams moaned that we were too physical. Many years later when I was at Newcastle we played Stevenage Borough and they moaned that we were too rough. Things certainly seem to have changed since my days. I suppose Alan Shearer was a bit physical at the time but it was still a surprise how the wheel had turned.

We lost 1–0 to Southend in a very good game when we missed our chances. Two years later at Swindon there was a very strange incident. It was a massive game for us and we took about 1500 supporters to Wiltshire. We were playing quite well and were a bit unlucky to be losing 1–0 at half-time. Just after the break I tackled Swindon's golden boy Paul Rideout. He was the up-and-coming star, a leading light in the England youth team and tipped for the top. I'll never forget what he said to me – 'Get back to your fucking nine-to-five job.' A few words were said and I doubt that he would even remember having an exchange with an electrician from London. But I remembered and two seasons after that I was playing for Coventry and he was on the bench for Aston Villa. I can't say how tempted I was to go over and say,

'How's the nine-to-five now? You can't even get a game.' But I didn't. I bit my lip and let the moment pass.

It still happens. When things become a little fraught on the pitch, the professional will often turn round and ask the non-league player who has been bugging him just how much he earns. It's a pet hate of mine because I've been there. I remember Garry Birtles did it when we played at Forest. We had gone to a non-league ground for a game to mark them getting floodlights. Garry was kicked and he turned round to this plumber and told him to get back to his proper job. I thought it was rich coming from a former carpet layer and I turned on him and told him to behave himself and grow up. He was out of order, especially as he had been through the mill himself.

I enjoyed my non-league days and I am glad that I came through that route. I wouldn't have it any different. I feel that I served my apprenticeship. I don't know whether I would have carried on playing football for so long if I hadn't had those five years. In a strange way I thought to myself that as I missed five years at that end of my career I would make up for them at this end.

One thing it taught me was the value of a £10 note. Even now if I am driving on empty I will pass a petrol station that is selling petrol at 84.9 if the next one is selling at 83.9. I could afford to go to any garage and pay whatever price they're asking, but why should I? I would rather go to the guy who is going out of his way to sell his petrol cheaper.

When I joined Coventry I became very pally with Trevor Peake, to such a degree that he was best man at my wedding much later on. He had played non-league at Nuneaton until he was 21. You could tell by their attitudes who had been non-league players. Kirk Stevens and Cyrille Regis were classic examples. There was a mile of difference between them and the kids who joined straight from school. Others such as Graham Roberts, Ian Wright and Andy Townsend had done the rounds. They made it late in the game and fully appreciated what they had.

Big clubs should scout around the non-league for the better players. They could pick them up cheaply and if they don't make it, the chances are that they could still sell them on, usually for more than the initial outlay.

When I was briefly manager at Nottingham Forest I tried to sign a young non-league player called Courtney Taylor, recommended to me by an old Forest team-mate Steve Wigley who was then manager of Aldershot. Steve had played against Naylor in a game against Dagenham. I trusted Steve's judgement so I rang Dag's manager Ted Hardy and asked if he would be interested in sending the player to me for a month. I thought that if Courtney Naylor had half the attitude I had when I joined Coventry City, he would be worth it. Ted Hardy wouldn't even consider it. Whether he wanted me to dive straight in with a couple of hundred thousand I don't know but he gave that impression when he added that in a year's time a big club would come in for the player and pay a lot of money. I asked him to let the lad know that a Premiership club was interested. By one of those strange coincidences I was at Dagenham with the England Under-18 team a couple of years later and I asked after the player. I was told he had gone off the boil a bit and had been sold on to Enfield or somewhere like that for a few quid. Who knows what might have happened had the manager allowed him to spend a few weeks at Nottingham Forest and he had impressed me?

I put myself in his place and wonder what would have happened to me if no one had told me that Coventry were interested in buying me. They paid £25,000 and although it was good money it wasn't the difference to the club between collapse and survival but to me it was everything.

There had been plenty of rumours but I ignored them until we played an evening game at Yeovil. Our centre-half came up to me and told me that the Coventry manager was there to look at me. He told me that our manager knew and so did most of the team but they weren't sure whether to tell me or not and he had taken it upon himself to let me know.

I doubt whether it spurred me on because I always gave my all anyway. On the Friday of that week, Bobby Gould was in touch with the club and offered them £25,000 for me. I learned later that Gould had originally asked his scouting staff to find out who the best left-backs were in non-league. It was a position where they were lacking; in fact, they had no left-back.

The connection was Brian Eastick whom I had trained under at QPR as a kid. He told Gould I was the best – the right age, 21, and as good as he would get. Gould lived down the road from Yeovil and took his wife to the game to run the rule over me personally. The story he tells is that he watched me for 25 minutes, saw me kick the winger over the stand and said, 'He will do for me.'

Coventry were playing Arsenal at Highbury that weekend and he took the opportunity to pop round to our house in Kingsbury to talk to my dad and me. I think he was concerned that now it was out that he was after me, someone else might step in. They didn't.

I was the recipient of well-meaning advice from all the old pros at Wealdstone – Ray Goddard, a goalkeeper for Millwall for 500 games, Paul Price from Arsenal, in fact almost everyone in the team apart from me had league experience. They all had something to offer, mainly to ask for a £25,000 signing-on fee and a king's ransom for wages.

I sat down with Gould and I told him what I was getting from the club and council, adding up to £230 a week, and that I would like £250 a week and £25,000 signing-on fee. Gould looked up and said, 'There's the door – use it.' I thought, 'The bastards didn't tell me this at Wealdstone. What do I do now?'

'I don't give signing-on fees,' Gould said. 'I never got one so I don't give them to anyone else.'

There were no agents then and here I was, an electrician who was being given the chance to play against the likes of Liverpool, Manchester United and Arsenal. He knew that. He knew that if he offered me a tenner a week I would have grabbed the paper off him and signed it there and then. It was not really about money. After all, how could I go back to the council and tell them I hadn't signed because I couldn't agree terms and could I please have my job back as an electrician.

It was Bobby Gould's second season at Highfield Road and he had signed a load of players, including Trevor from Lincoln, Terry Gibson and a lot of others who were desperate to play in the top division. I discovered later he had used the same line on all of them, apart from Ashley Grimes whom he signed for £200,000 from Manchester United. No one else got a signing-on fee from Bobby Gould, just the chance to make it at the top level. The rest of us had to swallow it and take what was offered.

It was rumoured that there were other clubs watching me but Bobby Gould was the one who took the gamble. Certainly if I go back into management I will look around for non-league players. I would want players of the right age and with the right attitude. I would give them a chance because I was given that chance myself.

CHAPTER 4

sent to coventry

Going from Wealdstone straight to Coventry in the first division was beyond my wildest dreams. Of course I heard the whispers but my yardstick was the trial at Hull City. If I was going to turn professional, I expected it to be with a third- or fourth-division club, another step on the ladder. Alan Batsford called me into his office and said, 'We have just accepted an offer from Coventry City of £25,000 for you and you go with our blessing. Good luck to you.' It finally struck me that I had achieved Utopia in one step. All of a sudden, it was actually happening, the bid had been made and by the Monday the deed had been done. I was a professional with a first-division club. I had been sent to Coventry in the nicest way possible.

It was case of take it or leave it — £250 a week and a 2-year contract. I bit Bobby Gould's hand off once we had overcome that initial misunderstanding. Effectively, it was a 20 month contract and that, I suppose, represented something of a gamble on my part, giving up a steady job and leaving home. But in truth it was no gamble at all. How could you finish your life as a sparky knowing that you could have been a professional footballer? What's security when you're 21, single, living with your parents and paying your mum £30 a week? Where was the gamble? I was committed. In fact, I couldn't have written a better script. I'd got my qualifications, had experience of a job and if my tilt at full-time professional football failed not only did I have a trade to fall back on but also my governor at the council told me that he would keep the job open for me if things didn't work out in Coventry.

My first game was for the reserves under John Sillett at Blackpool. We drew 1–1 and afterwards Sillett told Gould that I was the best player on the pitch and recommended me for a step up. It suited Gould because he wanted to fast track me if he could, having no left-back. So after one reserve game I was promoted to the bench for the game against Stoke. There was only one substitute permitted in those days so I was that close to the team and my debut. I didn't get on. We won 3–1.

Gould came specifically to watch me at Rotherham in the reserves and because I didn't play very well he decided not to pick me for the away game at Birmingham that coming weekend. But he gave me my debut in the next game on 12 November 1983 at home against, of all teams, Queens Park Rangers – the team I had trained with as a kid and supported as a youngster. That wasn't the only coincidence for up against me was Gary Waddock with whom I had played in my district team.

I couldn't tell you whom I marked but on the Monday we watched a video of the game. I had a shot from about 40 yards and if the goalkeeper hadn't come out to collect it, it wouldn't have reached the goal. Everybody laughed and took the mick out of me, this raw, new professional trying to shoot from so far out and not even reaching the goal. We won 1–0 and I found myself involved in an unbeaten run that eventually stretched to nine games, including a 4–0 win over the mighty Liverpool, lifting us up to fourth place, high enough for a nose-bleed for Coventry. Terry Gibson scored a hat-trick against Liverpool and it was one of the upsets of the season.

That was my fifth first-team game. It was ridiculous. It felt easier than playing at Wealdstone and I was thinking to myself that this wasn't bad and I had settled in quite well. My feet were still firmly on the floor, however, as John Sillett, knowing my background, soon had me wiring up his stables. 'Sparky,' he said, 'come and do some work for me.'

In truth, it was not as easy as I pretended. Sure I did fairly well, but I found the step up to training every day instead of a couple of times a week very tiring. I ended up suffering a stress fracture of the shin in my second season, which kept me out for three months, and I am convinced that it was the change in training and playing routines that caught up with me. It was a pity because I had settled in so well, kept my place apart from the odd injury and quickly felt that I belonged. How different it might have been if I had walked into a losing team.

Results-wise I was brought down to earth as we slipped badly in the second half of the season. In fact, after the sensational win over Liverpool we won just one of our next 19 games and we needed to win three of our last seven matches to stave off relegation, a regular feature for Coventry then as it is now.

Around Christmas time in that first season, we hit the wall. We could not win a game to save our lives. We nicked the odd point here or there which just kept us in or around the relegation zone and our finish meant that Birmingham went down with 48 points instead of us. We drew at Luton, lost at Liverpool as they avenged their earlier thrashing by hitting us for five, and beat Norwich while Birmingham drew their last three matches. It was so tight that season that we were fourth from bottom with 50 points, the same as Stoke City and one fewer than four other clubs – Norwich, Leicester, Luton and West Bromwich Albion.

In that first season, I had already played for Wealdstone in the preliminary round of the FA Cup. I thought nothing of it until we drew Wolverhampton Wanderers in the third round. Then I realised that my game against Basildon four months earlier had cup-tied me. I was gutted. As a non-league player I had never gone beyond the first round. I was thinking surely this doesn't count. I can't miss a game like this. We won against Wolves after two draws and went out to Sheffield Wednesday in the next round. I sat in the stand and hated every minute of those four games.

Some of the reserve-team players at Highfield Road never went out of their way to make friends with me, and one or two of the first team seemed to resent my sudden arrival and immediate elevation. Trevor Peake wasn't the first to come up to wish me well but I discovered that those who came up first were also often the first to drift away. I later discovered why Trevor had been a bit cool to me when he told me that they had heard that I had turned down third- and fourth- division clubs waiting for the big one to come along. It wasn't true but that's how rumours get around, bits in the newspapers and whispers here and there. Trevor and I got on like a house on fire after I explained that the rumours were absolute rubbish. It had all started because I turned down Hull City as a raw kid. Sometimes you meet someone and you get on with them straightaway because you think along the same lines and have the same sense of humour. We just clicked and we will always be on the same wavelength.

Trevor and his wife Haddwyn put me up for a while when I was struggling for somewhere to live. It was a worthy gesture as Haddwyn was pregnant at the time. I had been punting about for digs. I stayed at a hotel for a couple of weeks before I was recommended to go and stay with a dear old couple who offered me a place. They were really good. I was no trouble and half the time I was travelling back to my parents after the game down the M1. But the age difference meant we had little to talk about and, inevitably, I became bored and decided to move on.

I moved in with Dave Bamber, who scored the only goal on my debut, but we were chalk and cheese. He was horse-racing mad and used to record any race on television. Every video in our house was of horse racing and he would watch all of them. He was ringing bets through rather than going to the bookmakers and as a non-gambler I discovered that was a sign that you were well into the business. Dave did the cooking and I did the washing-up. He wasn't a bad cook but I suppose most of it was Marks and Spencer, usually served with a huge mound of mashed potatoes. Despite our different lifestyles we managed to rub along quite well but when he was transferred to York City I didn't fancy keeping up the place on my own and once again I was on the lookout.

I had a spell in digs with Ian Butterworth and a Scot named Jim McDonald. Jim was a staunch catholic and had a picture of the pope above the bed. We had single beds next to each other and I would mess around with his picture when he was out. He was not too happy about that, but generally we got on well. Ian, with whom I eventually moved to Forest, was good fun and kept us all amused.

I went home at the end of the season and when I returned I was again having trouble finding somewhere to live until Keith Thompson, brother of West Bromwich Albion's Gary Thompson, invited me to live with him and his family. It was one of those casual statements when he remarked that if I was struggling I could stay with him. Unfortunately for him, I'm one of those people who take things at face value and I turned up at his house in Birmingham with my bags one day.

Eventually I found myself looking round again because of the drive in and out of Birmingham with its attendant heavy traffic. When I mentioned it to Peakey, he told me to come and stay with him and his heavily pregnant wife in a new house they had just moved into. Again it was probably one of those offers that was only half meant and I think it may have caused a bit of friction between them. But I made myself useful and, being a bit of a handyman as well as an electrician, I was able to help out about the place, mainly fixing things like scales and electrical things to walls.

It worked quite well until I was due to make my comeback after the three months lay-off with the stress fracture for the game at Leicester City two days before Christmas. I was due to ease my way back into the team as substitute. We did all the public relations bit about me returning and I was pictured in the local paper on the Friday holding up the number 12 shirt.

After all that nonsense, we trained and, of all people, I did Peakey going for a 50–50 ball in our usual north v. south match. It all became a bit spicy in the tackle as usual and he ended up on crutches with me driving him home. He couldn't even drive his car never mind play the next day in what was a critical match with us languishing a couple of places off the bottom.

We walked in through the front door and Haddwyn, preparing for Christmas, said, 'What's happened to you? Who did that?' Then I walked through the door and she said, 'It was you, wasn't it?' All I could say was, 'It was an accident. It was an accident.'

I finished up not only wearing Peakey's number 6 shirt at Leicester but also his captain's armband and what made it worse was that we were absolutely annihilated. We lost 5–1 and the man I marked scored twice. He was some raw, young kid named Gary Lineker. Happy Christmas! And it didn't get any better.

I missed the Boxing Day game with injury – we lost 2–0 at Luton – and then I was back in the side as we went down 2–1 at home to West Ham, which left us struggling in 20th place. In typical Coventry fashion, just when everything looked bleak we bounced back to beat Stoke City 4–1 at home on New Year's day and then we beat Manchester United 1–0 at Old Trafford in the next game.

In those days, the season didn't all finish on the Sunday at the same time. If you were behind with your fixtures, quite often you would play after the final Saturday. We had three games left – Stoke on the Tuesday, Luton on the Thursday and the champions Everton on the Sunday. We were on 41 points and Norwich had finished their fixtures with a win against Chelsea at Stamford Bridge taking them to 49 points. It looked as if there was no way out for us this time.

As is recorded elsewhere in this book, we won the first game 1–0 when I scored with a penalty near the end, and Stoke's Ian Painter missed a penalty, hitting the bar; our centre-half Brian Kilcline scored from outside the box in the 83rd minute against Luton; and on the Sunday we beat the league champions 4–1 in a farcical game with the Everton players stinking of booze. I almost felt sorry for Norwich manager Ken Brown who was pictured walking his dog while our last game was being played. He had every right to feel that the gods were against him.

Coventry was a good, family club. I was pleased that I went there for my first taste of professional football. Even though they were first division, Highfield Road was a friendly place and I'm glad I went there before I joined Brian Clough at Forest. I was there for 20 months and it allowed me to bed down and get used to the pace of league football before the onset of pressure.

Bobby Gould was given the sack while I was there and the dour Scot Don Mackay took over. He was the one who eventually sold me to Forest. Brian Clough originally came down to look at our centre-half Ian Butterworth and finished up buying both of us.

Before that, we played a game at Nottingham Forest and a couple of us were down injured at the same time which meant that the Forest physiotherapist Graham Lyas came on to treat me. While he was bent over attending to my injured leg, he whispered out of the side of his mouth, 'How old are you, son?'

'I feel about 38,' I groaned.

'No, seriously son, how old are you?'

It transpired that this was the first or second time Brian Clough had seen me and he took a liking to me. When he had the chance to send on his physio, he told him to find out how old I was. He never missed a trick that Brian Clough. I couldn't believe what I was hearing. It was the sort of stunt that Clough pulled but he was only doing his job, even if it was a little unusual.

I still find it unbelievable that Coventry didn't nail me down on a longer contract. Even though there was no such thing as freedom of contract in those days, no one bothered to come and talk to me about staying or a new contract. I suspect that the changeover of managers was the reason. It was not until March, when I had a couple of months of my contract remaining, that they started talking to me.

Soon after that I was accosted walking up King Richard Street to the ground. I had parked my car round the corner, ready for a quick getaway after the game against Liverpool, when some fellow sidled up behind me, tapped me on the shoulder and said, 'I'm Alan Hill from Nottingham Forest. Would you be interested in joining us?'

I couldn't believe it. It was like something from a bad movie and just yards from the ground and a couple of hours before one of our biggest games of the season.

Then he said, 'Can I have your phone number? Brian Clough wants to talk to you.' If that was naïve of him, I was even worse because I gave this man I didn't know from Adam my home telephone number!

I played the game – which we lost 2–0 – and thought nothing more about it until one evening the telephone rang and there was the same man, Alan Hill, telling me to hang on because Brian Clough wanted to talk to me. Clough came on the phone and said, 'Hello son, do you want to play for me?' I muttered something about my contract being up at the end of the season and that I would love to play for him.

'OK,' he said. 'Tara,' and he put the telephone down. That was the extent of our conversation.

Luton, Leicester and Forest had all shown an interest in me but the only concrete offer I had was from Forest.

I wasn't at Coventry long enough to gain a full rapport with the fans but I really enjoyed my time there. We were blessed with a lot of good professionals and although on a bigger scale, it was a bit like Wealdstone in many ways. At Wealdstone, we had a lot of old players dropping out of the League; at Coventry, Bobby Gould trawled around for experienced players. He brought in seasoned performers such as Kenny Hibbitt from Wolves, Peter Barnes the old Manchester City and England winger from Leeds and big Cyrille Regis from West Bromwich Albion, and he brought Bob Latchford back from Holland. These were people I used to watch as a kid down at Loftus Road, and Bob Latchford was a cult hero when he was with Everton and England. They were massive names in the game and they came to join us at Coventry. I learned a lot from them in a short time.

We used to go out for a warm-up before games and when I asked Kenny Hibbitt if he was going to join us for a loosener, he looked up at me and said, 'Look, I have got to run around for an hour and a half out there. I don't need to go out for an extra twenty minutes beforehand.' He probably won't remember the conversation but I do. I never went to warm up after that. I could understand the logic – Why shatter yourself before a game? If it was good enough for him, it was good enough for me, and I followed that philosophy thereafter. The only times that ever changed was when there was a brief romance with plastic pitches and when I played for England under Graham Taylor. Graham insisted on all the players warming up together. I told him I didn't like to but as I was his captain I went out at Wembley for two minutes. Then I went back inside to do what I always did. I'm so regimented it's frightening.

My routine gradually moulded itself and, once set, rarely changed. It went like this:

* Arrive at around 2 p.m. Sit down to read the programme.

* At 2.15 start to get changed.
* 2.20 stretching routines.
* 2.30 find a quiet wall to kick a ball against to get a feel of it.
* 2.35 sit down again, flicking my legs out to stretch a little more.
* 2.40 work a set routine with the physio on yet more stretches.
* 2.45 pads on, prepare for the game and sit quietly getting my mind right.

Well, fairly quietly – the music came in to it, while the others were out warming up. I brought the tapes into the dressing-room at Forest so I played what I wanted (captain's prerogative). I also introduced the music at Newcastle until I heard Ruud Gullit outside the dressing-room door. The music on that occasion wasn't particularly heavy, not even punk rock, but clearly he didn't like it. I heard him say, 'What thee fook is thees shit?' I knew that was the end of the music in the Newcastle dressing-room but I didn't realise it was the end of me as well.

Musically Ruud and I were incompatible. Basically, I played it when the others were out and once I had finished with the physio. I would listen to the Clash, Stranglers and bands like those but a lot of people don't like that music so I compromised with Big Country, Oasis and Spear of Destiny. I would never sell out with crap like Garage. At 2.50 prompt it was music off and mind on football with no distractions.

When I went up to Newcastle with West Ham, I popped into the dressing-room to see the Newcastle boys and Alan Shearer pulled me aside and said, 'Listen to the music they play now.' It was soul and I looked at him in disgust. 'You've sold out,' I said. I was tempted to go and confiscate the machine but I suppose with Bobby Robson there they were lucky it wasn't Frank Sinatra or Vera Lynn!

I bumped into Bobby Robson and he was like a kid in a sweet shop. He asked me how my leg was (I broke it the day he started at Newcastle) and he took me out to look at the new stand. When you think of all the big clubs where he has been, he was clearly as proud as punch to be manager of Newcastle. What a nice man.

One of the most significant events during my stay at Coventry was meeting Liz, the lady who was to become my wife. When she left school, she worked in a hotel for a while in her native Wiltshire. Then she had the opportunity to work for international showjumpers Ted and Liz Edgar at Kenilworth in Warwickshire. While she was there she groomed for showjumpers Nick Shelton and Lesley McNaught. When Lesley moved on to join Paddy Lynch, Liz followed her. Paddy Lynch owned a big construction company in Birmingham. He was also Pat Cowdell's boxing manager. His daughter owned ponies and up-and-coming horses. When Lesley left, Liz stayed on at the Lynch house. I met Liz when Lesley dragged her along to a function at Coventry City. Lesley liked football but Liz had no interest. We met, got chatting and I have been with her ever since.

Up until then my social life wasn't that good. I moved around between digs and went back home whenever I could. It took an hour and ten minutes in my brand new Capri, a lovely thing which I still have. It cost me five grand for a spanking-new, black, two-litre S Capri; it was my pride and joy. My mother-in-law Mary drives it now.

The garage put a sticker in the back saying 'Sold and Serviced by . . .' For a game against Luton I pulled into the car park next to their coach. Their players looked out of the window and, according to Kirk Stevens who joined us later, they thought it was a sponsored car that I had been given after being at the club for just two weeks.

That car has been a lucky omen for me. Mary loves it as much as I do and calls it Cruella. It was a bit temperamental for me, a devil to start in the winter but for her it goes first time every time.

Until I met Liz my main pleasure was just the same as it was when I played for Wealdstone – having a drink with my mates in the local in London. In those days, Britain seemed huge and even the short run home seemed to take an eternity.

I met Liz in the February and in May Lesley said that they were off to Barcelona for a show and why didn't I join them. I said I'd love to and, being one of those people who tend to do what they say, I made the trip, much to Liz's surprise. She had taken the horsebox a couple of weeks earlier and driven through France and Spain, stopping in Gijon for a minor show before moving on to Barcelona where I planned to meet up with them.

I booked my ticket with a local travel agent and arrived at Heathrow nice and early for a 1.30 p.m. flight. I must have looked a right 22-year-old Jack-the-lad in my tracksuit, with my streaked blond hair, listening to music on earphones and having a few beers. I didn't look exactly like one of the horse set.

I began to get worried when the flight did not register on the departure board and at 1.20 decided it was time to ask about it. The steward on the information desk looked at the ticket and told me the flight was leaving from Gatwick not Heathrow, observing as he looked at his watch that I wasn't going to make it. He took pity on my plight, telephoned the travel agent and told them they had given the passenger the wrong information and that while he could put me on another plane, they would have to foot the bill as it was totally their fault.

There was another flight a few hours later and with time to kill I was lucky to bump into a friend who worked at the airport who pointed out that if I wanted a cheap beer I should follow his directions to the bar where all the porters drank. By the time my flight was called I'd had a good drink and I eventually arrived in Barcelona at around 6 p.m. a little the worse for wear and suddenly aware that I hadn't a clue where I was going. My only instruction was to go to the showjumping in Barcelona.

I spent the next hour looking for people who spoke English and asking them where I could find the showjumping. Eventually Air France gave me the address of a Polo Club on the off chance that it might be there and if it wasn't they could probably tell me where I could find the event. As luck would have it, they directed me to the right place and I arrived at this very fancy establishment in my black Sergio tracksuit, earphones around my neck and sports bag over my shoulder.

Despite sticking out like a sore thumb, I paid my entry fee and sat in the stand, looking round for where I might find Liz. I eventually saw Lesley sitting in the VIP area and immediately made my way across the seats calling out her name. She saw me and told me later that she said under her breath, 'Oh, my good God.' She quickly shuttled me out the back to where the horseboxes were parked and the horses stabled and then wisely washed her hands of me.

I found Liz and she was equally startled to see me. Clearly neither of them had thought for a minute that I would take them up on their casually offered invitation. I realised that if I hung around I was going to be in the way so I set about looking for things to do. I even managed to find a local greyhound track where they had an evening meeting. The way the locals looked at me they clearly thought that I was gay. I had a couple of beers and a bet and returned to the showjumping for a few more beers.

Liz was obviously embarrassed to have me there and continued to have as little to do with me as possible. I slept the first night on a settee in the horsebox while Liz had a bed with the horses where they were stabled. The second night I arrived back to find the horsebox locked. There were people sleeping everywhere so I found a sunbed by the swimming pool in the club leisure centre and slept there.

The rising sun and some irritating itching woke me in the morning and I jumped up to find that I was covered in insects and flies. I was startled to hear laughter from across the swimming pool and looked up to see all the grooms eating breakfast and falling about laughing at me. That didn't exactly raise me in Liz's esteem.

The next night Moet and Chandon, who sponsored one of the jumpers Nelson Pessoa, threw a party and all the grooms were on the free champagne in one of the horseboxes. I came out of there in a very happy mood and made my way back to our horsebox, where I slapped on a Bob Marley tape. Suddenly a head came up from the horse section and one of Liz's colleagues slaughtered me for waking her up.

That was the last night in Barcelona and rather than fly back on my own Liz asked if I wanted to travel back through Spain to Lyon in France and then on to Calais. By this time, I was wearing a white Sergio T-shirt, white Sergio shorts and a pair of trainers with no socks. I looked more like a tennis player than someone connected with showjumping or even football. We arrived at the border and the driver offered up the horses' passports and all the other documentation needed. Liz was out watering the horses and I was sitting with my feet up in the cab, earphones on, chilling out. The border guard appeared, opened the door and said, 'Move this wagon. It's in the way.'

I shrugged and told him I couldn't drive it but he was so insistent that he took his gun out to back up his request. I still shook my head and he demanded my passport. I reluctantly handed it over and he disappeared with it. I told another groom what had happened and he told me that I should go and recover my passport as quickly as possible because once they had received clearance they were gone and I would be left behind. He suggested I stay with the customs officer who had taken it. I did a man-for-man marking job on this Spaniard all around the control post. He kept looking over his shoulder at me, eventually telling me to go away. I turned but the moment he made his move I was back up beside him again. He turned round again, took out his gun and pinned me up against the wall, demanding that I leave him alone. I was only just in time with my passport. I think he was glad to get rid of me in the end.

We made our way to Lyon and a lovely racecourse setting, then on to Calais. They dropped me off at Dover and I made my way back home.

Despite the Barcelona experience and although Liz didn't have much time for football, or for my punk rock, we hit it off and got on quite quickly but the real catalyst was the move to Nottingham. By that time she had left her job as a groom and was nannying. I told her I was going to Nottingham and planned to buy a house, and I asked her if she would like to move in with me.

At that time I was off the road because of a drink-drive conviction, another unwanted entry on my CV. We had played at Norwich on 30 March and lost 2–1. On the way back in the coach I suppose I must have had three large cans of lager. In those days when we arrived back in Coventry we invariably went to a pub, and I had another drink, this time a lager shandy, before driving Micky Adams home. I was doing 40 in a 30mph zone and was pulled up for speeding.

The two policemen asked me if I had been drinking and I told them truthfully that I had had three cans of lager during a three-hour trip from Norwich. They tested me and I was fractionally over the limit. When Micky saw this he said, 'I'm all right from here. I can walk home,' and cleared off leaving me to handle the problem on my own.

I had originally planned to drop my car off and go out for the night. I was not a drink driver, even though it was not treated quite as seriously then as it is now. A lot more youngsters did drink and drive. I went down to the police station because they said that if I went for a blood test I might well pass positive because it was so close. On the way, I thought of a cunning plan. I was too clever for them, far too clever. I told them that I didn't like needles, I thought that if I went back to the club, I could pretend that I was on some form of medication that had pushed me over the top to get off any charge. I went to the club and asked the physio what I could say but he looked at me as though I was stupid and told me that there was nothing. I was gutted because I might have got off if I had gone through with the blood test. I ended up losing my licence at the worst possible time, when I was moving an hour further away from Liz.

Fortunately, Liz packed up her job and moved up with me. It was difficult for her and she found it hard at first. She is an independent girl and had been living away from home for a while and working with horses. Horses had been her whole life. When she joined me in Nottingham, she had no involvement with horses at all and sat around with nothing to do. That was just not her style. Both of us would admit to the fact that it was an awkward time.

I'm sure that it was fate that we met in Coventry, not hometown for either of us. I liked her as soon as I met her. I'm still a bit baffled about why she reciprocated. It certainly wasn't my music; she hated it. She was interested in horses and the country life while I knew nothing of either. Indeed, when it came to horses, I was scared to death of them. I was a bit of a Jack-the-lad, a city boy from London, thinking I was smarter than anyone else in the world. We had nothing in common but I seemed to have the ability to make her laugh. She was very shy, as I am until I get to know people when the guard comes down and exposes the real me. She is more homely than I am and while I love a holiday and travelling she is just as happy pottering about at home or in the stables. Give me the slightest excuse to climb on an aeroplane and I'm off. She may take a little persuading but once away she loves it as much as I do. The hard part is getting her there.

Not long after we arrived in Nottingham we took a retired racehorse on loan, an absolute lunatic. His name was Last River, hence his nickname Swim. He had been pulled out of racing because he wouldn't start, quite a drawback in that game. He would stand at the start and when the other horses went forward he went backwards. He was some character, completely barmy but Liz loved him. We stabled him up the road and spent a lot of time with him. That started my interest in horses and once you get to know them you fall in love with them.

We had a little flirt with horse racing and had a horse in training with Jenny Pitman for a couple of years. Once you lose the fear, it's fine but never lose the respect for them because you don't want to be kicked.

I also have to help out. I can't let Liz deal with the horses while I watch television. It takes two to tend to a sick animal of that size and when one of our horses contracted mud fever – that's developing little scabs on the backs of the heels when the ground is wet underfoot – I had to hold the horse while Liz treated the scabs. You have to be prepared for that sort of involvement or not have horses at all.

It's worked well. Horses provide a welcome relief from football and its attendant pressures. Managers seem to have the cares of the world on their shoulders. They think of nothing else but the job, walking round with it on their minds every waking minute. I remember the brief time I was in the job; I was in a permanent daze, thinking only of football. Sir Alex Ferguson and Kevin Keegan have both found a release in horses and I have followed that same route.

Fortunately, Liz appreciates that football is my life and, like most women, she says that I put football before her!

It made me laugh recently watching an interview with Manchester United and England defender Phil Neville and his new bride on their wedding day. The interviewer asked him if this was the biggest day of his life or was it winning the European Champions League. He was immediately on the backfoot. Every professional footballer watching knew that winning the European Cup was the biggest day. To be fair to him, he didn't say that getting married was the biggest day of his life; instead, he hummed and haa-ed. If I had been him, I would have lied. He finished up trying to wriggle out of it saying, 'The European Cup was a one-off.' That made me laugh and I asked his image on television, 'So your wedding isn't a one-off then?'

But when your life, and I mean your whole life, is football, winning a European Cup or a World Cup has to be the biggest thing. It would be like me asking Liz if she would swap all involvement with horses for the marriage. She could not and it would be unfair to ask.

We were together for a long time, around nine years, before we eventually tied the knot. I asked her to marry me a couple of times and she turned me down, saying she wasn't ready. Then Nottingham Forest beat Spurs in a League Cup semi-final to reach Wembley and when I arrived home that night I opened a bottle of champagne and asked her to marry me. This time she said she would. It was third time lucky and I mean lucky!

She has long been aware that football means everything to me and she has been prepared to adjust her life accordingly. On a Saturday morning, for example, if the telephone rings she knows I won't answer it, whoever it is, even if it is my mother or my dad. I don't talk to anyone on matchday mornings.

If we have friends coming to the game and they call at the house, Liz sees them and I stay in bed. I'm resting and I get up when I'm ready. Even with friends, I get into the car, turn the punk music on, have no conversation with them. They sit in silence while I continue to get my mind right. Football is on my mind, nothing else. Liz understands that and she deals with it.

Sometimes I listen to other players' wives and they don't understand exactly what their husbands require to give of their best. My diet and preparation routines have been in place for years. A football wife has to be aware of all that. There are routines I have picked up as I have gone along over the years. I have always been in bed by 10.30 on a Friday night whether it is at home or in a hotel. Sometimes you can hear the boys still chatting at midnight. Maybe that's what they do every night, but it's not what I do and I expect everyone to respect that. Trevor Peake used to have four cans of lager every Friday night before he played. He had done the same thing at Nuneaton, Lincoln and Coventry where he was one of our best players and close to an England call at one stage. When I went to live with him and his wife, he asked me if I wanted a beer and was surprised when I declined. I'm strong enough to know what's right and what's wrong for me. I personally thought that he was wrong but that was his business.

I learned quite a few bits and pieces from England coach Glenn Hoddle that he, in turn, had picked up from Arsene Wenger when he was manager at Monaco.

Mary, my mother-in-law gave me a good tip. She put me right when she said, 'A horse wouldn't have a meal three hours before a race. So why do some athletes?' She was right, of course, and gradually I worked out a diet that suited me. When I'm away on the day of a game, I have a raw carrot, raw broccoli and beans on toast for breakfast. The others might have a fry-up. Nutritionally, that's rubbish but it's what they have always done. A lot of it is down to habit. I have a pre-match meal at the same time every matchday – for a three o'clock kick-off it will be at 10.15 on the dot – and I have been doing that for a number of years now. Previously I was like all the others having my pre-match meal at 11.45 because we knew no different. Everyone is looking over his shoulder at what the next man is eating and you end up having what everyone else does so as not to be different. As you get older you become wiser.

The game is changing quickly, though. That came home to me when I went with the West Ham United team to Newcastle for a league game. There were a lot of youngsters on the trip including a player the Hammers had signed from Arsenal. Arsene Wenger is meticulous about what players eat and what vitamin pills they should take and this lad had been at Highbury since he was 14. But when he came down for breakfast at the hotel, he saw the older players having a fry-up so he followed suit. The physio spotted it and asked him if he would have done that at Arsenal. He, of course, admitted that he wouldn't but when he was asked why he was eating it now he said, 'Because it's there and it looks nice.' You have to be strong and he wasn't.

Liz knows how professionally I take my job and, in turn, I know how she is in dealing with horses. I wouldn't say I am like that in everything I do in life but in football I have to be prepared properly and she understands that. You go into the players' bar after a game and there will be players' wives there who don't know the result and don't care. They don't even know which way the teams are kicking. I used to go away from there and tell her I couldn't live with someone like that. She appreciates how I am and it has rubbed off on her. She knows that if we have been stuffed or if I have played badly, it is no use saying that it's only a game and suggesting that we go out for a meal or a few drinks. She is aware that I will have the hump and won't feel like going anywhere.

In some ways we are not compatible in our backgrounds, our hobbies and many other areas but in other ways, such as attitude and professionalism, we are totally on the same wavelength. I am thankful that I have someone alongside me like that. People may say I have a one-track mind or that I am a chauvinist but even the strongest person needs some support and she has been brilliant for me.

Another important factor was that we didn't have children until we were well into our 30s. I have never understood how players can be focused on their careers when they have a family. At times I find it very demanding and hard work.

When Chelsea came along it was a bolt out of the blue. We had not planned or tried for a family. When Liz discovered she was pregnant it once again emphasised the support I receive from her. She discovered on the Thursday that she was carrying but because we were playing at home against Arsenal on the Saturday she didn't tell me until the Sunday in case it put me off my game. I appreciated that. It represented real support.

On the Sunday morning she said, 'I have something to tell you.' I said, 'What's that?' expecting she had spent more than she thought she should have done on a coat or some such thing. She stunned me when she said, 'I think I'm pregnant.' There we were, two 36-year-olds who had been round the block once or twice, and I was so staggered that I did not know what to do or say. It was so unexpected. I started laughing, that nervous laugh that just sometimes happens.

She asked me what I thought and I said, 'Ask me Tuesday. It's done me up. I need a couple of days to think about it.' It wasn't the best or the most thoughtful of responses and Liz, understandably, burst into tears. We had our own lives and although there had been children around, we had never considered it. We had all the excuses. It knocked the pair of us for six for a while. It wasn't that we didn't want children but for both of us it was always later, let's think about it later. Both of us were terrified.

When Chelsea was born, I loved her to bits but I couldn't have done it when I was 21. Physically, I would have coped but I don't know what detrimental affect it might have had on my career.

Brian Laws at Forest used to go swimming with his kids on the morning of a game. I couldn't have done that. Even when I was young I would stay in bed on Saturday morning and my parents and later Liz knew that I was preparing myself. Even now that I am further than the back end of my career, I wouldn't dream of doing anything on the morning of the game.

I'm not saying that young players should not have children but I'm convinced it must have a negative effect on their careers. For a start, there is no doubt that when you have children your diet suffers. You end up having burgers and chips because it's easier.

Liz is an outstanding mother. I knew she would be simply by the caring way she tended the horses in her charge, not that she hoses Chelsea down or puts a cold pack on her leg when she is poorly. I have to confess that I'm a doting dad. I used to take the mickey out of other couples with kids, telling them that they ruled their lives. I joked how I hated those little boys who come up to you, shove a scrap of paper under your nose and say, ''Ere Pearce, sign this.' Now the boot is on the other foot and they are poking fun at me. The funny thing is that I don't mind.

When the baby finally arrived it was a case of finding a suitable name. We were a bit stuck at first as most parents are. We produced a short list with the names we both liked. I liked Tallulah but Liz thought it sounded like a streetwalker. I also liked Toulouse but that was put on a back shelf as well. In contrast, I also liked the traditional name of Victoria and, when we looked at a baby book, the name Milan caught my fancy.

I was slightly worried about the football connotations with Chelsea and Milan but then I thought what the hell. I was nearing the end of my career and in a year or two no one will think twice about it. It is just the names I like, not the football clubs, and I never once thought of calling her Queens Park Rangers or Nottingham Forest. They didn't roll off the tongue like Chelsea.

There is no doubt that Chelsea has changed our lives. What a different sort of love a father gives to a daughter. I see bits of Liz in her, I see bits of me and I see her own individuality. It is all very exciting.

I was lucky to have a solid home life with my parents and then moved almost straightaway into an equally solid home life with Liz. She doesn't go to as many games now we have Chelsea but she was a regular at Forest and I think she enjoys football. She will even watch it on television although she prefers it when someone she knows is playing.

When I broke my leg the first time, I didn't want her to hear it on the radio. I telephoned and just told her I had broken my leg. There was no panic. At least she didn't have to call the vet to have me put down.

We have discovered a common bond in travel, although as I said, she sometimes takes a little persuading. For me it started with Coventry when we went on a pre-season tour of Scandinavia. I thought to myself that this couldn't be bad, being taken to Sweden to play football, all expenses paid, and drawing a wage at the same time. But my interest in having my passport stamped was really aroused when I joined Forest a year later. Brian Clough would have us pack our bags at the drop of a hat. If he had an 'earner' (a friendly that paid the club good money) he would tell us on Friday that we were flying to the Middle East immediately after playing the league game on Saturday. It was phenomenal. Two years earlier I had been changing fuses for Brent council and now someone wanted to take me to Tenerife for a mid-season break or to Saudi Arabia to play football. More of that please!

Football not only put pages of stamps in my passport but also gave me the bug for travel. I quickly decided that the world was too large to go anywhere twice and I vowed that I would always take my holidays in different places every year. I have been to Bermuda, for example, and while I loved it I don't feel the need to go back. I want to go somewhere else. Liz wasn't too enamoured when I first started dragging her round the world with me, but now she appreciates it.

We are too protected from what is going on elsewhere in our comfortable homes in Europe, and it is an eye-opener in many respects when you start widening your boundaries. One of our most fascinating trips was when we went to Zimbabwe on safari. Because of what we had been force-fed on television and in magazines, we were of the belief that all animals should be preserved, especially as we are both animal lovers. I didn't believe that they should be hunted down or culled. What we didn't know about was how a herd of elephants might trample through a village, destroying precious crops and wrecking people's homes. A television documentary doesn't tell you that. Travelling gives us both sides of the argument and the opportunity to make up our own minds. It doesn't mean that I now believe all elephants should be shot but I can see someone else's point of view.

The attraction of travelling is that you see people in their own environment and can begin to understand why they behave as they do. As soon as we walked out of the airport in Sri Lanka it was a real culture shock. It was India without quite so much poverty. We travelled to our hotel in a minibus and instead of being held up by traffic jams we were stopped because there was an elephant in the middle of the road. That's the norm there. Driving into the capital Colombo, there might be a herd of cows sitting in the fast lane of the dual carriageway. Then a bus will go careering past with people hanging off the sides, doors and roof. When I drive to work from my Wiltshire home to West Ham, there may be an eight-mile traffic jam because a horse has escaped or because there is a sheep on the hard shoulder. It's a different world and I want to see as much of it as I can. You don't see anything if you stay at home.

I can never understand it when I hear people in their 30s saying that they have never been abroad. I know that I am fortunate in having a career that has made me financially secure and given me the opportunity to travel, but I would say to everyone, if you get a chance to travel – go! Just going to an airport is exciting. I love the buzz, the atmosphere, the coming and going. You can sit in a bar in an airport and see the whole world go by. The place has a special feeling. I'm so sad I get excited just flying out to Dublin or up to Glasgow.

My favourite spots in the world so far are Zimbabwe and Sri Lanka. Bermuda was idyllic with beautiful weather and beaches, but the other two places offered so much more, particularly when you sit in a safari camp with perhaps 14 other people swapping stories. The experience is imprinted on the memory. On our first night in Zimbabwe we were in our high single beds by around nine o'clock because of the early start and lay there terrified, listening to the noises of the night. It was like being in Jurassic Park. It didn't help the next morning when we emerged into the sunlight to find cheetah paw prints going through the camp.

The camp was on the edge of Lake Kariba. We got up at six, went out with the guide until eleven, then back for breakfast followed by a little rest, out again at around 3.30 and finally back before the light went for dinner at six. We sat round a big table under the stars in the jet-black sky, chatting to the guides and the other guests – a couple of South Africans and a group of Europeans.

One guide, Steve, used to work for the government before he acquired his own camp and he told us tales that made our hair stand on end. When he was on the anti-poaching squad for President Mugabe's government, protecting the rhinos, elephants and other endangered species, he claimed that he had shot and killed 14 poachers while doing his job. He further claimed that he left the job because the last poacher he shot was a relative of the President! True or not, it beat sitting around and watching soap operas on television.

Sri Lanka was also a great experience with lovely people and wonderful sights. The people are also lovely in Mauritius. That is, in the main, a beach holiday but I had the experience of going horse racing while we were there. They are fanatics. The crowds were incredible. The place was full of Indians, Chinese and Africans with the only white faces belonging to the jockeys, the owners and us. The two things they care about on Mauritius are their horse racing and English football. It suited me because I love both and add that to the fact that the people of Mauritius are probably the most racially integrated and friendly in the world and you can guess we had a pretty good holiday.

With our growing interest in horse racing, Liz and I have also been making an annual pilgrimage to Ireland, combining holiday with hobby. We look around all the studs with friends of ours who buy and sell horses.

There is, of course, a vast difference between going on holiday and travelling with a football team where the strict regimen means that access is restricted for the most part to airports, hotels, training pitches and the match ground. In any case, footballers are basically lazy bastards and even when there is time to spare on tours, they prefer room service in the hotel and a wine bar for entertainment. I have been incredibly fortunate to travel to China, Hong Kong, Australia, New Zealand, Thailand and many of the football-playing European countries, but I didn't see as much of them as I would wish. Things are changing slowly and players opening their eyes to the outside world.

When we went to China we were taken to the Great Wall as a squad and walked round. That evening Gareth Southgate, a couple of FA officials and I asked Terry Venables if he minded us hiring a taxi to go and look at the infamous Tiananmen Square. He gave his blessing and asked the rest of the squad if they wanted to join us. Everyone else blanked it. We had a look around the Secret City and the place where the students were massacred, and while it was chilling, it was a phenomenal experience. I found the attitude of the others very blinkered. They were happy to sit around the hotel and do nothing. If I thought the sightseeing would take away from my job, I wouldn't have done it but it was a couple of days before the game, involved a short taxi ride and a minimal amount of walking. What's more it keeps the mind fresh rather than stagnating.

With Brian Clough, we ended up going away an average of four times a season, usually a couple of times to Cala Millor on Majorca where he had an apartment. They were just jollies, a couple of beers and some rest and relaxation. These were also the money-spinners I've already mentioned, flying out to somewhere exotic, playing a game and flying back again. That was a ridiculous way of preparing for a league match but it made the club, or someone, a lot of money so we did it.

The players got blasé about it all. One time we had played about four games into a new season when he called us down to the hotel bar.

'Skip,' he said. 'The players are looking a little jaded. They need a trip.' The season had only just started and he was obviously poking fun but I responded.

'I think you're right, Boss.'

'Right,' he said. 'We'll go to Tenerife. That's what we'll do. Who wants to go?' I was always up for a trip and was first in line with just four others out of a whole squad of 20, including a fair number of single boys. Clough looked in dismay and spat out, 'I can't fucking believe you lot. Fuck off, all of you.'

Then he turned to the five of us and asked, 'Do you want to bring your wives?' That was even better as far as I was concerned. Liz would always think of a million and one reasons why she couldn't go before actually agreeing, and off we went, five players, their wives, Clough and some of the staff.

I thought it was unbelievable that when someone was prepared to give you a few days off with the sun on your back, in the company of your wife and pay for it all, people turned it down. It was alien to me. I don't understand that mentality. It wasn't the only time it happened. The players made excuses and said that it was because Clough would be in their face all the time and they would prefer to do their own thing. Bad excuse. In five days away with Liz, I would hardly see the manager. If you wanted to stay away from him, you could, and it was no problem having dinner together, especially if his wife was with him.

Moving to Forest was great for me. Brian Clough collared me at the right time. Even when I went to Forest, I was still unsure of myself and whether I could make it as a professional footballer. There was always that nagging doubt.

At Coventry, Bobby Gould was a big influence on my career. However, all the Coventry managers of that era were so busy looking after their own jobs that they didn't have much time to help others. When Bobby was replaced with Don Mackay, he was instantly under the same pressures. Coventry were always down among the lower clubs. But I was happy there – as happy as I was at Forest – and if they had offered me another contract I would have bitten off their hand. I could just as easily have played at Highfield Road for 12 years.

It was not until after a couple of years at Forest and the England Under-21 call-up in 1986 that I was finally convinced that I had made it as a professional footballer and that no matter what happened I would be able to find myself another club. They question mark hung over my head all the time I was at Coventry. I had a two-year contract and no one was talking to me about extending it.

I remember telephoning a friend when I signed for Forest and saying that I had signed a three-year deal and if it did not work out, well, I would have had three years. I carried on with my electrician's work; it was a common-sense thing to do.

CHAPTER 5

forest fire

Football was definitely a gamble in those early years of my professional career and I was glad that I had my trade to fall back on in case I flopped or was struck down with injury.

I kept my hand in at Coventry, doing some work for John Sillett, Peter Barnes and Kirk Stevens. Kirk wanted a light fitted in the bedroom. On the face of it there was no problems. It was a bowl-shaped fixture with a chandelier effect hanging from it, to be fixed to the bedroom ceiling with three screws. I did the job, jumped off the bed and said to Kirk, 'There you are mate, a lifetime guarantee with that little lot.' No sooner had the words left my mouth than the whole lot came crashing down on to the bed where, a few hours later, Kirk would have been lying with his wife discussing the mysteries of the universe. I had over-tightened the screws and they cracked the glass so that the screws stayed up but the light fitting did not. We both fell about laughing and it all turned out well as the shop replaced the fitting because they thought it was faulty.

The work for John Sillett was a little more robust. He lived out in the rural part of Coventry and he needed an armoured cable laying down his drive and into the stables.

When I moved to Forest I thought to myself that if I started a little electrical business it would be security in case the football didn't work out. I had been a professional for less than two years and nothing was certain. I went to Brian Clough and told him what I had in mind and asked whether he would mind if I advertised in the matchday pro-gramme. He had no objections and it brought in a few bits and pieces, so much so that after a few months it became too much with all the training and playing demands at Forest. The little jobs were not a problem but I rewired a friend's house in Coventry and the effort of training and then travelling to and from Coventry plus working on my own became a bit of a strain. In the end, I asked Forest team-mate Brian Rice to come and help me out and I paid him a daily rate for working with me up in the loft.

I also worked in a hotel where I met a builder who offered me some contract work with him. He looked after a chain of banks and hired me to clean all the light fittings in a local branch. Again it was too much for one person and I pulled in another of the Forest players, Billy Reilly, to assist me for the accepted daily rate.

After we had played Brighton in the League Cup at the City Ground I took a call on my business line from a Brighton supporter who wanted to know whether it was THE Stuart Pearce. He was an electrician himself and was delighted that I was in the same business earning an honest living as well as playing football.

Far from putting any obstacles in the way, Clough brought in his iron and his kettle for me to repair, although when I told him it was cheaper to buy a new iron rather than replace the element he began to doubt whether I really was an electrician. Mind you, it could have been some Clough master plan to rebuild the club from the inside because as well as me, he took on Gary Crosby who was a carpenter and Garry Birtles, a carpet fitter.

My first season at Forest involved not just bedding into a new club but becoming used to a completely different type of management under the colourful Brian Clough. Within a year I was captain. It was basically a very young side. With hindsight, I was a natural choice for captain – there was no one else on that bus whom he could have approached and asked. Even though I was a professional of less than three years, I was still a senior player.

My stature grew in the dressing-room over the years, far more than it did with Clough. It was never a nice, friendly partnership – I was his captain and left-back and he was the boss. It was a working relation-ship. My reputation grew within the club without me even realising it.

Like Mark Hughes, I am a different person on the pitch compared with off it. I like to do my shouting on the pitch during a game, although I have had my moments off it! Your career shapes your personality, especially when you are in the limelight. I enjoy the way I have done it and I agree with Mark's approach, fiery on it and quiet off it. I am not an Ian Wright type with all that cockiness and confidence in themselves. Sometimes I have my doubts about that type of character and, when I meet someone who is outlandishly over the top, the first thing that springs to mind is to ask myself what they are trying to hide. For some, that's how they are but my feeling is why are they giving it big? Why not let your football do your talking for you? But that's just the way I am.

I may have been quiet away from the ground by this time, but the dressing-room was my court and once I had my feet under the table people came in under my terms and if there was any mickey-taking I would be at the forefront.

Even at Coventry I was organising the odd function, bringing my non-league roots with me. After a couple of years at Forest, I was involved in everything. After a while you know everyone at the club and you become happy with the workplace. My rapport with the fans was great. It was a lovely place to go to work. To me that meant a lot. If you're happy with your surroundings, you're happy in your life and I was.

Of course, I was concerned that we weren't winning league titles. We finished third in 1988 and 1989 and thought we could go on from there. It was only Liverpool, who were the big side at the time, keeping us out and we expected to move on. But we didn't. In my first six seasons we never finished lower than ninth, but we could not push on. While we were successful in the cups, we were short of a couple of international quality players such as John Barnes or Peter Beardsley who were both around and available at the time. We needed a couple of individuals of that stature. But when Liverpool went in for players, they usually got them ahead of us.

Make no mistake, we were big with four players in the England side. We were short of players in the same way that clubs are now.

Aston Villa, for example, are the modern-day equivalent. Gareth Southgate took so long to ask for a move because he felt that Villa were only one or two players short of being a top side. It's the old story. They are not far away but the difference between winning titles and being a decent side is vast.

Clough brought in some foreign players including Johnny Metgod and Hans Segers, but I'm not sure that was the answer. What we needed at the time was another midfield player – keep Neil Webb and add a proven striker of quality. We were a young squad and lacked depth when things went wrong or when we suffered injuries. What we didn't have were a couple of 30 somethings to come in and settle the ship when things were going wrong.

But if you listen, every club in the country is a couple of players short. We were good enough for me to enjoy being there. I was getting international recognition and we were doing well in cup competitions so I had no regrets about not seeking to improve my lot with a so-called bigger club. Forest remained a strong side, very competitive and always challenging until we were relegated out of the blue.

Perhaps it was the success in the cups that took our attention away from what should have been the major target. In fact, sometimes when we went to Wembley it papered over the cracks of the team not being strong enough. We thought we had got away with a bit when we had the League Cup standing in our cabinet, one of only three domestic trophies available.

Everything hit the fan in a big way in 1992–93. There were never any real signs of us going down but the house collapsed like a pack of cards. On the other hand, someone should have realised because neither were we realistically challenging for the title. After a sequence of finishing third, ninth, eighth, and eighth, we went from losing 1–0 to Manchester United at Wembley in 1992 to being relegated a season later in 22nd position.

It is nothing you ever plan, to do well in cups. It is often inexplicable when you see Brighton taking Manchester United to a replay in the Cup final and being relegated in the same season. Where is the logic? Even now I still cannot say why we did so well in cups but the reason why we did not push on in the League was because we were short of a couple of top-class players. Here was a side who, 13 years earlier, had lifted back-to-back European Cups, relegated out of the top flight. A lesson to anyone but a lesson that never seems to be learned because you can never see it coming until the day it arrives. Just ask Manchester City.

Our best finish in the League while I was there was third and, give or take one or two better players, we might have been a bit closer to pushing a tremendous Liverpool side all the way. Had they not been as good as they were, we would have undoubtedly won more.

Brian Clough was clearly building a side for a tilt at the title. We finished eighth in my first two seasons there, 1985–86 and 1986–87, and third in the two following seasons as Des Walker emerged, Nigel Clough came in and Neil Webb proved to be a sensational buy. Garry Birtles came from non-league and did well, as did Dutchman Johnny Metgod. But, as I say, we were still a couple of players short of having a serious go and we couldn't get near enough to Liverpool for love nor money. We weren't good enough to get past them. They were head and shoulders above everybody at the time, although we gave them good games and beat them on occasions at our place.

There was a lot of bad feeling between the two teams, certainly there was on my part. It was probably jealousy where I was concerned because they always seemed to be in our way.

From my point of view, I would have played in Europe on three or four occasions but for the behaviour of some Liverpool supporters at the Heysel Stadium in Belgium, as a result of which we were all banned from playing in Europe. Personally, I thought that was very unfair. Liverpool should have suffered for what went on at Heysel, not Nottingham Forest or Norwich City, who hadn't put a foot wrong. That was an injustice.

We lost FA Cup semi-finals to them in 1988 and 1989 and what was really annoying was that had we been drawn against any of the other semi-finalists we would probably have beaten them and reached the final but both times we drew Liverpool. It stirred up a lot of feeling between the two sides because of the intensity of our meetings. Before the first of these two semi-finals, I was sitting in my car in the Forest car park with the radio on waiting for the draw. It was our luck. We had been drawn away in every round, beating Halifax, Leyton Orient, Birmingham City and Arsenal, but the semi-final was to be played on a neutral ground and we felt that if we could avoid Liverpool and draw either Wimbledon or Luton Town we would make the final.

We went up to Hillsborough, which we didn't mind, especially when a whisper went around the dressing-room that the Sheffield Wednesday groundsman had asked our club how we wanted the pitch: did we want it wet or dry?

We were a young side with Des Walker, Nigel Clough, Franz Carr and myself, against the likes of Bruce Grobbelaar, Alan Hansen, Peter Beardsley and John Barnes.

Some say that the worst thing is to lose in the final but as far as I am concerned the first round is the worst. I would rather go as far as I can every time and if I am going to lose, make it the final. We just weren't good enough to get there. John Barnes caused havoc. He was up against Steve Chettle who had been tucked up by a journalist in the previews to the game. He was playing out of position and was asked how he fancied reaching the final. He said that he was looking forward to it. Then when he was asked what he would have for his breakfast on the morning of the match he replied, 'Beans on toast.' The headline the next day was: 'I will have John Barnes on Toast'. It wound up John and he ran Steve ragged; not that Barnes needed stoking up. He was the best player in the country at the time. That individual battle was one of the main factors in the result.

It was a very tight game. They scored first through John Aldridge who then got a yard on me and scored a second. Nigel pulled one back for us and we gave them a couple of hesitant moments. But it was not enough and once again Brian Clough was left wondering about the FA Cup.

Clough could be calm or livid in defeat; it varied according to the performance. On that day he couldn't say a lot because we played as well as we could and were beaten by a better team. It was straight back on the coach, as ever.

I often wondered what would have happened, how the club would have risen in stature if we had won that semi-final in 1988. We were sniffing around the cups in the eighties and early nineties – semi-final, semi-final, third round, final, quarter-final in the FA Cup in successive years from 1988 to 1992. That's a good run for any team and on top of that we won the League Cup back to back in 1989 and 1990.

We were back at Hillsborough exactly a year later, hoping this time that we could overturn them. We had been playing for five or six minutes when people began spilling on to the pitch from the Liverpool end and my first thought was, 'Bloody Liverpool supporters again.' I am not ashamed to admit that because it's what I thought as the referee took us off the pitch. We didn't realise what was going on and all I could think of was that Liverpool and their supporters were stopping me from plying my trade in Europe and now they were keeping me from playing in a semi-final. We were protected from the horror of it; we didn't know what was going on out there.

The semi-final was eventually played at Old Trafford. Brian Laws scored an own goal and once again Liverpool got right up my nose as John Aldridge ruffled Brian's hair in mock congratulations. Little things like that, added to the fact that they were in a different class from us, riled me no end. When we beat them in the League, not one of them wanted to shake our hands but when they beat us they were in our face, wanting to shake hands and pat us on the back.

Everyone was saying to us that there was no way we could win the semi-final at Old Trafford and that even if we did, everyone wanted Liverpool in the final. That wasn't my attitude. I wanted to beat them even more than before the aborted Hillsborough semi-final. People will probably say what a hard bastard and that is taking football beyond sport. But having been banned from Europe for so long, I was aggrieved that they had stacked the entire nation on their side, again through no fault of ours.

Not long afterwards we went to Anfield for a league game and lost to a late John Aldridge penalty. Before the game Aldridge apologised to Brian Laws for rubbing him on the head. The game was a bit nasty to say the least with a few tasty tackles flying round and I was guilty of losing my head on one or two occasions. Ironically, it was Laws who brought Aldridge down to concede the penalty. Unbelievably, Aldridge rubbed him on the head again after apologising only a couple of hours earlier. I told Laws that I wouldn't have accepted that. I would have chinned him there and then on the pitch.

John Barnes recounted the story when we were both at Newcastle and according to his version Lawsy was having a go at Aldridge when Pearce came running up shouting, 'Never mind Aldridge, forget about him . . . get fucking McMahon, get McMahon.' It was true that I disliked Steve even more than I did Aldridge!

After the penalty, I was chasing a ball out to the sidelines and just couldn't get to it. Already steaming at the injustice of the whole thing, I smashed the ball into the crowd as hard as I could. I am not a good loser at the best of times. A few days later the Nottingham Forest secretary brought me a letter from the fellow I had hit. Apparently, it had knocked him out cold and he came around just as the whistle went. He went on to add that the guy sitting next to him suffered with a heart condition and that if the ball had hit him it would probably have killed him. He was complaining that my attitude was a disgrace. We are in this game to win and sometimes you can go over the top in the heat of the moment.

I understand that Liverpool were a good team and like most top sides they had a nasty edge to them. They could look after themselves just as the current Manchester United side can. It's part of being winners. In 1989 we got to Wembley in the League Cup and won, beating Luton Town 3–1, and once you get a taste for it you get a little nasty streak because you want to win again. We were young lads and we weren't used to winning but once we'd got there, it seemed a lot easier to get back. Statistics show that to be true for lots of clubs. Whether you grow in stature or you get used to it I don't know. But after my experiences against Liverpool, win, lose or draw, whatever the game, I leave the pitch straightaway. If someone crosses my path and wants to shake my hand I will do so but I won't go out of my way,

The perfect throw: practising the essentials.

More dribbling than tackling: me in my first year.

Hardly Psycho: me as an angelic schoolboy.

Silverware and long hair: the Fryent Primary School team and some of our trophies. That's me fifth from left on the back row.

Still me to come: my parents with Pamela, Dennis and Ray.

The original hard man: eldest brother Ray, who quit boxing and took up refereeing.

Putting on the style: brothers Ray and Dennis all set for a trip to the West End.

Making my mark: my first Player of the Year award with part-timers Wealdstone.

Champagne and cigars: manager Alan Batsford enjoys a puff as Wealdstone celebrate winning the Southern League.

Someone even older than me: Coventry City keeper Steve Ogrizovic and I go for the same ball. (*Coventry Evening Telegraph*)

Going blond: a moment of madness saw me dye my hair just before my trip to see a surprised Liz in Barcelona. (*Popperfoto*)

Turning it on: even after I joined Nottingham Forest, I still advertised my services as an electrician in the match programme. (*Nottingham Evening News*)

Of all people! John Aldridge, never my favourite player, settles our fate in the 1988 FA Cup semi-final at Hillsborough with his second goal. (*Colorsport*)

Wembley here we come: the end of a cold, wet semi-final against Bristol City at Ashton Gate, celebrating quietly with manager Brian Clough and the ever-present Alan Hill.

Derby day: yet another tussle with my old Derby County rival Ted McMinn. (*Popperfoto*)

The tragedy unfolds: when the problems began at Hillsborough during the 1989 FA Cup semi-final it was all at the far end of the ground, so the Nottingham Forest players were not really aware of what was going on until much later. (*Popperfoto*)

No quarter: a battle with rival defender and England team-mate Steve Foster in the 1989 Littlewoods Cup final against Luton Town. (*Colorsport*)

And again! Celebrating retaining the Littlewoods Cup, this time beating Oldham. (*Colorsport*)

The old one–two: celebrating another Stuart Pearce goal courtesy of my mate Nigel Clough. (*Bob Thomas*)

Beauty and the beast: I introduce Princess Diana to manager Brian Clough before the 1991 FA Cup final against Spurs. (*Empics*)

Take that! Lee Glover moves Gary Mabbutt out of the wall to give me space to score the first goal of the final against Spurs after Paul Gascoigne's injury. (*Popperfoto*)

purely on what I saw John Aldridge and other Liverpool players do. That to me was not sportsmanship. It was hypocritical. I am of the opinion that while I will try to kick lumps out of opponents, I can accept it without whingeing when they do it back to me.

Brian Clough was funny about Liverpool, as well. His opinion was that they were the sort of club who put things in your tea. He used to tell us, 'Don't drink the tea. The cheating bastards probably put something in it.' At Liverpool, he wouldn't drink anything that wasn't sealed.

The ill-feeling between Liverpool and Nottingham Forest culminated for me in a little spat at the end of the 1988–89 season. Arsenal took the League at Liverpool in that memorable 2–0 win at Anfield. I was in Scotland at the time with the England team for a friendly. We were preparing to play Poland at Wembley in a World Cup qualifier. We won that game but afterwards I had an argument with Steve McMahon. He was a spiky little devil who was not afraid to leave his foot in; mixed with my natural aggression it proved to be a strong cocktail that sometimes went to the head! It was a minor incident, soon forgotten. For my part, I put it down to losing those two FA Cup semi-finals. I was bearing a grudge because twice I had been a gnat's whisker away from reaching a Cup final, the only trophy Brian Clough had never won. I make no excuses and no apologies.

In fact, if I was asked what I regretted most it would have to be losing four semi-finals, those two, the World Cup in 1990 and the European Championship in 1996. If I could have any results changed, it would be those four to give me a tilt at winning the World Cup, the European Championship and the FA Cup. Each time the same teams thwarted me – Germany and Liverpool.

The first time we reached Wembley in the League Cup final, in 1989, we beat Bristol City in the semi-final. At Bristol in the second leg it was freezing cold and pouring with rain, the coldest conditions I have ever played in. We had drawn the first leg 1–1 and we squeezed through with a goal from Garry Parker in extra time. Before we left the pitch, we went over and clapped the crowd. As I went down the tunnel, Clough, back at Wembley for the first time in ten years, grabbed hold of me and said, 'Son, son, come with me, come with me,' and promptly took me back to our supporters. He wanted to give them a clap but didn't want to go on his own. Make of that what you will. It was a proud moment for me because I was his captain and we had taken him back to Wembley.

The key word for him was respect and I had that in abundance. Of all the good names I have worked for I held him in the greatest of respect. Ted Edgar, Liz's former employer, was very similar in his approach – unpredictable, having a go when you least expected it and holding back when you thought he would have a go.

Clough was a good man to work for. At Forest I had eight years under him, six as his captain, and then four years with Frank Clark. The press drummed it into us all the time that Clough had never won the FA Cup and being his captain I would have loved to have won it and said, 'This is for you.' Pictures of the European Cup winners were scattered all around the club and, indeed, all around Nottingham and I would have been ecstatic to have added ours with the FA Cup. I would have liked to have said to him, 'Here you are. The others couldn't win that for you.' Although I wasn't there when Clough won back-to-back European Cups, in 1979 and 1980, I was still very proud of the achievement. I know that some players and managers have no time for the past but without history you cannot have a present.

I have the same feelings about the achievements of an individual. When Brian Clough did what he did for the club, they should have named a stand after him straightaway and not waited until he retired and was in ill health. It was the same with Bobby Moore at West Ham. He was the captain of the winning World Cup team and the most famous player in West Ham's history. Why wait until he dies to honour him?

There is no accolade that the city of Nottingham or the club could have bestowed on Clough that would have been over the top. He put them on the map as much as Robin Hood did. They could have named the entire ground after him. He did more than any other manager at any other club, apart from perhaps Bill Shankly at Liverpool.

When we reached the League Cup final for the second time, in

1990, we played Coventry in a two-legged semi-final. That was a big deal for me against my old club and I scored a goal in the first leg from a free kick in the inside-right position. It went in off the underside of the crossbar and gave us a slender lead to take to Highfield Road. We drew at Coventry and were overjoyed at reaching Wembley. We arranged to go round to goalkeeper Steve Sutton's house for a party to celebrate and it was the early hours of the morning when I finally rolled home.

The next day we could hardly move and Clough was furious, perhaps because we hadn't included him. He made us do five laps of the pitch as a punishment and he was screaming at me to run harder. I couldn't resist shouting back, 'I got you to Wembley.' He ignored me.

When Forest went to Wembley, nothing was organised in terms of big celebrations. Whether that was based on superstition, I don't know. I went to Wembley twice with Newcastle and there were parties after both games. At Forest, if anything was arranged it would be by the players meeting in a pub and having a few sandwiches laid on, or a few drinks in the boardroom. That was the case even after the 1991 Cup final when Tottenham beat us 2–1 after extra time. There was another club I hated losing to but we always had good open games against them. We often won at each other's ground because both teams' style suited the one playing away.

The 1991 Cup final was a big day with Princess Diana and Prince Charles as the guests of honour, particularly in retrospect with the sad events that were to follow.

I believe Clough picked his favourites instead of the best side that day and I was not alone among the players in that belief. We were surprised at his choice, particularly as in the past Clough had even selected his strongest teams for testimonials. Nigel Jemson was a bit of a loud mouth but was playing well at the time; Clough dropped him in favour of Lee Glover. Jemson was not even selected on the bench and he was in tears on the morning of the final. I think Clough did it because he thought Jemson was a bighead. He certainly always called him that. Jemmo always had a lot to say but it was softened because he was funny with it. Clough probably thought that he was teaching him a lesson.

He also left out Franz Carr. Forest were in negotiation over a new contract with Franz's agent and his father. Clough didn't like agents at the best of times and he showed it. Franz's dad didn't like Clough's attitude and from what I understand stood up to him when Clough bad-mouthed him, and told him forcefully, 'How you talk to my son is up to you but if you talk to me like that I will sort you out.' That was the background to poor Franz being dropped and the suspicion is it was the reason he was dropped. We felt he could have given Spurs problems with his explosive pace. Clough also left out Steve Hodge, another who was playing well at the time.

It was a bad day for a lot of people, that final. The game hinged on Paul Gascoigne. Because of him the hype for the final was incredible, much more over the top than I could remember before. Our manager had never won the FA Cup and Gascoigne was playing his last game before going to Lazio for £8.5 million in a high-profile transfer. The expectations were high but, in truth, it wasn't a very good game at all. It will always be remembered for what Gazza did, not for the brilliant football of which he was capable. His tackle on Garry Parker was so bad that he caught Garry in the chest but it was nothing compared with the horrific challenge on Gary Charles. He should have been sent off rather than carried off but that wild tackle had a massive effect on his career. It put him out for a year and God knows what effect it had on his electric pace. He was never quite the same player afterwards.

The first tackle on Parker gave an indication of what lay ahead. Everyone should be up for a Cup final but he was way over the top. I knew Gazza and I knew what he was like. He had a remarkable run in the competition that season. He took them to the final almost single-handed and few will forget the two goals he scored in the fifth round to put Portsmouth out. He was the player we were most worried about because we knew he could turn a game on its head. We started quite well for the first 15 minutes. Then Gazza was carried off and his foul gave me the chance of a free kick on the edge of the box that I buried – 1–0. But after that we didn't play. The game was finding its feet for the next half an hour; they were trying to settle down after losing their best player while we thought it was too easy.

Nothing was said in the dressing-room. We were one up, Gazza was off and we felt all we needed to do was to play the second half out. I don't know whether it was complacency or whether we thought we had something to hold on to and sat back. We ended up letting them back in the game. Paul Stewart equalised in the 54th minute and then, in extra time, Nayim, who had replaced Gazza, took a corner. It was touched on by Stewart and Des Walker, our best player on the day, headed through his own goal.

Receptions to glorify a defeat are not my scene, but I told Liz I would see her back in the boardroom at Forest where something was laid on. The players' coach arrived back first and I was having an orange juice when the directors' coach arrived. They had sunk a few beers and were well on the way. I remember saying to John Hickling, who came in smoking a cigar as happy as Larry, 'It's fucking small-minded bastards like you who make this club what it is.' I liked John and bore him no malice but I couldn't understand someone being happy when we had lost. He was talking about how he had met Princess Diana, what a good day he had had and all the rest of it. It was a red rag to a bull.

By the time Liz arrived I was in a towering rage. I was captain and I had gone to Wembley to win. I guess I was just a bad loser. I said my piece and got it off my chest. Fortunately, John was understanding and apart from telling me to calm down took it no further. At some clubs I would have been given my cards.

We didn't see Clough at the back of the coach. He sent a few messages down to us, one of them telling us that we need not go in for training until Thursday. Had we won, we would probably have been in the next day just to keep our feet on the ground. That's what happened after winning the League Cup.

If we had won the 1991 FA Cup, Clough could have retired then at the top instead of waiting to be booted out when the club was relegated two years later. He would have gone out the complete hero having won everything. He is still a hero to most in Nottingham but relegation somewhat tainted his image.

I collected autographs in a book when I was a kid and when I looked at it a couple of years after joining Forest, I saw I had Margaret Thatcher and Brian Clough on one page. There were two people with the same attitude and aura about them – strong characters. It was dated 1974 and I have no real recollection of getting the great man to sign my little book. I was a ball boy at a Vase final and I took my autograph book to the Banqueting Suite after the game. The Prime Minister and Brian Clough were there among all the other celebrities, so it must have been then. It must be rare to have two such diametrically opposed people, in terms of their political leanings, on the same page.

We all knew how much Clough would have liked to win the FA Cup but he never spoke about it to the players. In fact, the games he was most revved up for were the East Midlands derby matches against his old club Derby County. He hated losing to them. I can understand that in part – I don't like losing to clubs I used to play for. It was emphasised for him because of the bad feeling when he left the old Baseball Ground.

He was always desperate to win that one and in all my time at Forest we lost to them just once and that was 1–0 at the Baseball Ground the year Derby were relegated. It is amazing how it becomes instilled in you that you must win a particular game because of the manager's attitude. Even in the short time I was manager at Forest I told the boys that whatever happened in the rest of the season we couldn't lose at Derby, and we nicked a 0–0 draw. I was passing on what I had learned from Brian Clough.

The old Baseball Ground was tight and compact and the touchline was very near to the crowd. So much so that when I took a throw-in I would have coins thrown at me and was regularly covered in spittle. This wasn't a group of wild teenagers or louts in their 20s; this was all sorts ranging from little old ladies down to six-year-old boys. I loved it. It stoked me right up. People ask me if I find certain grounds intimidating and I can honestly reply that I have never once felt intimidated at a football ground. I love a hostile atmosphere. No one is going to come on and kill you, so what have you got to fear?

I hear people outside the game say that places like Turkey and the old Eastern Europe must have been scary. What rubbish. It may be for the spectators who are unescorted in the city before games but the players are shepherded to the ground, escorted into the dressing-room and policed on to the pitch. It might not be brilliant for goalkeepers, who have things thrown at them from behind the goal, but for the rest of us, we stand more chance of being hurt by a bad tackle than by an angry supporter.

At Derby you could sense the hatred from the home supporters and I would wind them up by running straight over to the Forest fans before the kick-off to give them a clenched fist salute. They would respond with a massive cheer while the home supporters would chant 'Bastard Stuart Pearce'. Old ladies, whom you would normally help across the road with their shopping, would call me things that would turn a navvy's face red. The tension and the hostility was tremendous, much better than playing in a nicey, nicey atmosphere.

It was just like that one day when I was marking Ted McMinn, a tall, leggy Scot. He was on the wing and I was full-back, so we spent a great deal of the game confronting each other along the touchline. I went sliding in for a typical tackle right on the touchline and we both crashed to the ground in a heap, him on top of me with my head level with his chest. It was a spur of the moment thing but I couldn't resist the target staring me in the face. I bit him right on the nipple as we lay on the ground. Ted jumped up and screamed at the official, 'Ref, he's just fucking bit me!' I looked at him and started laughing. He saw me out of the corner of his eye and he started laughing as well. The whole thing was just too ludicrous for words. This, I hasten to add, was pre Tyson biting off Evander Holyfield's ear. That little episode gave my kind of love bite a bad name and only a fool would try it now.

It reminded me of stories my brother Ray would tell of when he played for a working men's club in Harlesden. The centre-half would go up for a corner, head the ball and land in a heap on the ground with the centre-forward attached to his leg by his teeth. Maybe I took a bit of that with me. In my younger days when I played with Ray, if anyone tried to sort me out he would go and take care of them, even though I would protest that I could look after myself. The game has changed a lot since those days when local football was a lot more robust.

Nowadays if a player was caught biting another player the way I did, he would be called uncivilised, a savage, an animal and mad. It makes me laugh. When Tommy Smith scythed someone down it was brilliant but when Vinnie Jones did the same thing he was an animal. It's that nostalgia thing. Why is one brilliant because it was in the old days but the same thing terrible now?

Two incidents occurred within weeks of each other when David Beckham was sent off for a powder-puff tackle in a tournament in Rio while Robbie Savage could have broken Kanu's leg when Leicester played Arsenal, but he escaped. I don't support tackles like that and I would have shed no tears if the Leicester player had received a ten-match ban. It was what the tackle deserved.

At club level when two teams who are at loggerheads clash, even players with no knowledge of past conflicts pick up on the hostility and are soon joining in, saying, 'C'mon. Let's have some!' This sort of game, particularly local derby matches, creates extra tension between the two sets of supporters.

When I went in to see Forest chairman Irving Scholar about leaving Nottingham Forest, he expressed a concern that I would go to Derby or Leicester. Kevin Mason, my agent, butted in, 'With due respect, you have no idea of the politics of the area. If you think Stuart would play for Derby after leaving Nottingham Forest you are seriously mistaken.' I hadn't said a word to Kevin but he was a man who was born in Derby and now lived and worked in Nottingham so he knew the intensity of the feelings.

He had it spot on. If I didn't have a club to go to and Derby was my only option, I would rather go on the dole than join them. I do not mean to be derogatory to Derby and probably if I had played for Derby for 12 years the situation would be reversed. The longer you are at a club the more those rivalries become ingrained. If I had said to those 24,000 supporters who attended my testimonial that I was going to join Derby in the future, a great many of them would not have bothered to attend and pay their money to see the game. I could never walk in Nottingham or go to the ground again if I signed for Derby. I am sure that the Nottingham fans respect me staying when we were relegated and I can still go there and not have a bad word said about me. They are not concerned about Newcastle United or West Ham. Some have made the switch – Archie Gemmill and Steve Sutton – and that is their choice. I couldn't kick those Nottingham fans between the legs by playing for Derby. Liverpool, yes . . . Derby, definitely no.

Scholar couldn't understand that. I doubt whether anyone outside football would understand it. Football, even though it is now plc, is not company business. It is about flesh and blood, emotions and feelings.

Despite my loyalty, if I were playing against Nottingham Forest in the last game of the season I would be desperate to beat them even if it meant sending them down.

I had my opportunities to leave the City Ground long before I did with two of Britain's biggest clubs making overtures to me. Just before the 1990 World Cup in Italy, my contract was nearing its conclusion. England captain Bryan Robson spoke to me as we were preparing for the tournament and told me that Alex Ferguson was interested in taking me to Manchester United the following season. Graeme Souness, who had recruited several top English players four years earlier before the Mexico World Cup, also told me that he would like me at Rangers. It sowed a little seed, not a big one because I was settled and happy at Nottingham Forest.

As a result I went in to see Brian Clough and hammered out a very good five-year contract that would carry me up to ten years service with the club and a testimonial. We were getting to Wembley regularly; Manchester United were winning nothing at the time. We were an up-and-coming side ready to challenge for the major honours while United were not the side they were to become ten years later. It was even rumoured that Alex Ferguson was under severe pressure for his job.

Rangers, on the other hand, were winning everything but I wanted to play my football on the competitive battleground of English football and not have just the occasional high-intensity game north of the border. I was happy living in Nottingham, as was Liz, and I was contented with life at the City Ground.

On the reverse side of signing a five-year deal, I had a problem three years down the line when wages accelerated that much that I was left behind; not massively because I was well paid but significantly enough for the long-serving captain of the side, who was also captain of the England.

I was first named captain on the 1986–87 pre-season tour of Sweden. Ian Bowyer, the previous long-serving captain and a player whom I held in the greatest regard, had left the club at the end of the season having been through all the glory years. We jumped on the coach to take us to the airport and Ronnie Fenton made his way down to the back. 'The gaffer wants to know if you would like to be captain,' he said. I was well pleased. It was an honour but it might have meant just a little bit more had the man himself asked me. Even so, I was as proud as punch. He obviously saw in me someone who could lead on the pitch. I had something to say for myself, although not too much when Clough himself was around. Without being boastful I think he made the right choice. I enjoyed the responsibility and organising. I am always ready to do my fair share.

A high for me was the rapport I had with the fans at Nottingham Forest. Arguably the support I had from them during the highs and lows was as good as any player who's ever played the game. I could walk off the pitch having had a stinker and no one would complain. I think most people realised that I was not the most gifted player in the team but I have a fair amount of ability and I always give 100 per cent. I'm totally committed to any team I play for.

I also have a theory that the fans see a little bit of themselves in me – a bit of a park player, a bit of this and a bit of that. Forest supporters knew I had the love of the club at heart and put them first. I gave the same to every club I played for but because I was at Forest so long that relationship grew and grew. It has never ever been just a job of work.

You are representing people who have hopes and dreams for the club. There will always be fans at the City Ground. It's a lifetime thing for them.

I listen to a radio talk show while I'm driving to West Ham and one morning they were discussing how hard it is for some players to settle at a new club. I can't understand that. I don't think I could ever go to a club and not settle. At Newcastle I had a bad time under Ruud Gullit but I loved the North East and I loved being part of Newcastle United Football Club. If you go to a club and don't settle, it's down to the player, no one else. You have to be open-minded. If things are not going right on the pitch, you have to work to put them right by your performances and not blame managers, surroundings or the other players.

Coming back from the World Cup having missed that penalty, I could not believe how the fans supported me; and not just fans from Nottingham but from all around the country – even though a few weeks later those same people slaughtered me with chants of 'Stuart Pearce is a German' from the stands at Chelsea and Derby among others. When I came back all I wanted to do was get out and play for Forest. Even now I still have a massive mailbag from Forest fans. I have a soft spot for the club and the supporters, but not necessarily for Nottingham Forest plc.

Liz seems to think that I am the unluckiest footballer around. With some players it seems as though their careers are scripted, but Liz and her brother Chris think I'm jinxed. To them, it's bad enough being on the losing side in a World Cup semi-final but it's worse to miss a penalty in the same game. Losing in the semi-final of the European Championship reinforces that theory as does reaching Cup finals with Newcastle and Forest and losing them both. Liz calls me the 'nearly man'. She says, 'You're nearly a legend but you're not because you keep messing up at the final hurdle.'

The fact is that I can get a big high out of winning 1–0 in what to others is a meaningless league game. I have been on the winning side in semi-finals and the atmosphere has been really quiet. At Newcastle it was almost an anticlimax when we returned to the dressing-room after beating Sheffield United at Old Trafford. I remember saying, 'Come on lads, it doesn't get better than this.'

Reaching the League Cup final and going to Wembley for the first time in 1989 was memorable. Going to Wembley was the next best thing to winning the League. To me it didn't matter what competition it was. Clough had the same attitude and we went to Wembley for some of the most obscure Cup finals ever to be played and won most of them. There was the Mercantile Credit Trophy in 1987–88; the Simod Cup the next; and in 1992 the Zenith Data Systems Cup, the same year we were runners-up in the League Cup final to Manchester United. We even took part in a Wembley tournament to mark the Football League's Centenary Year, and won that as well. In all, we went to Wembley eight times and won all the games but two. Unfortunately, one of them was the FA Cup final.

Give us an obscure Cup final and we would win it because Clough would always play his best team and demand that we play it for real. We were on no bonus scheme for trophies like the Simod Cup – we had never heard of it and so it wasn't written into our contracts – but I seem to remember Clough buying the wives a box of chocolates each, almost certainly from his own shop!

We won the Guinness Soccer Sixes two years out of three and reached the final the third year; and he took the Nottingham Senior Cup seriously, lifting that as well. Clough would never belittle any competition the way Newcastle did when I was there. Newcastle played a reserve side, of which I was a member, in the Northumberland Shield, as most teams would. I was taking my coaching badge at the time and the FA coach supervising the course would laugh when I had to shoot off early to play at somewhere like Scarborough, which was important to me because we wanted to stay nine points clear in the reserve league. When I told him I was off to play Blyth Spartans in the Northumberland Shield he fell about. I told him not to laugh; I wanted a winner's tankard to put next to my medals from the Simod and the Mercantile Cups. Play to win, otherwise why play at all? I probably have the finest collection of obscure medals of any professional playing at the moment thanks to Clough's philosophy.

Before the FA Cup final against Tottenham Hotspur, we were all concerned not to get injured but the flipside when Clough was about was that if you weren't trying you would be out of the team. Clough had promised that he would play Notts County in a testimonial across the Trent on the Monday before the Cup final on the Saturday. He took the full team and played us for the full 90 minutes. What's more, he spelled it out that if we didn't play and didn't play well, we wouldn't be appearing at Wembley. What other manager would do that five days before the Cup final? Fortunately, we all came through safely.

I'm not saying he was wrong because his philosophy worked. Footballers are creatures of habit and there is no better habit than winning games. It came home to me many years later at West Ham when Igor Stimac was one booking away from being suspended for a possible League Cup semi-final. He played in the reserves instead of the quarter-finals and was booked. But we were knocked out in the quarter-finals and so he missed an important league game. When you start planning ahead and being smart you invariably land on your backside.

If I start thinking to myself that I haven't been injured for a time, I can guarantee that something horrible will be lurking around the corner for me. The old saying about taking every game as it comes is worth taking note of, and the one about the important game being the one you are playing in. That's what I tell anyone asking for advice. Never look down the fixture list because it always works against you.

You can be successful in your own little world. For me playing for England counted as one of my greatest successes. Being the most capped player while at Forest made me very proud and it was one of the reasons I preferred to stay at the club. I was player, captain, union representative and manager, I scored and led the side to a 2–0 win all during one day at Nottingham Forest. There was only one way after that – downwards! There wasn't much else I could have done for that club. I didn't sweep the dressing-rooms but that was only because I didn't have time.

When we beat Aston Villa 6–0 at home, Clough came in at half-time and pulled me to one side. We were three up with the game won, but he said, 'Dip your bread.' I asked why I should keep steaming forward when there was a chance for other players to express themselves. He looked at me and repeated, 'Just dip your bread. When you can, dip your bread, dip your bread.' His message was clear – keep playing to the best of my ability and never let teams off the hook. If you have scored three, go on and score four and so on. As a youngster, you don't appreciate these things.

Some people can coach for hours to get across the same message; Clough could get it over in one sentence or even a couple of words. It is another little thing to pass on. It teaches you the game and your job if you are prepared to listen. It's great coaching to my mind.

My best feeling is to do a good day's work, go home and put my feet up. The older I get the more satisfaction I gain from it. I prefer not to go out on the town, have a few beers and glorify the victory with every sycophant in town. It's nice to go home, walk round the garden and enjoy the moment.

Going to Wembley was success because it had to be earned the hard way. The first time I went there was to play Luton Town in the 1989 League (Littlewoods) Cup final. Luton were no pushover; they had been there the year before in the same competition and beaten the favourites, Arsenal. Few of us at Nottingham Forest had played in a Wembley final before and, in that respect, we were the underdogs.

I have always maintained that to reach Wembley you need the luck of the draw. For those two FA Cup semi-finals against Liverpool we believed the luck of the draw had denied us a Wembley appearance. In the finals we have reached, generally the draw was kind. If a club the size of Forest draw Arsenal or Manchester United away, the odds are that you are going to go out. In 1988–9, we played Chester City home and away, scoring ten goals in the process; then beat Coventry City 3–2; Leicester City 2–1 at home after a goalless draw away; QPR 5–2; and Bristol City on a 2–1 aggregate over two matches in the semi-final. They were hard enough games but there was no real bummer. We would settle for playing any team from outside our division in the semi-final, especially over two legs.

We reckoned we were a better team than Luton and so it proved with Nigel Clough scoring two in a 3–1 win. It was a great atmosphere and to go as Clough's captain and finally break that barren spell for him was special to me. It was also the first major triumph for the club since the European days and it meant so much to the club and to its supporters. It was the start of a succession of visits to the famous old stadium and not just for those small cups.

It always makes me wonder when players and managers belittle the League Cup. They go out of Europe, out of the FA Cup, can't win the League and suddenly they wish they were back in the old League Cup again. The League Cup final was, to me, as important as the FA Cup final.

I find cup finals strange days. There is so much pressure on you. Often younger players do better than established players. They can go and enjoy it. People don't remember a youngster having a shocker but the club captain or an established player feels the weight of the club's and fans' expectations.

We were lucky. We won that first one fairly comfortably, beating Luton with something to spare. The next year, we wanted to succeed even more, having gone out at home to Manchester United in the third round of the FA Cup. The draw wasn't particularly easy. We beat Huddersfield on away goals; Crystal Palace 5–0 in a replay; Everton 1–0 at home; Spurs 3–2 away after a 2–2 draw at the City Ground; and my old club Coventry again 2–1 on aggregate in the semi-final. That left us facing Oldham in the final, again a team from a division below us. We won 1–0 and although it was hardly a classic it was another win.

With no banquet, as usual, I arranged a little session in a local wine bar near the ground. We had a few glasses of champagne on the coach back; then I persuaded all the lads to chip in £50 each to cover the food and drinks and to subsidise the young players. The youngsters were soon at it and when they realised it was free they were ordering up champagne and anything else that they could think of. I made certain it was all going well and then Liz and I slipped quietly away. I was knackered. When I went in to the ground the next day I discovered that the bill had gone over what we expected and I quickly had another whip round of a tenner each to cover the extra costs. Everyone put in except Tommy Gaynor. Even though he had played in the final and picked up his £6,000 bonus, he refused to pay the extra because, he claimed, he had eaten only a chicken leg and drunk a couple of Budweisers. I told him I had probably had about the same and it wouldn't hurt to help pay for the youngsters. But he wouldn't hear of it and no one else was prepared to back me on the issue.

The nearest we came to an official party was when we went to the Council Buildings a couple of days after the 1991 FA Cup final. None of the players wanted to go after losing to Spurs, but it was one of those events that Clough decreed as compulsory. To make it worse, they organised an open-topped bus ride. I have only been on three and all were after losing! They are nightmares. It's the last thing you want and it should have been organised on the proviso that if we lost it would be cancelled. The fans turned up in their thousands and that was terrific of them, but I would have happily gone to Market Square on foot and signed autographs as a thank you. To go on an open-topped bus around the city was an embarrassing farce.

I vowed I would never go on one again but, sure enough, Newcastle organised one after we lost in the Cup final. I was sorely tempted to say no but I realised that it would have put our manager Kenny Dalglish in a terrible position had one of his players refused to go. So I swallowed my pride and tried to smile.

Sometimes I remember the bad times more than the good times. I can recall more about the three times that Clough substituted me than I can about the four major cup finals we played in. The good times can look after themselves; you have to work harder to eradicate the bad.

One of the biggest disappointments was the 1990–91 FA Cup final, losing 2–1 to Spurs. We had quite a history with Spurs in cup competitions, having beaten them on the way to our second League Cup victory. Those two games had a total of nine goals. With such open games, it always seemed that the away side had the better chance but this was different. We were playing on neutral territory.

On the run of play we probably didn't deserve to win. It was an uninspiring game, dominated by Gazza's injury. People remember that and not the fact that I scored direct from the free kick on the restart. I doubt whether a neutral would remember any of the three goals. It will always be remembered for Paul Gascoigne and his extravagant fouls. That guy was always likely to do something ridiculous one way or the other – getting himself carried off or being sent off through overexcitement or winning the game on his own.

At the time, we were pleased to see him go. I am not aware of any of our players visiting him, but why should they have done? I was friendly with him but I can't say I really knew him well. We had no idea of the extent of his injury and, in any case, sympathy was a bit short as he had tried to maim two of our players.

It was one of those situations, like Hillsborough, where you are focused on your own job and I was oblivious to almost everything else. I certainly didn't rush over and ask him if he was all right. I am not the most compassionate of players, especially when I am in the heat of battle and about to take a free kick from the edge of the box. If I had spoken to him it would have been to shake his hand and say thanks for the free kick that was right in my zone.

We went home with what we deserved – nothing at all. The dressing-room was deathly quiet.

Whether Brian Clough lost or won in finals he stayed quiet. I can't remember him whooping and hollering around the dressing-room when we won and it was the same when we lost. He might have come over and kissed Des on the head after the Tottenham defeat or he would come and have a word with me as his captain. He was a past master at building players up and motivating them; he also stuck by his players in times of crisis. When Gary Crosby was the fans' whipping boy and his form and body language cried out for him to be dropped, Clough stuck by him and kept playing him. Whether it did the lad any good in the long run I don't know; it didn't always help the team. Clough would say, 'I don't care what thirty thousand fans are saying. I pick the team not them and if I say that Gary Crosby is playing, he'll play.'

But if things were going well, he loved to put you down. If I did well in the England side, I knew he would be after me; and if I gave a big interview to the press, he would ask me if I thought I was a big hitter. Yet no one manipulated or used the press the way he did.

I don't think he enjoyed his players talking to the press. He preferred to do that himself and he was a regular columnist in the *Sun* whenever there was anything to say about Forest or, come to that, football. I don't suppose he did that for nothing.

In the end I got used to him. He was predictable in his unpredictability. If you lost a final he would be quiet and polite and likely to give you the week off but if you won he would be down the back of the bus telling you to turn the music off and to report for training the following morning, even if it was a Sunday. If you lost he would be there to help you out and lift you up but if you won he would be banging on your door trying to keep you down.

Des Walker was certainly down after the FA Cup final defeat, shattered by the experience and there wasn't a lot Brian Clough could do to lift him that day. Des was there for me in the World Cup when I needed him and this time I wanted to be there for him. I appreciated his support just by being there and I hope that in some small way I repaid him that day. We didn't say a lot. We didn't need to.

We walked off Wembley as a team and our thoughts were that we had been beaten 2–1 and not that Des had scored an own goal. If he hadn't got his head to it someone else would have been there behind him. He was distraught, absolutely gutted. I told him that we were in it together. It was a year on from when he did the same for me. It must have been even more difficult for him in Market Square the next day. God knows the rest of us were pissed off but for Des it was murder because in his own mind he had to face thousands of fans thinking he had cost us the game.

The person that the press and the public know and the Des that I know are two vastly different people. With the media and in public he is silent and almost forbidding whereas to me he never stops talking and can be a bit of a smartarse who is never wrong. But he is a terrific friend. When I lost my licence, it was Des who drove me to and from London, dropping me off to see Liz in Coventry on his way back. We got to know each other pretty well through that and through learning together at Forest, even though I am a little bit older than he is. We have grown up together in football terms not only with Forest but also with England and I suppose I have played more games with him than anyone else. When we went to the 1990 World Cup he was almost certainly the first name on Bobby Robson's sheet. In other words, he was a very good, very consistent player.

We are both from London but more importantly we respect each other as professionals. I can't get on with someone I can't respect. With Des it hurts him to be beaten as a footballer even though he appears a bit unemotional on the pitch. He likes to come to work, get the job done by giving it his best shot and then go home. He loves football when he is playing it, and when he is away from the game he doesn't particularly want to talk about it.

Outside football his passion is for cars and his latest fad, motor-bikes. He scared Liz and me to death when he roared up our drive dressed in his black leathers, helmet and biker's gear. We didn't know anyone who rode a motorbike and couldn't think who it was until he took his helmet off. Typical of Des he not only had a motorbike, he had the fastest motorbike, the only one made in the world, and he had just come from the local airfield where he had been doing wheelies at 120 miles per hour.

Without any doubt he was the best player I played with at Forest in the five years we played together. He left for Sampdoria a year before we were relegated and that speaks volumes. He was a huge loss to the club.

Going to Italy was a great move in every way for Des. He was career-minded and he wanted to play in the best league in the world, as it certainly was then. He wanted to see how good he was and he enjoyed playing against the best players in the world. He did as well as any defender in Italy. He didn't endear himself to the Italian press because he didn't bother talking to them. We were of a similar mind.

I had been tucked up once or twice early on with misquotes and silly headlines and it turns you sour. I thought to myself that if they were going to do that I wasn't going to play their game. Just before the 1988 European Championship I had been out injured and when I came back in a pre-season tour of Italy a journalist collared me coming out the hotel and asked me how the injury was. I told him that it was coming on fine. He asked me if I would be playing soon and I answered that I sincerely hoped so. When I telephoned Liz she told me that her cousin had called her about a piece in the *Sun* under the headline: 'I want your place Kénny'. Kenny Sansom was the current England left-back. It went on to give the quote I gave which had no mention of Kenny Sansom. The headline had nailed me to the wall and made me out to be a bigheaded bastard. I wanted no part of that with my family and friends believing that I had gone over the top. It annoyed me. As far as I knew, the journalist was at fault. I didn't realise at the time that someone else wrote the headlines.

So I shut off from the press and, to be honest, it suited me. I did not elbow the media completely. I built a working relationship with the Midlands *Daily Express* writer John Wragg after warning him that if he messed me up a single time our relationship would be over. I wasn't asking for someone to say I had a good game when I had a bad one, I just wanted him to be honest and in return I gave him an interview when he wanted one. He knew the boundaries – be honest with me and I would be honest with him. We worked well together and if it had been like that across the board I would have been quite open and I'm sure that goes for a lot more professionals.

Five or six years later, the *Sun* carried the same headline only this time it was Tony Dorigo who was supposedly wanting my place. I looked at it and burst out laughing. I knew Tony and I knew what he was like and I thought to myself, 'You've been tucked up just as I was.' And so the cycle continues.

It is annoying but the older and hopefully the wiser you get the more comical it becomes because you know exactly what's going to happen. Build the player up and when he is selected knock him down and start promoting someone else. I have been through that not once but several times.

When I made my international comeback at the age of 37, I made a personal appearance for the England players' pool at the Nationwide Building Society with Gareth Southgate. England had just been drawn against Scotland in the Euro 2000 qualifying play-off and a flood of journalists turned up looking for a good quote. I was ready for them and, sure enough, one of the Sunday tabloid writers started on a line of questioning which suggested to me that he already had his story written in his mind and just wanted a comment, preferably from me, to stand it up. I fenced with him until he finally had to ask me outright, 'Can you make it? Tell the fans, can you make it to the European Championship finals.' I knew he wanted me to stick my head out at the age of 37 and tell the world that not only would I help knock out the Scots single-handed but I would be in the finals. Having been around the block several times I just looked at him and laughed. Ten years earlier I would have fallen right into it and answered yes, leaving the way open for him to add his words. This time I wasn't biting and eventually he realised and gave up. He probably wrote it anyway.

That sort of interrogation displays not only a lack of professionalism but also a lack of originality of thought. But it goes on and will no doubt continue to do so.

Of all the highlights I enjoyed at Forest my most memorable was the evening of my testimonial match against Newcastle United in May 1996. Obviously, if we had beaten Spurs in the Cup that would have been it, but we didn't and while the other Wembley occasions were big, they could not overshadow that night of my testimonial.

I wanted it to be a big event, not just for the money it would bring but for me to thank the Forest supporters who had backed me so brilliantly over all my years at the club. I wanted the best possible opposition for them, and for weeks I talked to Walter Smith, manager of Glasgow Rangers, and always there were excuses about the police not allowing it because of security reasons. So eventually I cleared it with the Nottingham police myself and they promised to back me, but then the excuse was that the police in Glasgow wouldn't stand it. I thought I had sidestepped the excuse but I hadn't.

It was a wasted couple of months and when I was stonewalled by Walter I had to look around for someone else. I suppose Rangers must have hundreds of these requests because they are a massive club but a straightforward and quick no would have been a much bigger help.

I telephoned Kevin Keegan at Newcastle United around January time and he agreed. At the time Newcastle were 12 points clear of Manchester United and I had my fingers crossed for them to win the League. Having dealt initially with Kevin, Arthur Cox took over. I was as nervous as hell particularly when their lead at the top began to crumble. All the tickets had been printed and sold and I kept ringing Arthur to make sure it was still on and he kept saying, 'If Kevin has said he'll do it, he'll be there.' The pair of them were so good to deal with and despite losing the title to Manchester United Kevin not only honoured his word but brought the full side to play – everyone including Tino Asprilla and David Ginola. Unfortunately, my England team-mate Peter Beardsley was injured but such was the support that he came down on the night anyway. What's more, both Kevin and his assistant Terry McDermott came on as substitutes and made cameo appearances. Nigel Clough and Des Walker returned to play for Forest and Coventry's Gary McAllister made a guest appearance.

Newcastle being there helped fill the ground. The kick-off had to be delayed for a quarter of an hour to get everyone in. I had been there for 11 years and it was all the good times encompassed in one night. Even the local radio stations were telling people that if they didn't go to another game, they had to go to this one because of what I had done for the club. It was nice and touching and it made it my biggest night. I had a nervous build-up, rushing around trying to keep everyone happy. A couple of the guys from Madness turned up to present me with one of their platinum discs. The score was 6–5 and while players weren't busting a gut, it was semi-serious and a lot of good football was played. The big crowd appreciated it. That night was as much for me to say thank you to them as it was for them to say thank you to me. To cap it all my brother Ray refereed the game with a couple of his friends running the line; that just tied everything up nicely. By the time the game was over and I'd had a couple of drinks, I was knackered and ready to go home.

To put it in perspective, in the March of that year we played Aston Villa in the sixth round of the FA Cup and had 23,000 fans through the turnstiles. When we played Newcastle in my testimonial we had over

24,000! Ian Bowyer, European Cup winner, League champion and the rest, had 6 or 7,000 against Derby when he was the beneficiary, and goalkeeper Steve Sutton was the next to be honoured with the same number turning up, again against Derby, the club he was playing for at the time.

It all started to go wrong at Forest long before we were relegated. We had a real high from 1988 up until the 1991 Cup final when things began to wane. Then Des Walker left and we started papering over the cracks. Selling Teddy Sheringham after he'd scored 20 League and cup goals in his first season was a monumental mistake in my opinion.

Clough was Clough. He ticked along while the fans were demanding he sign new players and we realised we had lost too many quality players to maintain our previous high standards. In typical style he ignored the demands and the obvious failings. It wasn't until March that he brought Neil Webb back to the club where he had made his name, but he wasn't the Webby who had left us to go to Manchester United. Clough also signed striker Robert Rosario and, to be honest, that didn't work. Robert simply wasn't the sort of goalscorer to lift us out of trouble.

I suppose the fact that we reached the 1992 League Cup final – losing 1–0 to Manchester United – put off the inevitable. Two weeks earlier we had won the Mercantile Cup at Wembley, beating Southampton 3–2. I was injured in that game in a tackle with Glenn Cockerill after about 20 minutes. I carried on for a quarter of an hour but every time I sidefooted the ball I suffered a searing pain. It transpired that I had damaged my knee ligaments. I didn't play again that season so I watched the League (Rumbelows) Cup final from the bench sitting behind Brian Clough. On the other bench was Manchester United's injured captain, Bryan Robson.

That was when I knew the writing was on the wall. Teddy Sheringham hadn't set the world on fire in that first season but it was obvious he could score goals. The potential was clearly there, as he has gone on to prove. Had he stayed and achieved the same level for us in a second season, we would have stayed up.

I thought Brian Clough was stronger than any man or board member at Nottingham Forest, so to me it was never inevitable that he was going to be the one to go. I didn't think that there was a board member strong enough to even suggest he should be sacked. People at the club conspired behind his back because they were afraid to do it face to face.

In the dressing-room, the players knew that things were going badly with no signs of getting better. I couldn't see a way forward. From Christmas onwards we were a relegated side. We were miles adrift and there was no way we could catch up. We seemed to go without a fight.

Even so, the sacking came out of the blue. It was terribly sad coming on the back of the Championship, the European cups and our revival in the eighties. Now we were facing the unthinkable of relegation. People were saying that we were too good to go down but in truth we were shocking. We weren't good enough to stay up.

The only bright spot for the club was the incredible form of the young and versatile Roy Keane. When he was playing centre-half it meant we lost a great midfield player and when he played in midfield we lost our best central defender. I can't speak highly enough of him. He was a young, up-and-coming player who was new to the club. When he first played for Forest, I didn't know who he was. I was injured and missed the fixture at Liverpool. We lost 2–0 and the next day when I asked the physio what had happened, he told me that Roy Keane had played on the right wing. I assumed that he was a Liverpool youngster as I had never heard of him and asked why Ray Houghton hadn't played! Roy had been signed just the week before from Ireland and, because I was injured, I had never even trained with him.

Basically, he stayed in the team from that moment on and he was brilliant. He is a strong character and that showed through even at that early age. I had the impression that he didn't listen to Brian Clough or the senior players much but it didn't affect his form. He was outstanding.

Maybe by then Brian Clough didn't have the same aura about him. His powerful influence had diminished and players were no longer frightened of him. Things had changed dramatically. I heard on the car radio that Clough had been sacked.

The last home game of the season was against Sheffield United and the atmosphere in the ground was creepy. I had a really eerie feeling and I've never worked out whether it was just me or generated by the crowd. I was in the stand watching with Liz and there was a real buzz around the ground and a tingle when he came out. Here was an institution and this was his last home game after 18 years or whatever it was. Suddenly it was all over. We lost to a team managed by Dave Bassett, the man who was eventually to take over from me. I was very aware that this was a momentous occasion and the end of an era.

I'd had my problems with him but nevertheless I found it all quite sad. We were down months before but our relegation was rubber-stamped that day. It was unfortunate that such a great man who had done so much for the city should go out on that note. It says a lot about going out, if you can, while still on top. I didn't go to the final game at Ipswich but thousands of our fans did and they turned the wake into a carnival.

CHAPTER 6

hillsborough

Hillsborough, Sheffield on Saturday, 15 April 1989 remains strangely remote in my memory. It was something that happened to someone else in some other place, not to me.

That, of course, was the day when 96 Liverpool supporters lost their lives, most of them just a few yards away from the dressing-room where I sat, or rather paced about waiting in vain for our FA Cup semi-final against Liverpool to restart.

We didn't have a clue what was going on. All we knew was that referee Peter Williams had called both teams off the field after six minutes as supporters began to pour over the fence behind Bruce Grobbelaar's goal. As far as I was concerned or knew, it was another case of football hooliganism. As I've explained elsewhere, I was always ready to hear and believe the worst about Liverpool because they were our nemesis, so much better than any other team in the country, a constant barrier between Nottingham Forest and silverware.

I must say that I wasn't best pleased when, on the Monday lunchtime after our quarter-final win at Manchester United, I listened to the draw on my car radio in the club car park, just as I had done the previous year. Bloody Liverpool again. Why couldn't it have been either Everton or Norwich, two teams we fancied we could beat? I drove away trying to convince myself that sooner or later we were going to beat them. After all, hadn't underdogs Wimbledon beaten them at Wembley the year before? But I knew that, if anything, that defeat probably made them even meaner. They were still winning everything in sight but we were a year older, a year more experienced and we were very, very hungry for success.

The venue was to be Hillsborough again and, with its good pitch and the high terracing behind the goal where our supporters would be massed, that was fine.

Liverpool began well and Peter Beardsley soon hit the crossbar. The nerves were twanging but the game was gradually beginning to sort itself out. Then I saw one or two spectators come on to the pitch behind the Liverpool goal from the Leppings Lane end, then a few more. I was cursing the Liverpool fans under my breath as the referee took us off the pitch.

From the far end where I was stationed, it looked like no more than another of those frustrating pitch invasions, a blight on our game for a few years. As a player that was one of my pet hates. I am so dogmatic and careful about my preparation for games and when referees started coming into dressing-rooms and telling us that kick-offs had been delayed it threw me. Mentally I wanted to be ready to go out five minutes before the kick-off, fresh and ready to go bang like a boxer coming out for a fight.

This, if anything was worse because we had already begun, the adrenalin was pumping and the muscles becoming loose. We were told that there was going to be a delay of ten minutes and the instructions were to keep warm, keep loose and not let the delay blunt the competitive edge and take our minds off the game. Then someone else came in and told us fifteen minutes more. We still didn't have a clue what was going on outside. All we knew at that stage was that Liverpool supporters had come tumbling on to the pitch and forced us off.

There we sat in the dressing-room, still in our kit, waiting for an hour. It was five o'clock by the time we had bathed, changed and climbed into the coach. During that time I never left the dressing-room and no one had explained why such an important game was being delayed for so long and then called off. It was only when our centre-forward Lee Chapman boarded the team coach that the first grains of doubt were sewn. He said that he had seen scenes of devastation, with people injured, and been told that there may even be some deaths. He was very upset but, to be honest, most of us took this news with a pinch of salt. People didn't get killed in English football stadiums, at least not since the Bolton disaster way back on 9 March 1946 when 33 fans perished while the game played on. This was a football match, not a war; as far as I was concerned, it was a silly rumour. Perhaps I didn't want to believe it. I was still livid because I had turned up to play in one of the biggest football matches of my life and my own eyes told me that some supporters from the Liverpool end had caused the game to be cancelled. Had I been convinced that it was that serious, I would have been worried for Liz's safety. She had gone to the game with a friend of mine from Coventry, Jim Connolly.

I rang Liz on the way back to see that she had got home safely and it was only then that she told me what she had been watching on television. Liz had watched the incident develop from her seat in the stand. Jim, wisely, had quickly summed up the situation, decided that the game was not going to restart and driven them both back to Nottingham.

It was only when I watched it on television that I saw what had been going on while we were in our dressing-room as bodies were carried away on makeshift stretchers and placed side by side in the club gymnasium. It was surreal, like watching an earthquake in Russia. Was I there? It didn't feel as though I had been there at all because I didn't see any of it. I felt strangely detached from it all, even then. It was as though I was watching something that had nothing to do with me. I had seen none of this.

At no stage did Brian Clough tell us anything of what was happening out there. There were two different reactions – Lee Chapman and one or two others had heard that supporters had died and they were devastated while others like me could only think that Liverpool, who had stopped us playing in Europe, had now halted a semi-final. That was the only information I was taking in. The anger was building in me. We were told to stay in the dressing-room but Chappie ignored the instructions and found someone to tell him what was happening. He went down the tunnel and glimpsed the dreadful scenes. Me? I was, as usual, cocooned in my own world trying to maintain my concentration in case the game restarted. I was annoyed because I didn't know the facts. Brian Clough had a go at the Liverpool supporters after Hillsborough and I felt the same way until I read all the accounts and began to understand what went on and how many had died. Clough should have kept his mouth shut until he knew all the facts. I was glad that I did.

Those chilling facts emerged slowly, the deaths of innocent men, women and children. People were giving their versions and the blame, in those early days, was spread around. Some said the police were at fault, others blamed the fans themselves; for a while, drink was suspected to be the main cause; an accident on the motorway caused spectators from Liverpool to be late, a gateman opening his gates to let the crush of latecomers in. You paid your money and took your choice. I felt it was unfair at the time to heap all the blame on to the police. In our society that happens all the time. If you are in trouble or your house is broken into the first people you ring are the police, yet they get it in the neck.

It was horrific but I cannot say that I was affected or mentally scarred by it. Most people there saw a hell of a lot more of what happened than we did and even those who watched the horror unfold on television as it happened knew more about it than us. That is why on the Monday morning I found it ridiculous that the police came to interview us about what went on. I felt aggrieved at the waste of police time, going through the charade of questioning all the players, none of whom knew anything about it. The police interviewed me, when I saw nothing, but didn't want to talk to Liz who saw everything. I was up in arms about it and considered refusing to co-operate. I felt that they wanted to interview me just because I was Stuart Pearce; it certainly wasn't because I was an eyewitness. They knew full well that we were in the dressing-room for an hour and a half but sometimes these things are done for appearances, just for the sake of it. Interview the journalists from the press box, the stewards, the programme sellers, all of them will have seen 98 per cent more than any of the players.

I wouldn't say I am a particularly religious person and when Liz and I attended the memorial service in Nottingham I told Liz I felt a bit of a fraud being there at all. But I appreciated that if the captain of Nottingham Forest or the manager had not attended that would have been pounced upon by the media who, not unnaturally, were wallowing in the tragedy. There were television cameras in the church and I felt that I was there for their benefit. I didn't want to be seen doing things for the sake of doing things. I was never one to court publicity. It was a strange scenario.

I didn't have the same emotions that Lee Chapman had or those who had witnessed it. I felt that I was paying lip service. I don't want to give the impression that I didn't care. I did. But I felt the same emotion that I would have done if it had happened at some other game on some other ground, desperately sorry for the bereaved and for the game of football but not personally involved. I am not a heartless person. I saw nothing. I had no first-hand knowledge of what had happened. I felt great sadness that innocent people had been killed in an incident at a ground where I was plying my trade.

The game was eventually played at Old Trafford on 7 May and between the tragedy and then all kinds of options were offered, everything from cancelling the competition for that season to giving the FA Cup straight to Liverpool. I was in a Catch-22 situation. I wanted to win the game even more. As a professional sportsman that was only right. Yet the whole nation wanted Liverpool to win as a mark of respect. I found that unfair on Nottingham Forest, just as unfair as our ban from Europe after Heysel. I had total sympathy for the Liverpool supporters and the bereaved families but to say that I didn't care whether I won or not would be lying.

Within the club, I tried to stoke up my colleagues so that we wouldn't go out and lie down if and when the replay took place. The game and the football public deserved more than that. Some may say that it went beyond sport but if that was the case then they should have scrapped the semi-final altogether and given the Cup to Liverpool as some suggested. It was not right to use us as stooges. I pleaded with the players not to go through the motions when we eventually played and told them not to give up the game because of what had happened, something which was not only out of our control but out of Liverpool Football Club's control as well.

The atmosphere at Old Trafford was terrible. There was a dull edge to the game that made it a bit of a non-event. We did not play well but we tried and Liverpool won on merit, which was the right way. How would the Liverpool players have felt if we had rolled over and let them win? I can't imagine one of them would have enjoyed that. Maybe everyone was relieved in the long run and Liverpool went on to win the Cup.

There were no instructions from anyone to take things easy in view of what happened and that was right. My game is built on aggression; it is one of the aces in my armoury. I am not pacey and I am not blessed with an abundance of skill. For someone to tell me not to overdo it in a semi-final against Liverpool would have been akin to telling me not to play at all. We were there to beat them and get to Wembley and in the end we were beaten by a very good side and, apart from the needle over the Aldridge business with Laws, it was played in the right spirit.

Afterwards I asked myself what I would have felt like if the boot had been on the other foot. Had it been the Nottingham Forest supporters who had died, I would have been devastated. I can understand the sadness and I thought the mourning of those people was phenomenal, the flowers and the work by Kenny Dalglish and the players with the bereaved were exceptional. But I couldn't share it with them because I didn't see it; I can't lie about my feelings and pretending would have been an insult to those innocents who lost their lives, youngsters and adults who had arrived at the ground early and were there to see a football match.

Chappie remained the one most affected by it all. On our end-of-season tour he was in tears talking about it in a bar with Steve Hodge and me. Had I looked out of the tunnel and seen what he had seen, I might have felt the same.

I didn't have those tears inside me and I was annoyed that we hadn't won. That's not being the hard man. I have cried over football and I have cried over a few other things in my life.

Sport may get nasty at times but the beauty of it is that it has all the emotions of life. It was a tragedy that so many people were killed; things like that shouldn't happen at sports events. But at least those 96 deaths were not in vain because grounds are now so much safer for everyone after Lord Justice Taylor's report. It's sad that it needed a catastrophe of that magnitude to bring it about.

CHAPTER 7

old big 'ead

Did I want to play for Brian Clough? Did I want to play for the twice European Champions Nottingham Forest? Is the pope a catholic? Of course I did! They sent a car to collect my Coventry City colleague Ian Butterworth and me at the end of my second season as a professional but I would have walked and, just as when I joined Coventry, money was never a consideration.

Brian Clough was a managerial colossus and, as a kid, when he wants to sign you, you sign. To be honest, he scared the life out of me as he did most of the squad, even the million-pound superstars. Trevor Francis used to hide from him in the laundry room or the boot room.

When I first walked into the office at Nottingham Forest with my Coventry manager Don Mackay, my first impression was the difference between the two men. I liked Don and whenever I see him we still have a chat but that day it seemed as though he was in awe of Clough. After we had signed, we travelled back to Coventry in the car and we couldn't stop talking about the charismatic Clough, repeating over and over, 'That's a manager, that's a manager,' until Mackay threatened to turn us out on the roadside and let us find our own way back. But you could see on his face the same admiration for the man that we had. This was a giant. When he walked into a room, people stopped talking. That was the strength of the aura surrounding him.

It was not only Ian and I waiting to see Clough but also Neil Webb from Portsmouth. Webby was a lot more worldly wise than me. He went in first and knowing that Aston Villa and other teams were after him he had bargaining chips. When he came out smiling I asked what he had asked for because I hadn't got a clue what I should be saying. He wouldn't tell me what deal he had struck (I later discovered he signed for £300,000) so when I went in I told Clough that Coventry had offered me £25,000 signing-on fee (strange that it should be the same figure I had originally asked for when I first joined) and £500 a week and if he matched it I would sign for him. I had already decided not to tell him that I had a drink-driving conviction and was currently banned from driving before putting my name to the contract in case he decided not to sign me. He clapped his hands and said, 'Done!' I suspect I was.

Once I had signed I plucked up the courage to tell him about my latest offence. He jumped on me straightaway. 'Have I signed a drinker?' he said, and, 'Shall I get you a bucket to drink out of?' He told me that he wouldn't have signed me had he known but then suddenly asked if I had a girlfriend. I told him I had, wondering where the conversation was going. He asked me if I was going on holiday that summer and I told him that I was going to Disneyland in America.

'Are you taking your girlfriend?' he asked.

'No,' I replied, 'I'm going with a mate.'

'What's the matter son?' he came back. 'Are you a queer or something?'

He had only just signed me but in a matter of minutes he had hammered me for being a lying bastard, for being a drinker and now for being a homosexual. I explained that Liz was too busy looking after horses and couldn't get the time off.

He signed five of us that pre-season – Scottish international John Robertson came back from Derby; Neil Webb was the big-money signing; Brian Rice came down from Hibernian; Ian Butterworth, an England Under-21 international; and me. By the time he added his son Nigel, although not quite ready for the first division, he had bought half a new team. Another one coming through was Des Walker who was a kid, a 17-year-old pup who was about the place but on the way.

We were all together on the ten-day pre-season tour of the south coast with the colourful Robertson immediately earning cult status among the new boys by turning up with a toothbrush in his back pocket and no clothes other than those he stood up in.

Clough tried to label me with the boozer tag but gave up after a couple of months when he realised how wide of the mark he was. He switched his attention to Webby who was much more a couple of glasses a wine man than I ever was. Maybe because Neil had cost the most, Clough gave him no respite; he hammered him. He was on his case all the time as if he was trying to make or break him. Selfishly, I was grateful because it took the pressure off Butty and me.

If you went away with Clough and he picked your name out of the hat, it became easy to see why some players wouldn't want to go away to Tenerife and other places with him. He could make life sheer hell. He would accuse his latest target of being a drinker, an idiot, a fool and worse; it was as though the rest of the team didn't matter and he was on to the one player all of the time. He was cute because he rarely dug out more than one player at a time and would play off the rest against his stooge. Ian Bowyer was his captain and a very well-respected player. Clough would have a go at Webby through him, saying while Webby was in earshot, 'Ey, Bomber, he's a fucking idiot. He doesn't know his trade.' It could have worked either way and often did – it made Neil Webb a footballer, an international footballer at that, but he had to suffer for a full season before relief came in the shape of another patsy.

My turn arrived unexpectedly and I could have cheerfully chinned him as he got on my case during a ten-day pre-season trip to Holland. He would stand there at the side of the pitch shouting, 'Stand up and tackle. You are always on your fucking arse,' 'You are an idiot,' 'You cockney bastard, always stealing this and that.' He would tell me that I ran funny, that I had a lopey stride, that I was always on my backside and so it went on. It was a nightmare. He made my life a misery. Why? I don't know. Little things seemed to annoy him.

I learned what it was like to be the butt of his comments and what he could really be like. It made me angry and I desperately wanted to fight back and prove him wrong but there were others who left the club because they couldn't stand that sort of abuse. It makes or breaks you. I hated him and there were times when I rang home and told Liz that it was a nightmare trip, club and manager and that I hated all of them. Every player went through it to some degree or another, even Des Walker whose standards were always so high. He was the most consistent player I have ever played alongside. If he had played for a more fashionable club or a London team he would have been in the England squad three years earlier. If he had a bad game it was memorable. Tony Cottee once scored a hat-trick against him at West Ham and Clough never let Des forget it, taunting him that he couldn't get near the little striker and doubting his lightning speed.

Des has the same footballing mentality as I have. We are different animals but he wants to do well at his job. Maybe he is not as dedicated as I am in certain ways but what he wants to achieve in the game spurred him on. For four years he was brilliant and then he had one bad game and Cloughie was down his throat for a week or two.

It was a myth that Clough wouldn't let Des go over the halfway line. I was flying down one wing most of the time and Gary Charles or someone would be flying down the other flank. Someone had to stay back and sort things out. That was usually Des. It became comical because Clough would talk about Des getting a nosebleed if he got too far forward. Before Des went to play in Italy for Sampdoria he did start venturing forward a bit more and, because he had never done it in the past, it became a big joke to the manager and the fans.

Not everyone suffered the barbs from Clough's sharp tongue. When I had been there for four years or so, Lee Glover forced his way into the team. You could name just a couple of players in the eight years I was with Clough whom he liked and respected. Lee Glover was one and Peter Davenport the other. They tried to do the right things, hold up the ball, turn and all the things that he preached daily. It suited them because that was their natural game. He loved Davenport; Peter never had to come in on a Monday when he pulled the rest of us in for extra training.

I had been Clough's captain for three years when, one day, I went in to see him in his office. Lee Glover happened to be with him at the time and, although he was no older than 17 or 18, he was telling the boss that he didn't want to play for the youth team and added what he would rather do. I waited for the explosion but it didn't come. Even as his captain, I would never say anything like that to him because he would have had me for it.

I don't know whether he liked me or not. It was impossible to tell. I did a job for him, sometimes I did it well and sometimes I didn't but I assume that he thought he needed me at the club for what I did professionally. He accepted me and that was how it was. There were times when I hated his guts and not just on that Holland trip. Sometimes you loved him for the things he did, like buying those tickets for me to go to America, and sometimes he would go out of his way to niggle you.

Because I was captain, he would always give me the players' complimentary tickets to hand out to the boys. I was late getting in one day before a game against Luton Town and Des Walker, being the vice captain, handed out the tickets instead. Tommy Gaynor asked him if there were any spares. Des replied that the only ones he had left were mine. Gaynor promptly told him that I had said that he could have my tickets so Des gave them to him and he put them on the door for his friends. When I finally arrived I asked Des for my tickets only to be told that Tommy Gaynor had claimed them. Des laughed because he thought I was winding him up but this just happened to be one of the occasions when I did need them.

By now I had the hump and when I demanded my tickets back, Gaynor just laughed at me. That was a red rag to a bull. I marched him up to the office and reclaimed my tickets off the door. Five minutes later I passed him in the corridor. He was standing with Franz Carr and as I walked past he laughed at me so I promptly threw a punch at him, missed him by a mile and he grabbed me in a headlock. It was over in seconds but when Clough came into the dressing-room before the kick-off he had been told that we had been seen having a scuffle and asked, 'What's been going on then, Skipper?'

I told him Gaynor was out of order but that it was a storm in a teacup and it was all over. He glared across the dressing-room at Gaynor and said, 'If you need some fucking help, Skipper, let me know.'

He almost certainly said it to me because Tommy Gaynor was more expendable than I was at the time. All the same, I appreciated his backing.

My respect for the manager, despite our ups and downs, was immense. He makes you into a player and if your standards fall he will have you out of the team. He would do it if you were a senior player to spite you. He substituted me three times during our years together when I was playing badly and every time he would hold the board up with my number on instead of leaving it to the assistant manager or the physio, as was the norm.

I can even remember the games, the memory is so vivid. The first was away at West Ham when he was up on the touchline making a big show of holding up my number. When I came off I tried to look him in the eyes but he wasn't paying attention; he was back in the dug-out. I was livid and he knew it. I count it as a personal insult to be taken off even if I am having a stinker – and I was. No one plays well all the time and I have had my share of stinkers.

Another occasion was on the last day of the season at home against Leeds and the other was away at Wimbledon. He was right. I was woeful in every one of those games. The substitution served its purpose: he was not only showing everyone who was boss and that he could take his captain off when and how he liked; he was also posing the question to me, asking me if I could still do it. He knew that I would want to prove him wrong. It worked because every time I would roll up my sleeves and come back in the next game, even if it was the first game of a new season, to show him that he couldn't do that to me. It was brilliant psychology.

There was an FA directive some years ago which stated that the captain had to go to the referee's dressing-room at 2.15 to present the teamsheet and receive instructions. I loved going in with Brian Clough because the referee and his linesmen would be wetting themselves. That was the power of his presence. I would still be in my tracksuit because my habit was to get changed at 2.20 but any number of the captains would be half-changed and turn up in their flip-flops. That was fatal with Clough; he would deliberately stand on a bare foot. We would be there for three or four minutes and, throughout the entire time, Clough would stand there with his foot nailing down the opposition captain who would be too embarrassed to say a word.

The officials would also be very deferential to him but he would not reciprocate. He would say, 'I don't want any shit from you lot. They have a shithouse playing for them who kicks my centre-forward.'

I was glad I had him there with me. He wasn't an extra player but having his presence was a lifting factor because you could never let your standards drop when he was around.

Forest was totally dominated by Clough in the time that I was there. He dominated a succession of chairmen like no other manager at any club. Sir Alex Ferguson is clearly the boss at Manchester United while Don Revie was all-powerful at Leeds and Bobby Robson ran Ipswich from top to bottom but none of them ruled a club in the way that Clough ruled Nottingham Forest. If he had wanted, he could have got rid of the chairman because the club didn't even have a proper board of directors at that time. He was the boss.

Certainly players who stepped out of line or who didn't fit the bill were out on their ears no matter how much they cost or what their potential was. Before I arrived, Gary Megson arrived with a fanfare but lasted just a couple of weeks because Clough was forever in his face. He couldn't stand it and had to move on. I saw it at first-hand when he signed Dave Curry from Barnsley. He lasted for no longer than a month. I knew what was coming the day I was in an away dressing-room with Curry, Clough and a handful of others. Clough turned to Curry and said, 'Ey, son, have you got yourself a house yet?' Curry said, 'Not yet, Boss.' Clough gave him the all-time put down. 'Don't bother!' he said.

It made Curry laugh because he thought Clough was joking but the lads who had been around a long time knew different. I looked across the dressing-room at Des Walker and we both knew he meant it. Sure enough, Curry was soon on his bike.

John Sheridan was another. He joined Forest from Leeds United and was there for a couple of months before Clough decided he was wrong for the team and moved him on.

The offending player would do something that convinced Clough he was not suited and Clough would blame his assistant, Ronnie Fenton, for signing him. All the bad ones were Fenton's fault. Teddy Sheringham was a classic case. He signed in 1992 and scored 20 goals without playing particularly well. He eclipsed Nigel with his goals. In those days he didn't play the link role as he does so brilliantly nowadays; he was a penalty-area player who wanted the ball on his head. You couldn't argue with his goal record. However, Clough had made up his mind about him that season and again I knew that Teddy was for the chop.

I was injured just before the 1992 League Cup final and sat behind Clough on the bench at Wembley listening to him criticising Teddy non-stop from start to finish. He was unrelenting, saying things like, 'He shouldn't get in my reserve team never mind play at Wembley.'

Teddy was still with us on our pre-season tour of Ireland, but there were rumours that he might be going to Tottenham. He was still there for our first game of the season and curled one into the top corner to help us beat Liverpool 1–0. He played one and a half more games and he was gone, sold to Spurs. That year we were relegated and Clough was sacked. It was all because Clough had made up his mind that Teddy couldn't play and sold him before he had sorted out a replacement.

It also worked the other way, of course, and he was just as quick to decide when someone could play. He made his mind up about Roy Keane in an instant when he arrived from Ireland as a raw kid, because he was so good in the air. Clough's philosophy was that if you could head the ball you could play. I don't know where he picked up that idea, whether it was from someone else or simply from watching the game. Keane was one of the best headers of the ball I have ever seen and Clough decided that he was his man and put him into the team as soon as he arrived. No one else had heard of him.

Clough helped to make Roy a rounded international, as he did with Neil Webb. In the couple of seasons before he went to Manchester United, Webby was scoring 20 goals a season from midfield, including a spectacular hat-trick against Chelsea. In fact, Webby was the first of our little group from Forest to be called into the England squad by Bobby Robson. He was playing so well he couldn't possibly be ignored. He was in the England squad for a year and a half before I was selected. That was what Clough was like. If you were career-minded and prepared to take some flak he could make you. In many ways he made me.

He never lectured but would suggest things, instead, asking if maybe you should have done this or that. Then he'd leave you to think about the wisdom of what he had said. I equate it to a couple of young horses we have at the moment. When you are breaking in young horses, you give them a short lesson, finishing on a good note and turning them out into the field. The same applies to young footballers. You don't have to preach to them until they get bored. Instead you plant the seed, let them think about it and then get them back. If they are any good they will come back with the right answers.

A typical team-talk would be for Clough to throw a towel in the middle of the dressing-room ten minutes before the kick-off. By then everyone had done his warm-ups and stretches and was ready for the game. You could hear a pin drop as we waited and anyone walking in at that moment would think we were at a wake or saying our prayers. He would then put a ball on the towel and say, 'This is what we play with. Go and get it.' That was it. You could feel the tension vanish. One of his big thoughts was that you could not play if you were nervous.

Brian Clough was no great organiser and often we would start the season not knowing who was in the wall or who was picking up whom. Sometimes we would work it out ourselves or one of the coaches, Liam O'Kane or Archie Gemmill, would pull us to one side and try to arrange basic things. But if Clough spotted them he would shout across, 'What do you think you're doing? What are you telling them?' It was all very strange. Most of the time we played off the cuff and got away with it because there was so many good players. But it hit the fan in 1993 when we didn't have enough good players and suddenly discovered that we could no longer get away with it.

Clough didn't coach; he ruled by fear. But the few words he used and the little throwaway phrases were better at times than hours of coaching from another manager who could not get his point across so succinctly. When early on he told me to stay on my feet, he did not labour the point on the training ground but it was something he might scream at me one week and say quietly the next. I went away wondering what he meant; then I would dive in and the winger would nick it past me. The realisation hit home and I knew what he meant. I could make ten good sliding tackles, miss one and he would have me for the missed one. That was his way of coaching. If I laid the ball off first time and it went astray he would say, 'Stop the ball.' Because I was in awe of the man, the penny dropped, quickly. He would have had me soon enough if it hadn't.

The little line he would throw at the forwards was, 'When you get the ball, turn.' He wanted them to turn all the time to face the goal. Once a forward has turned, he has half a chance, and I can vouch for that as a defender facing them. Little things like that I will certainly take with me into management.

You can't work for eight years with a man of his domineering personality and not learn something. Tactically he was very cute but I would never say that the man was a great coach. Coaching sessions on the training ground were unheard of. Basically, our training sessions comprised a few sprints, a warm-up and a five-a-side. You found your own level. If you were good enough in his eyes, you survived; if you weren't, your feet wouldn't touch the ground.

Only Clough could arrange the sort of pre-season we had at Forest. I came back from the 1990 World Cup with only an eight-day break between the last match in Italy and our return for pre-season training. I went to see him and asked if I could have an extra week off, explaining I was fully fit and just needed a rest rather than a hard pre-season.

'I have signed the contract. We are going to Sweden and you will be there,' was his response. 'But what I can do for you is give you the week off before the season, when we go to Italy.'

Play on a Saturday and he might say he would see you next Friday for training. Come in Friday, play Saturday, if that was what you wanted. It didn't suit everyone's needs and some would ask Liam O'Kane to put on a session for Tuesday. Liam would come in and we would please ourselves. It wasn't always like that but if the players looked tired or jaded or the performances weren't as good as they should be, Clough would give players time off instead of pulling them back in for extra work the way other managers did. The worse the performances, the more he would go the other way. It takes a strong man to follow that route.

Clough probably had it right. Come Christmas, everyone was as fit as players in other teams. You have had enough games by then, whatever the pre-season arrangements.

Players who say they weren't scared of him are almost certainly lying. Many were relieved to be out of his way and avoided him if they could. Look at the strong players he dominated even before I arrived, including Larry Lloyd and Kenny Burns, big names and hard men. But if Clough saw a head-to-head conflict in the offing, he would sidestep it. A classic example was when he took the first-team squad to Porto Benuese in Spain for a six-day break. There was rarely a curfew and normally it was very much come and go as you pleased. This time he said that he wanted everyone back at the hotel at ten o'clock. It was unheard of. But what the man asked for, the man got and at 9.30 we were all gathered in a bar, before heading for the coach that was picking us up. Fifteen minutes later, we struggled to our feet ready to go, all that is except Garry Birtles who, having had a few drinks, said belligerently, 'I'm not moving. I have a wife and three kids and I'm old enough to make up my own mind when I go to bed.' Ian Bowyer tried to persuade him but he refused point blank and shouted after us, 'You're a load of fucking boy scouts.'

We knew Clough would miss him and, sure enough, he was waiting for us at the pick-up point and immediately asked where was Birtles. Garry received a reprieve when the coach failed to turn up and we all trooped back to the bar where he still sat nursing his drink. Instead of walking up to the bar and hammering the still aggressive Birtles for going against him, Clough joined the rest of us for another drink and ignored Birtles completely. He knew that Birtles was a stubborn guy and if he had confronted him, there would have certainly been a row that he might not have won in the circumstances.

It was the same when he used to substitute me. I would walk off muttering obscenities loud enough for him to hear but he would avoid all eye contact with me and would never jump up and ask what I had called him. He wouldn't always sidestep but he knew when to take someone on and when not to.

At the end of my first season, we went away to Cala Millor. I lived in the same village in Nottingham as Neil Webb and we had the crazy idea of reporting to the airport in Bermuda shorts and flip-flops with hair greased back and sunglasses. It was raining cats and dogs and cold when we drove to the ground to catch the team bus to East Midlands airport wearing all our gear including mirrored sunglasses so that Clough wouldn't be able to see our eyes when he confronted us. Clough was going straight to the airport and when we climbed on the coach Ronnie Fenton said, 'Good joke lads, now take the stuff off or he will go mad.' We stood our ground and said it was a holiday and end of season and even though it was May and freezing cold, there was little we could do about it as all our stuff was in our cases.

We queued up at East Midlands airport shivering and everyone thought it was hilarious, except Brian Clough.

'What are those fucking idiots up to,' he raged. 'What the fucking hell do they think they're doing?'

He wanted to send us home there and then but Ronnie and Liam managed to persuade him that we were just having a bit of fun at our own expense.

The Walsall team were in Cala Millor at the same time as we were and early one evening they joined us at our table where we were playing music and having a few beers. A short while later, Clough and the coaches arrived. There were no spare seats so our manager just pulled the chair from under Walsall striker David Kelly. He yanked it so hard that Kelly shot across the road and landed on his backside. Clough sat down, reached over and turned off the music. Kelly leapt to his feet not knowing whether to hit him or keep quiet. Wisely, he chose the latter course of action. It might not have been his manager and he might have been seriously wronged, but this was Brian Clough. We were all half-cut having been there for most of the day enjoying the sun and the beers. Clough sat there silently for 20 minutes with no music and not a word said. Just as suddenly as he had arrived, he stood up, said, 'See you later,' and shuffled off into the night. The music came back on and everyone just sat open-mouthed, amazed at what had happened. No one blamed Kelly for not reacting and the Walsall players were as much in awe of the man as we were.

One time, when we had just beaten Queens Park Rangers in the quarter-final of the League Cup, a group of supporters ran on to the pitch celebrating. Clough hated supporters on his pitch and he lashed out at them, landing punches on two or three of them. Those lads made a big fuss, threatened to sue him and have him arrested. In typical fashion he invited them into the club on Monday morning where they met the players. If they thought that they had been called in for an apology they had another thing coming. Clough laid into them, telling them that they shouldn't have been on the pitch. He didn't apologise but they did.

Who else would have got away with that? Instead of being pilloried, he received letters of support from a Chief of Police and Labour leader Neil Kinnock, and the FA offered to hold the resultant tribunal in Nottingham instead of London! He was fined and briefly banned from the touchline.

However you look at it, he was a remarkably successful manager with two unfashionable clubs. He won the League championship with Derby and reached the semi-finals of the European Cup, and at Forest he won the League and, most incredible of all, back-to-back European Cups, taking on and beating the multi-million pound giants of Europe. That's what makes him the man he is – the success he has achieved.

Local derbies between Derby County and Nottingham Forest were always fierce affairs on and off the pitch. The local rivalry was intense. Brian Clough is among the few who made the switch and after his acrimonious departure from the Baseball Ground he had more than enough reason to be all fired up whenever the two clubs met.

One midweek in the early nineties before a home game against Derby he was worse than usual and instead of posting the team up in the morning he told us to come in at 6.30 and he would tell us then.

When I arrived in the dressing-room the boys were laughing and when I asked them what was up they nodded towards the showers and told me to look for myself. There was Brian Clough, one of the most feared and respected managers in the game, sitting in the tub fully clothed.

I asked Liam O'Kane what the team was but he shrugged his shoulders; he still hadn't been told. We ushered the players out to look at the pitch, leaving Liam to try to glean the information from the boss but when we returned things had gone from bad to worse. He had moved from the bath to the sauna, still fully clothed, and he had a big yard shovel, the sort the groundstaff used to clear the snow, by his side. What he had the shovel for God only knew but I suppose he might have been using it as a sort of walking stick or a crutch.

The unpredictable things Clough did, when analysed later, often showed not just his eccentricity but his brilliance as a motivator. One such occasion was when we were going to play Millwall at the old Den in the first division. At the time Millwall were under the spotlight because of some crowd disturbances and, sure enough, they had some hard supporters who could look after themselves. A mile from the ground Clough ordered the driver to stop the coach and told us all to get off. He led the way and strode on, swinging his walking stick as he made his way through the hordes of Millwall supporters down Cold Blow Lane. We are thining, 'What's going on? I don't want to be here.' The supporters were just amazed. He marched us through. The message was that they might have a reputation but they weren't going to intimidate him or his team. At the same time he was telling us that there was nothing to be afraid of.

We had no hassle at all and the Millwall supporters seemed to enjoy it. Mind you we kept close to the manager; no one wanted to tail off in case they suffered a rogue one! It was clever psychology and all part of the Clough mystique.

On another occasion we were driving to London when he saw a truck driver with his cab down looking at his engine. He called to our old driver, Albert, to pull over and took a plate of sandwiches, prepared for after the game, to the stricken driver on the hard shoulder. He stuck his head under the hood and said, 'Can I help you?'

'Fucking hell, you're Brian Clough,' said the amazed driver.

'That's right young man. Can I help you?'

Clough knew nothing about repairing a broken-down lorry and he must have been quietly relieved when the bemused driver said he could manage. Clough gave him a couple of salmon sandwiches, got back on the coach and off we went. As we drove off we could see the lorry driver watching us, shaking his head and obviously thinking that his mates down the pub would never, ever believe his story.

Albert had more points on his licence than any other football coach driver because Clough would be forever telling him to get us to the game on time. If the police stopped us, he would tell them, 'Get off my fucking bus. We're late for the game.' Even the police were frightened of him, but unfortunately not of Albert. If Clough had told him to drive over the grass verge and through the supermarket he would do it – or get the sack.

Motorways seemed to bring the worst out of Clough. Albert once broke down on the M1 on his way back to Nottingham after a game at Tottenham. The engine was spluttering and sounding very unhealthy, forcing him to pull over on to the hard shoulder. Albert made his way up the middle of the coach to climb through the trapdoor to get at the drive shaft. When he was up to the waist down the hole the bus suddenly started moving off. We thought he must have left the brake off but when we looked down the aisle there was our manager driving the bus up the hard shoulder with the needle creeping past 30 miles an hour. The police were quickly on the scene and when he spotted them Clough put on the brakes, jumped out of the driver's seat and back into his own just behind it. Albert was struggling back up the coach when the police came knocking. I don't know whether they knew it was Clough driving but the boys were rolling about on the floor laughing.

I had a friend with me that day, having asked the manager for the favour of allowing him to ride on the team bus, a rarity for me because I didn't like owing the boss favours. He didn't believe what he was seeing and even those of us used to Clough's peculiarities were stunned. It scared Albert. I don't think he was laughing too loudly.

Clough did lots of things that normal people just wouldn't do. Having arranged a trip to Spain a couple of weeks hence, he suddenly decided that the coach should pull off the motorway at junction 24 so that we could drive past East Midlands airport and wave. 'We'll be there in two weeks' time, Skipper. Give it a wave, give it a wave,' he said. All we wanted to do was get back to Nottingham and we'd gone half an hour out of our way just to wave at an airport. What's more, it wasn't the only time we did it. Imagine grown men sitting on a coach waving at an airport.

The peculiarities extended way beyond our frequent coach journeys. He was in the habit of taking the boys for a walk on the morning of a big game and would suddenly come across a tree.

'This,' he said, pointing at the tree, 'is a punch tree. You have got to punch it. It's lucky.'

There was never a boring day, never a dull moment. Often he would invite you to join him for a drink at the oddest moments. He liked having people around him. When I first went there I would have half of Guinness so as not to upset him. Clough didn't mind if his players had a decent drink when they were at the bar at his invitation. Neil Webb liked a drink and he would occasionally down a bottle of red wine over dinner. He was playing well and claimed it relaxed him so Clough took no notice. When Webby went to Manchester United and Alex Ferguson found out that he was drinking a bottle of wine on a Friday night, he was not impressed. Personally, I thought it was unprofessional. It was down to Webby but I have to say he was magnificent when he played for us that first time around. Had he not played well Clough would have held it against him.

When we played at home we used to play deep; I thought that was wrong. I felt we should push on and if they had a throw-in near their corner flag, push in, squeeze it and win the ball early rather than let them bring it out and play. I had the nerve to mention it to Clough and it worked for four or five games. Then we were caught out and lost a match. He turned on me.

'You twat. Push on, push on, idiot, idiot,' he shouted.

He didn't mind when I told him but he used to store things up and turn on you when it went wrong. He always liked someone else to blame. He has an incredible memory and I had given him a noose to hang round my neck by opening my mouth. I thought it was for the good of the side. I didn't suggest anything again.

One evening before our first away game of the season he rang round our rooms and invited us all to join him in the bar for a drink. Chris Fairclough, Ronnie Fenton, Neil Webb, Nigel Clough and I were there with others. He always let us drink whatever we wanted, a Guinness or a glass of wine. I would have an orange juice and sit with him for half an hour before slipping off to my bed. But on this occasion as we sat chatting among ourselves, one of the customers, who had been sitting with his wife having a drink, came over and said, 'Hello Brian, you have put on a bit of weight.' I looked at Chris Fairclough and we started counting one, two, three, four . . .

'What the fucking hell did he say to me, Skipper?'

He knew exactly what the man had said because he was standing right next to him but I repeated it. Then he turned to the unfortunate fellow.

'What did you say to me?'

The man started to splutter something but Clough cut him short.

'What job do you do?'

'You don't want to know what I do.'

'What fucking job do you do?' Clough repeated a couple of decibels louder.

'I'm an undertaker, Brian,' he eventually ventured.

We were biting our lips by this time, trying desperately not to fall over laughing as the manager gathered himself for his riposte.

'Well fuck off and die then.'

The man returned to his wife and said loudly, 'What a fucking rude man he is.'

Just because he had seen Clough on television he thought he knew him but it was like going up to someone in the street and saying, 'You are a fat bastard.' You just don't do it.

Celebrities used to pop into the dressing-room now and again.

When Elton John was chairman of Watford first time round, he always used to come in whenever we were at Vicarage Road. After one particular game, Clough had gone to have a bath and was all lathered up when Elton popped his head round the door. Ronnie Fenton shouted through that Elton was here to say hello. Elton was chatting to one or two of the boys when Clough bellowed back, 'Tell the fat poof I'll be out in a minute.' All the players started laughing and, to be fair, so did Elton. The next minute Clough appeared, naked but for the soapsuds, and gave Elton a big cuddle. For all the players, Elton was a massive star and we were in awe of him – but not Clough.

I have been to see Elton in concert and backstage and I really do like him. He is definitely a man of the people and I liked the way he took Brian Clough at face value when other so-called superstars might well have been upset and walked out.

Geoffrey Boycott came into the dressing-room once to see Clough. We were playing Sheffield Wednesday at Hillsborough. He walked in after the game and you had the feeling that both were talking and neither was listening to the other.

'Eh, by 'eck, that centre-half of yours is a quick lad, isn't he?' said Boycott.

'Do you mean Dessie?' asked Clough.

'Aye,' said Boycott. 'He's quick – but I'd still run him out though.' That brought the house down.

As I've said, I don't think that Brian Clough liked his players talking to the media. He never came out and said as much but we got the drift that this was his province and for us to leave it alone. Neil Webb and one or two of the others liked having their names in the paper, but I didn't and neither did Des Walker, Nigel and a few of the others. If anyone said anything ridiculous in print or on radio or television, he would pounce on them and leave them in no doubt that they were fools to be trampling on his territory.

What he did say to me and to others was that we could use him as an excuse for not speaking to the press and that suited me. It was easy to say that the boss had banned us from talking and, knowing him, everyone believed it.

When I went with England for the first time he repeated the instructions and that delighted me. I didn't want to talk to the press before such a big game – it was against Brazil in the old Rous Cup – and have them turn something against me to upset my preparations on the morning. They were already building me up as the hot head, saying that it was a big risk to play me in an international. I knew I was in for my first cap because Kenny Sansom was injured. I just didn't want to worry what they would write if I commented.

The big story the next day was that Brian Clough wouldn't let his captain talk to the press. That was fine. He had done me a big favour, shielded me from what could have been a difficult situation. Not that he was particularly generous about my international call-ups. When I was first pulled into the squad by Bobby Robson he called me into his office.

'Son, you're in the squad are you?' he said.

'Yes, Boss.'

'Do you think you'll play?'

'I don't know, Boss,' I replied, knowing that I would.

'Do you think you're good enough?'

'I don't know.'

'I don't. Get out.'

He meant it. He didn't think I was good enough to play for the country. In fact, he didn't like his players playing for their country much anyway because he thought we came back as smartarses, comparing wages with other players from bigger clubs and of course, for that period we were outside his influence. But he never tried to stop anyone playing. He would tell them that if they didn't want to play he would back them up by reporting that they were injured, but in my experience he never once told anyone, 'No!'

One time I was due to head out for Saudi Arabia with England for a friendly. Des Walker was injured and pulled out, as did Steve Hodge and Neil Webb, leaving just me from Forest and I had just had a nightmare of a game. It was the one against West Ham in which I was substituted. I was gutted and Clough offered to pull me out if I wanted. I was tempted but I quickly put the idea out of my mind. It would have meant giving up another England cap for one thing and a trip on Concorde for another, not to mention a first visit to a new country. Those were three good reasons to go. I went, played well, got my passport stamped and travelled on a great aircraft.

It wasn't the best game. We scrambled a draw thanks to a late goal from Rodders, but I had a decent game and safeguarded my place for the next one. Bobby Robson took the flak for our performance. The press climbed all over him with the memorable and unfair headline: 'For the love of Allah, Go!'

That taught me the greatest lesson of my international career. I was a total idiot for even considering pulling out and I told myself never, ever to consider it again. I never did. It annoyed me to this day that I even thought of backing out.

A lot of players do back out. Talk is cheap. When they say it's a pleasure and an honour to play for England, that's lip service. Some pick and choose their games, especially when they know they are not going to play. I spent two years sitting in the stand waiting for my chance to come back when Graeme Le Saux was in the team. Terry Venables gave me the chance of retiring honourably, indicating that I wasn't going to get back in his team. I remembered my lesson, bit the bullet and stayed patient. As long as he picked me in the squad I was going to turn up and if Brian Clough had suggested different we would have had a row.

I don't know how the physiotherapist Graham Lyas coped with Brian Clough at times. Clough may have been happy to back up any international who wanted to cry off with an injury but if too many players were in the treatment room he would sometimes lock the door. The players would roll up, get changed and set off for the training ground. As we walked down the corridor, there would be the physio and the injured players standing around kicking their heels outside the locked door. When we came back from our training session, they would still be waiting. Two or three times while I was there Clough locked the treatment room for up to a week, stopping the physio attending to the injured players.

Graham became numb to it in the end; it just ground him down. He joined us from the County Cricket Ground next door and in the end he came in, did what he could and went home. If the door was open he would work, if it wasn't he had to find something else to do with the injured players.

I'm sure there was the odd shirker but I doubt whether Clough's ploy to get them out of the treatment room and back on to the pitch worked. Most players want to play and for someone whose career was terminated early through injury you would have thought he would have had a little more understanding, but it was in character.

Contact with the manager, even for the club captain, was limited to say the least. I went in to see Clough in the summer of 1992 about a new contract. When I asked him about the prospects he shouted across the table, 'Do you want to leave the club, son? Do you want to leave the club?' No I didn't. I had simply gone into his office to ask about upgrading my contract. The last thing anyone does is to go into Clough's office and demand anything. His reaction took me aback. I told him that I wanted to stay. My point was that I thought my contract was a bit outdated to which he replied, 'I do as well, son. I do as well. Come back and see me in the week.'

It was a week before the season began and there was a ruling in force at the time that if you signed a new contract it had to be done before the season started. I probably had it wrong but that was firmly in my mind so I told him and we arranged our meeting accordingly. The next thing I heard was that he had cleared off to Spain for a week, which carried us into the season. I was furious. I telephoned the PFA and the FA and asked for dispensation as it had been agreed that I would have a new contract but I had to wait for the manager to come back from his unexpected holiday. They appreciated the eccentricities of our unusual manager and agreed.

Clough then arranged for me to meet him before a reserve game at 6 p.m. I was there on the dot but there was no Clough and not even Ronnie Fenton knew where the gaffer was. He was nowhere to be found. We sat waiting in his office for an hour before Ronnie shrugged his shoulders and said to come back at half-time.

I had no intention of going back at half-time; I had been at the club for seven years and his captain for five of those. He had cleared off on holiday when he had arranged to meet me without bothering to cancel the appointment and now he was swanning around the ground somewhere and had left me waiting again. That was plain bad manners. The least he could have done was be there.

It was all building up inside me as I made my way home. I told Liz what had happened and said that I wasn't going to go back at half-time as Ronnie had suggested. We put the answer machine on and, sure enough, the phone rang exactly on half-time. We leaned over the machine and we could hear Ronnie saying, 'He's not in, Brian.' Then I heard this voice shouting in the background, 'Not in? Not fucking in? What do you mean, he's not in?'

I turned to Liz and said, 'That's going to cost us a lot of money.'

Clough and I never talked properly again. I blanked him because I felt that I had been treated like dirt. I had never fallen out with a manager before, but once I have made up my mind I am obstinate. I would walk past him in the corridor, he would say hello and I would ignore him. That went on for an entire season and my form suffered because of it. From February until the end of the season I was out with injury, a groin strain that needed an operation. We were relegated that season, my form was rubbish and he was given the sack. It didn't help either of us.

He had lost me by then. In his autobiography he slaughtered me. Certainly his recollection of events is very different from mine.

Away from home, the coaches, the manager and me in the dressing-room made for a frosty atmosphere, but I was as stubborn as he was. At Maine Road before a game against Manchester City, he said to me that we should sort things out. I told him there was nothing to sort out, he hadn't bothered to turn up, and so the standoff continued until he left. When he went we were still not talking and there was still a bad atmosphere, certainly from my side. I felt aggrieved and hard done by and judging by his comments he thought I was a greedy bastard.

Everyone has their own side of the story. I can only tell it as I saw it and maybe I'm off the mark somewhere. But I was mad with him for that entire season and afterwards as well. I told him he had messed me up and messed up my family. I have mellowed a bit since then.

When Frank Clark took over, he not only had the problem of Forest being outside the top division but also the problem of me and my contract to solve. The chairman, Fred Reacher, obviously knew that there had been a massive gulf in that last season between the captain and the manager and, naturally, he wanted to sort it out. It hadn't helped that he and the other players had witnessed Clough saying, 'Hello Skipper,' and me ignoring him. No one blanked Clough – but I did. I wasn't trying to be the big shot because I couldn't touch the manager in terms of stature and achievement; I was just being true to myself, right or wrong.

This wasn't the Brian Clough I knew. He wasn't in the best of health but the saddest thing was that the club was going to be relegated and he seemed to do nothing about it. He had sold Teddy Sheringham at the start of the season and not only had he not replaced him, he had not signed anybody at all until March. We went slowly down and down and were relegated without a fight.

I have to hold up my hands and admit I was part of the cause. I played poorly up until February and then played no part at all. Clough, in his book, suggested that at the time they thought I was shirking and it was only when I went into hospital for an operation that he realised how serious my injury was. I don't believe that the situation would have developed a few years earlier when he was still on top of the game. Things were allowed to fester all season whereas he would have sorted it out or kicked me out. I'm not proud of it and have to take my share of the responsibility for Nottingham Forest being relegated. Neither was it the way I wanted to end my association with Brian Clough, a man and a manager I had respected above all others. I was mad at the time but it is water under the bridge and with time I have recovered my respect for the man.

I have stayed in regular touch with Nigel and I always ask after his father. I'm sure Nigel knows the problems I had with him, but he is diplomatic and lives his own life. We have always got on well together with a great deal of respect and no animosity. If I get a job in football management, the first person I will ring is Nigel Clough. It was the first thing I did when I was caretaker at Forest.

There is plenty of contact there but none between his father and myself. But then I never really had any social contact with him before. He managed and I was captain. We were never friends, I was never invited to his house and we didn't we even swap Christmas cards. He was my boss and I was his workman. That was hard and fast and it suited both of us. I'm sure he didn't want me as a friend and I wouldn't have been comfortable sharing confidences with him. I was always on my guard with him because he was that sort of person.

I caught up with him at a dinner where he was being honoured. I sat with Nigel and his wife Margaret and Brian's wife Barbara and was delighted at how well my old manager was. His acceptance speech was brilliant and brought down the house. I managed to snatch a few words with him after the function and he was charming, telling me to look after the leg I had broken for the second time. If he held any animosity it didn't show. I guess he was the type who would have a fall-out and forget all about it the next day. He didn't give a toss.

CHAPTER 8

forest after clough

The technical side of my game has improved and the proof of that is that throughout my career I have been sent off only three times. Unless you are technically decent you don't play for England, certainly not the number of times I have played and for so many different managers.

Sometimes when a player is considered over-robust, his technical qualities tend to be overlooked. I am not talking solely about myself but others of the same ilk such as Julian Dicks, Mark Dennis and Neil Ruddock. There is no sweeter left foot than Ruddock's but because the main weapon in his armoury is the physical pressure he puts on other players that quality is often forgotten. He is a strong player who intimidates opponents and that is what has made him such a good professional footballer rather than that superb left foot that can drill 40-yard passes.

You have to be cute, you have to learn and you have to evolve. Technically, I have a good left foot and a virtually non-existent right foot. I have been able to get away with it because my left foot is so good that if the ball is between my feet or to the right, I can hit it with the outside of my left foot and with pace as well. I can comfortably take a corner with the outside of my left foot and whip one in. There are not many of us left-sided players about because of the way the game has changed and that is probably why I stayed involved with England for so long.

For my height I jump well; I don't lose a lot at the far post when it counts. If you are not going to win the header, it's important to prevent the player you are marking from scoring a goal, even if it means having to put your head in his face.

Obviously Clough helped my technique with his odd remarks and observations while Don Howe, a coach with England for much of the time I was there, has a vast knowledge of defensive football. I dipped into that as often as possible. I had respect for Don and once you have that you hang on to every word the coach has to say. He has been around for years at the very top level. I remember coaching sessions when he would be looking after the back four and he was so committed to what he was doing, almost dogmatic, that you could not help being sucked in. I find myself coaching some of the sessions the way he did. That I can remember them after 12 years shows what an impression he made.

As much as the game evolves and technically improves over the years, the basics stay very much the same as they have always been. A player or manager has to change with the times but good play never changes. That was something Clough would always hammer into us. If you are defender, then defend. Don't look where the player is; look where the ball is. The ball can hurt you far more than the player. Midfield players have to win the ball and turn and if you are a forward you have to score goals. If you are in trouble, put the ball in their half of the pitch and don't mess around with it in your own penalty area. There is nothing wrong with putting your foot through the ball and kicking it 80 yards at the right time. These things haven't changed since the game was invented. Heading the ball is a basic and so is playing the right ball, playing it simple, playing what you see, playing what is on.

Watch a video of Pelé in the semi-final of the 1970 World Cup in Mexico, against Uruguay. Pelé was the best player the world has ever seen. He was capable of running through ten players but what does he do? He gets the ball, commits a defender, and rolls it to his mate Rivelino who strikes the perfect goal. Pelé saw what was on and played it. If you are coaching youngsters I would say show them that goal first rather than Diego Maradona running through the entire England team and scoring in the Mexico World Cup 16 years later. They will no doubt prefer the Argentina goal but then explain why the first one was better. Pelé took the right option, played the right weight of pass and was aware of what was going on around him. Pelé stuck to the basics that day while Maradona personified the ripples on the top. You can tinker with the bits and pieces of the game, those ripples on the top, but never with the basics.

Respect is the key to coaching and management. Whatever other ingredients go to make the ideal manager is anyone's guess and vary from person to person. Respect can only come with time; it's not something you can order up or simply acquire. Once you have it and the players are listening and want to work for you, you are on the way. If the respect or confidence goes, then there is a problem. The players stop listening.

There is no better example of the dramatic contrast that there can be between successful bosses than Brian Clough and Don Revie, two totally different characters, yet enormously successful with Nottingham Forest and Leeds United. However, they were not successful everywhere they went. Revie failed as an international manager while Clough did not command the respect of the players at Leeds, the same players who had played under Revie. It's that sort of thing that makes our game so fascinating.

At the clubs where they were successful, the individuals they worked with hung on every word and didn't question what they were told to do. Revie was very dogmatic in his approach; Clough was often perceived as casual. Who was right? The answer is, of course, that they both were. If those two were at either end of the scale, Bob Paisley fitted right in the middle, and he was even more successful than the other two. To copy any of them is to court failure. All three were their own men.

I have learned something from all the managers I have worked for. Some players would not be as benevolent towards Ruud Gullit but despite what happened at Newcastle I still learned things from him and I'll use them when I go back into coaching or management. I'm not too proud to give credit where it's due.

Life at Nottingham Forest after Brian Clough and relegation looked bleak as the team began to break up. Nigel Clough went to Liverpool and the priceless Roy Keane to Manchester United. Nigel had made up his mind to go and many thought he had no choice after what had happened to his dad. One of the directors had placed a derogatory story in the newspapers and dragged Nigel into it as well.

I would be lying if I said I didn't think about leaving. One of my concerns was my England place and I confess that I telephoned manager Graham Taylor to ask him what effect dropping down a division would have on my position as his captain and my place in the team. It was only when he gave me some assurances that I went ahead with a meeting to discuss my role at the club and a new contract. Taylor's only concern was that I was happy at the club and I was able to tell him honestly that I was.

Chairman Fred Reacher and Frank Clark, the new manager, called me into a meeting to sort out my future at the City Ground. I told them that I had felt badly let down by the club, not just by Brian Clough but by the chairman as well because he knew everything that was going on and he sat back and let it all happen. We talked for a long while, resolving the problems that had festered for a year. I finished up signing a new contract and I am not ashamed to admit that I used the situation to improve the terms. I was sorry to saddle Frank with the problem and tried to make it plain that it was more to do with the chairman than him. He sat back while I thrashed out the deal with Fred and once that was done he and I had a talk.

Some players seem to think that when they sign they should be told of all the clubs plans, who they are going to sign and what colour they are going to paint the toilets. To me it's far plainer – sign, play and do your best. Once you start suggesting signing this player or that you are asking for problems. Unless I was asked I wouldn't dream of venturing an opinion. Certainly Frank never asked me. The job is hard enough without me putting my five pennyworth in.

There was a lot of pressure on Frank to succeed from the off as he spent money not just on me but on new players as well. He signed Stan Collymore and Colin Cooper. I had never played against either of them. Stan was an up-and-coming lad with a bit of a reputation and Colin had been earning his wages in a lower division with Millwall. So I really wasn't sure of the quality of the players replacing the engine room we had lost.

Unfortunately, we did not start that well and it wasn't long before we all knew that we weren't going to win the League. By the end of October we had lost five games and drawn four, slipping down to 19th place at one stage. We lost Colin Cooper through injury after just four games.

Millwall beat us at the City Ground on 3 November but after that we turned things around and lost just three more league games all season. We finished second to Crystal Palace, nine points ahead of third-placed Millwall. Steve Stone came into the side and did well, and we also signed Lars Bohinen. In retrospect, staying at Forest and winning promotion was one of the highest points of my career.

I liked Frank. It was a hell of a job taking over from Brian Clough even though he was the man Clough had always said should eventually have his job. Frank had been his captain through some of the glory years, a reliable defender and a student of the game. He was given the job and virtually told get promoted or get out. That was tough. He is a nice man and I have never met anyone who has a cross word to say about him. He knows his football and he is easy to talk to, as I do whenever I bump into him. Frank coached a little but was more of a manager. Some managers want to be hands on, coaching on the pitch all of the time. I saw Frank as an ideal general manager. As a manager, I could have worked under him a lot more easily than I did Dave Bassett.

We needed a point from our third-from-last game at bottom club Peterborough to be sure of automatic promotion and avoid the lottery of the play-offs. The Posh are not that far from us and we filled their little ground to overflowing as 14,000 people crammed in. The atmosphere was brilliant but the nerves were jangling to such an extent that before we knew it we were two goals down and what was supposed to be a promotion party threatened to turn into a wake.

Stan Collymore scored just before half-time but it was not until about 15 minutes from time that a cross came over, Chettle headed it on and I scored the equaliser with a diving header which carried me into the back of the net. The celebrations were ridiculous and to cap it Stan scored a wonder goal with the last kick of the match. The ball had hardly reached the back of the net before the fans were spilling over the fences in wild celebrations and the referee, wisely, blew for time.

The police eventually came into the dressing-room to tell us that we would have to go out and see the fans or they would never be able to empty the ground. We went up into the directors' box and gave them a wave.

For a nearly man, things worked well for me that day. It vindicated my decision to stay and it was a great occasion, totally satisfying. For everything it symbolised, that game at little Peterborough is one I'll never forget.

To be fair, we weren't a bad side. Stan came in firing on all cylinders and we finished third in the Premier Division the next season, as high as I had ever finished under Brian Clough.

Frank had his work cut out with Stan. I felt a bit sorry for him. He couldn't let things brush past him like Clough could. When Stan first came, he was a bit of a handful but not too bad. Frank had ten other players who would graft, people such as Steve Stone who ran up and down the wing, Colin Cooper who worked so hard that he won himself an England cap and Bryan Roy who came in for that first season back in the Premiership; and I was not playing too badly. All the average players were playing to the top of their form. Frank was conscientious and sensitive, aware of the other players and their feelings, so much so that he came to me on one occasion to ask me what I thought he should do about Collymore and whether he should fine him.

He ended up throwing fines at Stan all the time and I don't think Stan could give a toss about money. Stan is Stan and will do stupid things but for Forest he played phenomenally well for two seasons. I remember saying to Frank, 'I know I have been around the dressing-room a lot longer than most and from my perspective I couldn't give a shit what he does. If he scores me a winner on Saturday, he will be my best friend.' I didn't care what he did with his life or whether he came in for training or not. In two seasons he helped us to win promotion to the Premier Division and get into Europe. I believe we had his two best-ever seasons.

Forest bought him for £2 million and he scored 24 goals in that first season. The next-highest scorer was Scot Gemmill with nine. Promotion made us millions. He scored 25 in the second season, giving us the prospect of earning more millions in Europe, and we sold him on for £7 million to Liverpool. Since then he has not achieved anything. After a good start at Leicester City he was dreadfully unlucky to break an ankle.

He was two-footed, good in the air, and in my opinion, he is one of the best players ever to play for Forest. There are a lot of critics who would pooh pooh that statement but it's fact. Ten of us would defend like hell and when we got it forward he would beat two players and score two goals at somewhere like Sunderland and that would win us the game in our promotion push.

I found Stan bright to talk to and I could never understand why he brought trouble to his own doorstep, especially when things were going so well on the football field. Sometimes he'd do silly things like just not turn up for training and when Frank asked him where he'd been he would throw in a stupid excuse like his grandmother had been poorly! That was the nature of the man. As far as I was concerned, it was thanks for two great seasons and £5 million profit, on you go and good luck to you.

We would have loved to keep him for at least a third season and I honestly didn't think he did too badly at Liverpool where he scored some spectacular goals. But he is not the sort of person to mix the way Liverpool reputedly requires you to do. He is his own man who does his own thing. You have to accept it, although that's easier said than done if you're his manager. Managers have to worry about what other players may do if one is allowed to get away with eccentricities. We used to have a players' Christmas party and Stan would be the only one not to come. What do you do? Get on his back? What was the point? It was his choice.

I wouldn't say we had a great deal in common. I once heard someone ask Sir Bobby Charlton if he got on with George Best, rumours having indicated otherwise, and Bobby said, 'We got on all right but we were totally different people. While he was at a nightclub I would be at home with my wife and family.' It was the same sort of thing with me and Roy Keane and Stan Collymore. We were a different age group and I would go home to Liz while Roy would like to go out clubbing. Stan liked to go back to Cannock and have a beer with his own mates. I always quite liked him and whenever I see him I laugh and ask him, 'Keeping out of trouble, Stan?'

'Trying to, Skip, trying to,' he says.

I'm afraid the game is riddled with might-have-beens and could-have-beens. When I turned professional I drank at a pub where everyone knew someone who was a lot better than I was. To me that does not mean a thing – you have to do it, not talk about it.

The next year, 1995–96, we went into Europe on the back of Stan's goals and enjoyed an incredible run. We played the first three rounds in the UEFA Cup and conceded just two goals. We lost the first leg of the first round 2–1 to Malmo in Sweden, but Ian Woan's goal in the 1–0 second leg was enough to take us through. We followed it up by winning 1–0 in France against Auxerre and drawing 0–0 at home, and reached the quarter-finals by beating Lyon 1–0 at home and drawing 0–0 away. Basically, we just defended. Away from home we were incredible and at home we had the attitude that we were the under-dogs. Everyone was playing well, especially our goalkeeper Mark Crossley who was on fire and kept us in it more than once.

The game in Auxerre was the most one-sided game I have ever played in. Steve Stone scored a breakaway goal with what was our only shot of the match. In contrast, they hit the post four times and we cleared three off the line. We hardly got out of our half, particularly in the second half. I walked off laughing because it was ridiculous. Even in the return, we spent the entire 90 minutes defending.

Against Lyon it was not a lot different. The one goal came after my penalty was saved and young Paul McGregor followed up to put in the rebound.

We were eventually found out in the quarter-final against Bayern Munich. I had been out for six weeks with a calf problem and it was only on the morning of the game that Frank told me he wanted me to play after a workout on Bayern's training ground. An hour before the kick-off I discovered that my leg had swollen up and when I pressed

No fear: a diving header between the flying feet of two Peterborough United defenders as I score the goal which clinched our promotion back to the elite in 1994. (*TBF*)

Thanks a million: an emotional moment at my testimonial as the crowd show their appreciation along with the two teams. My eldest brother Ray is the referee. (*Empics*)

One of the best: this story may have had an unhappy ending but Pierre van Hooijdonk was one of Forest's best signings as far as I was concerned. (*Empics*)

Another good week: the joys of being a manager – not fit and unable to play I express my emotions in the dugout. (*Alex Livesey/Allsport*)

Gone but not forgotten: although I had left for Newcastle United I was still remembered at Forest as the boys retire my No. 3 shirt to the 'Hall of Fame'.

Happy days: Rob Lee helps me celebrate my goal against Dynamo Kiev in the Champions League. Neither of us were quite so happy six months later.

One in the eye: Arsenal's Christopher Wreh catches me with a leading arm, cutting my eye on a day when little went right for me or Newcastle. (*Colorsport*)

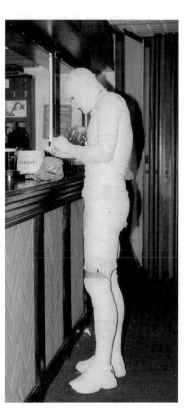

The invisible man: never one who liked to be seen at the bar, I was heavily disguised for this Newcastle United Christmas party.

In action for West Ham in February 2000 following my first broken leg. After my return to the England side earlier in the season, I still hoped I could make it to Euro 2000. (*Empics*)

Not again: I break my leg for a second time during the 1999–2000 season soon after my comeback from the same injury. (*Solo Syndication*)

or the first time: I win
the header against
Müller to set up the
goal for Lineker to
mark my international
debut against Brazil at
Wembley in May 1987.
(*Bob Thomas*)

Team-mates: the
Nottingham Forest
quartet of Steve Hodge,
Neil Webb, myself and
Des Walker, who were
regulars in the England
squad but played
together just the once,
against Denmark in
September 1988. (*Bob
Thomas*)

That penalty in semi-final

Placing the ball on the edge of the spot nearest to the keeper.

Keep your eye on the ball.

The ball flies straight and true...

...but Illgner gets
his legs in the way.

f the walk to the penalty
spot had been long and
nerve–wracking, the
walk back was a
nightmare.
(all *Popperfoto*)

Peter Beardsley tries
to console me.
(*Colorsport*)

Forgiven: thousands turn out at Luton airport and on the route to our hotel to welcome us home after our penalty shoot-out defeat by West Germany in Italia 90.

Captaining my country: leading out England for the first time at Wembley against France in 1992. To my right is Basile Boli with whom I had a coming together a few weeks later in the European Championships. (*Empics*)

my thumb into it, it left a big depression. I showed Frank, who had already put the team in to the referee, and he called in Doctor Jarrett. We went into the showers away from the other players where he advised me not to play. I was almost in tears as the doctor kept telling me he couldn't advise me to play while Frank was insistent that I should give it a try.

In the end, we reached a typical British compromise and it was decided that I should go out and give it a try and if there was any reaction I should come straight off. As it turned out I played for 90 minutes in the Olympic Stadium and we did ourselves proud. Steve Chettle equalised a goal from Jürgen Klinsmann but, ironically, sloppy defending cost us the game when Mehmet Scholl scored what turned out to be the winner just before the break.

We really fancied our chances in the return, as we needed to score only one goal and keep a clean sheet to go through to the semi-finals. We went into a game thinking we had to win and instead of defending as we had done in all our previous games, we went at them and were slaughtered 5–1 with Klinsmann scoring two more. We lost to the much better side and Bayern went on to crush Bordeaux 5–1 in the two-legged final.

We had our chances early on as we lobbed balls into the box where Jason Lee caused havoc with his head and elbows, the famous pineapple hairdo flailing everywhere. If we'd had Stan up there we might have gone all the way. We not only missed his goals but Bryan Roy was not the same player without him. From the time Stan left we began to slip. The average players who had been overachieving went back to being average and worse. Instead of playing to capacity, there were too many players performing below par. We finished halfway that season.

One Friday morning just before Christmas 1996, I took a telephone call from Alan Hill telling me Frank had resigned and the club wanted me to take over as player-manager. I felt sorry for Frank. The club were in the middle of a financial takeover, they were floating on the stock market and there was no money available for him to buy the players we needed. Various parties played tug-of-war, each of them making different promises. They even tried to drag me in, asking for my support but I wouldn't get involved in the party politics.

The players Frank had brought in didn't work. Kevin Campbell from Arsenal was riddled with injuries, Chris Bart-Williams did well to start with but faltered, and we hardly got a game out of the Italian Andrea Silenzi, a 6ft 3in Roman who was bought for ridiculous money from Torino and played one full league game. So Frank resigned and suddenly it was down to me.

To say it was a bolt out of the blue would be understating the situation. It was five days before Christmas and we were playing Arsenal the next day. We were bottom of the table and hadn't won a single League match since the opening-day victory against Coventry City. Hill hung on the telephone waiting for my answer but I told him that I couldn't get my head round it and that I would see him when I arrived at the ground in 15 minutes' time.

Liz was mucking out the horses.

'You're not going to believe this,' I said.

'Frank has just resigned and they have asked me to be manager.' She looked at me as though I was crackers.

I drove straight to the ground and went to see temporary chairman Irving Korn – Fred Reacher had stepped down by then – and I eventually agreed to take over until the end of January.

The players were clearly surprised at this dramatic turn of events, but I had little time to gauge their reaction. The first thing I did after training was to ask Alan Hill to ring Manchester City and sign Nigel Clough on loan. He was doing nothing at Maine Road and it not only meant a new face but it would also mean I had someone on my side.

It was a whirlwind of a day and when I finally arrived home I sat down to try to work out my best team to play against the League leaders the next afternoon. I felt I couldn't go with the same team. I needed to change things if only for change's sake. The team that Frank turned out most weeks was, I believed, our best team but it was simply not good enough. I had Nigel to bring in and I started from there. I made a positive change of tactics by picking three at the back and after trying at least 20 times I finally came up with a team that looked right.

I showed it to Liz and she sat there staring at it for a long while before saying, 'Why have you dropped Mark Crossley?' Of course, I hadn't. I snatched the paper back and realised to my embarrassment that I had picked a team without a goalkeeper. No wonder the team looked strong. I had five at the back, three in midfield and Bryan Roy behind the front two. It was a shambles. I had worked for an hour and a half to come up with a team which covered every eventuality except keeping out the goals.

The next day was difficult to say the least. All of my routine, my careful pre-match preparations, went completely out of the window. I went in early to talk to the coaches, tell them what team I had finally picked and then meet with the players. It looked ominous when Ian Wright opened the scoring for Arsenal in the 63rd minute. Then Wright fouled one of our defenders and was sent off and we took advantage to win 2–1 with two goals from Alfie Haaland. The winner came a minute from time.

The trouble with winning like that is that you have immediately set yourself standards and if I thought that the job was easy I was put right five days later when, on Boxing Day, Manchester United beat the same team and the same formation 4–0 at home. David Beckham and Nicky Butt scored in the first half and Ole Gunnar Solskjaer and Andy Cole in the second. It made me wonder whether I should have changed a winning team for the game. Should I have matched them up 4-4-2? Everything was going through my mind. Liam O'Kane said to me, 'Look at it this way. We have had Arsenal, the top of the League, and Manchester United, second in the League, in the space of five days. Would you have settled for two draws before we played? Of course you would. On that basis, we have one more point than we could have hoped for.' It was good logic and I slept a little better than I might have done.

After that we went to Leicester and Nigel scored the first goal before we slipped behind. But we showed our character and with a minute remaining Colin Cooper scored an equaliser. We followed this up with a trip to West Ham and won that one with a goal from Kevin Campbell.

It is amazing. As a player I could hardly remember one game to the next but I can remember every detail as a manager, right down to who scored the goals and when.

We had built a bit of confidence and that improved even more when we drew Ipswich at home in the third round of the FA Cup and beat them 3–0. Then we beat Chelsea 2–0 and I scored a goal. Bryan Roy scored two to sink Spurs. We also knocked Newcastle out of the Cup. In the middle of all this, I was made Manager of the Month for my first month in the job.

I had to make a decision about whether to stay on. I could have walked away then and everyone would have said I had been brilliant while I sat back and watched someone else get the team relegated. Despite our success, all we had done in this time was to re-establish contact with the other teams battling against relegation. But everything had gone right for us, including a couple of good draws in the Cup and an increase in confidence. I stayed on.

One of the problems I faced was that the chairman Mr Korn was on the telephone to me all the time telling me had the bank manager on to him and he wanted to sell my players. I told him that if he wanted to sell goalkeeper Tommy Wright and Chris Bart-Williams to Frank Clark, now manager of Manchester City, to go ahead but without my consent and that when the fans asked me why I had sold them I would tell them that it was the chairman not me. I explained that if we sold anyone we would certainly be relegated. He backed off but told me we needed a quarter of a million pounds quickly. Naively, I thought that was his problem.

I had signed a new playing contract when I became manager and the club were in such dire straits at the time that they asked me to defer my signing-on fee for a few months until the takeover was complete. As manager I thought I ought to do what I could. So I allowed them to put it off until the spring. It didn't help and the pressure from the bank to sell players grew and grew until one day I went home and stunned Liz by telling her that I was thinking of lending the club some money, around quarter of a million pounds just to keep the bank off our backs and to keep the club solvent.

She thought I was crazy but rather than lose one or two of our better players I was tempted. In the end I decided that it could become too messy with new owners, especially if they decided that they wanted a new manager.

I walked into the chairman's office soon afterwards and he was filling in his lottery card.

'Tell me things aren't as bad as that, Irving,' I said. 'If they are, I hope you have a winner.' At least it raised a smile.

I didn't wave my new title in the faces of the players. I still changed in the same place. I'm not sure all the players liked it, nor did they particularly like having Nigel around because they thought he was my man and would tell me everything that was being said behind my back. But I didn't want to change, especially as initially I thought that I would be doing the job for just a month. Liz carried on sitting in her usual seat with the other players' wives. I didn't use the manager's office, before, during or after the game and tried to run my life as closely to normal as I could.

Joe Royle, then manager of Everton, left a message one day asking me to ring him back and when I called he wanted to buy Alfie Haaland. He knew the player was out of contract in the summer. Alfie had made it clear to me that he was waiting to see whether we were going down. Joe offered me £200,000, pointing out that Haaland would go for nothing at the end of the season. I laughed.

'Joe, to be honest with you,' I said. 'I don't care what you're offering. It ain't my money and I need Haaland or we will definitely go down.'

It was a pity that we didn't have a bit more umph. After beating Spurs 2–0 we didn't score two goals in any other league game for the remainder of the season.

I missed the Cup defeat at Chesterfield through injury but told the players that although they were two divisions below us they would turn us over if we didn't have the right attitude. We didn't and they did! It was a shame because had we won we would have drawn Wrexham at home in the next round and then Middlesbrough, who weren't playing at all well, in the semi-finals. We had the luck of the draw but simply didn't have the players to do anything with it.

It was difficult but I enjoyed the experience. I had always enjoyed the responsibility of being captain and this was an extension of it. Of course, it was hard work and time-consuming. Half the time I walked round like a zombie thinking of teams and training. I was able to take the training as I wanted it done; not jolly up training but stuff that was enjoyable *and* meaningful. I needed to get the enjoyment back into the club because everyone was so down. The morale needed lifting more than anything else.

In March the club was floated and Irving Scholar came in as chairman of the new consortium who were running things. I went in to meet the former Spurs man on the back of a run of poor results. We had lost a couple to Coventry and Everton, drawn with Aston Villa and beaten Spurs. That was to be our last win of the season. We had also gone out of the Cup at Chesterfield.

The first thing Scholar asked me after I had explained that I had promised to stay on as manager until the end of the season, was whether I would like someone in to help me. Playing was still the most important thing to me so I saw that as a good idea.

'What about someone like . . . someone like . . . someone like Dave Basset? Do you think you could get on with Dave Bassett?'

I asked him why he had mentioned Dave Bassett in particular and when he said Dave could be interested, I sat back and laughed.

'You've obviously spoken to Dave already,' I said.

He admitted it and clearly Bassett was primed to come but Scholar hadn't wanted to walk in, kick me out of the job and appoint a new manager. It was much better for him to have me on board rather than have the supporters on his back but I would have appreciated him being a little more honest.

It was difficult for Dave. He was a seasoned manager and had his own ideas. In hindsight, perhaps I should have said there and then that I would stand down and perhaps the arrival of a new man would have given the players a second wind. If I had thought that Dave could have kept us up, I would have handed over to him like a shot. As much as I enjoyed it, it wasn't an ego trip on my part. Dave ended up coming in and trying not to tread on my toes. He said he didn't want to interfere and that he was there if I needed any help.

He sensibly sat back and if, as happened, the results went badly he wouldn't be the one to shoulder the responsibility. He made sure that when he went into press conferences everyone knew who had picked the team, especially when we lost! He liked coaching and I quite often used to pass over a session to him because I could see he was kicking his heels and wanted to get his teeth into organising set-pieces and the other things that he is good at.

The disappointment at the end of the season was not so much that I had failed in my first effort as a manager but that the club I loved had once again been relegated.

One of the legacies Irving Scholar and I left Forest was a certain Dutch striker Pierre van Hooijdonk. We were in desperate need of a striker and we drew up a short list with Irving throwing the Dutchman into the equation. He was a lot like Stan Collymore and the club had a couple of good years out of him, helping them out of the First Division. We probably got more out of Stan, who was a better player, but the club couldn't legislate for a player going on strike to demand a move. Pierre helped and we took some decent points in a succession of drawn matches but in our position it was not sufficient to save us. We had left ourselves far too much to do.

When we were relegated I received a call from Dave telling me that West Ham United were interested. The very fact that he felt he needed to pass on this information sowed the seeds. I decided that I was going to leave in the summer. My agent Kevin Mason and I saw Irving Scholar in his London office and told him that I thought it was time to move on. He wasn't impressed. He sat and listened as I explained my reasons.

I had three years left on my contract and I told him that at 35 and with what I had done for the club over 12 years, I would like to go on a free transfer and pick up the signing-on fee I was due in 13 days' time. He agreed to let me go for nothing but refused my other request. I thought that was ridiculous; I could sit on my backside for 13 days, collect my money and then go. I decided not to go down that route, as the obvious retaliation would be for them to try to get the money back via a transfer fee.

There had been rumours around Nottingham that I was being hounded out of the club and, as part of any deal, Irving wanted me to write a piece for the local paper denying it. It wasn't true but I had not bothered to dispel the rumours before by denying them. By the time I left his office he had agreed to a free transfer but not my signing-on fee. When he telephoned me and asked about writing the article to get him and Dave Bassett off the hook, I answered that I would do it if they reinstated my signing-on fee! I thought it was comical but he didn't seem to see the joke. Seriously then, I told him that we all knew the truth and that they should survive on their own merits.

I have never worried about what's written about me in the papers. Providing I'm doing the right thing and can look in the mirror in a morning, I am happy with my life. My philosophy has always been take me for what I am; what you see is what you get.

I certainly had nothing against Dave Bassett and I would say to any First Division club that if they want someone to lift them out of that division they couldn't find anyone better. It is uncanny the way he gets teams up. He signs players at a certain level such as Neil Shipperley who are good First Division players, but, without being unkind to him, when he gets his teams up he carries on buying the same type of player. He doesn't step up. I doubt if he has ever had a world-class player playing for him. He knows the lower leagues like the back of his hand. He has good set-pieces and is well organised.

To prove my point, Dave got the team straight up again. If the board knew we were going down and they brought him in to bring us straight back up, it was a brilliant piece of business.

There was no animosity between the three of us. It was just the right time for me to go, but it was a sad day when I left the City Ground. We lived 15 minutes away and it had been a big part of our lives. I did it the right way. I hadn't gone looking for a club first before asking for a move. I like everything neat, sorted out and above board. Kevin talked to Kenny Dalglish, sorted out the contract and after a lifetime at Nottingham Forest I was off to play for Newcastle, a team in the European Champions League.

CHAPTER 9

out of toon

I had been tempted to leave Forest in 1995 when my agent Kevin Mason came to me with an unexpected offer from Japan. The club was in the city Kobi, recently devastated by a terrible earthquake. They wanted me to play for them in the newly formed professional J-League that was booming at the time.

With my love of travelling and the fact that I was unable to force my way into Terry Venables' England team, I gave it some serious consideration. They were offering a million US dollars a season, more than I was receiving in England. I chatted to some of the officials from Kobi and went to see Frank Clark with Kevin. He was none too pleased about me wanting to go, especially as I wanted a free transfer to make the deal worthwhile financially. The Japanese had made it clear that if they had to pay £400,000, they would take that out of the package they were offering. Frank was quite firm. He didn't want me to go and he especially didn't want me to go for nothing.

It was a good opportunity and something that appealed to me, but I was not sure that Liz would be happy living that far away from her family. I liked the idea of going somewhere totally different from everything I had been used to, a different culture and a different way of life. In the end it wasn't a workable situation. I certainly didn't hold it against Frank. I probably got on as well with him as any of the dozen or so managers I have worked for.

When the time came to move on from Forest, I talked to West Ham United as well as Newcastle. Dave Bassett had already told me of their interest. Harry Redknapp was keen, saying he couldn't see anyone coming down the wing with Julian Dicks and me there. I was honest with him and told him about Newcastle. They had been one step away from the championship and they were going to be playing in the European Champions League. I suspected where I would be going.

I told Newcastle that I wanted the same three-year contract and the same money I was earning at Forest. We finished up by agreeing a two-year contract with a year's option. This meant that if they wanted to keep me for a third year, I would stay at an agreed fee, and if they wanted to get rid of me they had to pay a set fee for me to go. It safeguarded my last year. It was a decent deal for both of us, considering they had signed me for nothing.

I had been used to playing for family clubs, Coventry and Forest, and walking into St James' Park was a different feeling altogether. This was big, big business. Kevin, Liz and I walked up to the offices and waited in a reception area before being shown into a private room. Kevin acted as the go-between, going into the office to talk to the secretary, coming back out to talk to me, going back in and so on. It was all very impersonal. In the past I had always gone into the manager's office and talked it out for myself.

Newcastle arguably have the best supporters in the world. Outside the doors of the ground everyone knows you; inside it was like being in a big city office. No one appears to know you at all.

Having agreed a deal with Newcastle, I didn't want to waste Harry Redknapp's time. We pulled into the first services on the A1 and telephoned him straightaway. He was brilliant and wished me all the luck even though I hadn't given him a chance by going to West Ham to talk to him. But he could have thrown twice the financial package at me and I would still have gone to Newcastle just for the chance to play in the Champions League.

I talked very little to Kenny Dalglish before I signed. Newcastle were playing a friendly in Birmingham and stayed overnight on a Friday. Kevin and I went to their hotel to see Kenny and Terry McDermott. We gossiped and laughed and the only time we talked about football was when Kenny said to me, 'I don't need to tell you how to play football.'

My first game for Newcastle was at home to Sheffield Wednesday and I was amazed. It was a full house, as it always is these days. The ball was on the centre spot and the noise built to a crescendo as kick-off approached. I have played at Wembley and for England in some pretty big stadiums but this was a bit special. It was very uplifting. We were kicking off a new season on the back of finishing second in the League and as I waited for the start I thought to myself how much I was going to enjoy it.

I have played with and against John 'Digger' Barnes over many years. When he was at Liverpool he was one of the best players in the country. But when he, Ian Rush and I went to Newcastle almost together, I felt that I went as a professional to further my career while they went to finish theirs. Ian was given a one-year contract, Digger two and myself three. Neither of them were automatic choices and while John was surprised, I wasn't. The two of them had won everything and had lost some of their edge – and Digger was also looking a little plump around the edges – but I hadn't and this was the biggest club I had ever been to. I still had something to prove and was a regular, apart from injury, in that first season. The difference I suspect lay in the motivation and I was possibly more motivated than either of them; that is probably why I carried on for so much longer in the Premier Division.

Ian played half a dozen times in his year and John wasn't in the team at all when Gullit arrived. He had played up front when Alan Shearer was injured, filled in in midfield and did whatever he was asked, starting in 22 games for his old team-mate Kenny.

If Kenny had stayed, I suspect that I would have been around a lot more in that second season while I doubt whether John would have been. He is a great fellow to have around and I like him immensely. You can talk with him about any subject in the world and he will always have something to say. Whereas some footballers can be blinkered, he has an opinion on anything and everything. I just liked being in his company. I would have loved to have played with him ten years earlier. He was probably the Gascoigne of the eighties. I used to tease Digger that he was the only upper-class Jamaican I ever knew, born with a silver spoon in his mouth. I always liked holding that against him – in fun, of course!

I loved the playing side, the fans and everything about the club except the plc, which was cold and businesslike. It was something I had never come across before but now pretty well every club in the Premier Division is that way.

We started off quite well. We won the first two games against Sheffield Wednesday and Aston Villa, both at home. I was pleased with my form but then in my first European game, away to Croatia Zagreb, I turned and chased someone and my hamstring went. After eight days it felt fine and I was sprinting but on the eve of a match against Wimbledon it went again and kept on going and I was out of action until the end of November.

I had a lump the size of a golfball on my hamstring. It confounded everybody. I had scans and all sorts but no one knew what it was. At the end of three months I was whipping balls over when I felt a twinge again. This time I had a cortisone injection, something I was loath to have but that seemed to clear it up. Even now, the one leg is different from the other. When I showed the physio at Nottingham he had seen nothing like it. It seems as though there is a piece missing.

We qualified for the Champions League proper and I missed out on the opening game against Barcelona at St James' Park. It was an incredible evening with Tino Asprilla scoring a hat-trick and putting on a performance as good as I have ever seen. You can see in their faces when defenders are frightened of a forward and he was running them scared, and this was Barcelona, one of the biggest clubs in Europe.

I also missed PSV Eindhoven home and away. I managed to get myself fit eventually and played in the away game against Barcelona at the Nou Camp, coming on for Darren Peacock after 35 minutes. By then we were already out of it, unable to qualify. The last game was against Dynamo Kiev, the winners of the group, and I scored in our 2–0 victory. This is what I had joined Newcastle for but, for me, it was over before I had started. It was a big disappointment that we didn't qualify.

To balance that we reached the Cup final, which was only the second time that had happened in my career. The draw was kind to us with an ordinary Everton side in the third round, then non-league Stevenage, Tranmere Rovers, Barnsley and, in the semi-final, Sheffield United, all from lower divisions, before we faced Arsenal in the final. It gave us every chance, avoiding the big hitters on the way. You need that help. Newcastle were down the wrong end of the League in the second half of the season, hovering around 15th or 16th place. We had some big, important games and the Cup run was something of a relief.

Unfortunately, on the big day at Wembley we didn't play well and got what we deserved from the Gunners in a 2–0 defeat. Up in the commentary box, Ruud Gullit slaughtered us and talked at length about Alan Shearer looking unhappy and not playing well. What an irony that Newcastle were back a year later under Gullit with Alan Shearer looking even less happy than he had a year before. Gullit was asked what he would do if he was Newcastle manager and went on about how Shearer needed the right sort of service!

We didn't deserve to win the Cup that year. The only decent team we played beat us and we could just as easily have drawn Arsenal in the third round.

I was taken off with about 20 minutes to go and replaced by forward Andreas Andersson as we chased the game. It had slipped away from us with goals from Marc Overmars and Nicolas Anelka. We changed our system to suit Arsenal and instead of playing with a back three we played a flat back four because the manager was so worried about Overmars' pace and skill.

All in all it was a disappointing season and we had greater hopes for the next one under Kenny. But that might have all become an irrelevance and I might never have played another game for Kenny, Ruud or anyone else after a brush with death.

The team had gone off on a pre-season tour to Ireland and I had stayed at home with a niggling little injury, not enough to worry about but something not to risk unnecessarily before the season started. I was about three miles away from home on my way to visit my accountant. It was a winding road and I suddenly saw a massive garbage truck coming towards me, completely out of control. It was just far enough away to give me time to decide whether to pull over or carry on and try to swerve past it. I stopped but by this time the wagon had toppled over and started rolling, straight towards me. There was a little bit of verge on either side and I could have tried to dive out, or reversed. If I had climbed out I would have been a dead man. Time appeared to stand still; it was a slow-motion replay to beat all slow-motion replays as sparks began to fly, adding to my anxiety as I thought that it had caught fire. I thought, 'I'm going to take one here,' and decided in that instant to lie down flat in the hope that it would roll over the car. Naive, to say the least, but what do you do when a thing of that size is bearing down on you like a fire-breathing demon from hell? Perhaps I had been watching too many James Bond movies.

Thank God there was no one in the car, particularly Liz who was five months pregnant at the time. I lay down across the passenger seat under the dashboard level and just crossed my fingers that the hit I was about to take would not be a fatal one. Then there was an almighty bang as the truck hit the car. I opened my eyes and looked up to see huge rear wheels on either side of me. The truck's drive shaft had come through my sun roof. Had I been sitting up in the driver's seat, or even leaning to one side, the drive shaft would have killed me.

As luck would have it, the strongest part of the car, the suspension, took one set of wheels and the engine the other. The truck had come down wheels first on top of the car. If it had landed side down, roof down or almost any other way, it would have crushed the car and me. As I was lying across the seats I felt a weight on my back and for a moment I was frightened that I was holding up the entire dustcart. I reasoned in the moment of panic that if I moved it would come down on me. Then I thought I saw flames and all I could think of then was getting out.

The driver, unhurt apart from some nicks caused by broken glass, had come round to the car window, convinced that he was going to find a dead body. The only place untouched was the passenger side; lying down had saved my life. He was pretty shaken himself having been thrown around as though he was inside a tumble dryer.

Having survived the crash, I wasn't going to burn to death and I shouted at him, 'Get me out of here you fucking idiot.'

I didn't want to open the door in case it was load bearing. The window was slightly open and while I pushed, he pulled until the glass shattered. I scrambled out, ripping my jeans and sustaining a small cut – the only injury I suffered in the entire episode. I went for the driver, thinking he had been reckless, but fortunately calmed down as he apologised before I did him any permanent damage.

In the meantime, another car had pulled up without me noticing and when I saw this other man I went for him as well thinking he had been in the cab. He backed off, saying, 'No, no, I've just pulled up.' I was definitely suffering from a case of road rage.

The police were there very quickly and things had fortunately settled down a bit. I jumped out in front of the police car and told the officer to keep onlookers away from the vehicle in case it went up in flames.

Then I telephoned Liz. In her delicate state I could hardly tell her that a lorry had landed on my roof, so I just said I had suffered a minor bump in the car.

I was taken to hospital in an ambulance as a precaution because I had a stiff neck and felt that I needed a general check-up in case there was anything else wrong, especially if there was a claim to be made. When I returned home having been given the all clear there was a reporter in my driveway and that, with Liz inside the house and pregnant, was like a red rag to a bull. They had given me a neck brace as a precaution, and that excited the man from the *Sun*, although he was probably disappointed that it was not a bit more serious and newsworthy.

The local policeman came round and told Liz that I might suffer nightmares for a while because it had been such a narrow escape, but I was fine. I even took off my underpants and said to Liz, 'Look, nearly killed and no skidders.' That night I slept like a log while Liz lay awake tossing and turning, thinking how close she had been to becoming a widow with an unborn child.

When I looked at the pictures I also realised just how close I had been to death. Certainly had I sat where I was and covered my head with my hands, the normal reaction, I would not be here now. The cart had gouged a foot-deep hole in the ground just before it had reached me, causing it to leap in the air and come down on top of my motor. It was all a matter of inches where the wheels had landed.

The driver, apparently, had a full load on, hit the curb and started snaking before tipping over and starting to roll. He lost it and so might I have done. I must have been unhinged to think that by lying down the massive truck would have just taken the roof off my car.

My time clearly hadn't come and, for once, I was glad to be the nearly man. But I didn't really think much about it afterwards. I'd had a crash and survived. I suppose I am a bit unemotional about things. I filled in an insurance form and it asked what had happened. I just wrote that I had pulled up to a halt and a garbage truck landed on my roof. There were other silly questions and I thought I should just send a picture and let them see the damage for themselves.

Up until then I had been pretty lucky with all the driving I do. The nearest I had ever come to an accident before that was when we parked in a public car park. On our return from a bit of shopping, I noticed this car with the rear bumper pulled so far out it looked like a rhino horn. I was really sympathetic until I discovered it was my car.

Kenny Dalglish rang me having seen the pictures of the wreck and expressed his wonderment that I had escaped. I went to work in Newcastle the next day, travelling by train, and I sat looking at all the other passengers reading their newspapers with me and my wreck on the front page. Rover were delighted because the car was so strong that it saved my life.

We started off the season by drawing with newly promoted Charlton 0–0 at St James' Park. It wasn't good because they had a man sent off well before half-time and still managed to hold us. Then we had a decent result with a 1–1 draw at Chelsea and suddenly Kenny Dalglish had gone.

Sacked? Resigned? We were only the players and we didn't know. Two games into the season! It was staggering. For that to occur at that time of the season simply made no sense. I don't think he was sacked.

He intimated that he wasn't getting the response he wanted from the players and the chairman went off at a tangent and began to look for another manager.

Everyone liked Kenny. He is a great man and good to have around. He has achieved just about everything in football both as a player and a manager, winning the double as player-manager of Liverpool and then taking Blackburn Rovers to the title. But he wouldn't figure on the list of all-time great coaches.

Before we played Arsenal at Wembley there was some concern among the players that we needed to work on one or two bits and pieces, especially our teamwork. There was a lack of depth in this department. You can't just throw 11 players on to the pitch and hope they gel. At Liverpool in Kenny's time there they *were* able to do that because they were all good enough to win most games in which they played. At Blackburn Rovers, Kenny had the good fortune, or good sense, to have Ray Harford alongside him, and Ray took the training, did the coaching and was a good organiser. Blackburn played well within the system they adopted. That was where we struggled. Kenny didn't want to go down that road. At Newcastle, he would have done well in the general manager's role with a good coach to do the other work. But Kenny enjoyed the training and joining in the five-a-sides and was very well liked by the players. If he did ask one of the coaches to organise something, Terry McDermott would be there messing about with Alan Shearer and Dave Batty and undermining what the coach was trying to put on. It was a good, happy camp but at the end of the day we had to get the results.

Even so, Kenny had not been there for very long and it was a bit of a sudden divorce. I didn't realise that it was going to affect me more than Kenny in the long term.

Ruud Gullit arrived and there was no hint of what was to come. He had us all in the office, Alan Shearer the rest of the senior players, myself and others, telling us that we must stick together and that if there was a problem to tell him and generally saying what he thought were the right things. It all sounded very good and matey but personally I wasn't brought up to run to the manager with every little problem. I wouldn't dream of walking into my manager's office and saying we should play this or that formation. I did it once with Brian Clough and had my fingers severely burnt. But I did appreciate it was the way the Dutch players did things, as we have seen over the years – they all have an opinion!

I played the first handful of games under Gullit and we had some encouraging results, beating Southampton 4–0, Coventry City 5–1 and Nottingham Forest 2–0. In fact, I played in his first 11 games. But it was a false dawn. I was to play in only one more league game during the rest of my time at Newcastle United. It was a most frustrating twilight zone of my career.

The catalyst to my future problems came in the game against West Ham United at home on 31 October when I was sent off. The ball was up in the air, I arrived a little late and caught Trevor Sinclair with my elbow. I expected to be booked but Jeff Winter sent me straight off and we went on to lose that game 3–0.

Winter had given a few bad decisions against us in the first half when we were drawing 0–0 and Shearer gave him a hard time coming out of the tunnel for the second half. I was walking alongside the pair of them when Winter turned to me and said, 'That's not fair, is it Stuart?' I just looked at him and blanked him. Three minutes later I'm walking back down the tunnel the other way having been shown the red card. I don't know whether he had the hump with me or not but I hadn't been booked before. It wasn't a deliberate elbow; Sinclair went down but didn't make a meal of it. I was left to wonder what might have happened if I had told him what a good, fair referee I thought he was and supported him against Shearer's tirade. I had disagreed with some of his decisions in the first half but it was Shearer having a go at him, not me.

Gullit called me into his office the night before we were due to play Manchester United and told me that, as I was going to be missing a few games because of suspension, he was going to leave me out of the game at Old Trafford and play Andy Griffin. I told him that was fine, that he was the manager and it was his decision. I went back to my hotel, rang

Liz and told her what had happened and that I doubted whether I would play many more games for this manager. Being sent off was exactly the excuse he needed to drop me and I wondered how much longer I would have lasted had I not been sent off. If he thought that I was too old or not good enough, why didn't he put me out of the side straight away?

Andy Griffin played well at Old Trafford in a goalless draw and had one more game before he, too, was left out and another youngster, Aaron Hughes, was brought in only to be replaced by Frenchman Didier Domi from Paris St Germain. In the space of a couple of weeks, I was suddenly a long way down the pecking order. My prophecy to Liz was proving to be accurate. I was training, being picked in the squad and then nothing. I would be named as one of the substitutes on the bench if there was a coachload of injuries but I would never come on.

I played in just the one game, against Liverpool at Anfield, and that was me finished with my first-team career at Newcastle. It was a strange feeling to be discarded so quickly and dramatically.

The older players could not understand what was going on, so much so that one day Alan Shearer came up to me and said, 'What's the matter? Have you been going to bed with his missus or something?' He asked me what we had said to each other and I told him, adding that I assumed the manager had left me out because he didn't think that I was good enough.

It was not going to make a scrap of difference if I went crashing into his office. He was hardly going to say, 'Oh, yes, I forgot you were around. What a good player you are,' and put me back in the team. That sort of thing doesn't happen and all I could do was keep fit, keep my nose clean and be ready if he changed his mind and decided he wanted me.

It was such a ridiculous situation. But I was careful to fulfil my part of the contract – I was always there and always available even though I was basically being ignored. I would wait until the team and the substitutes were posted and if I was not included I would sometimes drive home to Nottingham.

For one game Gullit had so many injuries that he had to pick me on the bench. For once, I went out for a warm-up, joining the lads who were already out there. The fans quickly spotted me and began to cheer and shout. I responded by running round giving them the big salute and causing great hilarity among the other players. I went out at half-time and helped work the reserve goalkeeper and then, with a minute or two to play, one of our defenders went down with an injury. We had already used the one other defender on the bench and Steve Clark, our coach, told me to strip off in case I had to go on. I was so far removed from my normal, dedicated professional approach that a wicked thought crossed my mind. I wondered to myself what would happen if I took Steve at his word and did not stop at my tracksuit but carried right on until I was standing there in my underpants. The timing was right – by the time I'd completed my strip the whistle would have gone and I could have gone down the tunnel and straight into the bath. It was almost irresistible but fortunately good sense prevailed. Had it been a few years earlier I might well have done it.

It came to a head at Derby at the Pride Park Ground on 3 April when we had Steve Howey injured along with I don't know how many other centre-halves. I felt this time I had to be given a game because no matter how much he shuffled the pack he was still going to be short in my area. There was simply no recognised centre-half. We had the team meeting on the afternoon of the game. He flicked over the teamsheet and not only was I not in the team, I was not even on the bench although Steve Caldwell, a 17-year-old who had never trained with the first team, was. Gullit had shuffled the pack so much that I had once again slipped out of the bottom without a word said to me.

It was the last straw. I knew that if he didn't want me then, he never would. As we were still living at Nottingham, I had someone drive my car down to Derby behind the team bus. When we arrived at Pride Park I walked down the coach, got off, got in my car, drove down the M1 and then the M40 and arrived at Aylesbury in time to watch our horse Archie run in the 3.30 race at a point-to-point meeting. Liz, of course, didn't know I was going but there I was, the best-dressed man on the course in tie and blazer. Everyone else was in sweaters, green wellington boots and hacking jackets. I confided in her that this time he was taking the mickey out of me and although I was acting unprofessionally, I felt that I couldn't do anymore if someone was prepared to go that far out of his way to exclude me.

In the midst of my problems at Newcastle, I received an unexpected call from Nottingham Forest coach Liam O'Kane. By this time Ron Atkinson had taken over from Dave Bassett and the club were again in dire straits. I knew what was going on from the local radio and television news and the local paper. My name had been mentioned here and there because I was out of favour with Gullit.

Liam asked me whether I would be interested in going back to the City Ground as a player. I told him of course I would be interested; I needed to play football at my age and not sit around. But there was no follow-up and I heard nothing more until I bumped into Big Ron at the Central Television studios in Nottingham along with Terry Venables. Ron said that he had wanted to bring me in but had found resistance at board level. I can only assume that Irving Scholar did not want me back. It was not surprising if this was the case. I would probably have done the same thing in his place.

On another occasion Alan Shearer had a quiet word with me, saying that a Midlands journalist friend of his wanted my telephone number for Ron because he was interested in chatting with me. That was a laugh because everyone at Forest from the laundry lady to the tea lady had my number and if Ron had looked it was probably on the noticeboard. I certainly did not need to pass it to him through a third party. It wasn't rocket science; if a club wanted me it would have been easy to go through the front door. I was out of the Newcastle team, they would almost certainly have got me on a free transfer and with my record I would have given my all to the Forest cause.

Some days were worse than others at Newcastle. I tried hard to be the complete professional I had always been, but I have to admit that when Ruud Gullit joined in the training matches I would go out of my way to lump him. The one time I did catch him, he went clean over my back. He was quite good about it – got up and played on. The lads found it amusing and Rob Lee, who was on Ruud's side, offered to leave his pass short to give me another crack at him.

There were times I would go in for training and think to myself what was the point. Gullit had made it plain that I was never going to play for him again and it seemed he was just trying to grind me down. Then there were other days when I went in with a big smile on my face and just enjoyed my training, happy to do what I did best and to be in the fresh air. That was my problem – I did enjoy training and playing football and still do. It hurt not to be playing.

The boys got to the Cup final that year beating Crystal Palace, Bradford City, Blackburn Rovers, Everton and Spurs without me being involved at all. Despite the success in reaching Wembley for a second time, the discord was growing in the dressing-room. A couple of the players had new boots on because of sponsorship deals. Ruud came across in his new adidas boots trying to tell them in his roundabout way not to get carried away with the commercial aspect of the Cup final. He told them how it was when he was with AC Milan and added that nobody won anything wearing flashy coloured boots.

'Apart from Martin Keown,' I chipped in, 'who won the double with Arsenal last year with those red boots of his.'

He said nothing, just walked off. It couldn't hurt our relationship anymore than it had already been damaged and he certainly wasn't going to pick me to play against Manchester United at Wembley. It gave the lads a good laugh because there were more than just me finding the former great Dutch player difficult to understand and get on with.

By the end of the season, we had not discussed the impasse. He seemed content to let me tick along because I wasn't being too disruptive or breaking his door down. I could go with the first team, play in the reserves or not play in the reserves. He left it to me. If his strategy was to try to grind me down, it was working. I felt that I couldn't sit there any longer. I wanted to do something. There was Liz at home with our new baby daughter Chelsea and I was staying in a rented apartment on my own – for what? My professional life had no end product.

But I had served my two years and the option in my contract now came into play. If they wanted to release me they had to pay me up, and if they didn't want to do that, they had to offer me a new contract for the year. I hadn't talked to Ruud about my contract at all but now it was decision time. I needed to know. I hadn't played for the club, apart from one game in December, for seven months. Surely there was no way they still wanted to keep me.

In the week leading up to the Cup final I telephoned the club secretary, Russell Cushing, to ask him what was happening. He told me that there was a board meeting in two weeks' time and he would tell me after that, adding it was nothing to do with him.

I waited. Nothing happened. I waited until the end of May and then telephoned the PFA and explained my position. Gordon Taylor agreed that he couldn't see them offering me a new contract and thought, like I did, that they would pay up as they were legally bound to do and send me on my way. Gordon offered to ring the club and when he came back to me he told me that they had to let me know two weeks after the season ended. But, he said, they had already written to me and sent the letter to my house. I didn't know what he was talking about. What letter? I had seen no letter. It turned out that they had sent the letter to my rented accommodation rather than to my Nottingham home where I had informed them I would be. The letter was telling me, incredibly, that they were offering me another year's contract.

They had made the decision to offer me a slightly higher salary, as they had to by regulations, but clearly more in the hope that I would tell them to stick it. I am nothing if not obstinate and having stuck it out for seven months, I was prepared to wait a bit longer. If they wanted to play cat and mouse, I was game.

I went back for the pre-season at the end of June and finally went to see Ruud. I asked him outright, 'Am I being released or are you giving me a new contract?' He shrugged his shoulders, refused to take responsibility and said that it was a matter for the board. I asked him point blank if he wanted me at the club and he replied that as far as he was concerned he didn't want me at the club. That was fine. It was what I wanted to hear. With that in my armoury, I requested a meeting with the chairman, Freddy Shepherd.

They messed around and the day they arranged to meet me they didn't turn up and didn't bother to tell me. A new date was arranged and this time when they failed to honour it I was told that Shepherd, chief executive Freddie Fletcher and the secretary Russell Cushing were out of the country. When they returned, I stormed in and demanded to know what was going on. I told them that the manager had told me that he didn't want me at the club, so would it be all right with them if I stayed at home in Nottingham and they just sent me my wages.

They laughed and said it could not be done. I had just wanted to make my point. To press it home, I told them that I was the only player in the Premiership who was a non-playing player, the only player in the Premiership this season or any other season who couldn't at any time represent their club. Gullit would never ever play me. I told them, 'Ethically and morally, the decision you have come to by giving me another contract is a pile of shit! You know that as well as I do.'

Shepherd denied it, saying that I was the sort of player they wanted around to bring on the youngsters in the reserves.

'Behave yourself,' I said. 'You know as well as I do that what you want is for me to tell you to stick your contract, walk out and find another club.' They now knew how I saw it so I went on to offer them an alternative.

'Rather than me staying another year, can we sit down here now and organise a payment that is acceptable to both of us if I can find another club, because if I sit here for another twelve months it is going to cost you a lot more than half a million quid.'

If I had followed it through, away from my wife and child for another season, I would have gone off my head but I wasn't going to tell them that.

We eventually agreed on a payment, a little more than half of what I would have been due. That agreed, I said, 'No offence, but I'm not leaving this office without having that in writing. I don't want to come back and tell you I have a club because you will try and get a fee for me.'

I assumed that Ruud had reassured them that I was too old and would never get another club and my agent Kevin Mason had told them that my best chance of continuing my career was with a foreign club. They must have been convinced that I was at the end of the road and they eventually gave me my written agreement.

I immediately got off my backside and telephoned Coventry City, Southampton, West Ham United, and Watford and left a message for Aston Villa to which they never responded.

At Watford, my former England manager Graham Taylor, hummed and haa-ed after I had spoken to coach Kenny Jackett but decided not to go with me. At Southampton, I talked to Stuart Gray who said they weren't particularly interested in signing me. Gordon Strachan was good at Coventry because he didn't waste my time. I talked to him directly and he got straight back after a couple of days and said what a pleasure it was not to deal with agents but he was sorry he couldn't take me on.

It wasn't looking at all promising and for a while it looked as though Gullit might have been right. I telephoned Liz from the Newcastle flat where I was still living and told her that I would decide on a cut-off date. If I hadn't found a club by then, I would pack it all in.

'I'm staying at Newcastle,' I told her.

'I can't leave and I'm not walking out for anything out of principle because of the way I've been treated. The cut-off date is 7 August.'

I had been sent a training schedule for a month's training in the close season. I did it to the letter, even though I hadn't played for eight months and there was no sign of playing again for another year. It made me feel surprisingly good.

Three weeks before the start of the season, a little castaway group of us who were never going to play while Ruud was there, went off with reserve-team coach Tommy Craig. There was Rob Lee, Nikos Dabizas, Alessandro Pistone, me and a couple of others. Tommy was as fed up as I was. His feeling was that Rob and I shouldn't be playing in the reserves at our ages because we were stopping young kids coming through. We did what we could for him. We'd been playing for him on and off during the previous season and we'd won the League.

Tommy was dreadfully unhappy at the pre-season situation. He would organise a training session for the kids and the pros who weren't in the team and then Ruud would come along and take the kids away to take part in a training match. He did this regularly leaving Tommy with six players, two over age, two foreign pros and a couple of youngsters. He would despair. We ended up doing a bit of training or a bit of head tennis and then we would go off for a walk in the park and Tommy would buy us an ice cream.

I had taken my foot off the gas for a couple of days and was genuinely contemplating my retirement from the game. I had no takers from the clubs I had talked to nor from Forest where I had dropped huge hints that I would be prepared to go back as a player and my deadline was fast approaching.

I thought to myself that if I had no takers by the start of the season I would go down to the Newcastle Youth Academy for a couple of days a week to help progress my coaching. It would keep me out of Gullit's way and it would also allow me to come and go as I pleased, permitting me to spend a little time with my wife and baby. I went to see the academy coach Alan Irvine, told him of my situation and asked if I could come down and help him out with a bit of coaching. I cleared it with him before I asked the manager or the board. He was delighted for the help.

Tommy Craig was one of the people who kept me sane in those dark days. He really boosted my flagging confidence when he told me, 'I'd love to see you playing in the reserves but if you don't want to, don't. You are a credit to have around. At your age you are working harder than the kids and if I ever need an example to show them I point you out and tell them to look at Pearcey.'

Tommy lived in Newcastle while his family was in Glasgow so he understood my situation. He basically left it to me when I came and went.

I went in for a double training session with Tommy a week before the season started. He was again saddled with our little group and we cleared off to the park with all the mothers and the kids still on their summer holidays and stopped the ice cream van. That was in the place of the morning session and we decided that golf would be a better alternative to the afternoon work. Just as we were preparing for the round my mobile telephone started ringing. It was Kevin Mason to tell me that Harry Redknapp had been given the all clear from his board to sign me for West Ham United – a one-year contract, the same money. It had all been agreed.

To say I was stunned would be to underestimate this dramatic development. Here we were, eight days from the start of the season and in my mind I was ready to get my head around coaching and wave my playing days goodbye. I telephoned Harry straightaway and it was all systems go. Then I called Liz to tell her that I was no longer a retired professional. Then I started to worry about having done no training for the past ten days. Needless to say my golf went to pot and I played my worst round of the year.

I telephoned Russell Cushing and asked him to telegraph the money to me that next week. I still was wary even though I had it in black and white. They possibly thought I was going to Raggedarse Rovers and when I told him to fax through my playing certificate to West Ham you could hear the astonishment down the end of the line. He sounded gutted that I had a Premier Division club, having to pay me to leave with the knowledge that I was still going to be in the same division to haunt them.

I was staying that night with the physiotherapist Derek Wright and by nine o'clock I was out lapping the local park. It was a crash course because Harry had told me the night before that I would be playing the following Saturday against Spurs in a London local derby.

It wasn't the easiest of times at Newcastle but I loved the football side of it. Even being out of the side I didn't moan or bellyache; I just got on with my job. I kept in some sort of trim by playing for the reserves, not always in the Pontins League, sometimes much lower. Occasionally I would decline to play and have a night back in Nottingham with Liz. I also used the time to study for my coaching badge but the entire situation was weird. I found myself older than the manager, the assistant manager, the coach, the club doctor and the physio. I don't suppose that has happened previously in the top division.

People thought that Ruud and I had had a bust-up but we hadn't. This game is subjective and he had his opinion. We never once rowed about it. Whether he was right or wrong, people will have to judge for themselves but after five games back at West Ham, Kevin Keegan, another Newcastle cast-off, called me up to play for England again.

I was totally committed to Newcastle United and when I first signed I went with the idea that we would move lock, stock and barrel to the north east. It is difficult for us because we can't just pick a house on an estate the way most people can. The horses come first. We need a place with land – more than a big garden, not as much as a massive farm. Finding the compromise between the two is difficult. We looked hard, even searching North Yorkshire. After a month, I moved out of the hotel I was staying in and found myself a nice apartment in Durham. We had a change of heart and decided to stay as we were. I was going home regularly and Liz would come up on a Friday for the home games. It wasn't ideal but it worked because Liz was so supportive.

I enjoyed Newcastle. When I was on my own, I would go to the theatre or try to drag one or two of the staff to see a concert. We even managed a trip to York to see the Stranglers. Theatre was a great night out, much better than knocking around pubs which I didn't really want. I managed to see some Shakespeare and one or two musicals. I would always check what time the curtain went up, arrive as the lights went down and leave while the cast were acknowledging their first encore. No hassle. I even persuaded John Beresford and Warren Barton to come to a couple of Royal Shakespeare Company plays.

Warren and his wife Candy were particularly helpful in showing Liz and me the town and having meals together. Warren had recently moved into a new house and he asked me if there was any chance of helping him fix a couple of lights. He gave me the keys and cleared off, leaving me to it. No wonder. Candy had laid out her chosen light fittings in every room in the house. It added up to more than a dozen. I was out of practice so it took me an exceptionally long time to work my way through them all and I was there all afternoon.

Normally I go into a room, make sure the switch is in the off position and work on it live. But there was one switch that had been taped over. I assumed that the decorators had done it so I untaped it. Immediately alarms went off everywhere. It was a panic button disguised as an ordinary light switch but no one told me. It was me who was in a panic. I telephoned Candy who told me to leave it and it would go off on its own.

That was all very well but the next thing I knew there was a policeman peering through the window, and then hammering on the backdoor. I went out, complete with my toolbelt round my waist, screwdriver in hand, and said, 'Sorry mate. I'm the electrician and I've just pushed the panic alarm by mistake.' He couldn't work it out. He looked hard at me and did a double take. Recognition flickered in his eyes but he couldn't nail it down. Who was I? A well-known electrician? A burglar whose picture he had seen on file? He didn't know. He went off shaking his head, having reluctantly taken me at my word.

When Chelsea came along things changed. I'd get back to Nottingham as often as I could. The night before I was due back in Newcastle, we'd be in bed by ten. Liz would get up and do the midnight shift and go back to bed. I would do the four o'clock shift, jump in my car and drive to Durham. There was nothing on the roads at that time and I was back in bed in Durham in an hour and a half, setting my alarm clock ready for training at 11.

I loved the fans and they would always ask if I was playing. I would laugh it off, particularly the week before the Cup final when I told them, 'As he hasn't picked me for the last seven months, I don't suppose he would pick me for that one!' They were kind and sympathetic. But if anyone asked me if I had made the wrong move I would say no. I have to add, of course, that if I had been playing well Gullit would never have been able to leave me out of his side. Usually that's straightforward but on this occasion I feel that the dice were loaded against me. Clearly I was not good enough in his eyes. There was no way forward for me but there was no percentage in looking back. I have never regretted a single move I have made, Newcastle included.

Looking at Newcastle now under Bobby Robson, I know I would have been given a chance. The other three of the ice-cream four, Rob Lee, Nikos Dabizas and Alessandro Pistone have all played a big part in the remarkable revival that my former England manager achieved after starting with seven defeats and a draw.

It reminded me of the time when, after three months out in the cold, Rob was sent over to join us. I said to him, 'Don't tell me you've been left out now?'

'Don't be silly,' he said. 'I'm suspended on Saturday and that's why he's sent me over here.'

It wasn't long after that Rob was relegated to the has-beens. We were both hurt deeply but as I was 35 I could take it a little easier than Rob who was three or so years younger. He had been the club captain before the armband was taken off him and given to Alan Shearer. It was very sad when Rob said, 'To think that a couple of months ago I was in the England World Cup squad – look at me now!'

That's how quickly it changes in football. If you don't keep up your standards you can soon feel the effects but that was not the case where Rob and I were concerned. It was something altogether more personal. I believe that Gullit would have got rid of Shearer as well, if he could. They didn't like each other and he tried to push Shearer into asking for a move. When we played at Everton there was public and press talk of a split and a possible move. Ruud was clever. He couldn't say he wanted him out or just go ahead and sell him, so instead he said things like if Alan Shearer wants to leave it will be his decision. It's the classic way of nudging an unwanted player, pushing them towards the door, tempting them to come in and ask what's going on and have a row that can only end one way.

There was no love lost between Alan and Ruud Gullit, as there was no love lost between a number of players and the manager. It was hard to penetrate Ruud's cold exterior – in sharp contrast to his predecessor with whom the players had a good relationship. Alan was in a similar position to me only he was playing and I wasn't. He is a professional and as long as he is at the club he loves he will play to his best ability. Gullit didn't like him at all, but it was a two-way road. It was no surprise to me that when Gullit left the club, Shearer suddenly found all his old touch under Robson.

It wasn't just me and other players who disliked the man; it was physios and even the boot man, Ray Thompson. That's hardly surprising when the manager would walk into the boot room, toss his shoes at him and say, 'Here, shine these!' Ray does the boots and does them happily but when someone demands he clean normal shoes without a please or thank you, that seemed to me to be sheer arrogance. The same was true at Chelsea from where he was moved on when his demands became too high. I am not sure that he is able to look at himself and see the faults, only the good points.

On the good side, he erected a noticeboard so you could see at a glance what you were doing for the next six weeks, when you were in and at what time. I like to think that I am professional in my outlook and I enjoy having things mapped out for me. I was able to look at the schedule and tell Liz when I would and wouldn't be able to come home.

I also thought he ran the club professionally from the diet to the training. I didn't think his training was bad. It might have been a little too hard, particularly for players who had played week in week out. We would do a running exercise on Monday and for someone like me who had done nothing over the weekend it was fine but for someone like Gary Speed who had worked his socks off for 90 minutes it was tough. He had to pound the ground alongside someone with fresh legs. I would have had Pearce running and Speed resting.

It was only when results were deteriorating that he became dogmatic. He couldn't cope with failure. Local boy Steve Howey ruptured his Achilles and was under treatment for months. Derek Wright and the other physios at the club worked with him day in and day out but one day they arrived to find Steve working out with someone else who was having him balance on a beam, something they thought he was still weeks away from. Derek was, understandably, amazed and confused, demanding to know whom this stranger was and what did he think he was doing. It transpired that Ruud had brought in an expert from Holland without telling the physios. For them, that was a real kick below the belt. He did something similar with the club doctor over Duncan Ferguson, sending him to someone else. Assistant physio Paul Ferris was always looking over his shoulder because he thought Ruud wanted him out.

Training became practice match after practice match, particularly trying to sort out the defence. That was probably his biggest downfall because it didn't work. I sat and watched from my place in the stand or on the bench. As a defender, I was aware that we were being run ragged because he hadn't found himself a natural leader. He had the United Nations back there who weren't able to communicate with each other. He needed someone in there to start bullying them. That was me. I could have done that job for him and the club but I was never asked.

Sometimes I would go in early and talk to Steve Clark, the coach Ruud brought from Chelsea. Steve hardly spoke at all but we did chat now and again, usually at my instigation. I would ask him how he thought a game had gone, just general chitchat. After we had been beaten at Wimbledon he opened up saying that they didn't do this or that and particularly that no one tackled. He said that the team needed someone to stoke them up and get in a few big tackles. I wondered for a minute whether he was taking the mick but he wasn't. The answer may have been sitting in front of him but perhaps he couldn't see it. I just said, 'There aren't many of those about, mate!'

The players had one eye on the Cup final for that game against Wimbledon and Gullit could have played me. I wouldn't have thrown a wobbly because I hadn't played for six months; I would have taken the opportunity to roll up my sleeves and show people that I could still play and make others play. My pride would have ensured that. Only I would have suffered by sulking.

Steve was not the buffer between the players and the manager that Terry McDermott had been for Kenny Dalglish and Kevin Keegan before him. Terry would be in with the players and then in with the manager, conveying what was troubling them and massaging any ego that needed massaging for players who were in and out of the team. Steve rarely said much more than good morning unless you pressed him. Ruud needed something more than that and so did the players.

That was something else I learned. Sometimes you are taught more by a difficult manager than a good manager. One thing, certainly on a personal level, is how to treat people when they are out of the side. Those who are being selected keep rolling along but I learned that you need to talk to players who are not selected and not ignore them. You never know when you might need them.

It was the lowest part of my career. I had gone to Newcastle as a professional footballer and finished up as a professional with the word footballer dropped. It was far worse than being relegated because then at least you are hands on. To sit there and never ply your trade is demoralising. Had they offered me a settlement in January when it became obvious that I was no longer part of the team, I would have quit amicably. But I am obdurate; it is a short career and there wasn't much left. I would certainly have stopped playing had West Ham not come in for me when they did.

The worst time of all was when I played badly for the reserves on a windswept Richmond Park. We looked for a wind machine in case one had been installed at one end of the ground – it was that bad. Imagine playing on a muddy pitch on the Monday after the rugby team had played on it at the weekend. We played Middlesbrough in what must have been the worst conditions for spectators to watch any game. The wind blew straight down the middle of the pitch, gusting so hard that the goalkeeper would put the ball down for a goalkick and then have to chase after it to give it a flying kick. There has never been a good game played in a gale and this wasn't a good game. To make it worse we were beaten by a last-minute goal. I can remember winning once on that ground, that's all, and our best results were away from home. It was so bad that we were mentally beaten before we kicked off.

I tried to do my best for Tommy Craig. He would go in the next day and report to Gullit, telling him who had played well. Gullit would respond, 'I saw your team last night – they were shit!' It was depressing for Tommy and I wanted to do well for him so that he could go into Gullit with his head held up. I could see in his eyes how much it hurt. Ruud would turn up occasionally and watch half a game and then get up and go for a pizza or whatever he did away from the ground. He said that he wasn't interested in the reserves or the youth policy and he wasn't. If anyone came through then fine but he wasn't going to bust a gut to look for the talent when he had the money to go and buy foreign players.

I sat in many a time when Tommy had a team meeting with the youngsters. It was soul destroying to listen to those kids saying that the manager didn't even know their names, that it didn't matter how well they played they were not going to be considered because they believed that the man who picked the first team didn't know who they were. What incentive is that for a 17-year-old? The youngsters thought that Gullit belittled Tom and them. I felt for them. I knew the situation Tom was in and knew that there was no way out until Gullit left the club.

I was desperate for Tommy to do well and, in the end, we won the League, mainly because we won the first dozen games and no one could catch us. There were old pros like John Barnes and myself in the team; John tried his best, too. There were others who didn't want to know at all. George Georgiadis, a Greek signed from Panathinaikos, was a shambles. He didn't want to be there and let everyone know it. He was regularly the worst player on the pitch. The kids would work their socks off to carry the passenger and then look in despair when he was put back in the first-team squad the following Saturday. He would play so badly that Tommy would substitute him and by the time we returned to the dressing-room he would have showered, changed and gone. He was a standing joke among the reserves.

I found it all quite sad and I kept telling the lads to keep working at their game and if it didn't work out for them at Newcastle they would have a chance somewhere else. Tommy would point at me and tell them how I hadn't broken through until I was 21.

He would also dig me up during a game if I played badly. In the dressing-room I could see he was unsure but he would have a go at me and he was right. One time I had arrived with the hump and it showed. He thought that if he dug the big fellow out and I didn't have a go back, he could handle the others more easily. I realised his position and told him, 'You're right, Tom. I have been an absolute joke.' I went out for the second half and played a lot better and enjoyed it much more.

No matter who you are or how much you try to keep up your own standards, sometimes it is good for someone to have a go at you and tell you that you can do better.

The next morning he came up to me at breakfast and thanked me for not having a go back. I told him I wouldn't have dreamed of it. It is not my natural reaction to have a go back; that's normally the reaction of someone who doesn't look at themselves truthfully. They tend to cover their own backsides. If I'd thought that he was wrong to have a go at me, I would have pulled him later on his own and not undermined him. I had also gone out of my way not to undermine Frank Clark at Nottingham Forest.

It was so depressing that many times driving home on the A1 after a reserve game I would begin to doubt my own ability and think seriously of packing it all in. I realised then that it is a hell of a lot harder the lower you go. You can scratch around in the third division and make no impression, whereas you can go up into the Premier Division and with a little know-how you have half a chance. That's another lesson I learned. A manager can go and watch the reserves and think that a player is not good enough but when he is given a chance in the first team he suddenly lifts his game several levels.

The reserves used to play a lot of their games on a Monday night. Tommy used to let me go home at the weekend, telling me just to have a run out in a local park. I took a ball home with me and some kit, as I often used to do, rather than not train at all over the weekend. I did my running and kicked the ball against a convenient wall. One day, a couple of youngsters were playing football nearby and they recognised me and came over to ask for an autograph. The ironic thing was that it was just about three o'clock on a Saturday afternoon and for sixteen and a half years I had been otherwise engaged at that particular time. There I was, pushing 37, having a kickabout with two ten-year-olds. I went over to my car and found a couple of brochures from my testimonial, which I signed, and I gave them the Newcastle United ball I had taken home with me.

All in all, it was a desperately unhappy club. When I left the dining room on a Friday afternoon, everyone was in there and yet it was as quiet as a morgue. We had everything there – the organisation, the diet, and the quality of players – but there was no atmosphere, no buzz about the place and this was just a few days before the season began. No wonder they started with only one point from their first seven games before Ruud Gullit finally packed his bags and left for Holland.

It was too easy for me to say what was wrong at the club at the time but it would have been seen as sour grapes so I kept my mouth shut. But the club and especially the supporters deserved more than that. I wasn't making a statement by not selling my story to the papers; that's just how I am. Let people look at it and make up their own minds is my philosophy, as it was with Irving Scholar when I left Nottingham.

I swear I was the only one who walked out with a smile on my face, not only on the day when I finally left for good, but on all those Fridays when I would wave and tell them I would see them on Monday as I was off home for the weekend.

Gullit could have treated me a lot worse. There was no dialogue but no problem. He could have worked me day and night and had me turn up for everything without playing me. But he didn't; he allowed me to do very much as I wanted and I respect him for that.

I am not sure how much dialogue he had with anyone. I know there were team meetings but I wasn't invited and I don't know what was said. I can't imagine that much was discussed because English players are different from their Dutch counterparts. After a bad game an English player will hold up his hands and take the blame, but a Dutch player will look for someone else to blame. This was evident at a succession of World Cups and European Championships. They are very opinionated. When England played against Holland in Euro 96 at Wembley I was marking Jordi Cruyff and when we went three up he turned to me and said, 'I cannot believe this is happening. I do not believe it.' I said, 'You better fucking believe it,' but thought to myself then that he seemed to be abdicating himself from all responsibility and perhaps blaming others for the fact that they were getting thrashed.

I also had an experience with a Dutch player when I was briefly manager at Forest. Brian Roy wrote in the local newspaper that he and I had different ideas on how football should be played when I left him out. My idea was that when I picked him he had to try to play reasonably well. If he didn't he would be out of the team because we didn't need a passenger when we had our backs against the wall. If his criteria is different from that then fine. When you're away from home scrapping for a result and someone is standing out on the wing, screaming, 'Give me the ball, give me the ball,' maybe we did have different ideas. The best players in the world also tend to be the hardest working.

It was certainly a happy day for me when I departed the club on that Friday. By the Monday I was at West Ham for the team photocall. I hadn't even completed my medical at that stage. Later they told me they stuck me on the end of a row so that they could cut me off if the deal fell through. I trust that was a joke, at least I hope it was!

On the Saturday I made my return to Premiership football. We played Spurs and won 1–0. What a start. What a dramatic turn of events.

CHAPTER 10

the broken hammer

It would have been easy for Harry Redknapp to ignore me when the opportunity arose for him to sign me the second time around. Fortunately for me, he is an honest man who bears no grudges. I was not the only one who had been nipped away from him by Newcastle. John Barnes, according to Harry, had even agreed terms on the deal before he signed for Newcastle. But Harry was brilliant then and has been ever since. He has lived up to everything I thought and heard about him.

I knew my time was limited at Newcastle. I was like a lost soul in limbo, still living in Nottingham and moving around the north east like some homeless person, trying to find somewhere to rest my head. I was constantly on the move, sometimes staying with physiotherapist Derek Wright, who would leave me the key to his front door, or with goalkeeper Steve Harper. Invariably if I stayed for a game of golf in the afternoon I would be on the mobile afterwards trying to find somewhere to lay my head that night.

There was a time in Durham when we didn't finish golf until 9.30 p.m. I telephoned Liz to tell her I was looking for somewhere to stay for the night. I told her that if I struggled to find Steve Harper I might even stay at the golf club, hide in the toilets until they locked up and then sleep in the nice reclining leather chair in the lounge and use the beautiful showers in the morning.

With no club coming in for me and the clock running on my own deadline, I had made up my mind that on the first day of the season I would commit myself to the academy, get out of Ruud Gullit's dreadlocks and try to make that last year of my contract as comfortable as possible. I could come and go as I pleased and would give up football, stopping training. There seemed no hope with either a total lack of response or 'no' votes from Nottingham Forest, Coventry, Southampton, Watford, Aston Villa and West Ham. I could have rung Manchester United all day, every day but I went in at what I thought was a realistic level.

Because of West Ham's interest in me the first time around, Kevin Mason was pestering Harry to sign me. He was ringing him morning, noon and night and it became so bad that even Liz chipped in and said that surely 'no' meant 'no'. Kevin had told me that Harry wanted to sign me but was trying to get his chairman to release the necessary money to pay my wages. The wages were very much the same as Newcastle but had they asked me to take a drop I would have done so to extend my football career. This had gone on for a couple of weeks and I had more or less given up and told Kevin to leave Harry alone. That was when I took the call on the mobile on the golf course and Kevin told me it was on.

I couldn't believe I was playing against Tottenham in a week's time. Harry was quite nonchalant about it all and asked if I wanted a reserve game first but didn't try to press me despite my lack of match practice over such a long period.

I trained with Newcastle on Saturday, secured my release documents from them and drove down the motorway to London that very day. I had played just the one game between October and August but at least Harry had brought in a fresh player and someone who was bursting a gut to prove someone else wrong. I desperately wanted to do the business for him because he had been so decent. I hoped for a minimum of 20 games for Harry and to do enough to sign for another season – until I was struck down by injuries!

How I enjoyed my move south. West Ham are a fascinating club, a bit of a throwback in football terms, rather like going back to Forest as they were 15 years earlier. I had come from the antiseptic St James' Park where sitting in the offices is like sitting in the dentist's waiting room, a plc probably run by bankers in London. The Happy Hammers are such fun and it's very definitely a family club.

I turned up for training one Sunday while I was recovering from my first broken leg. The kit room was locked so I had to hunt around for a pair of shorts, a sweat top and an odd pair of socks. Fortunately I had my boots with me. They are not the kind of thing that you leave around at Upton Park because they, like everything else, tend to go missing, as mine did once. In the dressing-room in the few months since I have been there we have lost three clocks off the wall. People just come in from the car park and help themselves to a souvenir. Before that someone unscrewed the picture of Julian Dicks off the wall and took that away with them. As for my boots I can only imagine the young kids took them. You couldn't leave anything. I came in from a workout in the gym, changed out of my trainers and put on my boots to go out for a run around the pitch. By the time I came in my trainers had disappeared. I checked all the players and found Joe Cole was wearing them. 'Joe, those are my trainers,' I said. 'I knew they were someone's – but someone has nicked mine,' he replied.

On another Sunday when I arrived the training room complex was heaving with all the kids and parents of the Under-12s and Under-14s teams. I eventually pulled on jock strap, sweatshirt, socks and boots but could not go running because there were no shorts. I eventually pinched a pair from a youngster who was having treatment and even then he had 'found' them and they turned out to belong to the physio who was treating him!

Shaka Hislop kept what the boys called a goalkeeper's fund which was basically a swear box, topped up regularly during training and used every now and again for the players to go out for a drink or two. He kept the money in his locker and, sure enough, he opened up one day to find it gone and in its place a McDonald's box with a half-eaten burger inside and the words 'Thank you' scrawled over the outside.

That's what it's like. It can be infuriating but it has a tradition about it; an aura that's unique. It's been the same for years and looks unlikely to change.

They do their little bit on nutrition but it is hardly top of the agenda. Over Christmas we played at Wimbledon on Boxing Day, missed a day and then played Derby County at home the next day. Any dietician will tell you that the most important time to get the nourishment in is immediately after the game or the next day. The team was in training on the middle day and I expected pastas, rice and all the usual stuff to be waiting for us at lunchtime. There was not only nothing brought in for the players but even if there had been there was no one to cook it. There was a packet of biscuits, jaffa cakes and mince pies to show it was Christmas! The dinner ladies were off because it was holiday time. It was against everything that had been learned over recent years and totally alien to my regime.

What a contrast it was after my miserable last few months at Newcastle, a very professional club with much of its heart ripped out. Harry and Frank Lampard have been at Upton Park for years as players and in their managerial and coaching roles and they are happy to maintain the traditions of the club. There is good team spirit and a nice atmosphere to work in.

I don't know what the foreign players must think of it all. The showers in the training ground are mouldy and grotty, scraped now and again and the odd tile replaced from time to time.

When the kit man went missing for a day, Shirley, who cooks the dinners, loaded up the machines with the muddy shirts and shorts and then went straight to the kitchen to prepare the meals.

The gym is total chaos. While I was recovering from the first broken leg, I was working on one of the bikes. The youngsters were thrashing a ball around when it flew very close to me. I punched it and glared at the young boy who had kicked it my way. His knees wobbled a bit and he looked very miserable. I was cross because I wanted to focus on my recovery. Then, a few days later, I was doing sit-ups when a ball hit me on the head, rolled down my face, down my body and stopped on the other side against the wall. I ignored it and carried on while the boys who had been playing left it. None of them had the courage to come and get it and they eventually left the gym with the ball still lying where it had settled.

It's bedlam but the club has its own identity. It's thoroughly enjoyable to be there despite all the bits and pieces and the ragged edges. The boys just laugh and get on with the job.

There is a young lad named Jimmy, who wanders in when the team are training. One day I walked in to see him running round the gym as fast as his legs would carry him before collapsing in a corner exhausted. A player had wound him up. Can you imagine that happening anywhere else in the Premier Division?

When I arrived I was told that training starts at 10.30 and in my first week I was, as usual, there on time only to find that I was training on my own with a young Bulgarian trialist. I had just changed with all the boys so I knew they were in and, sure enough, they began wandering out ten or 15 minutes later.

That first game against Tottenham was another experience. It was a big game, far bigger than I had realised from a distance, a real London derby for the fans with a lot of rivalry. I had also enjoyed some stirring battles with Spurs over the years and I always liked to beat them.

It was the usual nice warm opening day of the season. I was wondering whether I was fit enough without my usual pre-season build-up, having had just one full game at St Albans for the reserves on the Monday night and then only after Harry left it up to me whether I played or not. I managed the 90 minutes but it was in an easy game and did not stretch me nor test me nearly enough and I still felt that I needed a bit more. Harry once more left it up to me whether I should play in the reserves at Dover on the Wednesday. I played centre-back for 45 minutes and in both games it was a case of building up my fitness.

Then suddenly I was thrust straight into a London derby in front of a new lot of fans, many of whom must have been wondering whether I was too old and past it. The bigger the name you have, the more you have to keep up your standards. You can have ten good games and then one bad one and immediately everyone is saying that you are too old. The one wish is to get through the game without making a fool of yourself, and I hoped that I was up to the pace after only one outing in ten months. There was added pressure because the team had finished a very respectable fifth the year before, so the expectations were quite high.

I need not have worried. We kept a clean sheet and won that opening game 1–0. I was happy with my personal performance and, in fact, we had a very good start. The only problem was that, in attempting a clearance, I cleared out my own man, Ian Pearce, as I tried to tackle David Ginola. Our knees bumped and I put my fellow defender out for the season in the opening game. We immediately had to reshuffle, playing four at the back instead of three with me as a centre-half. I believed that was now my position, just as Terry Venables had predicted a couple of years earlier. As left-back I don't think I could do as good a job as someone younger, defensively perhaps but not charging up and down the line. For that you have to be an athlete in prime condition.

In the four and a half games I played, we won four and drew away 2–2 to Aston Villa. After the Spurs game, we beat Bradford away 3–0, Leicester at home 2–1, and Watford 1–0 when I was injured. Before the Watford game I had the call from England and everything in the garden looked rosy with Harry saying how well I had played to anyone who wanted to listen. He was good like that; if you do well he sticks up for you and shouts about it on television and radio. It was a pleasure to be playing and a pleasure to be giving something back to Harry. Even though I cost nothing in terms of a transfer fee, I still like to be seen earning my wages.

Watford was a funny game for me, full of mixed emotions. Watford manager Graham Taylor had made me England captain, and only six weeks earlier he had knocked me back, not wanting to take a gamble on me. I bore him no grudge. Football and its players are subjective.

I was enjoying the game and just before the tackle I hit the bar from a corner. We had a lot of chances but the score was still goalless ten minutes before half-time. There was a stoppage for an injury and, feeling full of the joys, I picked up a water bottle and sprayed it towards Graham Taylor on the Watford bench where he sat with Kenny Jackett, with whom I used to play Sunday football. Some water landed on Graham's foot and he turned to Kenny and asked him who had done it. Kenny pointed at me, a laughing Stuart Pearce. Ten minutes later I was laughing on the other side of my face, being carted off with a broken leg.

It was ironic; here I was trying to prove to Graham Taylor that he had been wrong not to take a gamble on me and at the same time trying to prove to Harry Redknapp that he was right.

Two minutes before half-time I took a throw-in and the ball came back to me leaving me in a 50-50 situation with Micah Hyde. The pair of us slid in and I heard a slap but I thought it was my shin pad. I wear very thin shin pads, about the size of a saucer. I have never been a lover of the big, thick ones that are in favour nowadays. When I first turned professional, I used those old-fashioned plastic things with strips of cane inserted at intervals. My dad bought them for me and I wore them non-league and also when I turned pro. Eventually I believed they were a good luck omen. In fact, I still have them, along with the pair of boots I wore in that first game for Coventry City. It was only when the old shin pads, stinking with all the liniment that had soaked through, began to fall apart after 12 years or so that I replaced them but kept to the same size.

I was two yards from the touchline when the clash occurred and my leg went numb. The physio came on and my old Forest team-mate Des Lyttle, who was playing right wing-back for Watford, came running up to saying, 'Skipper, Skipper, are you all right?' I was trying to put on a brave face and told the physio that my leg had gone numb. He pulled my sock down and manipulated my leg with a jarring movement and asked me how it was. I began to get a little feeling back and the pain was general rather than specific. I thought that maybe I had just hit a nerve.

One of my pet hates is to suffer an injury and be substituted and then five minutes later discover the pain has worn off, leaving me frustrated realising I could have carried on. Over the years, I have done some pretty silly things to stay on. Once I damaged my knee ligaments and cartilage after 20 minutes and played on until half-time; I did the same in a Mercantile final at Wembley and played on for another ten minutes. But one of the worst was when I was caught by David Campbell in a league game playing for Forest against Charlton. His studs went right through my little shin pads and split the muscle sheath. There was a distinct hole and then a little egg-shaped protrusion appeared. Liam O'Kane, who had run on, was nearly ill when he saw it. 'What the fuck is that?' he said. I didn't know so I just told him to spray some painkiller on it to get me through the last 15 minutes.

This time it was close to half-time and Harry solved the problem by saying to come off and he wouldn't substitute me before half-time. Personal pride dictated that I wouldn't go off on a stretcher, so I lifted myself to my feet and the physio helped me off into the dressing-room where the club doctor was waiting to have a look at the leg. He wriggled the shin a bit and repeated exactly what the physio had said – 'I don't think there's anything broken.'

They iced it for ten minutes and Harry came in for a progress report. I was getting some feeling back so I said I would have a little run. There is not a lot of room at West Ham at the best of times, so I made my way to the tunnel to have a little run before going back on to the pitch. But it hurt like hell and I came back in and told Harry it wasn't going to work; there was too much pain to carry on.

West Ham, by a strange coincidence, had just acquired an X-ray machine and I was the first one to test it. The operative took one look at the plate and said, 'I've a bit of bad news for you. You've broken your shin.' I had broken the tibia but it was a very straight break and wasn't displaced in any way. It was good news, bad news.

I went back into the dressing-room, limped into the shower, changed and telephoned Liz to tell her I had broken my leg. I was able to tell her that there was no need for me to attend hospital because the break was so clean. They gave me a plastic boot and sent me home. Two of the groundsmen played the good Samaritans with one driving me home in my car and the other following behind in his to take his mate back. It was a long way, two hours' drive, but they were happy to make the long journey from East London to Wiltshire.

We must have spent a year looking for the right place to live and received the details of properties in five different counties. We probably looked at a dozen before finding the perfect spot just outside Hungerford, deep in the heart of racing country. We had only been in the house for a couple of weeks and we were up in the air. It was a nightmare for Liz; she had the horses, a young baby and me. I was useless and couldn't even baby-sit because I couldn't climb the stairs to change Chelsea. Liz had to take the whole lot on and she coped magnificently.

But however I looked at it, it was a massive blow. We had started so well, we were unbeaten, playing in Europe, and I felt I was genuinely contributing. The timing was so bad. I could have broken both my legs at Newcastle and no one would have noticed or cared; I would have recovered before they even thought about it!

Fortunately, I am not one of those people who sit about and mope. You put the worst moments behind you and try to come out stronger. It doesn't help to sulk. It was a case of accepting what was done, spending a couple of weeks recuperating and then going onwards and upwards. I told myself that I was recovering and not that I was injured.

If you look at it as a long-term thing, at my age it could have finished me there and then. I have to admit that, at 37, if I hadn't just joined the club I would have been tempted to call it a day and hang up my boots, but I felt that I owed something to Harry and to myself to prove the doubters wrong. I decided instantly to carry on. I thought, 'Sod it, I'll stick around and show people I can play.'

There were three roads open to me – I could come back, break down and pack it in; I could come back and not be the player I once was and pack it in; or I could come back, play as well as I had been and go for England and Euro 2000. There was no doubt which route I wanted to take. But the first priority was to get fit, get back into the West Ham side and play as well as I could. As insurance I also enrolled in a two-week residential coaching course with the Football Association. You never know what is round the corner; I certainly never suspected the twists that awaited me or that there would be a fourth road.

I was pleased with my progress, no one tried to hurry me and I took my time making sure that the leg was right before I made my commitment. I worked extremely hard but it was nigh on five months from the time I did it until the time I was back in the first team. I played a couple of reserve games, took some hard bangs and went in for some strong tackles without any adverse effect. The first game for the reserves was an easy, gentle affair and a case of getting through it. There was not a great deal of tackling and my leg felt fine. The second one was more lively with plenty of tackling. Harry Redknapp watched half the game and told me on the Friday that he didn't feel that I was ready for the first-team game on Saturday. I played by Brian Clough's rules that you are fit or you are not fit without any grey area in between. I told Harry that he was the boss and that whenever he wanted me to play I was ready to do so.

On the Saturday at 1.45 he came up to me and asked me how I felt. I told him the same as I had told him 24 hours before: that I was ready when he was. He told me that he was going to play me against Everton. We were thrashed 4–0 but I don't think that it was down to me and, indeed, after the game Harry picked out Richard Gough and me, two 37-year-olds, as the only two who had performed.

I was gutted that we had been beaten 4–0 but, strange for me, I felt some satisfaction that I had played a full 90 minutes and had played as well as I had five months earlier. We had a game away at Watford, the team I broke my leg against, the next Saturday where we won and I once again came through it without any mishaps.

I was as happy as Larry to think that I had returned so quickly and so well. It was on my mind from then on that I had had a nibble with the England team before Christmas and if I could get a good run of form between February and the end of the season, I might still have a shout for Euro 2000, especially in view of the fact that, with the continued absence of the unlucky Graeme Le Saux, Kevin Keegan was struggling for genuine left-sided players. There was a berth there available and it was up to me. Kevin had kept my interest going when he invited me to join the squad in the February against Argentina. I was pleased to be along.

The next game was on 5 March against Southampton and it was an eventful day one way and another. Just as we were getting ready to go out Harry Redknapp changed me from the left side of a back three to left-back of a flat back four ten minutes before the kick-off. As we trotted out Roger Cross told me that I would be up against Marian

Pahars and to rough him up a bit early on as he wasn't the bravest of players.

Message was received and understood. In the first five minutes, the ball was played to his feet and John Moncur and I arrived at the same time with the Saints player finishing up in a heap as though a ten-ton truck had hit him. I went over to the player to help him up, lifted him up to his full height only for him to fall to the floor again.

The next challenge I went into was with Kevin Davies. I was to the ball before him as I slid in, kicked the ball against his legs and slid onwards clashing with his knee right on the same spot that I had damaged before. I knew immediately that I had a problem. It was either badly bruised or another break. I got to my feet as the ball went for a goal kick. I was hoping that it was just bruised and that I would be able to run it off but it was evident that was not going to happen and I limped off to meet the physios who were jogging round the pitch. I told them it was in exactly the same spot as before and asked if I could have an X-ray. If it was not broken I would carry on. They looked at me as though I was mad and told me that there wasn't time to do that and leave the team playing with ten men. I asked them to hang on to see if I could get some feeling back into it. But it wasn't right and they helped me off the pitch to the dressing-room where I had an immediate X-ray.

It was the same old routine again. They told me they had some bad news for me as they confirmed that I had broken my left leg in the same place. If I was gutted the time before, this time I was shattered. As far as I was concerned at that moment, my career was over, pack it in. How can a player, 38 in two months' time, hope to come back after two broken legs in the same season. I was almost in tears as I sat in the dressing-room feeling sorry for myself. The physios left me alone to my thoughts.

I had treated Liz and her mother to a day at a health farm and she was on her way when I telephoned her to tell her that I had broken my leg again and couldn't look after Chelsea as I had promised.

I am pretty philosophical and strong about most things. Neverthe-less, after five months' hard work I was very depressed, but when I woke up a few days later I was totally comfortable about the whole thing and prepared to accept whatever fate held for me. Harry telephoned and helped me a lot by telling me that if I could get fit, they would love to have me at the club for another year. That was a great confidence booster and gave me a target. Two mornings later, I had a telephone call from Kevin Keegan who was also very encouraging.

At first I accepted that I wouldn't play again but the leg healed much better this time around and after a couple of months there was no pain at all. There are two lines of thought from the medics. The first is that the leg wasn't healed properly or that I was just unlucky to have such a heavy blow on the same point again. I had been in much harder tackles before the break and they were unhappy to work on the luck theory so we have to assume that, despite how good I felt, I came back before it had healed 100 per cent.

I popped into West Ham every now and again but they let me work on my fitness at Newbury Racecourse in their gymnasium and every two weeks I went to a rehabilitation centre in Manchester for two days where they have a water flume. It is about ten feet long by five or six feet wide and you run against a current of water with the inverted sides allowing you to bound from side to side in the current. I was the first from Upton Park to use it but several of our players with bad injuries have followed me. I was quite happy to be used as a guinea pig.

I was determined to try my damnedest and give it a go while being prepared to call it a day if the leg let me down medically. I really wanted to get fit and give West Ham the season I was unable to give them when they signed me from Newcastle. Harry and the chairman agreed that they wanted to keep me on. I told him that I wasn't concerned about contracts or money at that stage and it was Harry himself who suggested that I sign a month-by-month contract until I had proved my fitness to myself at which time he would offer me a proper contract. I had a doctor's appointment on 12 June when he gave me the all-clear to begin running again and I really felt I was making progress.

One thing I did was throw away my tiny shin pads and replace them with a pair specially made for me at Lilleshall. I was away with

the England Under-18 squad and their manager Martin Hunter mentioned that a couple of the youngsters had their shin pads tailor made
for them.

Kevin Keegan kindly invited me to join the squad for the European
Championship but once I had decided to try to play again the next
season, I felt ethically bound to decline, particularly as the club had
already given me permission to do my two weeks coaching badge
course at Lilleshall in the summer for my A licence.

I would like to dedicate my last season to Harry and West Ham for
the way they have stood by me when they had no need to, and to Kevin
Keegan for his support.

Even after the first break, I had a couple of telephone calls asking
me what my plans were, with the clear indication that someone,
somewhere was thinking of me for a job in management or coaching. I
had a good idea about the identity of one of the clubs but not a clue
who the other caller represented.

In an ideal world I would rather play for as long as I can but if I am
not doing myself credit or not maintaining the standards I have set
myself, I'll stop. I wouldn't like to be taking wages and not be giving
something in return. It has irritated me that I have not been able to do
myself justice and earn my wages since joining West Ham.

If I had been offered a two-year contract at the start I would have
refused because I needed to prove to myself that I could do it and if I
couldn't I would not have enjoyed taking money for not doing the job.
Even with broken legs I feel a bit guilty about being paid but then I
think that I suffered the injuries in service with the club and they are
physical injuries, not an old man's complaint like rheumatoid arthritis.

Throughout, Harry Redknapp has maintained contact and given
me unstinting support. I have talked to him more than any other
manager. He has involved me at games and talked to me about
decisions. Against Aston Villa he came over at half-time and said that
Rio Ferdinand thought Paul Merson was getting too much space and
hurting us. I couldn't see that; Merse was picking up the ball but as
long as we were shutting him down before he could shoot he wasn't
damaging us. Harry agreed and told me to go and tell Rio. I enjoyed

the experience and it showed that Harry had confidence in me.

Once I was mobile I offered to watch players or clubs if he wanted me to. He took it in the spirit in which it was offered. Harry has done an excellent job and has so many good young players coming through that the future looks extremely bright at Upton Park. The one they were all talking about when I arrived was the young midfield play-maker Joe Cole. I played a couple of reserve matches with him when I joined and appreciated that he looked good but I wondered whether he influenced the game enough. Harry held him back, held him back and then gave him a run and he looked superb. He has built himself up and is now very strong and can fight his corner with the strongest. How unfortunate he was to break his leg towards the end of April after a dreadful tackle by Derby's Rory Delap. He might not have made the full England squad for the summer but was a certain starter in the Under-21 Championship finals.

I thought a lot of the publicity over young Cole was hype, but it wasn't. He is an outstanding prospect and what is more he is not alone. There are plenty of others at Upton Park who have caught my eye, especially Michael Carrick, another midfielder, but a different sort of player from Joe. Joe has all the circus tricks and silky skills while Carrick is a two-footed passer, tall, comfortable on both feet and in the style of a young Glenn Hoddle.

I have just a small window on a young player's life but personally I have no doubt that Joe Cole will go on to the full England squad. His natural flair is probably on a par with Paul Gascoigne's, complete with party tricks, and, like Gazza, he is not afraid to put his foot in when it is needed. Skill and forcefulness don't usually mix but with Joe they do. He doesn't, however, have that electric pace that Gazza had before he injured himself against Nottingham Forest, and also I cannot see him scoring as many goals. He is not an out-and-out natural striker.

Joe is making steady progress. People in the game were trying to rush him too quickly; they were talking about him playing for England before he had made his full debut for West Ham. That was ridiculous and unfair. He should have at least 100 club games before that happens.

You have to have a good head on your shoulders to cope with that sort of hype and fortunately he has. Most of all, he wants to learn and do well. He will train and train and train, come in and say that his knee feels a bit dickey but then go back out again after training to practise shooting. I keep wanting to tell him to take it easy, that there is a long career ahead, to train well but don't do extra. The games will take care of the fitness and on days off I advise him to put his feet up and rest. He is like a young kid; he wants to go and play all the time. But Harry is keeping a careful eye on him, giving him a run and then pulling him out. Joe won't like it but, in the long run, it will help his game and his future.

When you have a Michael Owen or a Joe Cole in your ranks it is very difficult to leave them out. It is easy to forget how young these gems are. You have to look after them and nurture them. The trouble is that the pressure is on managers to achieve results now, so what's the point of holding them back and leaving the benefits for someone else or risking the player moving on at the end of his contract?

It's great to see so many good young English players around. I have no doubt that Joe will make it to the England squad but it is impossible to tell what he is going to achieve. In any youth team, if you can see one or two coming through you have done well but West Ham seem to have a few more than that after their Youth Cup victory in 1999.

Rio Ferdinand is still a young man. When I joined the club, obviously I wanted to play well myself but I also wanted to help those around me, especially Rio. He is a very good player whose raw ability is wonderful. We do one-on-ones in training and he is unbeatable. No one can take him on, he's that good. But where he falls down is that he suffers the occasional lapse of concentration. When you are as good as he is, you can switch off because you have confidence that your pace and skill will get you out of trouble. But, at the top level, that's the very moment when you become vulnerable yourself. Harry said to me straightaway that he thought I could help Rio, simply by keeping at him all the time and making him concentrate, not bullying him exactly but shaking the fist in encouragement when backs are against the wall.

Rio has all the attributes and if he adds concentration to his natural ability he will be a phenomenal player. With his talent he should have been a regular with England for a while but he won't be until he is complete across the spectrum and able to apply himself for the full 90 minutes. The higher he goes the more important it is, as I found out to my cost against Brazil.

West Ham are a very quiet team with not too many natural leaders, something many top teams in the country are missing at the moment. There are very few Tony Adams around and every manager wants one. If I can get back and help Rio then Rio can help me with his young legs.

Harry told me when I arrived that he felt he had the best squad he has ever had and I am impressed. If I were a manager, I would sign Trevor Sinclair tomorrow because he has skills as a winger and will battle back for you. What more can you want from a player? Paolo di Canio will flit in and out of games but he has the talent to turn or win a match. Joe Cole can only improve with age while Shaka Hislop, another broken-leg victim, was playing as well as any goalkeeper in the country before he was injured. It is an exciting team to be involved with and I am not ready to call it a day yet.

When I finally stop playing, I don't want to look back and just be an old footballer; I want to look forward as a young coach or manager.

CHAPTER 11

that's entertainment

One of my biggest problems has always been to interest other players in punk music, to the point of joining me at concerts or listening to my music in the dressing-room before a game. Fortunately, being the club captain for so long gave me that little bit of authority that, on occasions, I was not afraid to use. Eventually at Forest, I succeeded with a handful of people although I suspect that the crates of lager I brought along were a bigger attraction than some of the bands. We used to load the lager on the borrowed team bus and pay the groundsman to drive us to and from the designated venue.

We would not have gone at all unless I organised everything. I used to buy the music papers to see who was on and if I spotted a band such as Spear of Destiny performing locally I knew that a few would come, most of them for the beer. It certainly wasn't for the girls. Punks used to come up and say it was good to see us there and that I was one of them. I didn't argue. I just liked the music and as far as I was concerned it was 'our' music not 'their' music.

There must have been around eight of us who went to see the Stranglers at Leicester University, taking advantage of an invitation to go backstage after the concert. We enjoyed a few drinks with the band and everyone was quite relaxed, so relaxed in fact that one of the band was on the old wacky baccy and demonstrating the best way to gain full benefit from smoking it to one of the young players. Fortunately, none of the Forest lads followed his advice or example.

Eventually the band excused themselves to load up their gear on the gig bus ready to move on to the next venue. Some of our lads were a bit disappointed because it was all so tame and they had expected action after hearing how these wild groups smashed up their dressing-rooms after a gig. So I said, tongue in cheek, 'Do you mind if we trash the room?'

'No,' one of them replied. 'Trash away, boys, trash away. Have this one on us.'

To be honest, you would do well to trash Leicester University dressing-rooms when they have had bands on. It could only be an improvement.

The first music I was into as a youngster was David Bowie's but it was not long before the punk thing happened in 1976–77 and that was when I really fell in love with music. I wouldn't say I threw myself into the punk culture body and soul – I drew the line at the spiky hair and the other outrageous symbols – but I lived and breathed the music and never missed an opportunity to go to listen to the bands. I suppose I was a bit of a closet punk.

It was a great release and alternative entertainment. It happened at the right time for me. I used to go to concerts straight from school, catching the number 52 bus to the West End for the Marquee Club or the Music Machine (now called the Camden Palace) and then ducking home early because of school next day. Three or four of us would go together to the gigs. It was the times as well as the music. Some of the bands have stood the test of time but a lot fell by the wayside. The times have changed and music with it.

One of the first times I went to see Stiff Little Fingers, a top punk band from Belfast and one of my favourites, was at Acklam Hall in Ladbroke Grove, a small room under the flyover. The stage was only a few inches high and at the end of the concert I asked the drummer if I could have one of his drumsticks. As a young kid, I was made up when he gave one to me and I have to confess that I still have that drumstick now.

Another concert I went to was the Damned at the Rainbow. They didn't come on stage until nearly midnight and by then a sea of punks were breaking up chairs and throwing them on the stage. The band arrived without the lead singer and the audience blew up. It was mayhem but, strangely, there was never any violence directed against each other. The singer came on and started picking up all the bits of chairs and lobbing them back into the crowd. The atmosphere was electric – you just had to avoid the flying chair legs.

I still go to see the same bands all these years later but the difference is that now I know most of them as friends. I have been to see the Stranglers pushing 40 times – they even named a record label after me, Psycho Records – and a hell of a lot of other bands as well. I have travelled all over the country to see concerts, just jumping in my car and going. I always telephone the venue to ask what time the main band are on and arrive five minutes before they start and stand at the back. No one fusses you and I am away as soon as it finishes.

We all seem to have grown up together; the bands and fans are the same age as me, pushing 40 or more, and still enjoying the music even if they aren't breaking up the furniture any more.

Jake Burns, the lead singer with Stiff Little Fingers, is a Newcastle United season-ticket holder. When I signed for Newcastle he was delighted and we met up regularly after matches when I was at St James' Park. Nowadays all of these angry young men have gone through the rebellious stage when they shocked people and are normal members of society; after all, the drummer of the Stranglers is over 60! I appeared on *TFI Friday* a few years ago and a guy came up and introduced himself as Manic Esso, the drummer from the Lurkers. We chatted and I discovered that he was doing a lot of work for kids and the disabled.

Every Christmas, all the old school friends and their wives and girlfriends have a get-together. One year we decided on Bath as a venue. A big punk festival was being held at Bath Pavilion, and Stiff Little Fingers were staying at the same hotel as us. I told Liz that we were meeting Jake and she was expecting some giant with a Mohican haircut and a nappy pin through his nose. She was stunned when he appeared sporting a little shaggy perm and wearing a flowery shirt and glasses.

Music remains a terrific release from what I do. I enjoy indie music, I still like Bowie, but it's mainly punk that stirs the blood.

I also went (and still go) to see some of the new up-and-coming bands, including Oasis when they first started off and another band called Green Day. They were excellent. The atmosphere was vibrant; they were all so much younger. It was the same sort of feeling I had when punk emerged on the scene. It was also good to go to a concert that was packed because, to be honest, the punk concerts aren't that crowded these days. I stood there giggling because all I could see were Doc Martens boots going overhead as they passed people down to the front and with the students jumping around like idiots and diving off the stage it took me back to my early days at concerts. There are pictures to prove it – I feature on an album cover of the Lurkers, standing in the audience.

I was on the young end of punk music so I didn't get involved in the drugs or booze. The high for us at our age was going to the concert and getting home in one piece. The biggest danger was not so much avoiding the drug culture but the teddy boys and the football hooligans who were looking for sport at our expense. There was violence between the punks and rockers but rarely at the concert venues.

Once I wore my Lurkers jean jacket to a Lurkers/Adam Ant concert, totally unaware of the friction between the two groups of fans until I was hit over the head with a lump of wood. I turned round and there was a group of skinheads leering at me. I immediately apologised for putting my head in the way of their piece of wood, hoped I hadn't damaged it and made a hasty exit. That was the only violence I have ever personally experienced. In the main it was a good-natured fun.

Punks were mostly white males with very few women other than the out-and-out punks, but there were also a lot like me who were just there to listen to the music.

Although I didn't look for a punk barber or stick bits of metal through my nose and ears, I tried to dress the part. Johnny Fingers, the keyboard player of the Boom Town Rats, always wore pyjamas on stage so I took my pyjama top to have Johnny Fingers and the Vibrators screen-printed on the back. God knows what my father thought about me going out to a concert wearing my pyjamas.

I used to have things like bath plugs or toilet chains pinned to my gear or wrapped around my neck. My little mate would sidle up to me and whisper in my ear, 'My snout in the punk world says that bath plugs are in.' In fact, his snout seemed to think everything I wore was 'in'. I also sewed zips into my white Dunlop plimsolls.

The Stranglers had an air of menace about them that made them even more appealing. I recently took my brother Dennis to the Shepherds Bush Empire to watch them. He had never seen them before but knew their records. As they played each song, my mate and I would tell him the background to the track, like it being made after the nuclear tests in Australia ('Nuclear Device') or after they were arrested in France ('Nice in Nice'). He was amazed at how much I knew about them. They still have a close-knit, cult following.

I found them an even more fascinating group of guys when I got to know them. Bass player JJ, for instance, has a black-belt in karate and fights around the world, while the keyboard player Dave Greenfield is into the occult and black magic. Jet Black, the drummer, founded the group, touring in his ice-cream van. He is mean and moody and if you stand in the way of him and his food he is likely to bite your leg off.

The early eighties were a barren spell for me in terms of music so I didn't go to a lot of concerts, but in the late eighties punk made a comeback along with groups such as Carter and one or two others. They rekindled my spirit. Of the modern bands, I enjoy Oasis and those with a cutting edge such as the Levellers. Liz is not into my sort of music. In fact, she's hard work to take to listen to punk music.

When I first joined Forest, I wrote an article about my likes and dislikes and one of the things I mentioned was my love of punk music. It prompted a guy named Kieron Egan to write to me and send me an album of his band called Resistance 77. He lived in Derbyshire and was a Forest season-ticket holder. I listened and while the music was a bit raw it wasn't at all bad. I even went to see his band in a miners welfare club in Derbyshire. As a result we got to know each other. I went to watch his band several times and he came with me to listen to other groups, which was good because it was becoming increasingly difficult to find someone who enjoyed the same music as me.

As I have matured my tastes have broadened. I am ashamed to

admit that I never read a book until my thirties. That is both sad and a crime. I was never a good reader and when it takes you months to plough through a book it takes some of the shine off it. Now I go from one book to another. I enjoy thrillers with a twist, *Silence of the Lambs* is one, and Sherlock Holmes stories. From there, I went to Oscar Wilde's *Picture of Dorien Gray*. I really enjoyed it and it encouraged me to experiment. I've tried such diverse authors as Patricia Cornwell and Tolstoy. It still takes me a long time to read a book. I might read ten pages on the train or in bed and then put it down for a week, but I'm enjoying it.

I have also fallen in love with the theatre, often going on my own. I have thrown myself into Shakespeare; I couldn't believe how good it was on stage. The Royal Shakespeare Company has a sell-out season in Newcastle every year and that was where I discovered the Bard's work. I used to telephone Neil Webb's wife Shelley, quite a learned and well-read girl, and she used to advise me on what to go and see. I loved it. I couldn't believe how good it all was. I really enjoyed Leslie Phillips in the *Merry Wives of Windsor*. I started with the lighter stuff first and graduated to the history plays.

One wet Wednesday afternoon, I had the choice of sitting in my flat on my own or going to the theatre so I went to see *South Pacific*. What I hadn't realised was that I would be the youngest there by about 50 years. It was half price for pensioners and it was more like the Derby and Joan club and almost totally sold out.

The theatre manager found me a ticket that he had been keeping back, one of seven near the front of the dress circle. The auditorium was full except for the six empty seats next to me and I stood out like a sore thumb.

I wanted to keep my head down and I was grateful when the lights eventually went down and the production started. All went well for about half an hour when one of the old dears suddenly stood up and started to move down her row. I thought what a time to go to the toilet. She climbed two steps and then collapsed at my feet. I had been uncharitable. She had been feeling faint and had struggled up to get some air.

Immediately all eyes turned in our direction. I didn't know what to do. I froze. Here I was wanting a quiet afternoon and there was this woman lying at my feet. Even the players on the stage were aware something had happened although, like good troopers, they carried on. Then a man ran down the stairs saying he was a doctor while others came to her aid. All of this was going on right around me. The usherette came down the aisle and said that we would have to move her, as she was a hazard. Three men picked up a limb each while a woman tried to lift the other leg. She was struggling.

I was sitting there saying to myself, 'Do something. Get up you effing idiot and help.' Eventually, I jumped up and relieved the struggling lady and between the four of us we carried this old dear up the aisle with the entire theatre watching the wrong performance. We took her outside into the foyer and I returned to my seat feeling more conspicuous than ever. I checked up with the manager later to make sure she was all right. It transpired she had suffered a heart murmur and had to be taken off to hospital but, thankfully, she was comfortable and on the road to a full recovery.

She was certainly in better shape than the theatre manager who had had a really bad day, having thrown out a drunk earlier who then came back and hit an usherette. I couldn't believe it – a matinee and all that excitement.

If I have a choice of doing something or slobbing about, I would rather be active. I remember going to Australia, New Zealand and Malaysia with an England team under Graham Taylor. When we were in Auckland we noticed that *Les Misérables* was showing at the theatre literally over the road from our hotel. We had a night off and Graham asked if any of us wanted to attend. I was one of only four players to respond. Nigel Clough, goalkeeper Tony Coton, defender Keith Curle and I made our way over the road but within five minutes Curle was up and off followed five minutes later by TC who announced to the rest of the audience that he was going for a beer. Nigel and I stayed and really enjoyed the show; in fact, it was so good that I'll remember it for the rest of my life. But the rest of the squad are not going to remember going to a wine bar in Auckland.

I would rather go to a theatre or a concert than to a bar. For a start, it's better for you to sit and relax rather than stand in a smoky wine bar when you are on tour or away for a match. That may sound hypocritical but even when I was playing non-league football and all my mates were down the local on Friday, Saturday and Sunday nights, latterly I would have a couple of orange juices to keep them company on Friday and then go home to rest. The alternative was to go to Wembley dogs either on my own or with a pal to break the monotony.

Football came first and because of my attitude I had my chance as a professional. There were so many players in the teams I played for on my way up who were better than me but they didn't go on to make it. A large dose of professionalism and, of course, a little bit of luck like being spotted when you are playing well, always help!

CHAPTER 12

the nearly man

Liz calls me the nearly man and if I browse through just my England career, never mind lost semi-finals and finals at club level, I can see exactly what she means.

- I was injured playing for England when earning my fifth cap against Hungary. As a result I missed the European Championship in Germany in the summer of 1988. It was all very innocuous. I went to push off on my back foot and immediately felt a very bad pain in my knee. I carried on playing and every time I struck the ball normally there was no problem but when I sidefooted it I suffered a severe reaction. At half-time I told the doctor what was happening and it was discovered that I had pulled my cartilage away from the bone and damaged my ligaments.
- I missed the crucial penalty against Germany in the World Cup semi-finals when we were on the brink of winning the biggest trophy of them all.
- For the next European Championship in 1992 we were half a game away from qualifying.
- Having reached the semi-finals of the World Cup four years earlier, we failed to reach even the finals in 1994. What made it worse was that I was captain and missed five months of that campaign through a groin injury, including the games against Norway and Holland home and away and San Marino at home. We had started that campaign really well but when I came back I didn't recognise the squad after a trip to America had drained the confidence. To add a

touch of farce, the nearly man gave away a ten-second goal against San Marino in Bologna in the last game.

- We went on to the 1996 European Championship when the Germans turned us over again on penalties when we were just beginning to fancy ourselves to win the title at home.
- I missed out on the 1998 World Cup squad for France when Glenn Hoddle rang me up after I had been out with a hamstring injury to tell me that I was too old, even though I was the same age as Ian Wright who had also missed a chunk of the season with an injury. The only difference was that I had played five months' solid football leading up to it and he hadn't!
- After being brought back by Kevin Keegan for the Euro 2000 campaign, I broke my leg not once but twice.

That's how nearly I am. There seems to be an awful lot of pitfalls scattered through my 78-cap international career interspersed with a few highs. But back to the beginning.

I remember my name being projected for my first England cap back in the spring of 1987 when the regular left-back Kenny Sansom was scheduled to have an operation that summer. I had long lined up behind Kenny who, previously, had appeared to be impervious to injury. Throughout the eighties I couldn't remember him missing a single squad get-together. But now he had a problem and I was being seen as a possible successor, even though I had not been in a squad at that stage. Being the person I was, I totally ignored the rumours and speculation.

The call-up finally came for a competition called the Rous Cup, named after the famous English administrator Sir Stanley Rous. The games were against Brazil and Scotland, a mouth-watering prospect against the best side in the world and England's oldest enemy.

I first heard about it when I was away with Forest on a close-season tour in Bulgaria. We were sitting around a swimming pool when a couple of the local Nottingham journalists who were with us came over and told me I was in the squad. The other players heard and came over to congratulate me. All I wanted was a bit of privacy with Liz. I just wanted to scream and shout because I was so thrilled, but I couldn't in front of the other players and their wives. I just had to sit there and pretend it was water off a duck's back, which I did until I reached the privacy of my room.

The nearest I had come before that was to play for the Under 21s as a permitted average player – I was 25 – against Yugoslavia the previous November. Bobby Robson picked me but Dave Sexton was in charge of the game, which was played at Peterborough. It was home from home; Des Walker, Nigel Clough and Franz Carr were also in the squad. I had a decent run out. It was obviously enough to keep my name in front of the manager.

I was thrilled to be picked for the Under 21s and went looking for Liz in a restaurant where she was working to tell her about it. She looked doubtful.

'But you're over 21,' she said.

'I know, I know,' I responded, 'That's just a technicality. The important thing is that I'm going to play for an England side.' She still seemed highly doubtful.

I was even more excited about being picked for the full squad. Think about it. We are talking about a boy who, five years earlier, was an electrician with Brent council watching players like Glenn Hoddle, Bryan Robson and Peter Shilton – my boyhood heroes, the demigods of English football. All right I was playing against them week in and week out by then but when I sat down for dinner with them the first time I looked on them with different eyes.

I once walked behind Bryan Robson at an airport coming back from Hungary and was in awe of his stature and presence. Whether that was just in my own mind or whether he has that aura I don't know, but he was the only player who was consistent in the eighties and one of the few who came back from the disastrous European Championship in 1988 with his reputation still intact.

I had so much respect for the England captain at that time. He was Manchester United's and England's best player and headlines game after game talked about 'Captain Marvel'. He scored goals at one end and cleared them off his own line at the other. When you played in the

Watch it! I tell Dutch defender Michael Reiziger exactly what I think of his attempted tackle during our 4–1 Euro 96 win over Holland. (*Popperfoto*)

Commitment: making sure I'm first to the ball whatever the cost in a tussle with Alfonso during the Euro 96 quarter-final against Spain.

Exorcising the ghosts: scoring our third penalty in the shoot-out against Spain and appreciating the positive side of spot kicks. (*Colorsport*)

Take three: Chris Waddle, Gareth Southgate and me in the Pizza Hut television advert which made light of our penalty misses. (*Pizza Hut/AMV.BBDO Ltd*)

Good evening, ma'am: I have the privilege of being introduced to Her Majesty the Queen as rower Matthew Pinsent and heavyweight boxer Lennox Lewis look on.

Treasure trove: a life's work and reward spread in front of me.

Late kick-off: marrying Liz in Nottingham in 1993 after a nine-year courtship.

A golden couple: my parents celebrate 50 years of marriage.

A special medal: enjoying my investiture as a Member of the British Empire at Buckingham Palace with my wife Liz and daughter Chelsea in March 1999. (*Charles Green*)

How it might have been: memories of my interview with the Army as I pay a social visit to the Sherwood TA in Nottingham.

Growing old gracefully: two ageing punk rockers, with myself on guitar and Stiff Little Fingers lead singer and Newcastle United season-ticket holder Jake Burns, backstage after a gig.

What a load of rubbish: how did I walk out of this? The garbage truck writes off my sponsored Rover as I crawl out of the passenger side unscathed.

Horsing around: Liz and me with mare Goose Green, yearling Key Witness and two-year-old Crystalline.

Sport of Kings: Man of the Match ridden by Rodney Farrant at Uttoxeter, finishing third, trained by Jenny Pitman. (*Colin Turner*)

Home life: Liz, Chelsea and me outside our house in the Wiltshire countryside, which ensures that Liz's horses have plenty of fields to run in. (*John Davies*)

Taken for a ride: Chelsea still relies on mum and dad to give her a push. (*John Davies*)

Teaching Chelsea: helping my daughter with her books – she isn't yet quite ready to help me with mine! (*John Davies*)

same team as him and he shouted at you to get tight on your man, you would want to do it for him because you didn't want to let him down. That's a mark of a good captain. You upped your standards because he demanded it of you. He talked sparingly on the pitch but led massively by example. Sometimes you can just look at someone and respect them, him more than most.

I also came to respect Terry Butcher and Tony Adams. I remember Big Butch facing a nippy little forward, not the sort a big man wants to mark, but he wouldn't hear of anyone else taking the job on, snapping, 'I've got him – just make sure you've got your man.' That's the sort of defender you want to work alongside, someone who will never hide or shirk. Those are the players I want in my side, big personalities who play for years and years to the highest standard.

Butch was a great motivator and he would start to wind it up in the tunnel when we were standing next to the opposition. He would be shouting things like, 'Come on, come on, we're England,' and 'Remember the three lions.' He wore it on his sleeve. Fans will never forget when he split his head against Sweden in Stockholm and played on with 16 stitches, a blood-soaked bandage wrapped round his head like a turban. Wild horses wouldn't have dragged him off. He was a strong man and a strong captain, like Bryan Robson.

Peter Shilton was another strong character in his own way. He had a one-track mind on the pitch and that was not to concede a goal. He was obsessed with keeping clean sheets. He was so protective of his goal that he would set up walls if someone were trying to shoot from 100 yards! Peter is a complex man but look at his record and see how many clean sheets he kept for England.

I suppose I was a little awestruck and wondering whether I was good enough to be in this exalted company. That was when Brian Clough called me into his office and told me he didn't think I was good enough to play for my country. It was a good job I wasn't the nervous type or I might have jacked it in there and then. I suppose every player harbours doubts over his ability to make that giant stride from club to international football and I was no different. I had no idea whether I could or not. But as far as I was concerned, if I was going to make my debut what better match than against Brazil in front of a full house of 92,000 at Wembley.

In those days, players could afford to be a touch reckless in their tackling. Nowadays, of course, you cannot get away with it and Bobby Robson showed great faith in me when many of the critics were casting doubts on my temperament and ability to stay on the field for 90 minutes in an international without being shown the red card. In a normal league game against someone of the quality of Pat Nevin, I would rattle him as quickly as I could. Within the first five minutes I would get as close to him as I could, upend him and leave a bit on him in the hope that it would quieten him down for the remaining 85 minutes. More often than not, I would have a lecture and warning from the referee but I would carry on being robust as it was part of my game, only calming it down if I received a yellow card. I would deal with it on its own merits. My record of three sendings off in 17 years of professional football is testament to the fact that I do have some brains and it's not all brawn. I was prepared to rough my opponent up until I received a caution and then it would change. It was no good for the team or for me if I spent part of the match watching from the tunnel because I'd been sent off.

I was sent off for two bad tackles against Leicester in a League Cup game in 1989, for accidentally elbowing Trevor Sinclair when I was playing for Newcastle against West Ham, which didn't deserve a red card, and the third time was for swearing. Paul Stewart of Spurs had upended Roy Keane with 90 minutes gone. Young Keane, who had taken a battering, was lying on the ground and the referee delivered a mild rebuke. I was incensed and let him know in no uncertain terms. He sent me straight off.

The consequence of my aggressive play was the speculation about whether I would let down my country if I were to be picked. Some people were quite strongly against the manager selecting me at all. Mike Langley at the *People* led a vociferous campaign against my selection. I went on to make 78 caps and, in my humble opinion, I do not believe I ever let England down either on or off the pitch. Sometimes it's better to give someone a chance to prove themselves rather than trying to stifle their international career before it has started. Incidentally, no one has ever written that they were wrong about me!

Bobby Robson ignored the entire clamour and picked me. It was a nice, warm May day for my debut as the 999th player to be picked for England and I quickly learned a bitter and valuable lesson in that first game. We had gone a goal up and I had played an early part in it by winning a defensive header. Tony Adams came over to me and congratulated me for my small part but about three minutes later, when I was feeling quite pleased with myself, the winger Muller drifted across me, spun inside, received the ball and crossed for Mirandinha to score. I remember Bobby pulling me aside at half-time and telling me to concentrate at all times. He said that I had missed my man and he was right. The lesson was the higher you go, the harder you must concentrate. I was thinking I had Muller but he made the run before that ball was on its way and by the time I realised he had reached the by-line and made his cross.

We drew 1–1 against a good Brazilian side and didn't play too badly. I was happy to come through it with only the one black mark against me. My philosophy from that game onwards was that if I played well it would be worth two caps, one for the game I played in and the next because I would keep my place. I roomed with Des Walker for many of my England games and we would always say to each other before the games, 'Come on, good game today. Two more caps.'

I kept my place against Scotland and we drew 0–0. Two games, two caps, two draws and when I think back it couldn't have been a tougher baptism. They don't come much bigger than those two.

England versus Scotland is a massive game at any time. I was gutted not to be involved when we played them twice in the Euro 2000, qualifier.

I must have impressed Bobby Robson in those first two games because I was in the squad after that, albeit as Kenny Sansom's understudy. I learned a lot from Kenny even though we were such contrasting players in the same position. I often wondered whether

Kenny remembered the time when my manager at Wealdstone embarrassed me at the PFA dinner by telling him I would take his place. He was a better player than me, cultured, stayed on his feet, and passed the ball well. He was the neatest winner of tackles I have ever seen. He did all the things well that Clough told me I couldn't do.

Basically, I stayed in the squad from 1987, picking up the odd cap when Kenny was out, and I learned my international trade.

My next appearance was early the next season, this time as a substitute against West Germany! All the big ones first. Talk about a baptism of fire.

The game was in Dusseldorf. We were losing with about ten minutes to go when Bobby Robson, who was known to get the odd name wrong in his time, started shouting down the bench, 'Gary, Gary, get warmed up.' I knew he was talking to me but I thought no, I'm not going to look at him, I'm going to wait until he gets my name right. Then I thought if I don't look up in a minute I'm not going to get on at all. My philosophy thereafter was no matter what name he shouted I would jump up and start warming up, even if he shouted Glenn.

That game passed me by. When I looked for a pass or looked down to play the ball, by the time I looked up again a German had moved from there to there and intercepted it. It was all that much quicker – not just speed of foot but speed of thought. You start to think that the quality and the speed are beyond you, but it's a case of getting used to it. Bobby Robson's yardstick was that after a dozen international games a player should be playing to his standard. I thought that was about right.

Bobby had been around for a while and was comfortable in the job despite an immense amount of pressure from the media. He had his old England team-mate Don Howe working on the defence. Don was an out-and-out defender; he loved a clean sheet every bit as much as Shilton. He would take the defenders away from the others and there would be a few moans and groans and we watched the rest go off for a five-a-side or crossing and shooting. We would be in the penalty area with Don. 'Swivel your head,' he'd shout, 'Get your head round,' 'Get your head on it,' 'Go and win it.' Rodders (Tony Adams), Big Butch

(Terry Butcher), me and the other central defenders would come off with headaches while the others had been enjoying a jolly-up.

But, when all was said and done, Don drummed it into every defender what it meant at this level. That was where I really started learning my trade, going from being a club player with potential to having Nottingham Forest and England after my name.

I managed to fit in two more games after West Germany, playing against Israel and Hungary and it was in Budapest that I damaged my knee. Silly really, just pushing off to run and slipping on the grass after 15 minutes. The doctor pulled me off at half-time, strapped me up and I went straight back home to have an operation.

That was me finished for a while. I missed the disastrous 1988 European Championship in Germany. I would have gone as understudy to Kenny but would almost certainly have had a game against Russia when we were already out and Bobby Robson made a number of changes. It was a massive disappointment. Even if I hadn't been playing I would have willingly gone and sat on the bench for every match because there are only 22 people selected out of the entire country. I was just proud to be in the squad.

I watched the tournament on television and, like all England supporters, I was disappointed that we did not play to our potential because of injuries and illness. It proved to be something of a watershed. Kenny and a few others retired from the scene, giving players like me the chance to establish ourselves in the side.

We had qualified well for 1988, building up high hopes. We qualified quite well, too, for the next World Cup two years later. In fact, in the eight years that Bobby was in charge, he lost only one qualifying match in both competitions and none while I was in the squad.

Paul Gascoigne was breaking into the squad and there were some good established players. Gary Lineker was scoring a phenomenal number of goals. Peter Beardsley was there and Clive Allen, Mark Hateley, Chris Waddle, John Barnes, Shilton, who had been around for a million years, and Big Butch at the back. Captain Marvel Robson was still in midfield along with Ray Wilkins, another of my heroes whom I had watched and admired when I was a non-league player. The closest I had come to him before was playing with his brother Dean in the district side when I was at school.

It was a big, big tournament but I had more than a dozen caps under my belt by then and was one of the seasoned players. In fact, by the time of the 1990 World Cup I had a couple of dozen and had not missed a match since I became a regular in Bobby Robson's team. Tony Dorigo was coming along, pushing me. He was an outstanding player and he deserved more caps than he won. I was glad he didn't get them because they would have been at my expense. That big, strong player Mitchell Thomas was coming through too, so there was plenty of pressure and I was always looking over my shoulder. My personal adage of playing for two caps at a time was never more appropriate.

Leading up to the World Cup, some journalists were still saying that I was too fiery and too aggressive for a competition of this nature and intensity. They were sure that I would land myself in trouble and cost England. It reached something of a crescendo after we had played a friendly against Yugoslavia at Wembley in December 1989. They had quite a talented young midfield player who was playing really well and I felt that I had to sort him out a bit. I caught him just in front of the trainer's bench on the halfway line. It was a ridiculously late challenge and I did clear him out totally but I didn't do it just for the sake of kicking him. He was dictating the game and I wanted to give him a jolt and upset his rhythm. There are those who will say it was a disgraceful thing to do, but there was method in my madness because he was threatening to tear England apart. I was booked and later substituted by Dorigo. After the game, I took a lot of criticism from the media. But, as at club level, I stepped up to a certain mark and tried not to step over it. Once I had been booked, I settled down. There were, and still are, others who didn't; they continued to play at the same intensity and paid the penalty.

There seemed to be a glut of fairly wild left-backs around at the time – the big Scot Doug Rougvie, Pat Van Den Hauwe, Julian Dicks, Mark Dennis – and I was slung into that category. They were players who liked to leave their mark. I admit that I pressed it to a certain level to make my job easier. If opponents were scared of me so much the better. I would do it coldly and deliberately; emotion didn't come into it. Others maybe didn't have that strategy.

I learned from an early stage and being sent off at Leicester probably did me a lot of good. Clough made it clear that I had let down both the team and myself. You either learn your lessons quickly and move on or you end up sinking. I have never had any manager tell me to kick anyone directly but when I first started off it was a known thing that you went as tight as you could and made life as unpleasant for your forward opponent as you could.

In my first season at Coventry City, Bobby Gould asked Terry Gibson before a game against Spurs whom he would rather play against, Graham Roberts or Paul Miller. When Gibson told him Miller, Gould asked why and he told him because Roberts would give him a bigger kicking. I rest my case. If someone doesn't like it, do it some more. If they enjoy it, you have to change your game plan and do something else.

Football revolves around little battles. You know you can scare the life out of some and others aren't troubled and you have to handle them differently. Some you let have the ball to their feet because you know they are not good enough to go past you; others you have to stand up tight on tight. That's when you say to Des Walker or whoever's playing that you can't cover him today because your man is a threat not only to you but also to the team.

The game has changed and the philosophy has changed but I haven't. It might seem cold-hearted but as long as I can look in the mirror at the end of the game and say that I have played well and done my best for my team then I'm happy.

Bobby had a word with me after the tackle in the Yugoslavia game and told me to calm down on the tackling and to use my head. He had seen an awful tackle from his left-back 20 yards in front of him and he didn't know what was going through my mind or how well in control I really was. He obviously thought I went too far because he took me off in that game and that meant that I had lost out.

Looking back now, I wish I had thought about the game a lot more then than I did, but that is all part of growing up. You have to learn and learn quickly and the higher up the ladder you go the quicker you have to learn. In some ways I have been lucky because if I were graphing my career it would show that I have gone up very gradually. I would have found it difficult if I had gone in as quickly as Michael Owen, for instance. He almost certainly has a wiser head on his shoulders than I ever had; at his age I was being arrested for bad behaviour.

The game has changed and the tolerance has changed. Managers are sacked after a couple of bad weeks and that was unheard of then. You have to be cute and change along with it. When the rules changed about a booking without a warning for instance, I changed straightaway and that's why I'm still knocking around. These days, you can go off for one tackle that less than ten years ago would have resulted in a finger-wagging admonishment from the referee. In all, I was booked five times for England and was never sent off. I consider that a fair return for an aggressive defender playing so many internationals, many of them of an extremely competitive nature.

A cheap booking is for swearing at a referee. I did it once and learned my lesson. I would never swear at a referee now. I don't even bother talking to them. I would rather get booked for kicking someone, which could help my game, rather than calling a referee a twat, which helps nobody.

I was lucky that once I left non-league I didn't really come across anyone who set out deliberately to kick me. They were queuing up when I was at Wealdstone and perhaps those five tough years moulded me and the non-league mentality I had served me as a good apprenticeship. I took that with me into the professional game. It was a case of stand up and be counted or you were out of it. There were a lot of nasty sods about 20 years ago.

At international level they can be a bit slyer, certainly a bit quicker, but there has never been an opponent who has physically intimidated me. There has been more than one who has been prepared to have a go at me. When I was playing in Europe with Forest against Bordeaux, I went up with the French international Yannick Stopyra and we clashed. I won the header but he thought I had elbowed him. The ball was quickly transferred to the other end and with everyone's attention elsewhere he promptly chinned me. I lost my rag but stayed in control. I waited for the next tackle because if I had punched him back it would have been me who would have gone off.

I have been able to keep a lid on it with everything except spitting. That's a habit I despise. The closest anyone has come was Savo Milosevic at Aston Villa. I tackled him, he looked at me, went to spit, and then changed his mind and spat at the floor. If it had hit me I would have done nothing then but I would certainly have gone looking for him in the dressing-room after the game and sorted it out. I'm usually able to deal with a situation later, when I won't be sent off.

If you live by the sword you have to be prepared to die by it. Opponents know they can try it on with me because I won't be running to the referee. John Fashanu was close to breaking my leg when he stamped on me. I won't stand up and shout my mouth off to the referee or to the press because I have given as much as I've taken. My career means too much for me to let someone walk over me. I have never broken anyone's leg, I have never been malicious and I have never deliberately gone over the ball when I've been face-to-face with an opponent. Somewhere among all of the clippings there are sure to be one or two to prove me wrong but they will be few and far between and they have never been on purpose.

I was lucky that in my international career, particularly in the early days, we played mainly 4-4-2 against sides who were playing wing-backs. It meant that I didn't have to face players who would take me on in a one-to-one situation like I did at home with genuine wingers like John Barnes, Chris Waddle or Pat Nevin who could dribble past you. I was never that exposed. It was more often the subtle things that showed me up, like the Brazilian winger Muller's move when my error cost us a goal and a win.

I've had my bad, indifferent and good games for England, as most have, but I have never gone away thinking that a player has destroyed me. For the two games we played against Holland in the 1994 World Cup qualifiers, when I would have been up against Marc Overmars, I was out injured and Tony Dorigo had to cope with him.

Now Overmars is the sort of player who can hurt you.

Qualifying for the 1990 World Cup was never easy but we went to Poland for the last game undefeated, wanting a point to be sure. In the last minute, a lad named Tarasciewicz fired in a shot that hit the bar so hard it rebounded to the halfway line. Peter Shilton said he had it covered all the way, of course! It's amazing how often Poland cropped up during my international career. I swear I have more Polish shirts in my cupboard at home than any other country in the world. In fact, if you took away Poland and Brazil I would be down to my last 60 caps. Funnily enough, while everyone wants that famous Brazilian shirt, the first time I played against them in my debut I wouldn't give my shirt to anyone. It was a proud moment and I wanted to keep it. The England shirt was a much more prized possession to me than any Brazilian shirt. I wasn't cute enough at the time to tell a Brazilian to come to the dressing-room afterwards so I could have given him my spare shirt. I wanted the one I had worn.

The 1990 World Cup finals was the next step up. Playing for your club is one thing, stepping up to international level is another, but going to a major tournament, and they do not come any bigger than the World Cup, is different altogether. You cannot go any further in football; it is the pinnacle of what you can achieve.

There was quite a lengthy build-up to the finals, so much so that we were able to invite our wives over for one of the weeks we were on the holiday island of Sardinia. Without being mean to Liz I told her that I would have preferred to be on my own. I explained it was a football environment and that I would rather have been there focusing on the job in front of me. All I was thinking about was the World Cup two weeks away and it didn't feel right lying on the beach sunbathing with Liz and the other players' wives. Probably further down the line I would have been more relaxed about it but not then. I am not complaining about the organisation, which was perfect, right down to moving hotels once the girls had gone. We left the quiet luxury of the Is Morus hotel, on the beach, for the more spartan and workmanlike Is Molas Golf hotel, further inland and, as it's name suggests, on a golf course. For a lot of players it was perfect. We had the odd meal out and we were still training, of course, but as I said to both Liz and Des Walker, I would rather be in a football-only environment.

The friendlies and bits and pieces were eventually out of the way and we played the Republic of Ireland, Holland and Egypt in our qualifying group. Not so long ago I watched those three games again as part of my coaching badge course. It was my choice. I thought they would be ideal because they were part of a tournament. Three worse games you probably wouldn't see. The Irish game, played on a bitterly cold, windy, wet night, was typically dour with Jack Charlton's team launching the ball up the middle. We took the lead, inevitably through Gary Lineker, but finished up drawing 1–1. The nerves struck us. I remember Bobby having a little go at me and asking what was the matter. I said it must be nerves and he responded that the reason he had given me more than 20 caps was that I didn't get nervous. It was spot on by him, but this was another big step.

We lost Bryan Robson early on in the second game against Holland and he had to go home injured. He had problems with his Achilles, then suffered a further injury to his toe in an incident in the team hotel. There was bad feeling over this with the press complaining that they had been misled and lied to. The result was that some of the players decided they weren't going to talk to the press anymore. It made no difference to me because I had used the old Brian Clough escape clause.

It became even worse later on when the *Sun* ran a story that some of the team had been out disco dancing with one of the World Cup hostesses and that three of the team had gone to bed with her. Bobby Robson called a meeting the night before and told us that he had been warned that they were carrying this story and that it named three players – Peter Beardsley, John Barnes and me. Everyone immediately burst out laughing. Barnes may have had a bit of a reputation, but Peter and me? They had to be joking!

I went back to my room with the right hump and telephoned Liz. I told her that I had been with England for six weeks going from my room to the restaurant to the video room to the swimming pool, to training, to matches. I had not even had a drink, out of choice. I was there to work. I told her about the story in the paper but she was not worried because she knew what I was like where my country was concerned.

I found it more than a little bit irritating that I was there representing my country and that family and relatives of Liz had to read this garbage. She laughed it off, as did Bobby Robson, but from then on my attitude hardened. If a youngster asks me what it's like to play in a big tournament I tell them that there's a cycle. The football season in England ends and until then everyone is concentrating on the championship and the Cup. Then for a couple of weeks not much is happening and the papers look for stories about players. When the first ball is kicked, that's all forgotten and everyone is concerned about the football again. You don't notice the pattern when you're at home watching on television but when you're away you realise that's how it works. I learned to keep my head down.

Invariably it forges a siege mentality. Even before the World Cup the press had been hammering Bobby Robson. On arrival they turned their attention to what we were up to, trying to find out what and how much we had been drinking. Then came the accusations about the hostess. Everyone in the squad turned inwards. As a bonding exercise it worked quite well, although I'm sure that's not what the papers had in mind.

We played seven games in that World Cup and it was only in the later ones that we really did ourselves justice. When we came home to a heroes' welcome, the early matches were glossed over. No one seemed to remember the stick we took in the papers over the way we failed to perform, preferring to recall only the semi-final when we were unlucky not to go through.

We had fun and games at the hotel, a big video, horse racing games, all sorts of things designed to kill time but at the same time to conserve energy. We were advised not to sit in the sun day in and day out, although some did. Gary Lineker could have swapped passports with John Barnes after a couple of weeks.

The biggest source of entertainment was Paul Gascoigne. He couldn't sit still for two minutes; he'd be up and down, here and there.

We were relaxing by the swimming pool one day when he disappeared yet again only to reappear minutes later having covered himself from head to foot in toilet paper. He dived off the board into the pool. Only he knows why.

On another day, sponsors Wilson arranged a golf day for us on the course adjacent to the hotel. In England clubs are a bit picky about what you must wear on their courses. They are more relaxed about it in Sardinia but not so much as Gazza thought. He tried to play his round in shorts and flipflops. He also upset a few by driving his buggy through the bunkers and parking it on the putting green.

Bobby Robson had his big day out when the RAF took him up in a jet fighter while we were there. He came back that night late for dinner and he was absolutely made up, with that same look on his face that he had when he took over at Newcastle United. He couldn't stop talking about it until he looked over at Terry Butcher, Gary Stevens, and Chris Waddle. They had persuaded the wine waiter to fill a load of empty wine bottles with water and they were sat at a table for four wearing everything back to front or inside out, with their hair greased back. They were there when everyone arrived and we watched in amazement as they ate their meal backwards, starting with coffee, dessert, main course, and soup while quaffing bottle after bottle of 'wine'.

When Bobby spotted them he stopped in mid eulogy and stared at his former Ipswich captain Terry Butcher sitting there with a full glass, surrounded by empty bottles and wearing a baseball cap inside out and the wrong way round. It was like a red rag to a bull. He thought they were drinking wine and muttered idiot, idiot until he twigged that he was being wound up. It was brilliant because no one knew that they were going to do it. At the end of their meal they stood up and said, 'Thank you gentlemen and goodnight.' As they emerged from the shelter of the long tablecloths, we could see that they had nothing on, apart from G-strings, from the waist downwards. They were applauded out of the room.

Little things like that get you through the long weeks. Another diversion much appreciated by everyone was a race night with Gary Lineker and Peter Shilton nominated as the bookmakers. The rest of the boys persuaded the physiotherapist Fred Street to have a peek at the penultimate race in advance and then pass the winner on to the lads. We received the nod for number seven and we all piled our money on, some putting on as much as £2,000. Everyone was on number seven. Halfway round, number seven was nowhere to be seen and we were all beginning to wonder if this was a double bluff to match *The Sting*. Fred was trying to reassure everyone but by the three-quarters stage number seven was still not in the frame. Shilton, a man who likes a gamble, was rubbing his hands in expectation. Then suddenly number seven appeared from nowhere and stormed past everything with the entire room going up and Shilts totally devastated. Gazza was doing forward rolls and everyone was giving it the high fives. You would have thought that we had just won the World Cup. Shilts honestly believed that he had been wiped out. His losses came to thousands of pounds and he looked ready to do something silly until we took pity on him and admitted it had been a wind-up.

We had the English newspapers delivered every morning. I used to take the *Daily Express* at the time but one day when I came down for breakfast all of the papers had gone. Steve Hodge and Paul Parker had taken them all to their room. I knocked on their door and Hodgey opened it half an inch and asked what I wanted. When I told him I would like to look at a newspaper he asked which one I wanted. I told him the *Express*. He wanted to know what I wanted it for. I told him that I wanted to do the crossword. The door closed and reopened minutes later and he handed me the crossword, neatly cut out of the paper but with no clues. It wasn't until late afternoon that they returned the papers. Goodness knows what they did with them.

Bobby Robson changed the team for the Holland game, bringing in Mark Wright as a sweeper and replacing Gary Stevens with Paul Parker. The word was that the deep-thinking Chris Waddle had influenced the choice. He was a senior player and strongly in favour of playing three at the back. It was revealed later that Bobby had made the decision a long time before, having been turned over by the Dutch in a European Championship game when Marco Van Basten scored a hat-trick. The way I remember it, Chrissie was pivotal in the decision.

Whoever made it, the plan worked and we were all very comfortable with the system. Paul Parker and myself were both pretty athletic up and down the wings, Des Walker, Terry Butcher and Mark Wright gelled while Gazza and Chris Waddle worked the midfield.

As a 4-4-2 line-up we hadn't really fired. We had been a bit predictable and I think even now that we play better with the sweeper system; it gives us a lot more flexibility. Although we drew 0–0 I 'scored' from a free kick with ten minutes to go from just outside the box. It was an indirect free kick but I thought I would hammer it goalwards believing that it would be a brave goalkeeper who would just let it go straight into the net. Hans Van Breukelen, the Dutch goalkeeper, dived but it went past him and in. I knew all along that it was indirect but it was as good an option as any. Van Breukelen told me that he knew it was indirect and deliberately let it in. I thought if that was true he made a bloody good effort to save it.

The Dutch team had all their stars playing, including Ruud Gullit, Marco Van Basten, Wim Kieft, Frank Rijkaard, Ronald Koeman and the rest, but when I returned to the dressing-room it was to hear Shilton ranting and raving at Des Walker, calling him a cheat because Van Basten had beaten him once in the game and got in a shot from 30 yards. I bristled on behalf of my mate and had a go back at Shilton. Des had nigh on marked Van Basten out of the game. One thing Des is not is a cheat. A more honest player you would never come across. We had the right hump with our goalkeeper but that was nothing new. He used to go through black moods and was often at loggerheads with several of the players.

We now had to beat Egypt in our final game to qualify. We would have settled for that at the start of the tournament. We didn't play well but we won with a Mark Wright header and we were into the next round against Belgium in Bologna.

We went into the game thinking we had a decent draw but they shook us. Enzo Scifo played brilliantly in midfield and almost put Belgium in front when he struck a post. There was little in it and as extra time ticked by penalties appeared to be a racing certainty. I believe that's where the Belgians slipped up. They thought the same deadlock was not going to be broken and they lost concentration. With a minute remaining, Gascoigne took a free kick near the halfway line and David Platt, who had come on as a substitute for Bryan Robson's replacement Steve McMahon, took the ball over his shoulder and volleyed a spectacular goal.

The pressure is on when you are in the knock-out stages, especially with England. Whatever the tournament, if you go out in the league stages that is considered abject failure. Once you are in the knock-out stages, you start to get a bit of momentum, dropping the nerves and beginning to feel that you are there by right. The more we progressed the greater was the confidence, especially when we heard that we were to play the surprise quarter-finalists Cameroon. Without any disrespect, we would have settled for that any day of the week and Howard Wilkinson, who had spied on them for Bobby, reported that we had as good as a bye. It turned out to be the hardest bye we had ever played and for a long time it looked as though we were going out.

We might have settled for the quarter-finals, having got that far four years earlier in Mexico, but when we drew the African outsiders we were expected to get through to the last four and we believed we could do it.

It was a long walk from the dressing-rooms in Naples. You go from the centre of the pitch at one side, behind one of the goals and up the other side. We walked out together and the African side were singing tribal songs. Some of our lads found it amusing; I didn't think that it was at all funny. After all they might just turn us over in a few minutes. I tried to stay focused.

Everything went to plan and we were very confident when, after 25 minutes, Terry Butcher sent me off down the right and I crossed for David Platt to score the sort of goal he was scoring regularly for Aston Villa. Usually when you score that first goal you are home and dry, particularly against the still-emerging African nations. Cameroon did not have the best of disciplinary records and had players sent off for fun in the early rounds. In fact, four of their best players were suspended.

Nevertheless, this was a team of giants. A very physical side, they came back at us instead of letting their heads drop. When Gascoigne brought down the veteran substitute Roger Milla in the penalty area, Kunde beat Shilton from the spot to equalise and then another substitute, Ekeke, scored from a pass from Milla. I tackled someone and received one of my few international bookings, which as it turned out sent me into the semi-final against West Germany, along with Gazza, on a knife-edge. When you are 2–1 down you tend to become a bit more robust because you think you may be going out anyway. It looked as though that's just what would happen but suddenly Gazza and Peter Beardsley began to play and slowly we forced our way back into the game. Even then it took two penalties to see us through and both times it was Gary Lineker who was brought down, the first eight minutes from time and the second 14 minutes into extra time. Each time he picked himself up and scored.

I remember just into extra time I left a back pass short and let Roger Milla in. It took a fantastic save from Peter Shilton to stop us going behind again and Shilton gave me an almighty rollicking. It did me the world of good, a real kick up the arse.

No England team had ever been to a semi-final in a World Cup away from England and the momentum was growing. We were beginning to think we were a team capable of doing something. The draw for the semi-final threw us up against our old rivals West Germany in Turin. We weren't afraid although we would have much preferred to play either Italy or Argentina at that stage. In a strange way the pressure was off us because we had reached further than anyone back home had expected at the start of the tournament. Cameroon had shaken us but we were through and began to fancy ourselves, with some justification.

We played as well against the Germans as we had done not only in the tournament but for the previous couple of years or so. Early on in the game I was man to man with their wing-back Tomas Hassler and when I brought him down I feared the worst. The Brazilian referee Jose Ramirez Wright just awarded the free kick and I breathed a huge sigh of relief.

I felt they were fortunate to be in front with a freak Brehme goal that spun over Shilton from a massive deflection off Paul Parker after an hour. We fully deserved our equaliser, an outstanding effort from Gary Lineker ten minutes from time.

So for the third game in succession we were taken to extra time, very draining in the heat of the Italian summer. Eight minutes into the extra period Gazza mistimed a tackle on Berthold and was booked. I thought the referee was influenced by the reaction of the German bench who were close to where the foul took place. Even then we might have won it. Waddle hit the inside of a post. Normally from that angle the ball will deflect into the net but this one came straight back out and we were heading for penalties and my historic miss.

Chrissie managed to exorcise some of his personal ghosts in the third place play-off game against Italy when he replaced Steve McMahon. Neil Webb took over from Mark Wright when we were chasing the game. We'd gone down to a Roberto Baggio goal a minute earlier after a Shilton mistake. David Platt equalised but Schillaci dived over Paul Parker's outstretched leg to win an undeserved penalty and with it the game.

I had the utmost respect for Bobby Robson who was, even then, an elder statesman of football. I could never see anyone fronting Bobby in the dressing-room in an aggressive manner. Everyone respected him. His decision not to play me in that final game did not cloud my judgement of him at all. He made decisions that were right for England; all I had been thinking about was Stuart Pearce.

That was his last game in charge of England and I could see how sad he was having had such a hell of a tilt at the title. World Cup quarter-finals and semi-finals, both away from home, and the loss of just one qualifying match in eight years – that's a tremendous record. We were disappointed not to win for him but were also disappointed for ourselves. Winning the Fair Play Trophy was hardly compensation – in fact for me it was a positive insult!

Just before Bryan Robson left we were sitting by the swimming pool and he was putting on a brave face, saying that he would be able to attend his brother's wedding after all, but it was clear he was devastated. He had been to both the 1982 and 1986 World Cups and this was going to be his last. He was gutted. He had tasted two World Cups and he was looking for more. He would have given anything to be on that open-topped bus going through the streets of Luton. I didn't realise how important the World Cup was for so many people until we came home.

We came back with so much more stature than when we went. We didn't know what we were capable of when we went but coming back we knew what we could have done – we could have won it. Had we drawn anyone else, either Italy or Argentina, in that semi-final we would probably have won because we were getting better with every match.

I am often asked who is the most difficult player I have faced over the years and people are usually surprised when I reply Mark Ward; some even say Mark who? Even West Ham supporters seem surprised that I have picked out one of their less lauded Hammers rather than Marco Van Basten, for instance.

Mark Ward was a direct little player who liked to run at you with the ball at his feet. It is probably through him that I have had more bad games at Upton Park than at most other places. I was up against him when I was substituted for one of the three times in my Forest career.

Pat Nevin was another difficult player. When he was on fire, he was tricky and direct with a few skills. He was probably on the receiving end of some of the worst tackles that I have ever dished out. He agreed with that when I discussed it with him recently but he bears no malice.

Every player throws up a different challenge and if you are not up to it you will be slaughtered whoever it is. The odds, though, weigh heavily in favour of the defender. The more often I play against a forward the better I feel against him. You get to know their tricks and style but if you are weak in character and you have a bad time against an opponent, the next time you will not fancy it.

How often do you see a player come into the League, a foreign player or a youngster, and he does really well in that first season? Gianfranco Zola is a classic example. He was outstanding in his first season for Chelsea and was named Player of the Year but, in his second season, teams were playing man-for-man against him. Defenders knew what was coming and he was not quite as lethal. But it's hard to be a surprise package in the Premier Division these days. To do my homework, all I have to do is switch on the television two or three times a week and there they are in front of me.

At international level, for the majority of matches we would watch our opponents on video. It would have been naïve not to. As a defender you don't want to be surprised.

Aggressive opponents have never bothered me. What I fear most, along with every other defender, is sheer, raw pace. It doesn't matter how quick you are, there is always someone quicker. Michael Owen is a case in point. On skill alone you fancy your chances but his pace is frightening and puts you on the back foot. His finishing is a bonus. If an opponent is tricky but not too fast, that's not such a problem because you simply get close to him. But if he's tricky and fast, you have to give him a few yards in case the ball is played over the top. If you are not tight he can get the ball to feet, turn and take you on. In the old days you could try to intimidate them but that is not the case anymore. You have to be a lot more artful.

Des Walker used to say that top international players always have one characteristic that lifts them above the others. With Gary Lineker and Alan Shearer it's their finishing, with Michael Owen and Andrei Kanchelskis it's their blinding pace and Les Ferdinand and Duncan Ferguson are the best headers of the ball in Britain. The first choice on my list of defenders was also the first choice of Bobby Robson's England team list for many years. Who else but my old friend and playing partner Des Walker? He was magnificent in terms of consistency for Forest and was one of the reasons why we achieved what we did and why I was able to go forward so often to join attacks.

In the modern game I love Jaap Stam of Manchester United. He defends strongly and well. He is a terrific player with good pace. In one Champions League game, a forward backed up towards the penalty area while waiting for a free kick from the halfway line. Stam just stood there and let the player bump off him as if to say to his opponent that he was going no further. It showed that he has something about him. I read that he loves his football, isn't too bothered about having a big flash car and is as happy going to the supermarket shopping with his wife as to a celebrity function. He seems to be an ordinary bloke and I like to think that he and I are a little alike. I reckon he was cheap at the price of £12 million that Alex Ferguson paid for him.

Tony Adams is another who stands up to be counted. In a rich vein of form he is a world-class defender. He always stands tall, shouting the orders and taking responsibility. When things aren't going right he can be exposed but ten times out of ten I would want him in my team.

As far as left-backs are concerned I favour those who offer something a little bit different. Tony Dorigo, who had electric pace and was neater than I was on the ball, pushed me for years. I admire the skills that he has and I haven't. He has been unlucky not to win more caps than he did, a bit like West Bromwich Albion's Derek Statham who had to follow Kenny Sansom around for so many years.

In international terms, in my spot I would pick Roberto Carlos of Brazil. He has stunning pace but people say that he can't defend. Sometimes when you can run as fast as he can, you can get yourself into the right positions, but I am not so sure that he can't defend. I certainly haven't seen too many forwards take liberties with him! For me the man can attack, defend, score goals and has that pace.

Kenny was another who had something I didn't. He was neat and such a clean tackler he never gave away free kicks. Forwards would run at him but he would stand up and just take the ball off them whereas I would back off and jockey, wishing I could do it like Kenny. When he won the ball he used it so well. I had aggression and was better in the air so I scored a lot more goals than he did – in fact, more than most defenders, with 87 in my career. But I happily acknowledge that Kenny kept me out of the England team by right because he was a hell of a better player than I was at the time.

It is odd that currently we have such a dearth of left-backs. It is nothing to do with the way the game has developed but simply cyclical. When I was in the side with Tony Dorigo breathing down my neck, he had Julian Dicks breathing down his. Julian was a player something like me – combative, a goalscorer. When he was playing well we were carbon copies. But it didn't end there; Mark Dennis was also a strong, powerful left-back and Arsenal's Nigel Winterburn earned an England cap while I was around. The only other time our paths crossed was when Dave Bassett tried to sign me for Wimbledon from Wealdstone, couldn't get me and signed Winterburn instead. It turned out to be one of his best signings. Nigel did well not only for the Dons but went on to win just about every honour for Arsenal, playing in what became a legendary back four with Lee Dixon, Tony Adams and Martin Keown or Steve Bould.

How strange it is that left-backs through the years have tended to be so much more aggressive than right-backs. Apart from those mentioned, Pat Van Den Hauwe and Doug Rougvie, name me a right-back in that same style. It is not easy.

CHAPTER 13

from bad to worse

Bobby Robson was the man who gave me my international chance and helped me to play in a massive tournament, falling short just one step from the final. He was succeeded by Graham Taylor and, while I am grateful to Robson for giving me my start, I am equally thankful to Taylor for making me captain of my country, a great honour.

Over my time England have ridden a roller coaster. We did badly in 1988 in the European Championships in Germany and then did well in the 1990 World Cup finals. We reached the European finals in 1992, where we were disappointing, and did even worse when we could not reach the 1994 World Cup finals, but then we excelled in the 1996 European Championships in England, before we failed to fulfil our potential in 1998 in the World Cup in France.

As a nation, we have too many troughs and not enough peaks, never having that remarkable consistency of the Germans who can turn it on tournament after tournament, which was why their dismal showing in Euro 2000 was such a surprise to so many, even though it was clear they were not the force they once were.

In this respect I felt sorry for Graham Taylor when he took over. In many ways it was like following Brian Clough at Nottingham Forest, because Bobby Robson had gone out on a high and come back to England a hero.

I thought Taylor was the right choice for England manager at the time. In fact, I will go further and say that every time an England manager has been chosen he has been the right one at the time. I have been involved for 12 years and I am sure the clever beggars will look back in hindsight and say they knew that the FA had picked the wrong one. But for me there is no doubt: Robson was the right choice; Taylor was the best at the time; Terry Venables was the right choice and so was Glenn Hoddle. Then few would argue with the selection of Kevin Keegan, although it might be argued that they could have brought back Terry Venables who was available.

It was unfortunate for Graham in that we hit such an all-time high in Italy and the only way to go was down. Bryan Robson played only three more times for England, while we also lost Terry Butcher and Peter Shilton, experienced cornerstones of the team.

I was in the frame to replace Captain Marvel as skipper, along with Gary Lineker plus two or three other outsiders. I have never talked to Graham about it but I am sure that in hindsight he would have gone for me as captain rather than Gary. In some ways I am more of a Graham Taylor player than Gary was. We are different people; he was good with the press, a model professional, and a good goal scorer without being blessed with a great deal of talent outside the box. Whereas I could hardly be described as being good with the press, although I would do it if I had to, and I had a bit of nastiness about me whereas Gary had never been booked. Public perception would have probably given it to him, but I was more of a captain on the pitch than he would ever be.

It wasn't until the end of 1992 that Graham Taylor finally came to me and offered me the captaincy. That was an unbelievably prestigious thing to have thrust upon you. There are few players who have the good fortune to be selected for England and even fewer who are able to say they captained England.

Graham, like so many managers, plays the odd mind game and, in summer 1991 when we went on tour to Australia, New Zealand twice and Malaysia, Gary was made captain for the trip. Taylor saw us beaten only once between Italia 90 and the European Championships in 1992. While we were there, Gary had to pop over to Japan for some publicity event and that was when I first captained my country against New Zealand, and I celebrated with a goal.

The first time I captained England at Wembley was in February

1992 against France. It was another proud moment, and Liz was due to come and watch. Sadly she had a strange problem to contend with and didn't see me lead the team out that night.

When we bought our house there were chickens and the previous owners asked us did we want them to put them down or did we want to keep them. Put like that there was only one choice and we kept them. I had to ask how to look after them and was told it was just a question of throwing a handful of corn down every day. I thought even I could handle that little chore.

But on the day of the game one of our horses, a thoroughbred named Archie, found it amusing to boot them when they came near him. All of these chickens were named after meals and Archie took it on himself to go over the top on poor Chicken Kiev, putting a big hole in his side. So Liz couldn't come to the game because she had to take the injured chicken to the vet's. While I was captaining England, Liz sat waiting her turn at the vet's with Chicken Kiev in a box and missed my biggest day. Not only that but she was also embarrassed when she had to answer the receptionist's questions. Imagine it: 'What sort of pet is it?'

'A chicken.'

'What's its name?'

'Chicken Kiev.'

'How do you spell that?'

'K-I-E-V.'

'What sex is it?'

'It's a chicken, so it must be female!'

At least Archie only kicked him once and then backed off. He had learned well and wasn't shown the red card.

Two years down the line, when Gary had retired after being pulled off in his last game in the European Championship, Graham telephoned me to ask if he could come to my house in Nottingham. In the back of my mind I thought that I was either going to be offered the captaincy or I was in for the chop.

He was very proud and passionate to be the England manager and I don't think the public realised just what it meant to him, because he didn't wear it on his sleeve all of the time. I knew because I was in the dressing-room all the time with him and I could see in his eyes how important it was.

I believe that, probably because of his background as manager of Watford, he was more comfortable with players like me around him than he was with the superstars who were always in the media spotlight. I wanted to work and would rather not see my face splattered across the papers. That made me Graham Taylor's sort of player. When he asked me to be his captain, it was phenomenal. I couldn't have been prouder.

But perhaps Graham overdid it with his selection of honest, hard-working players. When I look back over that period at some of those he introduced to international football I wonder where they are now. Players like Andy Sinton, Tony Daly, Carlton Palmer, Geoff Thomas, Keith Curle and others appeared under Graham and then vanished. When other managers picked players regularly, they generally stayed around a lot longer when a new coach came in.

Bobby certainly had more international class players, in some case world-class players available to him. For, in the main, England players – with a few exceptions on the periphery – pick themselves. It might be argued that Graham was not blessed with a good crop of players at the time, having hit a downward spiral after the semi-finals.

I must say, however, that I enjoyed my time working with him. It didn't go too badly as we qualified for the 1992 European Champion-ship in Sweden and a good many fancied us to win it. Graham, in fact, had a long honeymoon period before it went pear-shaped. In club terms, we would have won several championships as far as I was concerned, for in my 78 games, disregarding penalty shoot-outs, I can only remember being on the losing side half a dozen times, including a couple at Wembley against Uruguay and Brazil.

So the spirit in the camp was good when we went to Sweden and we quite fancied our chances. We opened with a 0–0 draw with Denmark and were then held 1–1 by France. It was similar to the 1990 World Cup when all the pressure was on the team in the group stage to do ourselves justice, live up to the nation's expectations and qualify. It is as simple as that.

In fact, Denmark hadn't even qualified for the tournament and their players were sitting on benches around the world when they were called into the finals after Yugoslavia had been thrown out because of the political situation there. That was the game we should have won, catching the Danes cold before they settled in but it was a pretty nondescript, poorish game.

England against France, like Scotland or Germany, is a grudge game and it was one we all looked forward to with great anticipation, but it was a big let-down and the nearest we came to winning was a 25-yard free kick of mine which rattled Bruno Martini's crossbar. The nearly man rears his head again! But it wasn't that incident for which I will be remembered from that game, because shortly before that moment I was head-butted by Basil Boli.

I was attacked because I left a little bit on their winger Jocelyn Angloma, who had come on at half-time. I had sorted him out on one or two occasions and Boli had spotted it and when the ball was tossed into the box he took retribution and did it well, I have to say. It was a bit like the old wrestler Johnny Quango as he butted me on the run and I went down, not because he'd knocked me down with it, but because I thought that the referee would see it and send him off. If someone puts the head on you are entitled to go down.

When I realised that the referee had not seen it I was extremely annoyed, but I kept it to myself, waiting for the right moment to gain a little of my own back if I could. The last thing I wanted to do was to chase an opponent, throw a punch and get sent off. Instead, I turned on the unsuspecting Angloma and said: 'That was you, you little bastard. I'm going to kill you.'

He was shaken to his boots and pleaded: 'Not me, not me.'

By this time he was frightened to death, thus making my job a lot easier.

A few minutes later we had a free kick on the edge of the box, perfect for the left-footer. It was mine, but the only problem was that the Hungarian referee Sandor Puhl had ordered me off because I still had blood streaming down my face from the cut on my cheekbone caused by Boli's head butt. I said to Lineker, who was standing over the ball: 'Don't you dare take that free kick. Wait for me.'

I ran over to the touchline, had it cleared up and vaselined and then raced back to take the free kick. By then I was steaming mad and Lineker said: 'Just smash it.' I did. It rammed against the underside of the crossbar, bounced on the line and out of the area. Where was the Russian linesman when you needed him?

It was late in the game and had that gone in we would have been through to the semi-finals. I can't remember hitting a ball as hard as that before or since. The whistle went soon afterwards and, as I left the pitch, with the blood still pouring down my face, I was stopped by the television people. I was the natural target mainly because the only two things that had happened of any note in the entire 90 minutes were Boli putting the head on me and then me hitting the crossbar.

As I was waiting for the interview to start Boli walked past me, but as I had cooled down by then and taken it as part of the game, I ignored him. Graham Taylor saw what was happening and sensibly dragged me away to the dressing-room to have my face cleaned up and gave me a little more time to cool down.

Those cuts always look worse on the face than they really are and all it needed was four or five stitches. I then told the manager that I didn't mind seeing the press as they had asked for me. I knew what they wanted and thought to myself if I had launched into Boli and said it was a disgrace and he should have been sent off, the tables would be turned on me and the cry would have gone up about my tackling Angloma. So I sat down at the press conference and told them that it was an innocent clash of heads. If I had told them I thought it was deliberate, I am sure that Boli would have been in a lot of trouble. But what was the percentage? We hadn't got to play them again and it was time I lived up to my adage of living by the sword. Had the incident happened now, I have no doubt that video evidence alone would have been enough to hang him and see him out of the remainder of the tournament.

Equally, if I had caught up with him and had the chance of gaining my revenge during what was left of the match I would have done so. But it was now all water under the bridge. I told them that I was more concerned with the free kick not going in and thought no more about it as we went back to our hotel.

Trevor Steven, who played with Boli at Marseille, later presented me with a fax that had come through to the hotel offices. It was from Boli, written in pidgin English, thanking me for my sportsmanship and wishing me well for the future. The press were desperate for the story but I had played it down and he appreciated it. I could understand his mentality. He had seen me whacking one of his weaker players and had come to look after him. I would have done the same thing, but I would not have resorted to head butting. That, like spitting, is for the thugs in the back street. Having something like that winds me up and gets the adrenalin flowing so that I play better. Certainly I wouldn't have hit that free kick as hard as I did without the Boli incident.

Having played those opening two games in Malmo, we then moved on to Stockholm to play the hosts, still needing a win to go through. We were nice and relaxed and had been to watch Bruce Springsteen in concert, along with most of the Swedish players, and I still quite fancied our chances.

I fancied them even more when David Platt scored from a Lineker centre after only four minutes and everything looked sweet. They made a couple of changes at the break and it made a difference. Central defender Eriksson scored with a header and Brolin scored the winner in the 82nd minute. But the big talking point afterwards was Graham Taylor's decision to substitute his captain Gary Lineker in the 64th minute of what turned out to be his last game for England, replacing him with Arsenal striker Alan Smith. I don't know whether there was any politics behind that decision – only Graham and Gary would know that – but I am sure that Graham would not have pulled Gary off unless he thought that he could win the match by doing it and England must always come before the individual.

Gary was clearly annoyed and made it look bad by taking off his armband and throwing it on to the floor, in my direction, as I was taking over the captaincy. There was no doubt at that stage the way the game was going that we were never going to score a goal and it needed a change. But everyone was asking: why take off the player who had scored 48 goals for his country and had pulled us out of the fire more than once? I didn't think that at the time; I just thought we needed a substitute, anyone. We were going route one at the time, so Alan Smith seemed to be the logical choice.

It was really weird going back to the hotel that night. On the way to the match we had been thinking of a semi-final in Stockholm against Germany, but instead we were going back to pack our bags and go home the next day. It was so different from the World Cup two years earlier when we had come within the width of a post of reaching the World Cup final. It was a total anticlimax.

I have never known a feeling like it. The dinner was quiet because we knew we were finished and out of there that next morning. I wasn't ready to leave; it was too early. But, in truth, we were a few players short of being a good team and we didn't play well in the tournament. There was certainly something missing.

I felt before we set out for Scandinavia that Paul Merson was going to make a name for himself in the competition. He hit a post in the first game against the eventual winners Denmark and had that gone in everything might have changed for him and the team. It didn't happen for Merson and it didn't happen for England. You create your own bit of luck, and had it gone our way in that first game who knows. It wasn't a great tournament with few decent games and even the final, when Denmark beat the favourites Germany 2–0, was only exciting because of the triumph of the underdogs over the favourites.

Despite our lack of success in those finals, it was still a good squad to be around. We did everything together and there was a good spirit. One night we went to see the West End show *Buddy*, based on the life of Buddy Holly, and afterwards we were given the use of a private room in a hotel where we had a nice meal and then a karaoke afterwards. I have memories, or is it nightmares, of Graham Taylor, with his shirt open to the waist, singing a duet with Paul Gascoigne of 'Singing in the Rain' with some of the players pouring water over their heads.

We also had Steve Harrison in the squad for his banter as well as his coaching, a bit like Terry McDermott with Kevin Keegan and Kenny Dalglish at Newcastle. The boys loved him. The stunts he would pull were fantastic. One morning we were leaving the hotel for training when we heard someone shouting: 'The bells, the bells,' and throwing gravel at us. We looked up and there was Steve on the hotel roof playing Quasimodo. On another occasion, he sat with John Barnes on the team bus. Digger knew him from old and knew he was up to something when he sat there saying nothing, just smiling. He had been round the hotel garden in the morning collecting worms and it was only after about 15 minutes he opened his mouth and let one of the worms crawl out, followed by the others. It was thoroughly revolting but memorable. Hence the saying 'soppy as a bag of worms'.

There was nothing he wouldn't do to make the troops laugh. He would come into the dining hall and say how thirsty he was, pick up the pitcher and pour the water all over himself. He would sit there soaking wet eating his dinner as if nothing had happened. The lads loved him and he certainly eased the tension with his antics. Graham had him in the squad, I am sure, to take the pressure off and loosen people up a bit, especially the new boys. He broke the ice with a lot of players. I am sure it helped having him acting the fool. He eventually carried it too far, but none of the lads would have a word said against him.

The other regular face about the squad was Lawrie McMenemy, who was quickly nicknamed the Big Bopper after we had been to see the Buddy Holly story. I have heard since that there was animosity between Lawrie and Graham, but I can honestly say that we were not aware of it at the time. That can happen; you have your head down and sometimes you don't see what is going on around you because you are totally focused on the football and nothing else.

Although we were slaughtered for not qualifying for the semi-finals, our overall results were still not bad and while we had been overwhelmed in 1988, at least we had taken a couple of points this time and lost only once by the odd goal. From there it was straight into World Cup qualifying after that, with me as captain, but it was a short campaign for me. I picked up a groin injury playing for Forest, which didn't seem bad at the time, but twice I tried to come back and twice I suffered a reaction.

It happened when I went running on the track at Forest in late January 1993. I went back into the physio's room and he had me doing the splits to see how far I could stretch. As I was spread, Liam O'Kane came in and pretended to kick one of my feet away. I jumped, my foot slipped and I have never suffered pain like it, not even with the broken leg. It transpired that I had ripped the groin muscle away from the bone. I was in agony; I could put my finger deep into the hole and I couldn't get up off the floor. That was me finished, club and country, for the remainder of the season.

Typical of the nearly man again, I was made captain in September and then missed five qualifying games and a disastrous tour to America. It was one to miss as they say. We lost to the hosts 2–0 in Foxboro, Boston; drew 1–1 with Brazil in Washington and then lost 2–1 to Germany in the Silverdome in Detroit. Prior to that we had drawn 1–1 with Norway at Wembley and beaten Turkey 4–0. I was injured doing forward rolls in training at Wembley before the game against San Marino that I missed but we won 6–0. It was not the sort of game where a left-back is missed.

It still went quite well after that with a 2–0 win over Turkey in the intimidating atmosphere of Izmir and a 2–2 draw with Holland after leading 2–0. Des Walker gave away a late penalty and that draw was to have serious consequences. There was another draw in Poland, when Ian Wright at last scored his first England goal, and we then ended the season disastrously with an awful defeat in Norway when Graham Taylor got our tactics all wrong.

When I left the squad, there was a good spirit and things weren't going bad. When I came back into the squad in September the atmosphere was totally different. The confidence and the self-belief had gone, not only in the players themselves but also in the manager. Suddenly, Des Walker was being vilified, after being the mainstay for the side over five years. He was no big favourite with the press because he wouldn't talk to them and so they jumped on him when he had a couple of poor games. He lost his place, something that was unthinkable two years earlier.

We had a decent result when we beat Poland 3–0 at Wembley that restored a little heart and a faint hope for qualification leading up to our crucial match against the Dutch in Rotterdam. I was again injured in the build-up, but I was told by the manager that whether or not I trained I would be playing in the game.

We lost 2–0 and were rocked by a decision by the German referee Assenmacher when Ronald Koeman committed the 'perfect' professional foul as he pulled down David Platt when he had only goalkeeper Ed de Goey to beat. Not only were we not awarded the penalty, Koeman was inexplicably allowed to remain on the pitch. To rub salt in the wound we couldn't take advantage of the free kick that was given on the edge of the box. Koeman then took massive advantage of his reprieve to score at the second attempt from an identical free kick at the other end of the pitch. Dennis Bergkamp finished us off with a second goal after a blatant handball. It summed up everything that was going wrong with us at the time.

The dressing-room was like a morgue, but totally different from Germany after the shoot-out. Then we felt we were unlucky. We had confidence in the manager and among ourselves, but I think after this one the players had lost a little confidence in the manager and he had lost a little confidence in himself.

Looking back on it, I have to say that Graham Taylor was an unlucky manager and sometimes it is better to be lucky than good. Nothing went for us in that qualifying campaign, including my injury as captain which meant I missed two-thirds of the games.

I am sure that Graham would rather have come in when we were at rock bottom – but he didn't. He was proud, passionate and honest . . . And unlucky. I don't think he deserved the criticism he received. I liked the man and that has nothing to do with him having made me captain. Some of the criticism he fielded was personal. Being called a turnip was naughty and unnecessary. It simply wasn't funny. People should make their criticisms at a professional level and not at a tacky level like that. It affected his ability to do the job, and so harmed England's prospects.

The major accusation about him was that he had never played at international level, but I don't think that is why we didn't succeed under him. He had players he liked and he picked them but they were of a certain standard and maybe they weren't good enough. I wish he had succeeded for England's sake and for my own sake. But we didn't and after the helter-skelter of Italia 90 we were faced with watching the 1994 World Cup in America on television. It was a bitter pill.

We finished off against San Marino in Bologna and to qualify we needed Holland to lose against Poland and us to win by seven clear goals. The nearly man struck again. They took the kick-off and with only seven seconds gone I gave away the ball and they scored an embarrassing goal. I saw the run by the right-winger and did everything right until I took my eye off the ball. It is the same old things at the highest level, even against a substandard side like San Marino. Lose your concentration for a fraction of a second and you are punished.

Thank god Holland won because we went on go win 7–1! But that wasn't the point. We were out and when I arrived home it was to be met by Liz and the first thing she said was: 'It had to be you again.'

But imagine if that mistake had been the difference between whether we went to the USA or not. Coupled with the penalty miss four years earlier it would have about finished my international career. It doesn't bear thinking about.

Graham Taylor knew that he would have to go after the San Marino game. I believe that the confidence was shaken out of him by not qualifying and that it took him a long while to regain it, probably not until he was back in the familiar surroundings of Watford at Vicarage Road. But one of the biggest mistakes he made was to make that notorious fly-on-the-wall film, with Phil Neal repeating every word he spoke and the bad language that was totally against the grain.

There were a number of people Graham had introduced during his time in charge. He brought in a psychologist, World Cup winner Alan Ball, a politician who acted as a buffer between him and the press, all sorts of people. But in the end none of it worked. England were out of the World Cup and Graham Taylor was out of a job. As for the nearly man, I had to wait and see who was going to be appointed and whether he would send me the same way.

CHAPTER 14

euro 96

Terry Venables didn't want me as his captain or his left-back. He told me as much in a telephone conversation when he opened the door for my international retirement. He was very honest about it. He told me that he doubted that I would be his first choice. I had the firm impression that he was telephoning me out of courtesy because I was the captain and perhaps he felt he owed me that at least. He asked me how I felt about it and I guessed that he was waiting for me to say, 'Thanks but no thanks. I'm quitting.'

Terry did not know me well. I told him that if I was good enough to be part of his squad I would like to be along. He was a bit taken aback. He was offering me the opportunity to tell the world via the media that I was retiring from the international game rather than being reduced from captain to an also-ran. I didn't relish the prospect of sitting in the stand watching the games but it was better than sitting at home and watching it on the television! I felt I was man enough to sit there and wait my turn. There was no question of my ego needing to be satisfied.

I was obviously disappointed. I had hoped the telephone call was to say that he was keeping me as his captain. But a new man has his own ideas. He brought in Graeme Le Saux as left-back and named David Platt as captain. I spent a year sitting in the stands but every time I was called up for the squad I responded.

It was tough and it was never tougher than when we went to Dublin to play the Republic of Ireland on 15 February 1995. The game was abandoned after 27 minutes and as I sat in the stands I was genuinely disgusted to be English. I thought that the hooligan problems were, if not resolved, at least under control. I am probably the face of English football – passionate, bulldog spirit and all the rest of it – but I also have a streak in me that respects other nations. For example, I hate it when our fans jeer other teams' national anthems. When we play away, apart from our closest neighbours, foreign supporters tend to respect our anthem. It irritates the English players and every England manager I have played under when our fans do not do the same. If there were one thing all six of them wish they could change it would be that lack of respect for the opponent's anthem.

There are very few people prouder than I am of being English but part of that pride is to respect others. Much of that has come about because of the travelling I have done. That night in Dublin disappointed me. I know Ireland and I like the Irish. There is plenty of good banter but that day it was all rubbish. I met a Forest fan who was almost killed when someone hit him on the head with an iron bar. It has nothing to do with football and everything to do with criminal behaviour. I was sitting not far away from the troublemakers but there was little I could do.

I was with the other non-playing members of the squad and some of the FA staff and I was concerned for them, particularly the women, because if the police had charged in indiscriminately they could have caused a stampede and in that old stand at Lansdowne Road there could have been hundreds killed in the crush. Sometimes we shoot ourselves in the foot with that slob culture and that was what happened that night. Football, and English football in particular, lost heavily.

But I was not going to walk away from something that had become part of my life. I turned up whenever invited, trained hard and settled for being number two left-back to Graeme Le Saux. I was still involved with England and my reward came a year later when Graeme suffered an injury. I was called in for Euro 96 and it turned out to be the best tournament I have ever played in. In contrast to that day in Ireland, this had everything that was good about English football.

My instant decision to stick around was totally justified. I was sorry for Graeme and would much rather have beaten him for the place in a face-to-face confrontation but the chance had come and I wasn't going to throw it away. That happens in football and it was why I hadn't let go.

There has never been a time before or since when I was so emotionally involved. I have never played in such a cauldron as Wembley in that tournament after freezing my arse off for a year. It was the best England team I have ever played in and that includes the 1990 World Cup team.

We played some superb football, particularly against Holland and Germany. Our victory over Scotland wasn't the best performance but it was an important result and produced a spark of pure magic from Paul Gascoigne.

I have never experienced anything like it. I thought that Skinner and Baddiel's 'Three Lions' song encapsulated everything. I remember the two comedians coming to the hotel and telling us that this was going to be our song. They played it and we all laughed and shouted 'rubbish, rubbish' but a couple of weeks later we were all singing it along with the rest of the nation. God only knows what it would have been like at Wembley, in London and around the country had we gone on and won that trophy. It was an incredible way to play football. In Italy and Sweden we were remote from the public reaction; here we were right in the middle of it all. Our families felt as much a part of the growing hysteria as we did. But to reach that euphoric state we had to go through that old familiar pattern in the build-up.

The season had ended and everything was quiet with no games, other than the odd friendly. As usual, the media were scratching round for something to write about, having a knock here and a dig there, picking up stories on individuals and, once again, succeeding in pulling the squad together.

Then came the ill-fated trip to China and Hong Kong. The Football Association were worried about going to Europe on a pre-tournament tour because of the potential for crowd trouble so we ended up travelling to the Far East. China was fascinating and a great adventure for me, visiting Tiananmen Square and the Great Wall. I didn't play in the game but I wouldn't have missed the trip for the world.

The fun and games began long before those extravagant stories of happenings in Hong Kong and on the flight back home. The day before we left, Rangers had clinched the Scottish double of League and Cup and Paul Gascoigne had celebrated in true Gazza fashion. He hates flying and so he topped up on the night before's intake before boarding. We were not even off the tarmac at Heathrow when he was asking for a Budweiser. The steward, preparing for take-off, was quite patient with him, finding him a beer, but when Gazza wanted another one he began to get a bit irritated and asked him to hold on. He was standing just ahead of Gazza at the time, looking after the row in front, so Gazza reached forward and to attract his attention patted him on the bum. The steward turned round and punched him straight in the face! He caught him a classic right in the side of the head. I was sitting close by with Steve Stone and we just fell about laughing. If you can remember that look Gazza had on his face in the World Cup when he was booked against Germany and for the second time in the tournament, that crumpled face and quivering lower lip. He looked exactly the same.

The steward strode off, leaving Gazza wondering what the hell had happened. A couple of the players sitting directly behind him started winding him up.

'You're not going to take that from him, are you?' they said.

'If Jim [five bellies] and my dad were here . . .' Gazza said, nearly in tears.

That just made it worse and the two boys behind dug the knife in deeper, trying to goad him into having a go back. We had a stopover in Copenhagen and we calmed it down with the help of FA official Jack Wiseman. The captain was threatening to throw Gascoigne off the aircraft. It was a public warning and it wound Gazza up even further, especially when the captain again threatened to put him off, this time in Russia. That made the poor boy even worse and both lips started quivering. He was whimpering. 'They're going to put me off at Moscow.' Watching the entire episode unfold was hilarious and far better than any in-flight movie.

For once Paul escaped the media spotlight because all of the journalists had flown at different times and with different airlines. Imagine the headlines that story would have made.

I played in the second game in Hong Kong. We won 1–0 but we played very badly. At the time I was rooming with Steve Stone, who was my team-mate at Nottingham Forest. Stoney was the typical Geordie boy, always up for a beer and a good time. The two of us sat with Gareth Southgate at dinner and I warned them that the night ahead was fraught with danger. I had seen it all before. There would be journalists looking for stories and it would be a good idea not to get involved. Gareth, a good professional who would have drunk no more than an orange juice in any case, agreed with me and we decided to stay at the hotel. Steve knew better, finished his dinner and went off into the night. We heard all about it when the boys came lurching back to the hotel – just another typical night out, getting smashed, ripping each others clothes off and sitting in a dentist's chair while having neat spirits poured down their throats.

Over the next couple of days the pictures were plastered over every newspaper and Gareth was thanking me for the best piece of advice he said he had ever had. The boys had harmed nobody but themselves and they had just had a good time, but this was before a big tournament and we had just played very badly.

I had even predicted what would happen when I telephoned Liz after the game. If you go out as a group, especially a group of England players, you are immediately the centre of attention whatever you do. That's not my cup of tea at any time never mind before a European Championship. Teddy Sheringham came out of the incident looking more like Ollie Reed than an international footballer!

As for my room-mate, Steve had gone out and joined in the fun but in the picture of the boys all standing together with their T-shirts ripped he was right on the end of the line and the picture was cropped, leaving him off. He was lucky. He had the night out and took no flak.

It was very naïve; the lads should have known better. It is not a lot to ask to keep your heads down for two weeks. After the tournament is the time to go berserk and have a drink and celebrate.

Even then the lesson wasn't learned. On the flight back I was sitting up the front reading and sleeping when there was a commotion from behind where the inevitable card school was taking place. It turned out that one or two of the personal televisions had been broken. There was no hiding that one because the airline, Cathay Pacific, were claiming damages from the Football Association.

When we returned to our base, Terry Venables called a meeting and told us that he could find out who the culprit was but did not plan to. He said that as we were a squad we were all in it together and every player would have to chip in £5,000 to pay the damages out of the bonus we had already accrued. I had a good idea of who had caused the damage because I knew who was sitting there. I didn't think the solution was fair but for the sake of squad harmony I kept my lip buttoned and put my hand in my pocket. Liz didn't agree when I told her but this was a team thing and sometimes you have to go against your natural instincts for the good of the whole.

We had arrived back under a real cloud after the drinking episode in Hong Kong and the damage on the flight back. It was incredible that the Gascoigne incident on the outward journey had never come to light. As so often happens, the siege mentality took over and we became a closer, tighter knit and better squad because of it, culminating in the cameo when Gascoigne scored his magical goal against the Scots and mimicked the dentist's chair.

Gazza was fortunate to have the ideal manager in Terry Venables. After the trouble going out, in Hong Kong and then his involvement in the nonsense coming back, he could easily have found himself out of the squad. Terry liked Gazza and Gazza respected him as a manager. They were able to extract the best out of each other. Terry was very shrewd; he knew that he could not squeeze the best out of his enigmatic player if he put constraints on him. He let him have his head and then reined him in with a few well-chosen words. He was right because despite all the daft things Gazza does, he means well and he was an outstanding, gifted player. At times you just had to stand back and laugh at his antics and at others you appreciated his God-given talents.

Gazza also has a heart of gold. Ask him for anything and if it was in his power he would do it. I asked him for a signed Lazio shirt when I had my testimonial and he said no problem. I thought, unfairly as it turned out, that the request would go in one ear and straight out the other, especially when I heard nothing from him for a couple of months. But, sure enough, he turned up for the England squad one day with the signed shirt.

On another occasion a group of us had taken the minibus from Nottingham to White Hart Lane to watch the Michael Watson–Chris Eubank world title fight which ended so tragically. We had played at Villa that day and the groundsman had driven us to London with a few beers on board. In the foyer I bumped into my England team-mate Gary Mabbutt. I asked him if there was anywhere we could have a quiet beer away from the public gaze. Basically, he said no, he couldn't think of anywhere. I was just about to go and break the news to the boys that we would have to find a local pub if they wanted a drink when Gazza appeared and asked us what we were doing. I told him we were looking for a beer and immediately he invited us to go with him. He took us to a nice big bar in a hospitality box overlooking the ring. By coincidence, our seats were just in front of where we had a drink. As we left for our seats I saw Gary Mabbutt and his mates having a drink at the same bar. I wasn't impressed with that sort of attitude. Certainly if fellow professionals had come to Nottingham, I would have put myself out for them. There was the difference between the two. Gazza was kind-hearted and always wanted to please. That's why he does stupid things, to make people laugh.

I was able to return one of his favours when he asked me if I would play in a testimonial for Steve McLaren. Playing at Ibrox in front of a full house was a real pleasure, especially to return one of his number of kindnesses to me.

I would do a lot for him although I would rather be alongside him laughing than at the end of one of his madcap stunts. He came close to discovering the less kind side of my nature one day when he came into my hotel room wearing an old man's mask. I was looking out of the window with my back to the door when he crept up behind me. Startled I turned and was just about to let one fly because I thought I was about to be mugged in my own room when he shouted for me not to hit him. I wasn't on the end of any of his japes after that.

A football squad needs a Gascoigne or a Steve Harrison because if everyone were totally professional for every moment of every day it would get pretty boring and add to the tension and the pressure. They are like safety valves. All the time I was in the squad, it was Gazza who provided the light relief. He was also the best footballer, a genuine match winner. When he was flying, he was world class.

I worry about his future. I count myself fortunate in the influences around me. With my wife and parents and others, I have a very stable life. In the north east it can be different; the mentality there is different. Things that are the norm in Newcastle aren't the norm in London or Nottingham or the West Country. I can't imagine Liz's grandmother or my grandmother, for instance, sitting down in a bar and drinking a pint of lager but Steve Stone's grandmother does. Gazza was brought up there and, from my experience, the attitude to life and the drinking culture are different.

When football is finished, he says he would like to coach but I can only see a club taking him on for the publicity or to stir up spectator and media interest. He is going to have to prove himself first. Steve Harrison is a good coach because he can switch off the tomfoolery in an instant. If Gazza can do that he can succeed, but Gazza never seems to switch off. Even on the pitch he pulls faces at opponents and jokes with the officials in the middle of a crucial match. But who knows what makes a good manager? I listen to the so-called experts talking about what constitutes a great coach and wonder why, if they know so much, they aren't top managers themselves.

Gascoigne gave a good hour in all of those games in Euro 96. He was not the player he was before his injury but he was still the one player who could turn a game for us. He enjoyed a renaissance under Terry's gentle but firm guidance. The relationship hadn't gone too well under Graham Taylor probably because Graham tried to get on top of him and change his way of life.

I had made up my mind before the tournament started that after it I was finally going to retire from international football no matter what happened. My reasoning was that I was coming up to 34, I was on borrowed time anyway and only playing until Graeme Le Saux was fit again. I hadn't at that stage realised how well the competition would go for the team and for me in particular.

There was no real indication of what was to come in the first game against Switzerland with that old nervous nonsense again. We were expected to win and we should have done so after Alan Shearer had given us the lead. But I gave away a penalty seven minutes from time and Turkyilmaz scored to level it up. I thought to myself, 'Hello, nearly man is here again.' The ball was kicked at me and I couldn't get out of the way. Referee Diaz Vega of Spain shattered me when he pointed to the spot.

Seven days later we took on the old enemy and by half-time it wasn't going the way we wanted it. We had cancelled each other out. Terry gambled by taking me off and putting on midfielder Jamie Redknapp. It changed the game.

I sat on the bench watching as Alan Shearer scored and just when I was thinking we were on our way we conceded another penalty. David Seaman made a magnificent save to keep out Gary McAllister's spot-kick. Gascoigne rubbed salt in the wound with his spectacular solo goal and suddenly we were on our way again. There was a touch of déjà vu about it all, reminding me of Italia 90.

I was delighted. We were through to the next phase of the competition but I didn't know where that left me. I had conceded a penalty in the first game and was taken off in the second. Jamie Redknapp had come on and influenced the game, laying foundations for Terry and England to build upon. Terry had played me as one of three central defenders and he told me at the time that it could extend my career by a few years. How right he was. I was not a good left-back anymore because part of that job was banging up and down the line for an hour and a half, but I felt I could do a good job at the back, especially as part of a three with two wing-backs. I don't know whether Kenny Dalglish would have taken a gamble on me without that, or even Harry Redknapp at West Ham. Making the switch was no problem because I had played at centre-back in my early days.

Terry decided to change the formation for the next game against Holland. He went with four at the back to counter their two wide players and one central striker. He is one of the most tactically aware coaches I have ever played for. His decision brought me back in and I had the pleasure of playing in what turned out to be the best performance of any England side in my 12 years' involvement. We didn't just beat the Dutch – we whacked them, a big footballing nation, 4–1. We played them out of sight. Teddy Sheringham and Alan Shearer scored two each. A fair result would have been five or six nil and I was aggrieved that we gave them a consolation goal.

It can be imagined what that result did for our confidence and for the supporters. They were delirious and so were we. The atmosphere at Wembley was like nothing I had ever known before and to be involved was very special.

David Seaman was outstanding, absolutely brilliant throughout the tournament, while Alan Shearer, after a quiet build-up, was on fire and Terry was getting the very best out of two of his old Spurs players, Teddy Sheringham and Paul Gascoigne.

We were now out of the league stage and into the knock-out section of the competition, drawn against Spain. I tried to convince myself that my old adage of playing for two caps would work, even if Terry changed the formation to fit the occasion and the opposition. But I was relieved when I found myself in the side for the quarter-final on the following Saturday.

Now Terry had a team bubbling with confidence and a crowd who were totally behind us. I told myself that as I had only ever lost twice at Wembley with England, the percentages were in our favour. I was certain that we could reach another major semi-final.

Spain played well against all the odds. They deserved more out of the game than they achieved and I have to admit that they were unlucky to have what looked to me like a good goal ruled out for offside. We dug in well, particularly the defence and Tony Adams in particular. It was a tough game, culminating in that penalty shoot-out. That emotional explosion after converting my penalty, came up from my boots somewhere; everything that had been generated throughout the entire tournament bubbled up. It was like an internal earthquake, a moment of release.

When David Seaman saved Miguel Angel Nadal's penalty, every

member of our team mobbed the brilliant Arsenal goalkeeper, except me. I remembered how I had felt six years earlier and so I went over to commiserate with Nadal. I didn't have it in me to join in the celebrations at his expense; it could wait until I reached the dressing-room.

I did the same with Teddy Sheringham a few months earlier when Nottingham Forest beat Spurs in the FA Cup on a penalty shoot-out. Mark Crossley made a good save from Teddy and took off towards our fans at the other end of the Spurs ground, followed by the rest of our players. I stayed back to shake hands with Teddy because I remembered how good the Germans were to me.

I cannot imagine enjoying a euphoric experience quite like that again. After the game, David Seaman and I were interviewed on television, me having scored that penalty and Dave having saved one. The interview was a long way from the crowd but we could still hear them singing 'Three Lions'. No one would go home. It sent tingles racing up and down my spine.

Terry gave everyone the day off after that game, to do whatever we wanted. I went to see the Sex Pistols at Finsbury Park. I dragged along Gareth Southgate and a couple of people from the FA. It was a blinding weekend for me, beating Spain, that great atmosphere and seeing a concert I thought I was sure to miss. We didn't trash the dressing-room afterwards – we were representing England. It was orange juices only!

Six years on and it's Germany all over again, but this time the thinking was totally positive. We are at home, on a roll and they were supposedly on that downward spiral after years on top. To add to the tension not only was there the threat of penalties but also the golden goal scenario where the scorer of the first goal in extra time won the match.

We played extremely well, not as well as against the Dutch but better than against Spain. Alan Shearer scored again, this time after only two minutes, meeting a little flick-on header from Rodders at a Gascoigne corner and we had our noses in front.

Then I thought we had half a chance of making our first final for 30 years. If I'm to be honest I have to hold up my hands and take the blame for the equaliser. It was just ten minutes or so after our goal and I allowed Kuntz to run across me, nip on and score. It was concentration again; if you don't concentrate for every second at this level you are punished. I saw him, thought 'I've got him, I've got him, I've got him,' watched the ball and he was in for a goal.

Golden goal is big pressure. For every corner, every free kick and every attack, you are on tenterhooks. If people tell me what a bad way penalties are to decide a game I would argue with them because no one ever turns it off on television. As for the golden goal, as a player there can be no better feeling than to score, knowing that the opposition can't come back. You can run round like a lunatic knowing that there is no more football to be played. But for the losers, there is nothing worse, knowing that there is no way back.

Darren Anderton hit a post and Gazza missed converting a cross almost on the goalline itself by a matter of inches. If either of those had gone in, the celebrations that day would have been something to behold.

We thought we deserved to win, especially with those two late chances, but suddenly it was penalties again.

As a coach, Terry Venables was one of the best. He was good at man management, too, in the way he handled Gascoigne and others. He had more than a few problems along the way. The business in Hong Kong and the broken television sets were not easy things to deal with. We had shot ourselves in the foot as a squad but he handled it well and all the players believed that he was on their side. We never felt as though he was double dealing, even though he has the reputation of being a bit fly. He was an ideal England coach in my opinion.

Terry came in straight after Graham Taylor who, in some ways, was too honest for his own good. Graham would become involved in a press conference, start talking and not stop. That's clever journalism and bad management. Sometimes you have to be like a politician – give so much and know when to call a halt. Too often Graham was led down a road for which he was unprepared. Terry was a different animal, very streetwise. He could play the journalists at their own game. He has had his fair share of nonsense but he has all the credentials and he could stand and fight his own corner.

Tactically, he was as good a coach as England has had, very astute. I was disappointed when he left. I had no axe to grind because as far as I was concerned I would have quit international football whether he had stayed on or not. If my dad had taken over at that point I would still have quit.

England and club football should be getting more mileage out of Terry Venables. He has been allowed to sit on his backside for far too long. He has such a wealth of knowledge that it is a waste for him to be working for some radio station. He knows the game inside out and is one of the best coaches in the country. He should always be in there working at the sharp end of the game and, if he's not, the Football Association should utilise his skills with the youngsters until he is back in full-time work.

Straight after the semi-final Liz and I packed our bags and went on holiday. I have a personal rule that if I'm playing in a tournament we book a holiday for two days after the final.

I did the same thing after Italia 90. It was straight back home, pack and off to Mauritius where we were booked into the fabulous Le Toueserok. In the reception when we checked in, Gianluca Vialli, Pietro Vierchowod and Roberto Mancini and their wives were doing the same thing, a couple of days after England had played against them in the World Cup play-off. I thought then what a small world it was but the same thing happened two days after Euro 96. At Heathrow Airport on our way to Zimbabwe, the entire German squad filed past carrying the European Championship trophy. We were too far from them to make contact. If they had been walking closer I would have shaken hands with them because I have so much respect for them as a football nation.

Funnily enough, I became known as 'The German' at Nottingham Forest that next season. It started when the opposing fans chanted 'Pearce is a German, Pearce is a German.' Ian Woan picked it up and started calling me Hermann the German and that was eventually shortened to the German.

At the Christmas party we had this little routine that we pinched from Derby County. Everyone would draw a name out of a hat and they would have to buy that person a suitable Christmas present. After Italia 90 I was bought German shirts, Nazi helmets and Freddie Starr-style German shorts with a swastika emblazoned on the leg. Whatever you were given you had to wear it all day at the Christmas party until the early hours of the morning.

I wasn't the only one to suffer. Steve Chettle had the reputation of being under the thumb at home so he was given a collar and lead. Kingsley Black pulled out Brian Roy and gave him a little puppet with a pea as a heart because Brian wasn't the bravest of players.

Fortunately, they eventually tired of the German gear and as I got older it was walking sticks and zimmer frames.

I took the idea with me to Newcastle, along with my music, and the first Christmas it worked like a dream. I pulled Warren Barton out of the hat and I bought him a hairdryer, nabbed a pot of cream out of the physio's room on which I stuck my own label which read 'Dwarf growing cream' and finished off the collection with a pair of trousers cut down to a pair of shorts with turn-ups.

The first present was because I had written in my column in a local paper that I had tackled him in training and knocked the hairdryer out of his hand. He didn't like that, nor the fact that the boys called him the Umpa Lumpa man because he had a long body and short legs, hence the other two gifts.

Goalkeeper Shay Given pulled out the Italian defender Alessandro Pistone and bought him a sheep's heart from the butcher. Duncan Ferguson drew Nol Solano and went round the north east of England trying to buy a llama. Honestly! As luck had it, there were no spare llamas around Newcastle. Andreas Andersson was brave. He made up a prisoner's suit with arrows for big Dunc while Alan Shearer was given a lovely Mary Poppins doll by Solano. The foreign boys really made an effort and it worked very well.

Rob Lee, not that much younger than me, drew me and it was back to the hearing aids, slippers and other senior-citizen accoutrements. It went with my retirement from the international stage.

CHAPTER 15

more comebacks than sinatra

After Euro 96, Nottingham Forest were playing a pre-season tournament at the City Ground when manager Frank Clark asked me if I would have a word with the new England coach Glenn Hoddle. I had the idea in the back of my mind that he might ask me to carry on playing at international level. Why else would the England manager ask to see me? When we met up, the first thing he said was, 'Can I ask you why you're not playing for England anymore?'

'I'm 35 years old, a new manager has come in and I thought it was the right time to retire.'

'For no other reason? No personal reasons? To spend more time with your wife and family?'

'No. Sometimes it's a wrench but the passion of playing for England and a short career outweigh the time it cost me with my wife and we have no children.'

'Would you consider coming back?'

'I'll think about it.'

'I'll need to know fairly quickly. Can you let me know soon?'

As soon as he said it I knew I was hooked again but I told him that I would ring him and let him know the next day.

'To be honest,' he said, 'I'm looking at playing three centre-halves and you're as good as any left-sided centre-back I've got. There's no one as good as you playing in that position. I can't guarantee you a game, but I would like you available.'

I telephoned him the next day and told him that I would come out of retirement. Basically, he picked his squad for Moldova, I was in it and what's more I played. I was also in the next squad against Poland at Wembley, which we won thanks to a couple of goals from Alan Shearer. The team didn't play particularly well but I didn't have a bad game. Then we played Italy at Wembley and lost to a goal for which I was to blame. Zola spun off me. Sol Campbell took some of the flak in the press but largely it was down to me. We were reasonably flat as a back three. Sol couldn't get near me and subsequently couldn't reach Zola quickly enough. After that I was left out of the side and they started to play very well.

I learned a lot from that game about playing in a back three. Glenn had a camera positioned above the stadium and he showed the defence, and the team, how the Italians defended as a back three with the markers so tight on Shearer that he couldn't move and the spare man 15 yards behind. They played the system really well while we were flat and not tight enough on certain individuals. It showed how we went to sleep when the ball was at the other end while the Italians were always alert.

I found Glenn very good tactically. I thought he was a good coach. He really understood that system and was able to pass on the relevant information. I also learned about improving my diet. You are never too old to learn about these things. He was obviously from the Wenger school of proper eating, having studied under him at Monaco.

He changed the side after that defeat and we won away against Poland and Georgia, both 2–0. They were among the best away performances I have seen from England. David Batty was outstanding in both games, sitting in front of the back four, mopping up everything and ratting around. The only away game I can remember that was better was a European qualifying game in 1987. I sat on the bench as a non-playing substitute when England beat Yugoslavia 4–1 in Belgade.

Hoddle had the team playing really well which didn't bode well for me. Apart from nicking the odd appearance as a substitute, I found myself back up in the stand again. There were no cast-iron promises and I had been around the game long enough not to expect anything.

Graeme Le Saux had come back from his injury and was playing at the back with Tony Adams and Gareth Southgate. It was a disappointing time for me but I was pleased to be around the squad and determined to see it through to the end of the 1998 campaign whether I was in the squad for France or not. I made myself available as promised and spent most of my time in the stand watching the side playing very well, culminating in that away game in Italy when the goalless draw clinched the place in the World Cup and forced the Italians into a play-off.

In the summer of 1997 we played in Le Tournoi and, surprisingly, I found myself back in the team against Italy for the first game, which we won 2–0. It was one of my best performances and my 76th cap. The next morning, I attended a press conference with Terry Butcher who was working for BBC Radio 5 Live. I was pleased with myself and Terry told me that I was getting better with age. I thought my old practice of playing for two caps had worked again and I was looking forward to the next game.

'You never know, Tel. That could have been my last game for England,' I joked.

'No chance,' he laughed.

The next game was against France and Glenn left me out. We finished up against Brazil and I was on the outside looking in again. Martin Keown played and injured his shoulder early on. I thought I was going on but rather than send me on in a straight swap, Glenn changed the side around and used Gary Neville instead. I felt it would have been a more balanced side with me there, being a left-footer. My joking prediction to Terry was right. It was my last game for Glenn and I was more than a little annoyed because I had played so well against Italy and was still dropped.

By the start of the next season, I had moved on to Newcastle and after starting pretty well picked up a hamstring injury that kept me out for three months. I wasn't available for three England squads, including the visit to Rome. I worked hard to get fit for my club and played quite well in the Champions League game against Barcelona in November when I came on as substitute. I stayed in the side for the rest of the season so had been playing regularly when what amounted to the England World Cup squad was due to be picked in February.

Glenn rang me and told me he was picking the squad the next day and he was leaving me out because he was concerned about my fitness when it came to playing games every three days. That was bullshit. He should have told me the truth, either that he thought I wasn't good enough anymore or that my legs had gone or whatever the real reason was for axing me. I would have appreciated that a hell of a lot more. I was old enough to see through his nonsense but I made it easy.

'Fine,' I said. 'I'm always available if you need me. I said that I'd keep myself ready until the World Cup if wanted and I will.'

I played from the end of November until May and missed no more than a couple of matches. There was no doubt about my fitness. By contrast Ian Wright, about the same age as me, had missed most of the last three months of the season but Glenn kept the door open for him. That rather destroyed Glenn's flimsy excuse. How much better if he had told me that I was out of the running and he would need me only if he had a lot of injuries.

In fact, the squad for February and March did suffer a lot of injuries and he called me back in for the game against Portugal. I turned up, trained but wasn't used in the side or on the bench. I lived in hope. It had worked for me in 1996 and I could always hope that it would work again.

It rankled me when he said that I couldn't play two games a week – I had been playing two games a week since I was six. I also couldn't understand why he would decide in February that I wasn't fit for a tournament that wasn't taking place until June.

I prefer straight talking but Glenn seemed to have a problem in that direction in this instance. Having been involved for the last ten years, there was an empty feeling when the World Cup came around. I went away on holiday. I wasn't really watching England as a supporter and felt very detached from it all. If there was a television nearby, I would make the effort but I'd been at the cutting edge for so long it was galling to miss out this time, especially as I thought I was so close to going at one stage. Only a month or so before, I had still been in the squad and clinging to the hope that I would go to France. It would have been a great way to finish my international career. I had been involved at the top level for so long, it was disappointing to have been to just one World Cup finals.

When we came back from holiday, we flew out to the horse sales in Ireland. Our flight was delayed and it meant I was able to watch the England v. Argentina game on a television in the airport lounge. Most people who came in were desperate to watch the football and were saying how glad I must be that the flight was delayed. I had to say yes but I wasn't. Of course I wanted England to do well because a lot of the players are my mates and I always want my country to do well. But I didn't feel any part of it. To go from those massive highs to fading out of it was hard to stomach. It wasn't the way I wanted to go. In fact, that was why I made my original decision to quit at the end of 1996.

I still feel that I was right to agree to play; after all I won an extra six caps for my country by doing so. What would I have done if I hadn't won those extra caps? I would have stayed at home and been bored stiff.

I don't bear Glenn any grudge other than wishing he had been a bit more honest with me. I met him at a dinner afterwards and we had a chat but I never did ask him why he hadn't told me the truth. I appreciate that a manager's job is hard work enough without players making it harder for him. I had never spent a lot of time with Glenn so he didn't know my character or my nature.

I watched in the lounge at Dublin airport and saw Graeme Le Saux come off injured and then the game go to penalties. It was a back-to-the-wall situation after David Beckham had been sent off and if I could ever have done England a service it was then. If he had taken me he could have slung me on when Le Saux came off and I would have rolled up my sleeves and taken a penalty for him.

I turned to Liz and said bitterly, 'Why the hell didn't he just take me?'

My place in the squad probably went to Rio Ferdinand and while it was great for Rio was it the right thing for England? Rio hadn't won a cap so it would have been hard to toss him on in that explosive situation. By contrast, I had been there, seen it, done it. In one or two quarters in the game, I was asked why I hadn't been taken when a game like that was so much up my street. I am not naïve enough to think I can change a game or win a game, but I certainly won't buckle no matter how much the odds are stacked against and I won't be intimidated.

Tony Adams is that sort of player and I really did become anxious when, in extra time, the old warhorse, played a one-two and went charging up the line. I was on my feet shouting at him, 'Tone, don't do it, get back, get back, we're down to ten men.' It was the only emotion I showed throughout the entire match. When David Beckham was sent off, that didn't mean a lot to me and I just thought that we were down to ten and that we had blown it. But the boys battled brilliantly and I was proud of them.

I didn't get involved in the controversy that surrounded Glenn Hoddle. Certainly I never came across Eileen Drewery when I was with England, nor was I asked if I wanted to pop in to see her. I suppose most people would look at my public persona and think that there is no way I would become involved with that sort of nonsense and, while that may be true, as a professional I can see that if there is an option and it will help just one member of the squad to be a better player and contribute more it is a good thing. It's easy to pick up on bits and pieces and criticise, and I must admit that Glenn rather left himself open because he has such strong views about religion and other related matters and was prepared to air them in public. But if they are your beliefs you have to stick with them and he would have looked even worse if he had shelved them just because he had been slated in the press. In many ways he was pig stubborn but you can't reach the top in his profession without being a bit that way.

Whenever something new is introduced it is open to criticism. Look at food and alcohol and how the perception in professional football has altered in recent years. Clubs are much more aware of the importance of diet allied with fitness and those players who take it on board tend to last a lot longer than those who abuse their bodies. I like to think that I have stuck around longer than most partly because I didn't go out and get blasted every Sunday lunchtime.

Hoddle took a lot of stick over the Eileen situation but I honestly believe that if one player was helped 5 per cent going with the team was justified. If an England manager rejected that opportunity he would not be doing his job. That can be the difference between winning and losing a game. Those percentages are becoming finer and finer as footballers become more and more athletic. Glenn was probably unfairly vilified but if people are seen to be different they tend to be pilloried.

It wouldn't have been the case had England been winning all of their games; none of that would have mattered. All those chinks in your armour are overlooked when you are successful but once you start losing they all come to the fore, especially if you have taken on the journalists. It is a fact of life that, if you treat people reasonably, when it hits the fan they will be more sympathetic than if you have taken them on as Glenn did. I felt he was a touch hounded, but if you are going to be sacked you might as well go knowing that you did everything your own way and Glenn certainly did that.

Like Terry Venables, Glenn has more to offer the England game at international level and should not be overlooked. I learned a hell of a lot from both of them, probably as much from Glenn as anyone else. I have been away with the England Under-18s and I know how much those boys would have loved to have someone along like Glenn Hoddle or Terry Venables, and how much they could have learned without it being detrimental to the full-time FA coaching staff.

Glenn is close to my age and you have to worry that the opportunity may have come and gone when the best years of his coaching and managerial career should still be ahead of him. It would be short-sighted if both he and Terry were ruled out when, perhaps in five years' time, either of them could be the right man for the job. But with the FA hierarchy you cannot see it happening. They would be too frightened to do it.

To stay in management in England for any length of time is an achievement on its own. As soon as results start going wrong, the chairman, the press and the supporters are down on you like a ton of bricks with all sorts of 'experts' from radio pundits to politicians demanding your head. Look how close Sir Alex Ferguson came getting the push at Old Trafford. Results picked up and he is now lauded as the best manager there has ever been in the British Isles. Howard Kendall at Everton was one game from the sack and then went on to win cups and titles at home and abroad.

It's criminal to dispense with knowledge too early. With ten more years' experience, who knows where Glenn will be. Maybe he wouldn't want to be involved again after the way he was treated. Considering it is the best job in English football, it is sad that so many England managers are relieved when they leave.

Kevin Keegan was out of the game for too long, but at least that was his own choice. I can't say I have had too many dealings with Kevin over the years, other than when he was brilliant over bringing Newcastle United to my testimonial at Forest. He was so straight down the line with me it was frightening. He said yes down the telephone and turned up six months later with a full team without needing to have any further dialogue. That, needless to say, impressed me.

When he was given the England job to succeed Glenn, he was the obvious choice. As far as I could see, only Terry Venables was in contention. At the time, I was wondering where my next game was coming from at club level with never a thought about international football. I was lucky to get back into Premier Division action with West Ham United and was concentrating on trying to keep my place with them when I took a call on my mobile telephone while travelling on the M25. I pulled over and was surprised to find that it was Kevin. My first reaction was that it was something to do with the Under-18 side with whom I had become involved or that maybe he wanted to have a chat about Joe Cole, Rio Ferdinand or a couple of the other boys at West Ham whom he might see as potential full caps.

'If I called you into the next squad, would you turn up?' he asked.

'Do what? You do know I have retired twice?'

'Yes, I know all that. I'm not bothered. I saw you at Villa and you're playing as well as any left-sided player in the country. 'If I called you, will you turn up?' I was flabbergasted.

'I'm just on the motorway on my way home. Do you mind if I get back and have a word with my wife and call you back?'

'No problem, but you do realise that you can't sit on this for days.'

I promised to ring him back that very night; not that I really needed the time. It was exactly the same as when Glenn asked me to come out of retirement. As soon as the words came out of his mouth, I didn't really have to think about it. This time, though, I had just spent more than six months playing for Newcastle reserves wondering whether I was still good enough to play at club level never mind international level.

I had been out of the international squad for two and a half years and played only three games for West Ham at the time of the call and I was still in the clouds when I got home and told Liz the unbelievable news. She told me that I had nothing to lose and I telephoned Kevin straight back and told him that I would be honoured if he thought I was good enough. He said that it would be great to have me along but, of course, could give no promises that I would be picked. On the other hand, you don't pick a 37-year-old to sit on the bench or in the stand. He realised that there would be some criticism but he was strong enough to stand for his own beliefs. There were important games coming up, not so much Luxembourg at home but those old enemies Poland away. I had certainly been there and had not been fazed by it.

When we first met up he didn't try to build up my hopes and I told him that I was happy to be along, play or not. But I did play in the first game and became the fifth-oldest player ever to play for England. It couldn't have gone better. We scored six and didn't concede one against the amateurs from Luxembourg. I had a goal disallowed, so the nearly man struck again. There always seems to be someone out there pulling the reins and making sure that I keep my feet on the ground.

I joined up with the squad, tried to get as fit as I could and went into the game with exactly the same attitude as when I played my first international – play well in this one and the next cap will follow. I had to show that I was physically fit and able to do my job.

Kevin Keegan can do me no wrong. I had nothing to prove and he couldn't upset me. He could have picked me for one game and then bombed me and it wouldn't have hurt. As long as I could help him out for one game for a payback, that was good enough by me. He had done me a big favour with my testimonial and then another by bringing me back to the squad. I was going to give him everything for as many games as he wanted me and then if he found a kid to take my place that was fine. There was no contract; nothing written in blood.

I was like a little kid. It wasn't like my first cap because this time I had nothing to lose. This was a bonus because these were caps I never dreamed I would win. It was a great honour and a bit like a testimonial, going back to an old club for someone's benefit match.

The games couldn't have worked better for me, starting at Wembley where I received a very emotional welcome from the fans. My first England manager Bobby Robson was the guest of honour. And the result was right. Then it was off to Poland and a make-or-break game that let us in through the back door for the Euro 2000 Championship. From a defensive point of view, we couldn't do more than keep another clean sheet in Poland and that we did. It was another of those backs-against-the-wall jobs that couldn't have suited me better.

Everyone will admit that it doesn't matter how you get there, but you like to do it with a bit of style. English football had stuttered since 1998 and it spluttered right up until that very last day. Let's hope we learned a few lessons from that bad 18 months.

The squad had changed a lot, not so much in personnel as in the way it was run and its professionalism. The media side had been improved; they had tweaked it a lot since I was on the players' committee in 1990. The changes were all for the better, the relationship was better with the press, it was much better organised and there was a good atmosphere within the camp, more like club football.

Kevin likes his training to be enjoyable and fun, and he likes to join in himself when he can. The players have a lot of respect for him; he is likeable man and a good motivator. Kevin is not one of the more technical coaches I have worked for, so he has Derek Fazackerley and Les Reid to do the coaching.

I chatted with Kevin and Gareth Southgate on the way back from Poland and at the airport I just said, 'Thanks. It was a pleasure to be along.'

When I broke my leg, both Kevin and Arthur Cox telephoned me shortly afterwards. 'Funny old game, isn't it?' Kevin said. He wasn't wrong. Arthur Cox checked with my progress and who knows what my status would have been when Graeme Le Saux was eventually ruled out for the season.

Missing the two play-off games against Scotland really gutted me. I thought I had done well enough in the two games I had played in to be involved in any play-offs in some capacity or other. When we drew Scotland out of the hat, I would have busted a gut to play.

Kevin did not discard me. He invited me to be part of the squad even though I was far from being fit and unable to join in any training. When they trained at Bisham Abbey, I trained on my own in the gym and then joined the card school. I felt part of it until the day of the game when I found myself creeping around, knowing that the players needed their sleep.

I was allowed to come and go as I pleased, even to the extent of being able to pop home to Wiltshire to sleep in my own bed and then join the squad the next morning.

To be honest, it gets no better than being with England. I recall Bobby Robson saying to me when I joined up, 'This is the best team you will ever play for.' He was right. Playing for your national side when you are English is something special. It was still a big honour to be around, after all my caps.

I attended all the team meetings and joined in everything I could. It became a bit of a joke with Alan Shearer and Gareth Southgate because they didn't know whether I was there as a coach or a player. One day I would appear in a players' training kit and that night I would turn up for dinner in a coaching top, only because that was what had been left outside my bedroom door. The players would give me an old-fashioned look and ask me what role I was playing now! I admitted to them that I didn't know what I was there for other than to enjoy myself and have a game of cards.

I travelled up to Hampden Park for the first match and I was proud of the result in what was as very, very big game. We rode our luck but we got everything right and to achieve a 2–0 result was tremendous.

Then came the Wembley game. I have never felt like that after an England match. I didn't think we played and, worse, I didn't think we played with any spirit at all. I was given a seat in the stand. The Scottish substitutes who weren't involved sat behind me and they were the ones who were cock a' hoop as the Scots outfought and, at times, outplayed us. I was boiling up inside because we were playing so badly. I felt like shouting didn't they realise that this was Scotland we were playing against. I wanted us to win this game 4–0 regardless of the first-leg result.

It was the Scots fans who went home happy, not us. I went into the dressing-room after the game and it was a very strange atmosphere. We had achieved our goal in reaching the finals but we had lost. Even Kevin was quiet. It was as though we had found a pound and lost a fiver. How much better it would have been to have reversed the result. We should have settled for a 1–0 defeat at Hampden and a 2–0 win at home. For me what mattered was that we had lost to the Jocks and I have never gone home from Wembley in such a bad mood. I was furious. I couldn't imagine players such as Terry Butcher and Bryan Robson allowing a performance like that one. Sometimes you cannot help losing matches but I felt as though we went out that day feeling that the job was done. We didn't start and didn't finish. It was the Scots who came away with all the credit.

Talk is cheap and too many players pay lip service to playing for their country. To succeed, we need the commitment of players such as Tony Adams and Alan Shearer and, even more, Viv Anderson, Tony Dorigo and any number of goalkeepers who keep turning up for the English cause in the knowledge that much of their time will be spent in the stands or on the bench. It's easy to win 30 caps, be dropped and then feign injury or announce your retirement, and even easier to suffer a little injury which keeps you out of an unappetising friendly with nothing on it. I treasure every one of my caps and will never forget that lesson of Saudi Arabia when all my Forest team-mates pulled out and Brian Clough offered to make the excuse of an injury if I wanted to withdraw.

Tony Adams, to me, epitomises the dedication and commitment all players should show when picked for their country. When I first met Tony he was the one being built up as the next England captain. He was young, he was loud and he knew he was good at his job. None of Clough's players were like that; they tended to be quiet. They turned up, did the job and went home. Tony would be in the dressing-room, shouting and hollering with plenty to say for himself. I was 25 at the time. He was some five years younger and, I thought, a bit full of himself and a bit noisy. He was already pushing for the Arsenal captaincy. But Tony, I learned, didn't shout for show. It was how he was. Now he is more thoughtful and concerned. He has been through lean times and has pulled himself together in spectacular style.

Tony is a one-club man and there are very few players who have that loyalty these days. I felt the same about Forest. It was only through force of circumstance that I left. Tony broke through at an early age and hasn't had it all easy. The drinking, according to him, became heavy when he was injured or, perversely, when the team were winning, so it wasn't true adversity that forced him into the bars and the clubs. Whenever he played the big games for England he was there to be counted, just like Terry Butcher before him. He could never be described as the most talented player in the England squad but when the chips are down, he is the one you would want on your side. The arrival at Arsenal of Arsene Wenger has given him a new lease of life and added years to his career.

I give him total credit for the way he has changed. Could you believe Psycho and Rodders sitting down sans alcohol to discuss the merits of Oscar Wilde or books of poetry? That's what happened. Tony suddenly stopped and said, 'Can you imagine this conversation between the two of us a few years ago?' I couldn't. I only had to think back to one of the gatherings in Manchester before an England game. The Arsenal boys had arrived in a hired stretch limousine and had enjoyed a good drink on the way. They were in the bar when I got there and by that time they were steaming. Tony was really bad-mouthing a barman who must have been well in excess of his 50th birthday. I felt embarrassed to be there, had an orange juice and went to my room.

Tony looks back on all that and cringes. I didn't read his book, not even the extracts in the newspapers, but I am amazed at some of the things he is supposed to have revealed about himself. All I can say is that, apart from the drinking, he hid it pretty well from me.

I am equally staggered that he can call himself an alcoholic. No professional sportsman playing at the level and consistency of Tony Adams could possibly be a full-blown alcoholic in the sense of being a constant drinker. It is physically impossible. Can a footballer playing in the Premier Division be an alcoholic in this day and age? My answer has to be no. Certainly Tony drank a lot, too much, but I know how I feel after a heavy night out. There is no way I could play football the next day.

I would define an alcoholic as someone who cannot do without a drink. Certainly, I never saw Tony drinking on the mornings of an international match. If he did, he was very cunning and not only hid the booze but hid the effects remarkably well. There were times with England when I looked at players and wondered how they managed to get that drunk. I've walked down the corridor on a Sunday morning and seen Tony's hotel door hanging off its hinges.

I don't have much sympathy with the drinking stakes. I believe that if you are involved in professional football, or any professional sport come to that, the least you can do is lead a reasonable life which gives you half a chance and doesn't lead down the road of drugs, drink or excessive living of any kind. The rewards are so high, the price you pay is slim and for such a short time as to be negligible.

It was the same whenever we went away for a tournament. I could never understand why players needed to go for a drink during that period. In six weeks' time they could drink themselves silly and no one, not the manager, the press or the supporters, would care or think any the less of them. I can count on the fingers of one hand the number of times I have had a drink when I have been away with England, and even then it's been just a few lagers. Mainly I stuck to orange juice because I saw how the players could become uncontrollable and let themselves and their country down.

Des Walker likes a drink but he would go on his own or to a wine bar in Nottingham rather than a flash club in London. He would rather have a drink at a students club. He always doubted the wisdom of deliberately going for a drink where you could be seen. When I go out, I prefer somewhere quiet, too, away from that goldfish bowl. Paul Gascoigne, on the other hand, would go for a drink in his England tracksuit. He might as well have waved a banner to make sure everyone knew he was there. But Paul likes being in the limelight; I don't. I can understand other footballers saying they couldn't live the life I live. That's fine. You have to be comfortable with yourself, sleep sound and be able to look yourself in the eye in the mirror the next day.

For near enough every game in my professional career I have been at the height of my fitness, allowing for things like flu or niggling little injuries. There is a tiny percentage of matches after which I had to admit to myself that I hadn't given my best because I'd had a few drinks too many over dinner on a Wednesday or Thursday evening. If I have a bad game, I want it to be because I have simply not played well and not because I have stayed out late drinking beforehand. If I've slept well, eaten well and trained well, at least I can look my manager in the eye and say I have done everything I can.

I see more relevance and parallels to myself with Tony Adams than I do with most others and if I were a manager the first player I would sign would be a carbon copy of the Arsenal captain. I would bring him in, make him captain and build the team around him. That is how highly I think of him.

All his problems are self-induced, as are those that have afflicted his former Highbury team-mate Paul Merson. But with Merse, despite following his story through the media and hearing from other professionals, I still don't know where the real problems lay: with gambling, drinking, drugs or a combination of all three. I haven't read either of his books. Of course, I know he likes a drink and a bet and he claims he has done drugs. If he's up against all those things, I salute him for having sorted them out and getting on with his career.

I believe we are all accountable for our own actions, on and off the pitch. I don't have a great deal of sympathy for players who have abused their profession and therefore I don't have a great deal of sympathy for Merson. I hope he has sorted himself out because I like him as a person and have always had a reasonable relationship with him. But liking someone and respecting them professionally is a different thing. It is not in my heart to forgive and forget, especially when we are in the same England side. While I have pushed the ability I've been given to the limit, Paul Merson has nowhere near the number of England caps he should have had with his talent.

In football, the performers carry a lot of hopes and expectations on their shoulders and as more money comes into the game, the more those expectations will be. I have a number of friends who are staunch Arsenal fans who loved Merson when they saw him in the local pubs drinking pints with the fans, but when all his bad habits became public knowledge they were the first to criticise him when his form wavered or when Arsenal had a bad patch. I told them they were hypocrites. The time to have a go at him was when he was drinking in the Holloway Road when he and the team were doing well.

The majority of professionals I know are good, honest pros. It's usually only the ones who stray from the straight and narrow who we hear and read about. The arrival of foreign players, particularly from Italy, has brought in good habits and they have helped to educate English players. Certainly the booze culture is alien to them and attitudes generally are changing.

When I was at Forest as manager there was booze everywhere and I told them I didn't want it. It had no more place in my office than it had in the dressing-room. I am a sportsman, not a rock star. I didn't even want it on the bus on the way home from games. The players can let down their hair together come the summer or club breaks and I believe that can play an important part in building team spirit. The pressures are so high that players need to rest and relax and maybe have a few drinks – but always at the right time.

When I started playing for England, we would always meet in the bar on the Sunday but that's not done anymore. It affected training on a Monday morning and the professionals have taken that out of the games. Twelve years ago I didn't know that drinking makes you dehydrated and more susceptible to injuries. We all have that information at our fingertips now.

I have watched Paolo di Canio at close hand and I am impressed with how he prepared himself at the ground. He stretches well, trains well, even if he doesn't like being kicked in a practice match. He is just as likely to walk off if that happens. I look at him and can see that the game means something to him.

Ray Wilkins and David Platt were model professionals and took their game to its achievable limits. Platt likes to say the right thing and be seen to do the right thing, which is very good public relations for football. But at the same time he has learned about the game and he has looked after himself. There are other old pros who have been knocking around since the seventies and their views of the game have remained unaltered since the day they hung up their boots. They are in a time warp. They're like a stick of rock – break them open and they're the same right the way through. Platt has been prepared to look at what is going on and change with the game.

As for Ray Wilkins, I can listen to him all night when he is talking about football. He talks such common sense.

When I was away with England, I asked Gary Lewin, the Arsenal physio, if it would be possible to go and watch Arsene Wenger taking training for a couple of weeks. It sounds ridiculous that as a West Ham player I should want to go across London to watch another club train, but I like what I have heard about the Frenchman and the things he does. More than that, I have seen the results in what he has done with Martin Keown and Tony Adams and others. It is easy when you have been around for a while to think you know how the game is played and that you know best. That attitude can be dangerous. Unfortunately, I think Glenn Hoddle has that problem. He comes across to many as one who knows best and is inflexible with it.

Ideally, in the next few years I would like to watch Wenger, talk to him and to other top managers in the game to see what they are doing. Even if you come away from the experience rejecting everything you have seen, at least you have opened your mind and given it a chance. David Platt said that when he packed in playing he would tour around

Europe watching the top coaches in action. It was good public relations again, but the concept was right.

Gareth Southgate is another good professional who pushes himself. When he played in midfield for Crystal Palace he was steady and would never have won an international place, but he earned himself a move by working extremely hard at his game. He has an old head on young shoulders, trains hard and wants to learn and succeed. I can see him going on into coaching and management. I would be very surprised if he didn't and if he wasn't successful.

CHAPTER 16

what now?

When I was younger and not in the public gaze, I enjoyed the company of my mates, being the centre of attention and playing the fool. That's the real me and not the image I have portrayed during my professional life. Even now when the old crowd meet up and we let our hair down, I will be as stupid as the next one.

With strangers, it's different. That's not because I'm miserable but because I don't want to be a celebrity. If I'm at work, I'll sign autographs and do anything necessary but away from it I value my anonymity. I didn't mind so much when I was known solely in Nottingham but since the 1990 World Cup I've become more easily recognised.

Both Liz and I are private people and we enjoy our life away from the game. Also football is such a high-profile profession, and generates such a lot of pressure these days, that I need time to myself all the more.

I'm not complaining. Football has brought me many things I would not have had as an electrician in London – an MBE, for instance. I am a royalist and, consequently, I was deeply honoured and thrilled when I was nominated in the 1999 New Year's honours list. I don't believe our royal family are as appreciated at home as they are abroad, but that's the British.

When the letter arrived, it was a huge surprise. It had not crossed my mind that I could be in line for something like that. It's something that happens to other people. I do a job that I love and I don't see anything special in that. For someone to give me an award for what I have done in football is a massive bonus.

It was announced on New Year's Day and I went to Buckingham Palace in March with Liz and Chelsea to receive it. We had a smashing day. There weren't too many from the world of sport, although I did meet the athlete Denise Lewis, but there were people from most other walks of life – firemen, schoolteachers, nurses, even lollipop ladies – all of them far more deserving of their awards than us so-called celebrities. It was a beautiful sunny day and apart from meeting a cross-section of the working community in Britain, I was also introduced to the Queen.

It was the second time I had enjoyed that privilege. Previously I had gone along to the Palace with a lot of other sportsmen and women, able-bodied and disabled on behalf of the British Sporting Trust, a charity endorsed by prince Charles. There were around a thousand of us invited and out of those a dozen of us were asked to meet the Royal family beforehand. That was quite an honour, too. When I looked around the room, I found myself in the company of some of the biggest names in sport, including Lennox Lewis, Henry Cooper, Prince Naseem, Sally Gunnell, and Steven Redgrave. We were all lined up and I was a couple down from Prince Naseem, listening to what was being said as Prince Philip was introduced to each person in turn.

The Duke of Edinburgh, obviously recognising royalty in the Sheffield boxer, asked in all innocence, 'And what do you do?'

The Prince looked at him and said, 'I beat people up, man.'

'Oh,' said the Duke, 'You're a boxer.'

'Yeah,' said the Prince, 'I just beat them up.'

It was all I could do not to laugh out loud it was so comical. It certainly broke the ice for the rest of us. It also brought home how difficult it is for the Royal family, meeting thousands of people and having to find something to say. What do they talk about to a footballer who plays for a club (Newcastle at the time) they have probably never heard of? But they sounded interested and I thought the entire event was very worthwhile to those of us who were there.

I have done my own little bit with presentations and I know how hard it can be. Multiply that by many times over with the added knowledge that the slightest slip or wrong move and you are all over the front pages the very next day.

Is it worth it? Ask the tourists who flock to the Palace, just as we go to see the Eiffel Tower or the Sydney Opera House. They were all at the gates when we drove into the courtyard to park our cars before the British Sporting Trust event. Palace officials parked everyone, from the canoeists in their Ford Escorts with the canoe strapped to the roof to the four-wheel drives. The only one they parked round the back was Prince Naseem's huge stretch limousine. One way and another, he certainly made an impact.

I enjoyed mixing with the different sportsmen and women, professional and amateur, at the charity event and I enjoyed meeting the other people when I was awarded my medal. I am quite shy when I don't know people, and I spent a great deal of time talking to a fireman from Hereford who had been working in the force for 30 years. My only complaint was that there was nothing to eat! It would have been nice if they had knocked up a few bacon sandwiches at that time of the morning but there was only bottled water.

As well as my visits to the Palace, I also had a couple of visits to Downing Street when John Major was in residence at number 10. The first occasion was immediately after Euro 96 when the entire squad was invited but I was the only one not away on holiday. When the Football Association asked me if I would like to go and take Liz along I jumped at the opportunity of seeing a bit more of British history at first hand. We had a guided tour of number 10 and then enjoyed a garden party outside in glorious weather. I was introduced to John Major and was impressed. He is a very nice man and certainly knows his sport. Whether you agree with his politics or not, you had to admire his apparent honesty and sincerity. He came across as a thoroughly decent bloke. What more can you ask from a politician?

There were a lot of celebrities and the Prime Minister had time for everyone, talking to each of us as we arrived. We must have made a big impression at the European Championship because a number of the showbusiness personalities took the time and trouble to come over and congratulate the team through me.

I was there again a year later when Mr Major invited the England squad back again when they were all available.

We are lucky to have a nice house in the country with a bit of land, away from the football environment. We used to live outside Nottingham but went into the town for shopping and entertainment. Naturally, having been there for so long, people would stop and exchange pleasantries or ask for autographs. I am never stopped to talk about football in the village where we live now.

As a player, I do tend to take the game home with me but eventually I can unwind and switch off. As a manager, I discovered that the game is with you all the time. You are thinking about training, buying and selling players, next Saturday's team and a million and one other related matters. It will be very important to have that stable home life if I go into management.

In my experience, if a couple get on really well, there's a convergence of opinions and an understanding of what's needed. Liz mirrors my professionalism in football in her work with horses. I admit that I can be a little bit slapdash outside football. But we have found a common interest in horses and I now gain almost as much pleasure out of them as Liz.

We have friends in the horse world who buy and sell foals, known in the trade as pin hooking, that is buying them young and selling them on at the sales for a profit. Liz went to the sales at Doncaster and bought a five-month-old foal who we named Man of the Match. The idea was to look after him until he was four and then sell him on. It didn't work out that way. Archie, as we call him, became a family friend and when he reached the age of four we decided to keep him for at least another couple of years, put him into training and see what he was made of.

We had looked around Jenny Pitman's yard and liked what we saw, especially in the care of the horses, so we sent him there when he was six. He had a couple of years at Jenny's, running three times in the first year and being placed third in the last race. In the second year, he ran ten times and was placed several times without ever winning a race. He was a very honest, very reliable jumper but without the pace to go on and win the top prizes. We had a lot of fun with him.

After the two years with the Pitman stables, we had an offer from Jenny Pigeon, based in Towcester, wanting to buy him. We didn't sell but it put the idea in our heads to send him to her point-to-point yard. It was a successful move. In his first year, he ran ten times, had three wins and a couple of places. In the second year, he had only three runs because of the lack of firm ground.

The nerves I suffer watching him are worse than walking out to play at Wembley. You are so scared that something is going to happen to hurt him. The nerves don't settle for the first two or three fences but, fortunately for us, he is such a good jumper that we were more concerned than him or his jockey, Fred Hutsby.

Considering he cost us only £1500 plus VAT, he has been marvellous value. When he finished at the national hunt yard we had an offer of £10,000 for him because of his jumping ability. Champion jockey Tony McCoy rode him once and Rodney Farrant was his regular partner.

The betting side didn't interest me at all. The first time he ran I had a tenner on him but it was no more than a gesture. What with being in the stables before the race and then in the ring, there was never time. Anyway, I have seen too many footballers go down that slippery route! A lot of footballers, past and present, own horses these days, but a lot of them are in it because of the betting interest. Betting to me is incidental.

We still have Archie and will keep him. We have just added another racehorse, a three-year-old by Be My Native, for the future. As well as these two, we have an 18-year-old mare named Goose Green (because she was born during the Falklands conflict). We bought her for Liz when we were in Nottingham. She was a hunter until an injury prevented her from being ridden. She has foaled three youngsters. There is a six-year-old named Crystalline, a five-year-old named Key Witness, whom we sold in 1999, and a yearling named Cracker. Seeing young foals running around is another special part of breeding horses. Now we have 28 acres of land we are seriously considering having resting racehorses when they have a couple of months off in May and June.

I enjoy going round the racecourses, especially Cheltenham. Every time we have been there I have had a great time. We usually go with

Mark Crossley and his wife and we have also taken Des Walker and Warren Barton and their wives. Everyone who goes enjoys the day, the atmosphere and especially the company of the Irish.

I don't come across too many other football people at the races. Alex Ferguson, Kevin Keegan, Mick Channon and the other big-name owners and trainers are mainly involved in flat racing. For me, jumping offers so much more and the flat holds no interest at all. By the time you sort out your horse, it's all over, whereas in national hunt racing anything can happen at anytime and usually does.

We fly over to Ireland every year for the Fairyhouse sales and take the opportunity to travel round the studs, looking at the stallions. In the evening we go out for a few beers before dinner. It's not solely owning the horses but everything that goes with it which makes it such a good occupation.

Liz has always been involved in horses and they play a large part in her life. She has had horses ever since she was a child. Her father, Maurice, is a retired farmer. Her mother, Mary Cole, used to ride in ladies races and won the first ladies race ever staged at Hawthorn Hill. Now she writes about equestrianism. Liz has two brothers, Joey, who is a contract farmer, and Chris, who served an apprenticeship with Richard Hannon before joining Vincent O'Brien in Ireland. He later rode in Australia. I cannot see her existing without horses. That became evident when we first moved to Nottingham. She is a country girl. She could never understand other footballers' wives whose lives consisted of getting up in the morning with no reason to go outside the front door unless it was to go shopping, often just for the sake of it. She says to me that I like football more than I like her but my answer is that she likes horses more than she likes me. It is a happy stalemate.

What makes a good coach or a good manager? It is a relevant question for me to ask because I hope that's where my future lies when I finally hang up my boots.

I really enjoyed my brief time in charge at Forest and relished the responsibility, just as I did as captain of most of the teams I have played for. Even in that first game for West Ham, Steve Lomas was injured and Harry asked me to lead them out. Something like that makes me very proud, as it would to be a manager of a professional club.

Ray Wilkins was a model professional, a genuinely nice fellow and someone I really like as a person. If ever I listen to a pundit on television I would prefer it to be Ray. He reminds me of Brian Clough in the old days, someone who knows the game inside out, talks well and has no obvious axe to grind as so often happens with some former players. Ray highlights the good things in football and only now and again points out the negatives.

So why hasn't he made his mark as a manager? Maybe it's because a manager needs a nasty streak, something that appears to be alien to Ray. Certainly Brian Clough had it and so do Sir Alex Ferguson, Graeme Souness and George Graham. Players are scared to cross managers like them because they are in awe of them. But this is a quality, if a quality it is, which has to come from within. It can't be manufactured as Trevor Francis, for one, discovered at Queens Park Rangers. He, like Ray, doesn't have that nasty streak in him.

There are enough decent men around who have been successful as managers and if it isn't there you have to manage without it. You are what you are and the reverse applies to the nasty manager who tries to be nice and falls on his backside.

Any manager needs a lot of luck on and off the pitch and particularly in picking up the odd young gem who comes through the ranks. Also of course, a manager must be shrewd with signings.

It is surely harder now to succeed as a manager than ever it was and the more time goes on so the harder it becomes. The modern manager is governed by financial constraints and the smaller clubs cannot succeed at the very top level anymore. They can nick a cup here and a cup there like Leicester City have done in recent years. It could even be said that they have been overachieving for their size. Their former manager Martin O'Neill was very shrewd and clever with his signings. He looked in depth at players' backgrounds and took on those who worked hard not only for themselves but for the team. Their attitude is that if you are going to lose then go down fighting. That's Martin O'Neill's legacy to Leicester and his promise to Celtic.

To be a successful manager it seems that you need a bit of everything. No one, no matter how good or great a player he has been, knows enough to take a management job and say he knows the right way immediately. You have to listen to experience and have people around whom you can trust and respect. I don't mean yes men. There are plenty of those around at the moment but they have no value compared with someone who will be brave enough to tell his boss he is wrong and to think along another line. I see some managers with coaches around them who are afraid to offer a different opinion or who will just give another version of the same story.

When I took over at Nottingham Forest, Liam O'Kane helped me a great deal. As player-manager I found it very difficult at half-time to make a speech after running around for 45 minutes. I told him that I felt I had to say something as soon as I walked in instead of getting a cup of tea and relaxing. He took over after a couple of games and I knew it was right because the things I had been thinking as I walked through the dressing-room door at half-time had changed by the time I'd mulled over them. I let Liam chat and then I would stand up and pass my opinions and talk to Liam about what we might do. When you are out there it's difficult to gain a full impression of what's going on all over the pitch. You have a different perspective from the man sitting on the bench or in the stand with an overall view.

If things are going well, like they were for Kenny Dalglish when he was player-manager at Liverpool, fine. More often than not, he would go into the dressing-room at half-time with the team in the lead and little more to say than carry on as you are. It was very much the same after games, and a jolly-up five-a-side in the week keeps things ticking over when you are that good and so far ahead of the rest.

But when you do not have a top club, the results might not have gone for you and you might not have played well yourself, it is far more difficult to come in and point the finger at someone else.

There was the time we played at Blackburn Rovers and I had taken winger Brian Roy off. He had a go at Liam as he came off the pitch and then he came down the front of the coach to talk to Liam and me to ask why he had been taken off. I told him to go home and watch a video of the game and he would see why. It was because he was doing nothing for the team. When everyone else was defending with their backs to the wall, he was standing on the halfway line waiting for the ball. It was a time when everyone had to knuckle under and graft. The conversation became heated and Liam knew me well enough to calm things down with a little kick under the table. He knew I would eventually lose my temper with Brian. In the end, I told him to go back down the other end of the bus and ask his team-mates whether they would pick him and to let that be his answer.

I was delighted when the FA called up half a dozen ex- and older professionals to help with the England teams from Under-15 to Under-21. I was assigned to the Under-18s and was thrilled with the appointment because, apart from the involvement with England, it was a big help in my desire to become a qualified coach. I was in the middle of my coaching badge course and it enabled me to gain practical experience. I also felt it was a benefit to the youngsters, who were able to look up to someone who had been there and done it.

Will I be a good manager? I don't know. I am not that conceited to say yes. I could be the worst manager there has ever been. Look at my track record – I was manager at Forest for six months and took them down.

I do not believe that there is a blueprint for a manager. You don't just need a figurehead; you need a good coaching team around you. Rather than ask what would make a good manager, perhaps the question should be what would make a good management team.

I would start with someone who has the respect of the players. They should be a bit wary of him; someone the players wouldn't cross. He would need a good assistant who would be prepared to tell him anything and not be afraid to say when he thought his boss was wrong, although never in public and never in front of the players. There should always be solidarity and if there is a disagreement it should be sorted out behind closed doors.

I also think that technically the manager needs to be on top, especially at fault finding. That was something that Terry Venables was particularly adept at. As an electrician, I would have to find out why a light wouldn't work. As a football manager, you have to do the same thing. You pick a team, plan your strategy and 20 minutes into the game find that it has all gone pear-shaped. All the things you thought could nullify the opposition have gone wrong and you have to change your tactics on the hoof, find out exactly why it hasn't gone to plan. Terry was excellent at that; he would spot a problem in minutes and change it very quickly before any damage could be done.

A manager also needs a good buffer between himself and the players. Kenny Dalglish and Kevin Keegan both used Terry McDermott. He would be in the dressing-room with the players and they felt at ease with him and could talk, giving him a feeling of what was happening. Steve Harrison did a similar job with England. Players don't talk to them thinking they are going to run straight to the manager; the conversation is just normal. It's up to the buffer how he passes on that information without dropping any individual player in the mire. He doesn't have to give names, just pass on the general feeling. If he put a name to every moan and complaint the players would become wary of him and the manager would inevitably finish up fronting anyone who complained too much and too often.

Quite often these days top players go straight into high-profile management without a scrap of coaching expertise behind them. Sometimes it can work but often it doesn't. Peter Shilton always said what a good manager he was going to be because of the depth of his experience but it didn't work for him.

I am not blessed with that self-assured attitude. I simply don't know what will happen. Anyone can bullshit but usually they don't last.

I suppose I have played under some of the great managers but I would never model myself on any one of them. I am sure that some players-turned-managers try to be dominant like Brian Clough. Big mistake. There is only one Brian Clough and it is foolish to try to emulate him. Brian could upset people for the fun of it but it is only the odd person who enjoys being disliked.

I think I would listen to the man on the terraces, not necessarily slavishly following what they say, but taking on board anything that I thought was beneficial. The same applies to anyone who can offer a crumb of intelligence that can be taken on board to help make the team better. That's why I would like to watch Arsene Wenger and talk to him about his philosophies. I quite like the things I hear about him and what he passes on to his players – the vitamins, the diet, timing the training, not over-training the players and other things like that.

With Clough we never trained a great deal, letting the matches take care of the fitness once the season was rolling with two games a week. Having an interest in racehorses I have seen how the top trainers race the best and then rest them. Footballers should be treated the same way.

I believe that training should be looked on more individually than it is. I wouldn't hesitate to have the defenders in one day while the rest went home and relaxed. I would make sure that I had specialist coaches. I would look after the defenders myself but I would have others to take care of the midfield players, the strikers and the goalkeepers.

I noticed when we trained at Forest, if Clough wasn't there there would be some slapdash training, particularly by those who were normally in fear of him. But when he walked through the gates the standard went through the roof. It was match training simply because they were frightened of what he would do or say. It is important to have that little bit of an aura but I also noticed that now and again it didn't hurt if Clough wasn't around and he let someone else take the session. He would always let the players wonder where he was, even allowing them to think that perhaps he was looking at a player in their position. More often than not, he would be away playing squash or relaxing with a drink but he didn't let his players know that.

I believe in coaching and learning more about the game. When I took my UEFA 'B' course, there were players there who thought they knew it all and didn't need it. They were only on the course to get the qualification. That is a bad attitude, very blinkered. I felt that I would go away with some added knowledge and whatever I learned I was better off doing that than sitting on my backside in front of the television. The most important aspect is not so much the certificate but the learning. Again I can use my experience of being an electrician.

There are books that tell you how to rewire a house but once you are in that house, it's a totally different ball game. No two houses are the same and no two footballers are the same. Experience and learning from other people will guide you to the best way of doing things and surmounting problems. Football is no different. There is a lot to be learned from other coaches and other managers. No one should ever stop learning whether they are the youngest coach in the League or the oldest manager in the Premiership.

Having experienced being player-manager I accept that the concept is a good one but in practice it is too difficult. By the very nature of the game you are rarely offered a manager's job when a team is flying. More often than not the new man is taking over because the team are doing badly. Quite often a top player taking the job goes to the club and finds that he is better than anybody else in his position. He might also have a chairman who has made the appointment thinking he is getting two men for one wage. It is very difficult for the new man to say that he is hanging up his boots to concentrate on management.

I found the job difficult at Forest. It was fine when we were winning. We were getting by on the enthusiasm of the players even though we all knew that there were things wrong that needed fixing. It gets hard when you are in trouble and you still have to go out and play. Training, for example, becomes a problem in itself. I wanted to take training but at the same time I needed to train myself and you can't do both properly. Once the game kicked off I couldn't influence things as a manager but at least I could try to do my job on the pitch.

As a player or a manager, no one can afford to have too many distractions. As a player, at three o'clock on a Saturday afternoon, you have to know that you have trained, rested and eaten properly. If you are going out looking at players, attending meetings and doing the hundred and one other jobs a manager has to do, you cannot be fully prepared to play. That's when you have to start delegating and then you are not fulfilling the role you have taken on. Even when you have staff you totally trust, eventually you still have to go to watch the player you want to sign yourself. If it is you signing; you cannot rely on someone else's opinion no matter how much you trust them, anymore than you can rely on the hundreds of videos that are pressed on you. God knows in those six months I was offered at least eight Maradonas and if you watched the carefully edited tapes you could believe them! A player that looks a world-beater on tape can prove to be useless when you have him with a ball in front of him.

Handling the press would be no problem. At Forest I sent up one of the coaches to cover the press conference but that was because my mind was a jumble trying to do two jobs. The pressures of playing and managing meant that the media were bottom of my list of priorities. If I had time, I would do it. I admit it wasn't ideal but I had my hands full and I simply had to delegate and prioritise. Training and getting myself fit were more important than doing a Thursday press call.

I understand the media's demands and if I become a full-time manager I accept and appreciate that they will be very much a part of the job. I will do what I have to do. It's not a problem. I know the faces and I know the ones to avoid and I think I now have a reasonable relationship with the press.

I have also thought about the future without football. I have to because there are no guarantees. My name might land me a job when my playing days are over, with word getting round that I am a decent professional with good standards. Once you have that first job, it is vital to be successful because straightaway if you don't achieve everyone is on your back. David Platt is the classic example. When he stopped playing, everyone was predicting what an excellent manager he would make, the perfect man for almost any job. But not everything went well for him at Sampdoria in Italy and when he returned to England it was for a battle against relegation with Forest. Suddenly he had gone from being the man everyone thought would succeed to being the object of the shaking of knowing heads. That's happened to managers who have a great track record, never mind newcomers. One bad run and then all the good results are quickly forgotten.

That's the game we are in. Loyalty will mean nothing and we all know it, as sad as it may be. I am under no illusions that I am going to be a great manager but I will give it my very best shot.

If I don't get a job in football, or if I fail, I cannot see myself going back to my job with Brent council. I doubt whether they would have kept the job open for me after all this time even though they promised they would if my career in football did not work out! I feel quite comfortable doing media work with television but it has to be within the game because football has been my life and my love for so long.

I have looked after my money reasonably well so I won't have to scratch around but I would like to be around football in some shape or form. It is part of me and in my blood. Everyone who plays football is in the sport because they love it and not because they came in thinking that this was a quick way to get rich. It may have changed a little but not that much.

I hope that I will be able to guide young players in football matters, from important issues such as diet down to learning to keep your mouth shut when things are going right because there are always bad times around the corner. I would stress the three criteria of training, resting and eating well. If your ability lets you down, you cannot help that. It is acceptable. What isn't acceptable is when you have the ability but one of those three vital ingredients is neglected.

I would tell them to listen to the experienced people around them. I talk to youngsters and go on coaching courses and I am often asked if I respect a certain coach. Sometimes the answer is no and certainly there are few who measure up to the Terry Venables of this world but whoever they are I will listen to them and argue my point. If you don't listen you don't learn.

Then there are agents. I am fortunate because I work with an agent I rate as honest, good at what he does and not pushy. I wouldn't have an agent I didn't think was honest or whom I didn't respect. I couldn't work with Eric Hall because he is so different from me. I would be embarrassed walking down the street with him. He is a self-publicist on radio and television, waving his big cigar about. I don't think I have ever seen Kevin Mason on television and I don't think I particularly want to. That's why we have a good professional relationship.

Equally if I were an agent, I would rather handle someone like me than a Stan Collymore who you know is going to let you down somewhere along the line. As a manager, I would have no problem whether the agent was Kevin, Eric or Paul Stretford who looks after Stan because I wouldn't be working for them. They would be selling me a product, representing their players. We would get on famously if any of them had a player I wanted in my team.

Working with agents is hard work for managers but then again I use an agent so I can't criticise the system. Kevin gets me better deals than I could myself because he can push my qualities and I would be too embarrassed to do so. He enjoys football and doing what he does and I believe he has enjoyed representing me.

Not all footballers are womanising boozers, not all journalists are disseminators of untruths and not all agents are evil. There is a mix-and-match in every walk of life and they are no different. If they want the best deal possible for their client, I have no problems with that, but if they want the best deal for themselves with their client a secondary consideration then, as a manager, I would have a serious problem. There are agents out there who are unscrupulous and that is bad for the game in general.

If I did go back into management the very first person I would call would be my old Forest team-mate Nigel Clough. I did it last time when I wanted him as a player two hours after I took over as manager but the next time would be for us to work together. He has enjoyed a similar football education to myself; we played together at club and international level. Professionally, I admire him and I respect his knowledge and opinions on the game. He is the sort of man who would not be afraid to turn round and, without criticising, say he thought different from me.

Nigel has been creating a name for himself with Burton Albion because he wasn't offered anything in the League. He is not too proud to start at a lower level and work his way up and he has a steely attitude about him. He is a quiet person, but he is a very strong character with a strong inner belief, very much like his father. Nigel, however, is a little more flexible than his dad. While Brian has one or two problems in his later life, I don't think you will see Nigel go down that road. He has too strong a personality.

He had to have to survive in football as his father's son. He, Jamie

Redknapp and Frank Lampard are a credit to their fathers and a credit to the game but Nigel undoubtedly had the biggest cross to bear. It must have been the hardest job in the world, especially when things were going badly. When they were trying to usher Brian out at Forest, Nigel behaved impeccably, not being drawn into taking sides or going to his dad with stories. No one could have handled it better; he had respect from the players and his father. The most important thing is that he knows his football and we both believe it should be played in a certain way. If you put us in different rooms and asked us questions on footballing situations, more often than not we would come up with the same answers. He could run a club from top to bottom.

Another thing Brian Clough showed me was the need to take a step back or to take a little time away. That can only be done if you have someone by your side whom you trust. I would know that I could leave everything up to Nigel and come back without having been stabbed in the back.

stuart pearce

- Born Shepherd's Bush, London, 24 April 1962.
- Transferred from Wealdstone to Coventry City October 1983 for £25,000.
- Transferred to Nottingham Forest May 1985 for £240,000.
- League Cup winner's medal 1989, 1990.
- Simod Cup winner's medal 1989.
- Zenith Data Systems Cup winner's medal 1992.
- Appointed caretaker-manager Nottingham Forest December 1996, resigned May 1997. Was first player-manager to play for England.
- Free transfer to Newcastle United July 1997.
- Awarded MBE December 1998.
- Free transfer to West Ham United August 1999.

SUMMARY OF APPEARANCES AND GOALS

Season	Team	Lg	G	FA	G	LC	G	EC	G	CW	G	UE	G	OC	G	U-	G	In	G
1983–84	Coventry C	23	–	–	–	–	–	–	–	–	–	–	–	–	–	–	–	–	–
1984–85		28	4	2	–	–	–	–	–	–	–	–	–	–	–	–	–	–	–
1985–86	Nottingham F	30	1	–	–	4	–	–	–	–	–	–	–	–	–	–	–	–	–
1986–87		39	6	–	–	5	2	–	–	–	–	–	–	–	–	–	–	2	–
1987–88		34	5	5	1	3	–	–	–	–	–	–	–	1	–	–	–	3	–
1988–89		36	6	5	–	8	1	–	–	–	–	–	–	5	3	–	–	10	1
1989–90		34	5	1	–	10	2	–	–	–	–	–	–	2	2	–	–	15	1
1990–91		33	11	10	4	4	1	–	–	–	–	–	–	2	–	–	–	11	1
1991–92		30	5	4	2	9	1	–	–	–	–	–	–	5	1	–	–	9	–
1992–93		23	2	3	–	5	–	–	–	–	–	–	–	–	–	–	–	3	1
1993–94		42	6	2	–	6	–	–	–	–	–	–	–	1	–	–	–	3	1
1994–95		36	8	1	–	3	2	–	–	–	–	–	–	–	–	–	–	3	–
1995–96		31	3	4	2	1	1	–	–	–	–	8	–	–	–	–	–	11	1
1996–97		33	5	2	–	2	–	–	–	–	–	–	–	–	–	–	–	6	–
1997–98	Newcastle U	25	–	7	–	–	–	4	–	–	–	–	–	–	–	–	–	–	–
1998–99		12	–	–	–	2	–	–	–	2	–	–	–	–	–	–	–	–	–
1999–2000	West Ham U	8	–	–	–	–	–	–	–	–	–	–	–	–	–	–	–	2	–
	Totals	497	67	46	9	62	10	4	–	2	–	8	–	16	6	–	–	78	5

Headings: League; FA Cup; League Cup; European Cup; Cup Winners' Cup; UEFA Cup

Other cups: 1 Simod Cup 1987–88; 4 Simod Cup (3 goals) 1988–89; 1 Mercantile Credit Trophy 1988–89; 2 Zenith Data Systems Cup (2 goals) 1989–90; 2 Zenith Data Systems Cup 1990–91; 5 Zenith Data Systems Cup (1 goal) 1991–92; 1 Anglo-Italian Cup 1993–94.

Under-21 appearance: v Yugoslavia

G = Goals

Note: All appearances include those as substitute, of which there is only one at club level – v Barcelona, European Cup, 26 November 1997.

FULL INTERNATIONALS

Became the 999th player to be selected for the full England team in 1987 and took over the England captaincy from Gary Lineker in 1992.

1986–87	Brazil, Scotland
1987–88	West Germany (sub), Israel, Hungary
1988–89	Denmark, Sweden, Saudi Arabia, Greece, Albania, Albania, Chile, Scotland, Poland, Denmark
1989–90	Sweden, Poland, Italy, Yugoslavia, Brazil, Czechoslovakia (1), Denmark, Uruguay, Tunisia, Republic of Ireland, Holland, Egypt, Belgium, Cameroon, West Germany
1990–91	Hungary, Poland, Republic of Ireland, Republic of Ireland, Cameroon, Turkey, Argentina, Australia, New Zealand (1), **New Zealand**, Malaysia
1991–92	Turkey, Poland, **France**, **Czechoslovakia**, Brazil (sub), Finland, Denmark, France, Sweden
1992–93	**Spain**, **Norway**, **Turkey** (1)
1993–94	**Poland** (1), **San Marino**, Greece (sub)
1994–95	Romania (sub), Japan, Brazil
1995–96	Norway, Switzerland (1), Portugal, **Bulgaria**, Croatia, Hungary, Switzerland, Scotland, Holland, Spain, Germany
1996–97	Moldova, Poland, Italy, Mexico, **South Africa**, Italy
1999–2000	Luxembourg, Poland

Note: **Bold** type indicates games as captain.

index